# PREY

---

The gate was less than twenty yards away. Behind him the rasp of furious breathing eased closer.

Three figures filled the gate's opening, blocking it. He made no conscious decision. Even the voice in his head had fallen silent. He put his head down and ran straight toward the figures.

He closed his eyes and shielded his face with his crossed arms just before he reached them. Like playing football . . .

He slammed into them and felt his shoulder drive against hard muscular bodies. One of them snarled. Then he was through. A surge of triumph quickened him as he whipped himself toward the safety of the tube station on the corner. . . .

The harsh light of a stunner beam caught him in full stride and locked his nervous system into a long, painless spasm. A fading sensation of regret filled him as he fell.

## BOOKS BY WILLIAM SHATNER

QUEST FOR TOMORROW
*Delta Search*
*In Alien Hands*
*Step into Chaos**

Published by HarperPrism

*coming soon

# IN ALIEN HANDS

## QUEST FOR TOMORROW

—

## WILLIAM SHATNER

HarperPrism

*A Division of HarperCollinsPublishers*

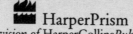

## HarperPrism
*A Division of* HarperCollins*Publishers*
10 East 53rd Street, New York, NY 10022-5299

Copyright © 1997 by William Shatner
All rights reserved. No part of this book may be used or
reproduced in any manner whatsoever without written
permission of the publisher, except in the case of brief
quotations embodied in critical articles and reviews.
For information address HarperCollins Publishers,
10 East 53rd Street, New York, NY 10022-5299.

ISBN 0-06-105743-6

HarperCollins®, 🔥®, and HarperPrism®
are trademarks of HarperCollins*Publishers*, Inc.

A hardcover edition of this book was
published in 1997 by HarperPrism.

Cover illustration © 1997 by Jim Burns

First mass market printing: September 1998

Printed in the United States of America

For further information about William Shatner, science fiction,
new technologies, and upcoming William Shatner books,
log on to www.williamshatner.com

Visit HarperPrism on the World Wide Web at
http://www.harperprism.com

❖ 10 9 8 7 6 5 4 3 2 1

# DEDICATION

It had started out as a hiss—a mere hint of a sound—something akin to the sibilant sigh of a serpent. Then gradually through the years, the sound inside my head increased in volume. It was like sitting beside a radio, searching for sound yet receiving none, giving only that empty static that spoke at nothing. I've heard of the music of spheres, but surely this was not it.

I found there was a name to what I was hearing: tinnitus, and it was driving me mad. I'd like to dedicate this book to those people I visited working in research and clinical studies. They have made the world once again a glorious place. To the doctors at the Oregon Health Science University, Robert Johnson Ph.D., and Jack Vernon, Ph.D., and the people at the American Tinnitus Association (they need research funding, by the way), and especially the kind, ministrating medicants at the University of Maryland, Dr. Pawel Jastreboff in particular. Thank you, thank you, thank you. May you help others as you have helped me.

# ACKNOWLEDGMENTS

---

To Bill Quick, in whose friendly hands this book resides. Other hands that helped along the way, or at least applauded:

Caitlin Blasdell
John Silbersack
Jim Burns

My thanks.

"A reasonable probability is
the only certainty."
—EDGAR WATSON HOWE

———

"Something magnificent is taking place here
amid the cruelties and tragedies, and the
supreme challenge to intelligence is that of
making the noblest and best in our
curious heritage prevail."
—CHARLES A. BEARD

———

"I too am a rare Pattern."
—AMY LOWELL

———

# CHAPTER ONE

## 1

Thargos, called the Hunter, contemplated the demands of his own gene pool. He was not without a sense of humor, at least what passed for such among the dour, saurian Hunzza. And so he understood that his reaction to what he had found in the wreckage of Delta's satellite was not entirely a product of the nature of the find.

"I hunt because I am," he murmured as he reviewed the results of his tests on the fragment he had found. Then he laughed. With Thargos, as with all of his race, much that was carried out verbally in other species was consummated for him with facial expressions. His laughter was expressed as a rapid, rhythmic blinking of the green compound eyes set on either side of his long, snouted skull. A Terran, coming on Thargos unawares, would have thought: *What a weird alligator, with those green softball eyes*.

"I am, therefore I hunt," Thargos added, acknowledging the modifications Darwin's iron hand had imposed on his DNA. It was in the fit of the two statements that he found humor. It was a very Hunzzan joke. He presumed his delight in it contributed to the generalized perception that the Hunzza had no sense of humor at all.

He stopped blinking and closed his eyes. The bits he'd snared offered only the gauziest of hints: shards of computer technology, not old or new, but different—a hint at the secret the Terrans were rumored to possess, and which had attracted his famous attention; and a name.

Jim Endicott. A human boy.

Thargos was not afraid to know when he didn't know. But he did fear ignorance in general and sought to erase it ruthlessly within himself. He knew the name and little else. The first stroke became obvious: find the boy.

In his experience, from small steps might come edifices of knowledge. Thargos privately regarded himself not so much a hunter as a builder. But he kept that conceit hidden from his fellows. Among the less refined of his own race, such creativity could be considered a deficit. Certainly it would be thought odd.

Better to let them believe he was only a hunter and a killer. They would understand that well enough.

## 2

**K**orkal Emut Denai rubbed his aching thigh. His people had once walked on four legs, and even after ages of evolutionary accommodation to the physical demands of intelligence, they didn't like to stand motionless for long periods of time. Getting older didn't help any, either, he thought.

"I told you, Captain Sir, it was an error. A mistake, nothing more. My ship is old and prone to breaking down. We didn't receive the beacon's automatic warning. As simple as that."

His voice was breathy. He had trouble wrapping his long pink tongue around the trickier consonants of the Terran language, but he could make himself understood. At least he thought so, though this stiff bonehead of a Terran Navy officer acted as if he couldn't understand a word of it.

"Remove your vessel from this restricted area immediately or we will destroy you," the officer said. This was his third repetition of the same mantra. Korkal was beginning to think he meant it.

"Yes, of course," Korkal replied. "We are having drive problems, you understand. It will be just a little longer."

"*Remove your vessel—*"

Korkal turned away from the screen and tuned him out. He looked at his chief intelligence officer, and said, "How much longer?"

The CIO interrupted her labors to say, "It's definitely Thargos. Shadowship technology, and the Terries don't have it. He's been here, but he's gone now. What else do we need?"

The black fur ruff surrounding Korkal's wolfish features seemed to quiver. "What else? Everything else! What was

he looking for? Did he find it? Where did he go? I can't stall this iron-backed captain forever. *What was that?*"

"Some sort of nuclear torpedo. Twenty-megaton yield. I think they call it a warning shot." The CIO sounded moderately shaken.

"Skypack in heaven!" Korkal turned back to his screen. "All right, we're going!"

The Terran commander nodded. "Very good, sir. We'll tag along to make sure you don't get lost."

"Yes. Why don't you do that?" Korkal closed his eyes. "Touchy pack rogue, isn't he?"

So the Hunter was here. How intensely . . . interesting. What was he hunting? And did he know another was hunting him?

Korkal felt the reaction drives kick in and allowed himself to relax a bit. So Delta and his satellite were both gone, and Thargos the Hunter had come sniffing around the ruins. But why Thargos, whom the masters of the Hunzzan Empire generally reserved for only the most important tasks?

Perhaps those masters now felt the primitive and insignificant Terrans were important? If so, that was worrisome indeed.

Because the Terrans *were* important. At

least Korkal's people, the Albagens, thought so. Which meant Korkal Emut Denai thought so, too.

*Find Thargos*, he thought. *Find the Hunter.*

## 3

Intellectually, Jim Endicott had been expecting it. Emotionally, it was a boot in the groin, and he hadn't expected that at all.

For a moment he thought his heart had stopped. Then he realized it was his heart that was pounding in his ears like a huge slow drum.

"So you're going back to Terra?" he said. He was proud of himself. His voice sounded steady and unconcerned. Very mature.

"Do you know your whole face just turned bright red?" Cat said.

"It's hot in here."

"Jim, we're outdoors. See? Sky, trees, park. And the breeze is cool."

She took his elbow and guided him toward a nearby bench. They sat, the perfume of gene-altered tulips rising about them. "Say something," she said.

"I don't know what to say." Should he beg? Yes, he should.

"Cat, please . . ."

"Jim, listen to me." She took his hands in her own. Her fingers were dry and warm. "Things are fine with us. Never better. Isn't this the time to let things end? People always break up when they're angry and miserable. Is that what you want to happen? Is that what you want to remember?"

He licked his lips and shook his head.

"I have to go. The Plebs need me. And I need them. You know it. You know why."

"You need them more than me?"

He saw the wrinkle of hurt in her eyes and wished he could take it back. But deep in his mind a tiny worm twisted awake and whined, *This can't be happening. I'm not ready.*

And suddenly he was sick of himself. He had never imagined himself to possess that snake of neediness whimpering, *Me. I'm not ready yet. You are, but I'm not. Me, me, me . . .*

For the first time in his life, Jim Endicott was appalled by himself.

"Oh, jeez, Cat, I'm sorry. I didn't mean that. Of course I understand. I do understand."

She squeezed his hands, and this touch of her strength pierced him as nothing had before. He felt tears well in his eyes.

"Oh, Jim. Don't cry."

She sounded desolate. He blinked. "No, I won't."

But of course he did, and this was the worst of his body's treachery, for try as he would, he couldn't help blaming her for it. His anger was unworthy of him—and her—but he couldn't escape it. Though he despised himself for it, it was his. And for a moment he hated her for making him see what he was, for unmasking this unexpected ugliness inside himself.

*Know thyself!* the sages taught. But if this kind of knowledge was part of growing up, he would rather stay a boy forever. The secret the wise men kept to themselves was that manhood was pain.

## 4

Home was . . . home. Everything here was physically still the same: the same familiar bed, the same brown curtains, the same orderly cabinets that held his things—the stuff he now thought of as the possessions of a dimly remembered child.

It was all different, invisibly clawed by loss. Everywhere he looked he saw the man he'd thought was his father. Carl Endicott, who had loved him, lied to him, and finally died for him. He didn't know how to deal with Carl Endicott's ghost.

The faint rush of conditioned air shifted slightly as his door cracked open. "Jim?"

"Yes, Mom."

He felt her come closer, and saw once again her tear-streaked fierceness as a flash of bright memory: she had snarled when she fought Delta for his life and her own. And she had forgiven him for killing the man she loved. That *he* loved. Why couldn't he forgive himself?

"Cat just told me she's going back to Terra."

"Yes."

"Oh, Jimmy." Her cool fingers touched the back of his neck, tangled themselves in his chestnut hair. "It hurts, right?"

He felt the warm huff of her breath on the fine hairs at the nape of his neck as she bent over him. "She does love you. You must try to understand that. But she has to go. And somehow you have to find it in yourself to accept that, to respect it. And to go on."

"I know, Mom. I know."

The bed creaked faintly as she sat. "I haven't told you what Delta told me when we were together."

"Mom . . ."

"I think it has a bearing on this. On everything. I debated whether to tell you at all, but I finally decided keeping it from you would be a mistake. Your father kept things from you for your own good. He meant well, but I think it was wrong."

Jim closed his eyes. That scab was not even partly healed, and he feared ripping open the wound again. Unconsciously he rubbed his stomach, as if the pain were there.

"You know your real mother hid a secret message in your DNA patterns."

"Real, Mom? My real mother? But what's real? You're my *real* mother—the only one *I* ever knew—and Dad was my real father . . . until I killed him. And you know what? Not one damned bit of it seems real at all. Especially whatever it is inside me that I never asked for and sure as hell never wanted. *That* was what caused all . . ." He grimaced. "All this."

"Jim. Look at me."

He swiveled slowly in his chair. Tabitha Endicott's features were set and bleak, as if she feared any expression. As if her face might break.

*"It isn't your fault. None of it. Not one bit!"*

"Mom, I *killed* Dad."

"Listen to me carefully, Jim Endicott. That was an accident. You act as if you murdered him. But murder comes from the heart, and there was no murder in you. Not for him. You were doing your best to protect us all. A sixteen-year-old boy. And Carl died because of that. If you have to blame anybody, blame him."

She licked her lips and spoke with an intensity that sent shivers up Jim's spine.

*"I blame him!"* she said.

"Mom . . ."

"I do, Jim. Your dad was a strong man. Maybe too strong. He kept things to himself. No doubt he thought it was for our protection. But he made that decision, and from it came everything else. If you had known the truth, you would have done things differently. You wouldn't have sneaked your application to the Academy and let Delta find us at last. If I had known, I would have told you. But I didn't know either. Because Carl Endicott didn't tell us. Do you understand what I'm saying?"

"Mom, you can't blame Dad. He was only trying to do the best he could."

"Our lives were at risk, and he never told us. Once, I told myself I understood that. But

Jim, it was a crime. In the end I believe he knew that. And he paid the price for it."

As she spoke, her eyes seemed to suck all the light from the room. Jim felt his muscles freeze with horror.

"Don't say that. Mom, please . . . I can't take it. I killed him, and you're saying it was all right. That it was some kind of judgment."

"An accident, judgment, whatever—as easy to say life killed him. Or Delta. Or that woman he loved a long time ago, loved enough to save her boy and bring him up as his own. Jim . . . sometimes things just *happen*. I don't blame him for that, only for some of the choices he made. He owed you—us—better."

"But I loved him, Mom. I still love him. I miss him so much. And I can't stand *knowing* . . ."

In the dim light he saw tears gleaming in her eyes. "I love him, too. But he died in an accident, son, an accident that had nothing to do with you except you were there. He might as well have been struck by lightning."

"I pulled the trigger. I fired the shot that killed him."

"No! That woman, your real mother, killed him, and I will *never* forgive her for that!"

Jim looked down at his forearms and saw goose bumps crawling on his skin.

"Oh, Mom, I can't . . . I can't . . ." He could hardly breathe.

"She put it in you. All the death came from it. From those who lusted for it. And worse, from those who *will* lust for it. It's still there.

And you know what it is, what it *has* to be, don't you?"

Numbly, he shook his head.

"It's the secret of the mind arrays, Jim. Nothing else makes sense. Carl knew, and he hid it from you. He knew Delta would tear the whole Confederation apart to make sure nobody else discovered the truth."

"It's worse than that, I think," Jim said slowly, realizing that on some deep level he already knew, and had known ever since Delta unlocked it and sucked it out of him. "It's the plans for better arrays. Stronger ones. Maybe even more dangerous. She had a year to work on them. Delta knew that." He looked down, suddenly ashamed without knowing why. "Dad must have known, too."

They stared at each other.

Finally she blinked. "Yes, of course. What else could it be? God, how I hate her."

"Maybe she didn't have any choice either, Mom. Maybe nobody has a choice. Not in the end."

She came off the bed and took him in her arms. Her strength was painful.

"You cannot—you must not—believe that, Jim. To be human is to choose. But for your father's death you had no choice. No choice at all. Someday you'll know that, and be able to forgive yourself."

"When, Mom? When will that be? I don't know where I came from. And now I don't know where I'm going."

She hugged him tighter, because she had no answer for that except her implacable love.

"My poor baby."

"No, Mom, not a baby. Not anymore."

For the first time he began to understand what he had lost. It was too great for tears. Like all the other childish things, even tears had been taken from him.

He had no idea what might be left.

## 5

### INTERORBIT CONTROL
#### INNER RING STATION:13:20 HOURS GMT

At any given time approximately twenty thousand shuttles, satellites, orbiters, transfer tugs, freighters, passenger liners, and fleet vessels were moving through the crowded inner orbital space surrounding Terra. No human mind could keep track of it all. The machines did that. Humans watched, and waited for the inevitable alarms when the machines found something they didn't understand.

"Take a look at this one," Junior Controller Monitor First Class Akwabi Sasteeka said to his supervisor, Gail Wakamoto.

"Take a look at what?" She leaned over his shoulder and peered at his screen.

"Right there." He touched a set of numbers that had begun to flash red.

"I see it."

"Nobody else does. According to the computers, it just vanished."

Her finely trimmed eyebrows rose against her ivory forehead. "What are you talking about? Ships don't just vanish."

"This one did."

"Scoot over."

He did. She scrunched in next to him, took his skull set, and logged herself into his monitor. "You're right. Gone."

"A ConFleet cargo ship."

She nodded, her eyes closed as data flowed directly into her mind. "Shut up."

Sasteeka watched Gail's lips as she unconsciously whispered aloud the conversation she'd initiated with Fleet Inner Ring Control. "You guys just lost a freighter. Says here its cargo is classified. How classified? What should we be worrying about?"

Her lips stopped moving. Sasteeka waited until she slipped off the headgear.

"What is it?"

"Start rerouting everything away from the projected flight path. Ten-thousand-kilometer globe. Till we can find out what happened."

"Huh? Gail, what was it?"

"Cargo vessel. Transferring nukes groundside from the damaged orbital forts."

"Jesus. Nukes?"

"Get busy. Get it done," she told him.

# 6

Thargos contemplated the advantages of advanced technology as he supervised the storage of the four nuclear weapons he'd salvaged from the destruction of the Con-Fleet cargo vessel. Ugly, primitive things that glittered like the children's toys they were. He stowed them inside oversize field cages that would entirely mask their crude radiation. When that was done, he reviewed the operation through which he'd obtained them.

After some thought he decided it had been a success. The energies he'd used should have been undetectable by the Terrans' rudimentary scanning capabilities, just as his shadow-ship was invisible to them. On their screens it would appear the freighter had simply vanished. One more mystery of the space lanes.

But the nukes might come in handy. He had discovered their location in the same place he'd found other data. The Terran information systems were not as secure as they believed. Not, at least, from beings who possessed modern technologies. And the Hunzza prided themselves on the sharp edges of their science, a science respected and feared by their neighbors and potential enemies.

Rightfully so, he mused. The nukes were indeed primitive, but if you intended murder, a stone ax might serve as well as a gravity disrupter. He didn't know yet whether he would be able to find the boy, or what steps he would take if he did. It might be that his only option would be to terminate Jim Endicott. If that turned out to be the case, a mysterious accident involving one of the Terrans' own nukes would betray no trace of his own claws on the matter.

When one hunted, it was best to be prepared for any eventuality. Thus far he was satisfied he had made the necessary preparations.

"Set course for the Terran colony planet Wolfbane," he instructed his chief pilot.

His lambent green eyes glittered with anticipation. The spoor of the prey burned on his tongue. One human boy. Not much of a challenge for him, but it would have to do.

He smiled. This baring of serrated fangs was not, among his people, a sign of friendship or humor. It reflected the white glimmer of a bonier, more basic hunger.

## 7

Everything around him was charged with memories. Once the Wolfbane spaceport had been just a place. Now it was crowded with recollections of fear. He had fled here and hidden here and escaped from here. Now he simply walked, Cat on his right side, Tabitha on his left. He carried Cat's suitcase. It contained everything of her life on Wolfbane with him and seemed much too small for that weight.

He carried that load inside himself as well, and it was choking him.

"Well, this is it. I guess." He heard his own words as a buzzing through distance. They stopped near the boarding gate.

"Let me take that," she said.

He handed the suitcase over.

"Jim . . ."

He put out his arms, and she stepped into them. The clean smell of her golden hair filled his nose with dry fragrance. Her bones felt thin and fragile though he knew they weren't. He buried his face on her neck. His lips moved against her skin.

"I . . . Cat . . . such a waste."

Her own voice was a warm sibilance against his ear. "No, Jim. Not a waste. I love you, Jimmy. But I can't love only you. I can't let you have my whole life. I just can't. Tell me you understand that much. Don't spoil everything now."

*But I don't understand!*

He wanted to shout it into her ear and somehow make her know the enormous losses he had suffered. His past was gone and his future, too, and now she was leaving and taking his present with her. He had nothing left but his anger, and he would die rather than show that to her.

"They say," he husked, "that if you really love something, you have to be able to let it go. I . . . think that's bullshit."

She moved against him. "You're not letting me go. You still have me. Here." She reached up and gently tapped his skull. "And here."

She stepped back and brushed her fingertips across his chest.

They stared at each other. Then her gaze smoked over, and she lifted her suitcase.

"A kiss," she said.

He bent forward. It was a polite peck on the lips. They might have been brother and sister.

"Jim, I . . ."

"No," he said. "I love you, Cat."

She stared at him. Then she nodded, turned, and walked slowly into the boarding corridor. He watched her shape diminish into perspective, though it felt to him as if he were shrinking.

"Jim?"

"What, Mom?"

She searched his face. "We should go."

He said nothing. After a while she took his hand and led him away as if he were still a little boy.

He was so angry.

## 8

Jim came out of the night searching for things as dead as the pyramids. He saw the fire first as a flicker, then a breeze-tossed beat of light against the dark. The eternal flame of the Spacer's Memorial.

His shoes crunched softly as he crossed the gravel verge, then went silent on grass black in the moonlight. As he walked a wind came up and licked his face with chill. He shifted his backpack uneasily. The reflection of the fire glimmered doubly in his eyes as he approached the great plaque and its list of the holy dead. The unread names seemed to whisper across vast reaches toward him; they cried out for remembrance.

*I have nothing for you,* he thought. *Do you have anything for me?*

The Solis Space Academy demanded his parents' genotypes, and they were either gone or unknown. The Academy had filed his own genotype, and it was a horror of secret knowledge. Without the Academy, the white ships would never be his. Did that mean the dream was dead with everything else?

He didn't know. Maybe only the dead knew. And so he had come here to stir the ashes of his hope, to listen to the silence in his heart.

An orca-owl cried out in the shadowed branches beyond the circle that cupped its portion of fire. Someone had cleaned the bronze plaque recently. It gleamed like a coin he'd already spent. He paused before the fire and felt its heat on his face as he bent toward it, but there were no answers in its dance.

All dreams die. Was that what he had learned? Was that what Delta and all the ghosts, old or fresh, had taught him?

He stood with his head bowed, unwilling to read the names imperishably inscribed on the cold metal. Not a tombstone. The corpses of these dreamers had not returned to earthly graves. Somehow that seemed fitting.

He turned as gravel muttered stonily behind him. At first he could see only another shadow dissolving out of the night. Then he thought: *What a weird alligator, with those green softball eyes.*

The creature smiled at him.

# CHAPTER TWO

## 1

—

**K**orkal Emut Denai walked briskly across the marble-clad inner courtyard of the High Chamberhouse of the Terran Confederation. He ignored the stares he drew from lines of tourists waiting to gawk at the famous places: the Chamber of Deputies, the Nations Council Room, the Confederation Court, and the formal offices of the chairman.

The humans near him fell silent as he passed their lines and entered the tall-domed rotunda that opened into the chairman's warren of cubicles. Humans knew vaguely of the existence of alien races, but finding an individual member on their home planet was still uncommon enough to draw their hushed attention. He felt their collective gaze on him as a myriad of small itches beneath his fur.

He veered to his left, away from the public rooms, and approached a small desk unobtrusively blocking an unmarked wooden door. To Korkal's practiced eye the uniformed guard who stared up at him was far too fit for a man who was supposed to look like a time-serving functionary.

"Your chip please?"

Korkal handed it over. The guard clicked it into a reader. A soft chime sounded. "Go ahead, sir."

"Thank you."

The door buzzed. Korkal walked around the desk and pushed through into a long, plainly carpeted corridor. Doorways opened along it into cluttered chaotic offices where staff people waved their arms and shouted at each other. He plodded past them without a glance and came to the end of the corridor, where he paused before another unmarked wooden door. He raised his hand and knocked softly. The sound was dull, betraying the steel beneath the wood.

"Come in."

He turned the knob and entered. The ante-room was medium-sized, hushed, and dense with the aromas of power. Two muscular males sitting on a leather sofa stood up and turned to face him, their expressions empty and watchful. The young woman behind her desk smiled at him.

"She's waiting for you, Mr. Denai."

"Thank you. Can I go in?"

"Let me check." The assistant lowered her head into an invisible hush screen. Korkal watched her lips move silently. After a few words she raised her head.

"Go right ahead, sir. The door's unlocked."

Korkal had learned not to smile at humans. For some reason they found Albagensian displays of fang unsettling. He didn't really understand this. After all, they did smile at each other. He settled for nodding at the two men as he moved past them. He noted with professional approval that one watched his hands and the other his face all the way in. He was also aware he'd been scanned by systems considerably more powerful than human eyes before he entered the outer hallway.

He carefully closed the door behind him, pushed aside a blue-velvet curtain, and found himself in the chairman's working office. He padded across a thick gold carpet and approached the woman seated behind a wide mahogany desk. The top of the desk was heaped with papers and chip cases and files. A half-empty bottle of a popular brand of beer stood next to her elbow, the malty scent of it strong in his nostrils. He found this detail charming.

She stood, smiled, and extended her hand.

"Mr. Denai, it's good to see you again."

Korkal made certain his claws were fully retracted before he took her fingers in his own stubby grip. Albagens did not shake hands with each other. They bowed their heads and closed their lips to show their fangs were hidden. Humans had always killed each other with their hands. In their earliest days his people had done everyday murder with their teeth. In some ways he understood the Hunzza much better than he did humans.

Prior to his only other meeting with this woman her guards had wanted to remove his vestigial claws entirely. Only his secret diplomatic status had saved him from that indignity.

"Chairman," he said, "as always you are beautiful."

By his own standards she wasn't pleasing—no human was—but he had learned that one could never insult a Terran female by calling her beautiful.

Serena Half Moon inclined her head in acknowledgment of his greeting, if perhaps not his sentiment. He found her hard to read. What the humans called a tough cookie.

Her straight black hair was rubbed with gray. It hung loose to her shoulders. Her skin was the color and texture of well-used leather, recalling the sunburned lives of her Navajo ancestors. Her dark brown irises focused the light strangely into her pupils, as faint white stars like those of certain sapphires. She was narrow, angular, and tall, with prominent cheekbones and a nose the pharaohs would have recognized.

"Sit down, Mr. Denai." She lowered her gaze to a screen concealed in her desktop. "I see you have rank among your people. I wasn't told that when we met before. According to this our equivalent title would be count. Would you prefer I use that?"

Korkal remembered she'd come to her present position after a long career in the diplomatic corps. He shook his head as he found the leather chair in front of her desk. "Whatever is the everyday title of courtesy,

Chairman. I don't use my ancestral honorific at home either."

"I see. Can I have something brought for you? A drink, a snack?"

"No thank you. Chairman, I think you and I have a problem."

"Oh? What kind of problem?"

"I've discovered evidence of a covert Hunzzan operation here in your system."

He watched the stars in her eyes go still. "Hunzza?"

"Yes."

"How do you know it was Hunzza?"

Korkal thought her a woman of acute intelligence, and he chose his words accordingly.

"I can't reveal the techniques involved, but I determined to my satisfaction that a craft using shadowship technology spent considerable time in proscribed areas containing debris from Delta's satellite. I was also able to identify the craft in question and therefore its likely commander."

"I see." She tapped an antique writing pen against her strong teeth, unaware, Korkal hoped, that her gesture had a specific and insulting significance among his people. "What do you think this means?"

"The commander is probably a Hunzzan agent named Thargos. I know him. We have dealt with each other on many occasions. He is not to be taken lightly, Chairman. His masters don't use him for trivial matters. If he is here, he has good reasons, and so do they."

"Is he still here?"

"I don't know. I'll need access to your traffic control systems. With that maybe I can learn more."

"I don't think I can permit that, Mr. Denai."

Ah. That was interesting.

"Can you tell me if Delta is dead?" he said.

"I don't believe I can tell you that either."

"Very well. Do you intend to tell my masters, if not me?"

She placed her hands flat on the desktop. Her shoulders stiffened. Korkal was somewhat skilled in reading human body language, but he couldn't tell whether she was angry, frightened, or just determined to reveal as little as she could.

"Please assure your superiors that the government of the Confederation will continue its ongoing dialogue with the Pra'Loch of the Albagensian Empire." Her tone was neutral.

"I will chase him anyway, you know," Korkal said. "Whether you help me or not. You should also know that when I tried to contact Delta through my usual channels there was no reply."

"I wondered why you had come to me personally."

"Yes. Do you think I should try to reach Delta again?"

"Tell me more about this Thargos. Perhaps you can change my mind about giving you access to our traffic systems after all."

That was plain enough. Even if Delta wasn't dead, Serena Half Moon had replaced him as the most powerful human on both

Terra and Wolfbane. She was no longer a fig-
urehead masking Delta's real power. Korkal
wondered what that meant for relations
between Terra and Albagens.

"Certainly, Chairman. I think that given the
changes in our mutual situation the more you
know about the Hunzza the better."

"Then by all means enlighten me, Mr.
Denai."

Korkal knew that, too, was a confession.
He just didn't know if it was a truthful one.

## 2

The Albagensian agent returned with some
relief to his own craft and found his chief intelligence officer waiting at the door of his private
quarters. He opened it, waved one hand at the
only chair besides his own in his small shipboard stateroom, and said, "Sit."

The CIO pulled the chair closer to Korkal's
cramped desk and settled into it. Her brown
eyes were red and filmy from lack of sleep. A
human would have found her odor offensive,
but Korkal merely sniffed the reassuring scent
of the ancestral pack.

"Thargos left Sol System three days ago
bound for Wolfbane," she said.

"You verified that?"

"The chairman's access codes let us look at
everything in their traffic control systems.
Shadowship technology relies as much on

spoofing large systems as it does on materials science. I looked for what wasn't there, and there he was. He wasn't exactly careless, but it was obvious he doesn't know we are looking for him. His traces would have been a lot harder to find otherwise. How did you talk her into giving us those codes, by the way?"

Korkal gnawed absently on his right thumb-knuckle. "The secret of Delta's computer systems is Terra's only bargaining chip that means anything to the Great Powers. Those Powers that know of it, at least. Essentially that means us. Without those computers the humans wouldn't be at the table at all. Delta used to control that chip, but the chairman wants me to believe she has it now. I don't know if that's true. She doesn't know much about the Hunzza. Or tried to convince me she doesn't. It's hard for me to tell when a Terran is lying. If she does know the Hunzza, she would hide it. She wouldn't want us to know she was talking to them.

"I hinted at my disbelief in Delta's death, and so she decided to give me a taste of her new authority. If Delta were still alive and in power, he would never have allowed us access to those traffic systems no matter what she said. But we got access."

"Would the chairman lie about Delta's own systems?" the CIO asked.

"Of course. Whether she has them or not, it's very important for her that our government believe she does. Delta has manipulated things so we've kept the big carnivores like the

Hunzza away from Terra's throat. She will want to maintain that attractive *status quo*. So emphasize that the Pra'Loch should test that as soon as possible. If those systems are gone, we need to know. Make a note of it for my next report."

The CIO raised her right wrist to show the red recording light blinking on her bracelink.

"Good. As for Thargos, three days is a strong lead. I'd pay a lot to know what he's after."

"I ran the usual probability correlation. Every result above 70 percent indicates a link between Delta's destruction and whatever Thargos is looking for."

Korkal's jaw worked against his fist. There was a callus on his knuckle from the pressure of his teeth over the years.

"One frightening possibility is that Thargos himself had something to do with the destruction of the satellite," he said. "It would mean the Hunzza have learned or at least suspect the reason for Terra's importance to us. Although the mere fact of our protection might be enough to attract Hunzzan attentions."

The tip of the CIO's tongue slipped from the side of her blunt muzzle, further evidence of her exhaustion. "Delta's mysterious computer system. We don't know anything about it except it works and is bigger and faster than anything we have. Or that the Hunzza have, from all indications. But frankly there have been times I doubted whether it existed at all. It seemed so convenient for Terra."

"It existed. Take my word for it. And now the question is whether the Terrans still have it or was it destroyed. Or has Thargos somehow gotten it for his masters, which would be an even bigger disaster. I'm torn, CIO. Should I try to dig up answers here or chase after the Hunter?"

"Thargos saw fit to leave, Captain. And he didn't head for Hunzzan space."

"Yes. He's still hunting. Something he found here sent him there. Very well. Wolfbane it is."

"I hope we're right."

"So do I, CIO. So do I."

## 3

Jim Endicott stared at the apparition striding across the grass toward him.

It reminded him of an alligator though it didn't look like one. It had a flattened head with a long protruding jaw beneath green baseball eyes set into thick ridges of bone. It was about his height. It was slimmer than he was and moved with sinuous grace on squat, massive thighs and calves. Its arms hung to its knees, had two sets of joints that made it move in an eerie, tentacle-like fashion, and ended in five clawed fingers, two of which were opposable. It wore a tight black suit, made of soft flexible material, and boots that bulged in odd places. Its jaw yawned wide to show double rows of teeth guarding a soft pale gullet.

Shadows rustled in the darkness beyond the circle of firelight. Abruptly Jim felt exposed, aware of how alone he was. It was a sharper feeling than the loneliness that had filled his thoughts before. Time began to slow for him as adrenaline poured into his bloodstream. He took a step back.

"Hello," he said.

The alien kept on walking toward him as if it knew him. Jim backed up another step and began to raise his hands. The alien saw this and immediately stopped about three feet away. A reflexive voice in the back of Jim's mind noted nervously, *Still in easy grabbing distance with those long arms.*

"Good evening, young human male," the alien said. Some part of Jim had expected it to hiss, but its voice was deep and richly colored with faint humming overtones. He had no idea if it was male, female, or some strange alien gender. He did know he'd never seen one of these things before, either in the flesh or in his exobiology studies.

"By your standards I am male," the alien said. "In case it helps you to think of me. Humans seem much concerned with sexuality. For my people that is hard to understand."

"You speak Terran very well." Was it reading his mind somehow? Jim wanted to move farther away but, trapped in his ingrained sense of courtesy, he was afraid that might seem impolite. At the edge of his peripheral vision he saw dim shapes pressing closer and heard the faint sliding whisper of feet on the dewy grass.

Thargos looked away from him toward the flame. "This is a place of memory, yes?"

"Yes. For those who died as humans entered space."

"A holy place then?"

"You could say that."

"My name is Thargos."

The requirements of manners took over again even though the voice in his skull was now yammering, *Run! Run away!*

"Pleased to meet you, Mr. Thargos. My name is Jim Endicott." He would have offered to shake, but the thought of setting his fingers into that cage of claws scared him breathless. He imagined flesh torn from the meat of his palms, ripped from the thin white bones on the back of his hands.

"I know," Thargos replied.

The nerves buried in Jim's spine fired a simultaneous burst that made his shoulder blades twitch. *How* did he know? More important, *why* did he know?

"I followed you here in hopes of meeting you."

Jim's uneasiness peaked. He realized he was shaking slightly, deep in adrenaline fugue, ready to fight or run. To hell with courtesy. He took two long steps backwards.

"Huhhh . . . I'd better be going now. My mom—"

Thargos flowed into the space between them as a snake suddenly fills a rabbit's burrow. His eyes seemed to glow. Jim found himself tangled in those eyes. Some kind of hypnotism? With an effort he broke eye contact. His pulse pounded in his ears. His lungs felt too big for his chest. He risked a quick glance over his shoulder and saw two more of the alligator things moving toward him from the rear. He lurched to one side, the long muscles of his legs bunching. He felt the night air touch his face again, colder as it brushed the sweat on his cheeks and forehead.

"Wait!" Thargos said.

Jim split the distance between Thargos and the two onrushing aliens at his back. *Watch it!* his inner voice rapped sharply. *The wet grass is slippery!*

Too late. His right foot skidded as he fought for traction. He half stumbled but didn't go all the way down, and this saved him. Something hot and bright sizzled above his head. He bounced one fist off the ground, caught himself, and spurted away.

The voice in his skull was screaming: *Whatthehell! Whatthehell! Whatthehell!*

He saw more figures coalescing out of the night. He curved away from them, felt gravel beneath his sneakers, then solid concrete. His shoes made slapping sounds as he raced across it. He pumped his arms and threw his head back. Cold air burned his throat.

The gate was less than twenty yards away. Behind him the rasp of furious breathing eased closer.

Three figures filled the gate, blocking it. He

made no conscious decision. Even the voice in his head had fallen silent. He ran in a kind of silvery limbo, absorbing the shock of his pounding feet with the resilience of his calves and thighs. He put his head down and ran straight toward the figures blocking the gate.

He closed his eyes and shielded his face with his crossed arms just before he reached them. *Like playing football* . . .

He slammed into them and felt his shoulder drive against hard muscular bodies. One of them snarled. Then he was through. A surge of triumph quickened him as he whipped himself toward the safety of the tube station on the corner.

Muted crackling sounds filled the night behind him. Flashes of light, shouts, a single cry of pain. A chorus of big dogs barking.

The harsh light of a stunner beam caught him in full stride and locked his nervous system into a long, painless spasm. A fading sensation of regret filled him as he fell. He felt the blow when his head struck the pavement only as a sudden pressure before darkness.

The last thing he heard was the dogs still barking and snarling. Crazily, he hoped the alligators wouldn't hurt them. Then nothing.

# CHAPTER THREE

## 1

**A**lthough Jim hadn't noticed, it was three members of an Albagensian penetration team he had barreled through as he raced between the gates of the museum. Later, Korkal's people had carried his unconscious form to the war wagon, a lightly armored grav-van they'd brought planetside with their squad. The van had been subtly altered so that it might pass as a Terran vehicle, since Korkal had decided the mission called for stealth rather than naked firepower.

Now he squatted anxiously over the sleeping boy. He was reasonably sure Jim had suffered nothing worse than a stun beam and a bumped head, but he worried that it was taking so long for the boy to come around. "We should have brought a medical kit for humans," he told his CIO. She panted softly from her recent exertions as she examined the swollen bruise on Jim's forehead.

"We didn't know we were coming into a firefight over this kid. That's the right word, kid, isn't it?"

Korkal nodded.

"It's a good thing we played it safe and came in the war wagon with a full penetration team, or we wouldn't have him now," the CIO said. She snorted. "Some spies we are. You'd think the Wolfbane authorities would notice a pitched battle in one of their public parks, wouldn't you?"

"It was only stunners, thank Skypack. Nothing got blown up. How is he?"

"He has a strong pulse although it's fast for a human. Natural enough, after what just happened to him. But he's young. If there isn't any skull damage, he should be all right. I think. I'm no medical officer, especially not when it comes to Terries."

Korkal leaned forward; by human standards he was mildly nearsighted. Beneath the harsh overhead light of the small grav-van they called the war wagon, the boy's face looked thin and drawn. There were lines beginning to form in the smooth skin at the corners of his eyes. From what he knew that was unusual. The boy must have endured stresses not usual for a child his age.

The CIO pushed a flop of Jim's hair out of the way for a better look at the wound. A brown crust had formed over a cut in the center of the bruise. At her touch the boy flinched and let out a soft moan. His eyelids quivered.

"I think he's coming around."

"Good. When he wakes up, maybe we can find out why Thargos rushed all the way from Terra looking for him. Nice job tracking down the Hunter so quickly, by the way."

"Thanks. He didn't know we were looking, and so he didn't take precautions, thank Skypack. He thought he was only dealing with Terrans and Wolfbane security. Now he knows better."

"Yes. It seems even the Hunter can succumb to complacency. No longer, though. I hope this Jim Endicott is worth blowing our cover."

"Thargos got away," the CIO noted.

"Of course. As soon as he saw our team coming through the gate he slithered in the opposite direction as fast as he could go. The Hunter hasn't survived this long by taking chances with his personal hide."

"Hunzza don't slither. And do I detect a hint of admiration?"

Korkal showed his fangs. "Mutual understanding. I'm fond of my hide, too."

"What happened?" Jim Endicott said. "Where *am* I?"

## 2

"**A**lbans," Thargos said. "What the Seventh Cold Hell were Albans doing there? And who were they?"

He and his battered snatch team were rising rapidly through the night toward the low orbit where his shadowship waited. He looked at the three with him. They were lucky to be here at all. That had been a full Alban penetration team. The first three through the gate had been followed by five more, all heavily armed. If they'd used anything more than stunners, he and his people would still be in the park, probably as charred black spots on the grass. He clicked his teeth in frustration.

Everything had changed now. He'd thought he had a clear field to snatch the boy, with no one the wiser. Terran technology would not be able to detect his ship. Albagensian science was another matter entirely. He turned to the comm unit that was his link to the shadowship.

"Security status," he said. His voice was soft but burred with tension.

A disembodied voice replied, "Buttoned up tight. We have class one spoofing enabled, and all watches on emergency status."

"Have you found that Alban ship yet?"

After a pause, "No. Their technology is equal to ours. Still, we ought to be able to find them if they are in single orbit, but it will take a while. And if they are hiding in that jumble of freighters waiting to off-load, we'll have to crack Wolfbane traffic control to see if we can search them out that way."

"Do it."

"Yes, sir."

Thargos turned away from the communicator. "Blast the luck!" Yet he knew that was an evasion. Luck was what you got after you did everything else right, and he'd made a major mistake in assuming it was only the Terries he had to deal with. The Albans must have found him with ridiculous ease. He was probably lucky they hadn't blown his shadowcraft out of orbit in some kind of spectacularly phony accident. If their roles had been reversed, he certainly would have done exactly that.

Alba and Hunzza weren't officially at war. Not yet. But elements of their fleets had been rubbing up against each other, and the number of fatal "incidents" was mounting. The politicians on both sides were still pretending a peaceful resolution was possible, but the fleet commanders knew better. So, evidently, did whoever was running the pack of Albans that had waylaid him. Discovering that was the first item on his immediate agenda.

Well, not quite the first. "How much longer?" he asked the pilot of the small shuttlecraft.

"Just about now."

The membranes covering Thargos's green eyes flickered. A moment later a loud clang resounded through the hull. Thargos waited while the ship-seals were initiated and then began to climb out of his seat. The round door irised into the wall and light flooded into the dim interior. Faces peered at him out of the glare.

"It's about time!" he said as he clambered through. "Ilgan, what kind of team did you bring?"

The master of the larger vessel cocked his head as if listening to voices only he could hear. "As you ordered, sir. A fully equipped battle company. Twenty troops and all their equipment. And this attack boat, of course."

"Good. Unless that thrice-damned Alban has landed something similar, we might pull this out yet. If we hurry. Make sure everybody understands that, if possible, the human boy isn't to be harmed. I want him in one piece. Of course you may kill every Alban you see.

"Sir?"

"Yes."

"What if it's not possible? To capture the human."

Thargos flicked his double elbows in and out of joint as he considered. After a moment he opened his mouth wide. His hummingbird tongue vibrated across his teeth. "If there's no other option? Kill him, too."

## 3

Korkal was impressed with the way the young human maintained his equanimity. The boy's green eyes focused on his own without wavering.

"I know what you are," the boy said. "You're Albagensians."

Korkal remembered to keep his fangs hidden and inclined his head instead. No sense in looking any more fearsome than necessary.

Over the ten Terran years he had functioned as the secret intermediary between Delta and the Albagensian Empire he'd made it his business to learn everything he could about humans, their ways of thinking, their cultures and histories, and anything else he could find that might help him to understand them.

His own masters wanted more from him than just a conduit for messages from the enigmatic Delta. They demanded his interpretations of those messages, the social and cultural contexts for them, and estimates of Delta's thoughts and intentions. It had been difficult for him because humans, though warm-blooded mammals as he was himself, were so different from the communal, pack-oriented Albans. Humans paid lip service to their communitarian instincts, but were capable of a kind of cold-blooded, antisocial egoism that was nearly beyond Alban comprehension. Yet as his understanding of this peculiar trait grew, Korkal thought that in some ways he had become a better agent, less dependent on consensus, readier to make critical decisions on his own. But something about this boy's calm made him uneasy. He tried to think of what it was.

An unsettling feature of human ecology was the pets they called dogs. These animals bore too much resemblance to Korkal's protoancestors for him to be entirely comfortable with them.

He knew that human reaction to his physical form involved a lot of intellectual and emotional processing around the concept of dogs as pets—although he didn't really resemble their dogs, any more than Thargos looked like their alligators. But each had features that reminded humans of both species, and so humans had a ready-made package of subconscious feelings and reactions when confronted by Albans or Hunzza.

Korkal had learned to manipulate these feelings somewhat, and this had come in handy on occasion. Humans and their dogs had loved each other so long that the primate half of the partnership had forgotten that their pets had teeth. Korkal had found the insight useful more than once. He wasn't sure whether this said more about humans or about him.

Would this boy see him as a friendly dog, or as a wolf? He knew the difference, although the idea of wild packs disturbed him on some ancient level. At least the boy was maintaining an admirable amount of composure in the face of what must surely have been a confusing and frightening situation. Korkal doubted if he could have done it any better himself.

But was it composure in the face of a pet, or of a wolf? Humans loved their dogs, but in some places they still killed their wolves without mercy.

"Yes," he said finally, "I am Alban. That's the short form of the word. My name is Korkal Emut Denai. Call me Korkal. What's yours?"

"Jim Endicott."

Good. At least he had the right boy. They'd watched Thargos rifle through the Wolfbane computers searching for that name. When he'd detected the Hunter's watch on the boy's house he'd set spies of his own, and had come when word arrived that Thargos was following the boy on foot. It had looked like a snatch from the beginning, and so it had turned out. But why? What did Thargos want with this youth?

"Jim, I don't want you to be afraid. You're among friends."

Jim turned his head and stared in turn at each of the shaggy Albans crowding the cramped interior of the vehicle.

"Friends? You mean like that alligator in the park? He told me his name, too. But I don't think he was my friend."

"No, he wasn't. He was going to kidnap you. And he would have succeeded if we hadn't gotten to you when we did."

The boy's tongue flicked across his lips. "You rescued me then." He raised his hand to push hair off his forehead, then winced as he touched the lump there. "Okay."

"I don't think that's dangerous," Korkal said. "Just a bump."

"Hurts like hell. How did I get it? Did you do it?"

"No. You got caught by a stunner beam and fell."

"Oh." Jim went silent for a moment, though his gaze never wavered from Korkal's face. Once again the Alban felt a sense of mystery about Jim Endicott, as if there were more to him than easily met the eye. To his surprise he suddenly realized he was a bit afraid of him. But that was ridiculous. What did he have to fear from one half-dazed human boy?

Jim moved his shoulder and slipped his

backpack down to his lap. His right hand rested protectively on the top flap. "Since you're my friend, you'll let me out of here now, won't you?"

"Well, I can't do that, but—"

"I didn't think so." Jim's hand moved with blurry speed, vanished beneath the pack flap, then reappeared wrapped around the butt of a huge handgun. Korkal shied back reflexively, cursing himself for his own stupidity. Why hadn't he thought to search that backpack?

A great invisible hand picked up the van and tumbled it like a child's toy. They landed with a crash that split the doors wide open, and Korkal felt himself flying through the air, the terrified howls of his CIO wailing distantly in his ears.

The flat sizzle of energy beams filled the darkness. *Those aren't stunners*, Korkal thought as he slammed onto the concrete and felt most of the bones in his right arm and shoulder snap like so many dry twigs. Then the blast wave skittered him like a flung stone across the pavement.

**4**

The explosion tossed Jim through the night in a low arc that ended in a thick, shaggy hedge. He landed unharmed, cushioned by the leafy branches. For a moment he lay in the bower motionless, catching his breath and his thoughts at the same time.

*What in the holy hell?*

His backpack was nowhere to be found, but the comforting weight of the S&R .75 still filled his right hand. He came to a cautious crouch and peered through the brush. Light and sound flashed and roared along the empty street. He saw the hulk of a vehicle overturned a hundred yards away. A pair of huddled forms lay limp beside it.

Something made him look up. A huge indistinct shape floated above him, barely visible against the dim glow of the star fields and Wolfbane's two tiny moons. He stared at it and tried to ignore the ache pounding in his skull. It wasn't just the darkness that shielded that amorphous silhouette—the longer he stared at it, the harder it became to see. It seemed to flicker in and out, just at the edge of his vision, like a ghost glimpsed from the corner of his eye. Yet he thought he was looking at it straight on. He'd never seen an attack boat using shadowcraft technology before.

As he watched, a bright rectangle appeared in the center of the thing. Dark figures plummeted down, sparkling with overheated light as they lanced the night with energy beams.

He took a deep breath. That overgrown version of a dog that called himself Korkal hadn't seemed all that bad, but this wasn't his fight. Making sure to keep the reflective whiteness of his face turned away from the revealing glare, he scanned the immediate vicinity and saw that he'd been tossed beyond the focus of the battle. The attackers were landing in the street and taking fire from the few remaining Alban defenders, who crouched behind whatever cover they could find. Jim didn't have to be a military genius to see how this firefight would turn out. Best to be gone before the inevitable ending occurred.

He slipped backwards, using the hedge for cover; then, still crouching, he scuttled in the opposite direction, toward an empty street running at right angles to the scene of the clash. The park offered no hope of safety; the alligators would no doubt search there as soon as they realized he wasn't with the other defenders. Likewise with the Albans, if by some miracle they prevailed.

He knew if he could get across the street unseen, he could lose himself in the houses and woods beyond. There would be a few moments of danger as he crossed the exposed emptiness, but that was a risk he would have to take.

He checked his pistol and shook his head as he saw the safety was still on. He flicked it off and scanned the empty street a final time. Something had shut down all the streetlights, but the rising glare of the battle around the corner gave some illumination, and in it he saw for the first time a crumpled figure across the pavement struggling to rise. He squinted. He couldn't be sure, but it looked like his avowed rescuer, the one who called himself Korkal. And he was hurt. It was obvious in the way he cradled his right arm gingerly against his chest. Jim could hear the Alban's moans—soft and panting with agony. The sound made him recall a dog he'd had as a child, a cocker spaniel named Duke. Duke had been crushed beneath a crumbling wall in an accident. He'd made sounds just like that while Jim cradled his bleeding head until he died. The memory was surprisingly sharp; he thought he'd forgotten, but the pain was as bright as ever.

A shadow wheeled around the corner and resolved into an armored alligator. It paused a moment as if sniffing the air, then ran directly toward the wounded Alban. Korkal saw him coming and tried to raise his hands. The sound he made was still ringing in Jim's ears when he lifted the .75 and blew the gator right off its feet.

He didn't realize he'd made the decision until after he'd crossed the pavement, scooped up the hapless Alban, and dragged him into the concealing shadows beyond the road.

"Shut up!" he hissed as he yanked Korkal along by main force, jerking him upright each time he stumbled. He was surprised at how little the alien seemed to weigh. Korkal was shorter than he was, but evidently he was also constructed on a less massive bone structure.

He ignored Korkal's moans of protest and then realized Korkal wasn't protesting, he was groaning because he couldn't help it. But the Alban seemed to have his feet under him now and was doing his best to keep up.

Jim felt a grudging respect. Whether friend or foe, this strange being was one tough little fighter. He kept them going until the sound-and-light show behind them had dimmed almost to nothing and a quick glance at the sky showed that the strange floating vessel was nowhere to be seen.

"Over here," Jim said, and led them to the protective overhang of a large kookananda tree. "Can they find us?"

Korkal was busy stripping pieces of equipment from his belt with his good hand. Jim saw a flash of white along the alien's muzzle and realized that Korkal was gritting his teeth. "I'm dumping everything they might be able to trace. Let's keep going."

Jim tensely checked the trees and houses around them while he waited for Korkal to finish. Lights were beginning to come on, and he heard voices calling querulously.

"Hurry up, we gotta get moving."

"I'm ready."

"Can you run okay?"

"If I can't, just drag me."

Jim glanced at Korkal and saw the alien staring back at him. "You saved my life."

"You said you were my friend." That wasn't the reason, not at all, but now was not the time to bring that up.

"I am," Korkal replied. "That might not have been technically true before, but it is now. Get us out of this, and you'll see. Better hurry though. I don't know how much longer I can stay conscious."

"Okay . . . Korkal."

"Good boy," Korkal replied.

Jim grinned faintly. "Aren't I supposed to say that to you, my doggy friend?"

Korkal's jaw dropped. So it was his pet-ness that had saved him. *Well, I can live with that. In fact, I have* lived with it. *Or because of it.*

"I owe you my life, Jim Endicott. I'll thank you properly later," he said, enunciating his words carefully to make sure the boy understood. In his own mind it was a vow that only death could break—and even then the burden of his life-debt would be passed on to his family and pack as a whole.

"If there is a later," Jim said. "Let's go."

# CHAPTER FOUR

## 1

Jim dragged Korkal stumbling and gasping through the darkness to the only place he could think of that might offer them immediate shelter. As the sounds behind him guttered out he remembered another time he'd run through a Wolfbane night while slaughter and destruction exploded at his back. He wanted all this to go away but knew it wouldn't. He would have to deal with it. *What about Tabitha? Would they be coming for her now? The bastards had done that before, too.*

"Sit there on that bench. I'll put my coat around you. It will help keep you warm."

"What is this place?"

"Tube station."

"Oh. Primitive . . ."

Jim raised his eyebrows. "I suppose. I don't know much about Alban technology. Or Albans, either—is getting warm good for you?"

"I'm a warm-blooded mammal just like you are. And I'm freezing because I'm in shock . . . *Awrll—careful!*"

"Sorry. I didn't mean to hurt you."

Korkal had begun to pant rapidly. His eyes

would drift out of focus, then snap back. "Is there some place I can get food?"

"Food? You're hungry after all this?"

"My body is repairing itself right now, and it's cannibalizing me to do it. I need to get raw material for it to use."

"Your people can regenerate? I never heard of mammals that could do that."

"We couldn't either till about three of your Terrie centuries ago. It's a . . . you call it nanotech . . . an intracellular micropackage with my soma-print carried in memory, right down to the atomic level. When something gets out of whack, the nanomachines kick in and start to fix the damage. The process dumps heat. That's why I'm sweating so much. At the moment I'm eating myself alive. Where are you going?"

"Trying to find a public axe. A communications access unit. Mine was in my backpack, but that's gone now."

A shudder racked the Alban. The ruff of fur around his muzzle was clotted with sweat. He gave off a sharp, damp odor. "But you managed to keep that gun, I see. Skypack! What is it anyway? It went through that Hunzza's armor like . . . I don't know what it was like. I've never seen anything like that before."

"Primitive technology," Jim said. "Like this tube station. But effective. Listen, I'll be right back. Will you be okay?"

"I still need food."

The bench was the farthest one from the main loading area, at this time of night deserted, shrouded in shadow. Korkal would be almost indistinguishable from a distance.

"There's a public axe near the entrance," Jim said. "I'll be right back."

Korkal began to pant violently again. He managed a nod, but speech was beyond him.

*God he looks bad.* Jim's thoughts swirled as he loped toward the front of the empty station. He was in a kind of shock, too, emotionally and intellectually. He had to trust his instincts. He had nothing else to fall back on, but they had served him well before. The first thing was to make sure Tabitha was safe.

"Mom?"

"Jim . . . what is it? Why aren't you home? Do you know what time it is? Why do you have the visual off on your axe?"

"Listen, Mom, get out of the house. Get out right now, just leave. Go to . . . uh . . . the last time we saw Dad. Got that? *The place where we saw Dad the last time.*"

"Jim, what's wrong? Are you in trouble?"

"Mom, I don't have time. You may be in danger. I don't know, but I don't want to take any chances. I'll call you again as soon as I can. But please don't argue with me, just do it. Leave right now, okay?"

Her voice changed, became tighter and tougher. "All right. It will take me a couple of hours to reach . . . that place. *You call me, you hear?*"

"Yes, Mom, I will. Now just go, okay? Just please get the hell out of there."

"I'm on my way. Jimmy?"

"What?"

"Whatever it is, be careful. I love you."

"I love you, too, Mom. And *you* be careful. Now get going."

The connection went dead. He was glad he'd left the visual off. He didn't know what he looked like, but he doubted that his appearance after getting blown up would have reassured her. He stood a moment at the axe unit and tried to order his thoughts. He didn't trust Korkal, but the alligators frightened him on a deeper, more basic level. Mammals and lizards had been enemies for eons, and though he didn't note that consciously, Darwinian inheritance was plucking strings of dread inside him. The riddle of the mind arrays wasn't the only thing imprinted in his chromosomal knowledge.

On a conscious level one thing was sure. Aliens were after him now. There could be only one reason for that. Delta had been terrified that the secret of the mind arrays would be discovered by nonhumans and thus destroy the only bargaining chip Terra held in the greater galaxy. And that secret now lay chained in the DNA within his own cellular core.

He could distill only one thought out of the chaos: he couldn't trust anybody. Of late it seemed the entire universe had conspired to shatter the smugness and conceit of his former life.

It was enough to make a person paranoid. But in the past year he'd learned something interesting about paranoia: sometimes the bastards really *were* out to get you.

## 2

"**H**ere. Eat these."

"What are they?"

"Candy bars. Bags of nuts. Out of a machine back there. High sugar content. And protein. If your metabolism is anything close to mine, they should help."

Korkal peered myopically at the little bars. "What's in them?"

"Peanuts, chocolate, a bunch of stuff."

"I don't have much choice, do I?" Korkal ripped away the plastic wrapping and gobbled several in a few gulping snaps. After a moment he seemed to relax a bit. "It should be okay. I can eat most Terrie stuff. The problem is allergies and toxins, not metabolic incompatibility."

"How are you feeling?"

"Better now. Give me a little more time, and I should be ready to get moving again."

"That's good because I don't want to hang around here. And you and I need to talk."

"Yes, we do. You know, you seem like a remarkable boy. I can't imagine one of our children handling this as calmly as you have."

"I'm not really a child," Jim said softly.

Korkal stared at him. "No, I don't think you are."

Suddenly the lurching exhaustion of adrenaline overload buckled Jim's knees and he sat down hard on the stone bench. The little alien stirred in alarm.

"Are you all right?"

"Just reaction," Jim said. "Give me one of those candy bars."

Korkal passed one over and they sat next to each other, jaws working in companionable silence. Korkal stirred as a couple of late-night travelers approached the distant loading area. Jim put one hand on Korkal's knee. "It's okay. They aren't paying any attention."

Korkal chuffed softly. As they waited a low whooshing moan began to rise in the air. "Grav-train," Jim told him.

A string of cars slid smoothly out of the far end of the tunnel, a single light like a great eye suddenly opening. The travelers boarded and the train greased silently past their bench and vanished.

"How do we get out of here?" Korkal asked.

"On the next train." Jim grinned slowly. Korkal thought the expression made him look even older and more tired. "If you hunch over and keep my coat wrapped around you, maybe people will think you're my dog. You know what a dog is?"

Korkal threw back his head and barked.

"That's good," Jim said.

## 3

Thargos stared at the CIO. The Alban female was near death. She'd taken two bad burns and major internal damage in the explosion that had cracked the Alban war wagon. The firefight itself had lasted only a few minutes before Thargos called everybody back to the assault ship. They had done their best to leave nothing alive behind them. It would make a nice little mystery for the Wolfbane authorities.

"Keep her alive. As long as you can," he told his medic. "But don't let her wake up. I think she's their intelligence officer. She's probably got some kind of suicide package we'll never find before she can activate it. I want her drugged to her eyes when she surfaces, no conscious control at all."

He regarded her thoughtfully. "Even that might not be enough, but we have to try. I want to know who she reports to. I'm beginning to get a bad feeling about all this."

The assault ship was considerably roomier than the tiny landing craft he'd used earlier. It had better communications links, too, and now he began to use them.

There was no penalty on size when building interstellar craft. For a variety of reasons such ships never landed on planets but only traveled from orbit to orbit. Since they never entered a planetary atmosphere or were subject to the harsh strains of a planet's gravity, they didn't need to be streamlined. They didn't even need to look very much like ships. Thargos's cruiser, for instance, resembled a long necklace of lumpy beads strung together. There was room aboard for two assault boats, several smaller landers, and a crew of five hundred Hunzza—as well as a large complement of the latest products of Hunzzan weapons research.

He would feel much better when he was safely back aboard his ship. He didn't fear the humans, but somewhere out there was an Alban vessel of which he knew nothing, and that did frighten him. As far as military technology went, the Terries were still playing with toys—but the Albans had the real thing. And despite their much-admired communitarian natures, when Alba sensed a threat against the Great Pack, Alba had no qualms about striking as hard as it could. Which was very hard indeed.

He eyed his captive. So far, his mission had been a failure. If he could get anything useful from this one, perhaps he might turn that around. But he'd lost the boy. And when he'd taken a body count he found that his team had left one scorched war wagon and six charred bodies behind them. This battered female was number seven. But a typical Alban penetration team numbered eight.

That worried him. They still hadn't located the Alban vessel, but without doubt that ship knew about him. Unless the Albans had sent down a short crew—and there was no reason to believe they had—somebody might at this very moment be telling the Alban ship about an assault boat full of Hunzza.

He imagined invisible weapons reaching out from hidden orbit with ghostly precision to lock on his small craft as it hurried back to the mother ship. He pictured some nameless

Alban gunner eagerly making ready to extract revenge for his murdered fellows. Thargos felt very much like a target. He didn't like the sensation at all.

## 4

The object of Thargos's worried conjectures popped the last of the candy bars into his mouth as he slumped in a huddle on a window seat of the empty grav-train car. Swathed in Jim's coat, he did somewhat resemble a large—very large—dog, if one didn't look closely.

"Any more?" He was beginning to feel better. His broken bones felt as if they were knitting nicely, and he'd been able to repress most of the pain with self-generated hormones that acted on the appropriate nerve centers.

"That's it. When we stop we can get more."

"When are we stopping?"

"The end of the line. Then we transfer to a long-distance train."

"Oh? Where are we going?"

"A place."

Korkal thought about that a moment. "Can I assume you don't trust me?"

Jim glanced at him, smiled faintly, and looked away.

"That's only sensible, I suppose, but I want to explain something. You don't know much about my people, do you?"

Jim shook his head. "Just a little from school. Exoanthropology isn't a large field of study yet."

Korkal nodded. "You don't know it, but you have a man you never heard of to thank for that."

"Oh?"

"A man named Delta."

Jim gave a tiny start. Korkal noted it and wondered. But he let it pass because he had more personal *skribbets* to grill.

"We aren't what you might call a warrior culture, but we do know how to fight. And when the Great Pack makes war it has traditions that predate our recorded history. By Terran standards it is a very old history."

Jim stared straight ahead, but Korkal thought he was listening.

"You saved my life, and you didn't have to. Moreover, you risked your own life to do it. And I have acknowledged that to you. Among our people that places me under an enormous debt to you, and not just me. The debt is owned by my family, my pack, and even, to some extent, the Great Pack itself—the entire Alban race. Do you understand what that means?"

"Among some of the old Asian cultures on Terra, supposedly if you saved a man's life you were responsible for him forever."

Korkal mulled it. "No, I'd say it's the opposite. That's a strange way of looking at things. Why did they do that?"

Jim's lips quirked. "I think the idea was that if fate had decreed it was time for someone to die and somebody else thwarted that fate, then the original victim was no longer a charge of fate but of the one who rescued him. You could sort of call it the revenge of fate."

"The revenge of fate? Yes, I suppose that makes sense. You humans never cease to surprise me."

"Do you know the meaning of the word condescension?"

Korkal thought about that and decided to change the subject. "Jim, what I'm trying to tell you is that I owe you. My family and pack owe you. Even my race is in your debt."

"A man once told me that races don't have morals or ethics, only interests. How much does your race owe me?"

Korkal found himself even more impressed. And he realized that almost against his will what he felt for this boy had changed from simple gratitude to growing respect. He decided to honor this new feeling with honesty.

"It's a debt, Jim. But not a suicide pact. Alba owes you something, but not everything."

Jim turned to face him. "Do you believe the ends justify the means?"

Korkal didn't know everything about humans, but even he felt the ethical mine field hedging the simple question. "Jim, I'm afraid to answer that question. For several reasons. Can we change the subject?"

"That's an answer. I guess. Sure. What else do you want to talk about?"

"You said you called somebody. Who was it? Why?"

"Korkal, I'm afraid to answer that question. For several reasons. Can we change the subject?"

*Game and set*, Korkal thought. But maybe not match. He had learned to enjoy the Terrie game of tennis.

"Hypothetically, if you called that person because you feared for them and wanted to warn them, I may be able to help. To offer some protection."

"Alban protection?"

"No. Terran."

"Oh? What would that be?"

"Would Serena Half Moon, the Confed chairman, do?"

Jim's eyes slowly widened. "You can do that?"

"Maybe. Probably. You want to find out?"

"It might make a difference," Jim said. "In how I feel about you."

*Match to me*, Korkal thought.

# CHAPTER FIVE

## 1

The night stars glittered in the chill mountain air like emeralds scattered carelessly on velvet, hard and uncaring. The tube station, never much used, was deserted except for their own presence.

Through the glass doors Jim could see pockmarks in the concrete apron outside, reminders of the bomblets the dead man he'd once believed to be his father, Carl Endicott, had exploded when he'd tried and failed to kill the strange deadly woman named Commander Steele. It had only been a few months, but it seemed like an eternity ago. Another life.

Korkal's voice lifted him out of his unwanted reverie. He stood a pace away—but out of view—from where the Alban was planted before an axe screen. Jim doubted the average human could have called the Confed chairman from a public unit and gotten through, but Korkal had spoken code words that turned underlings' faces pale and brought stammered guarantees of haste. It had taken several minutes, but eventually her famous face appeared on the screen. She looked tired, Jim thought.

Her voice was huskier and richer than what he'd heard of her public speeches.

She was plainly annoyed.

"A protection team? Why can't you tell me what it's for?"

Korkal murmured something Jim didn't catch, and the chairman's expression changed. "Oh. In that case . . ."

Korkal said something else. The chairman glanced off-screen, then nodded. "I'm told it will take about an hour." She raised one hand to brush an errant strand of black hair away from her forehead. Jim realized she must have been awakened to take this call, and his estimation of Korkal's influence suddenly expanded.

"You will furnish me a complete report about this incident, Mr. Denai," she said.

Korkal replied in tones that sounded agreeable. Serena Half Moon raised her chin, bringing her sharp features into high relief. She looked formidable. The screen went dark, and Korkal turned.

"Well, that's taken care of."

"You really do know the chairman," Jim said. He tried to keep his tone unimpressed, but didn't quite succeed.

"Yes. Not well, but evidently well enough." The Alban turned and headed for the door. "You said we have to climb. She says a special weapons protection team will be here in an hour. My own people should be here well before that. So you'll have a little time with whoever it is you want to see. But we'd better hurry."

Jim followed him out onto the concrete, then moved ahead to lead the way down a stair to the ground and a path that vanished into the dark trees.

"How come your people will get here first?"

"They're closer. And no doubt they're looking for me already." Korkal hoped that was true, that they hadn't written him off as dead in the wreck of the war wagon.

"I asked the chairman to contact my ship. She said she would." Privately, Korkal wondered if she would send the message before giving her own people a chance to arrive on the scene. He'd hung quite a bit on the issue of timing. Thanks to Thargos, things had turned tricky all of a sudden. Korkal knew he had a lot of questions to sort through and decisions to make, but first things first. He knew he wouldn't relax until he had Jim safely aboard his ship, concealed behind the toughest shields he could mount, and was shaking the dust of Wolfbane—and Thargos—from his heels.

His shoulder still ached, and he had to struggle to keep up with the boy's long strides. But the night air was clean and rich with the dark cologne of the trees. In some ways it reminded him of the carefully preserved forests of Alba, and this pleased him.

"What is this place we're going to?" Korkal asked.

"A bad place," Jim said, and walked faster.

## 2

In the dim light Jim saw that the cabin had not been repaired. The shattered roof still slumped drunkenly over part of the shell, and all the windows were dark, gaping maws. In one of them a faint glow showed that the place wasn't empty, and he felt an answering glow of relief. Nevertheless, he made sure the safety was off his pistol as he approached the front door.

"Mom?" he called softly.

He heard a faint rustle and sensed hidden eyes watching. "I'm here, Jim," came the low reply.

Jim put out one hand. "Wait," he said. Then he pried open the warped front door. Korkal winced at the sharp screech.

The Alban waited outside on the porch, but he could see through the window as a blond woman wrapped the boy in a powerful hug. They stood a moment without moving, then stepped away and faced each other. They kept their voices low, but Korkal's hearing was better than a human's. He could make them out clearly.

"Jimmy, what happened? You're a mess. That lump on your forehead . . ."

"I'm okay, Mom. Don't worry. Did anybody follow you here? Did you see anything weird?"

She shook her head. "Jim, what's going on? Why did you send me here?" She moved her head. "I don't have good memories of this place. I can't imagine you do either."

Korkal thought the emotions he heard in Jim's reply were twofold: shame, and a profound, inconsolable sadness. "No, Mom," the boy whispered, "I don't. But I couldn't think of anyplace else. And I didn't have any time."

"Come over here and sit down," she said. "Start at the beginning. Tell me everything."

"Okay, Mom. But I want you to meet somebody."

She stiffened. "Who? Who did you bring here?"

"Korkal!" he called. "Come in and meet my mom."

# 3

It quickly became obvious to Korkal that there was some deep complicity between the boy and the woman, something shared that had marked them so terribly that words were unnecessary. When Jim described the attempt by Thargos to kidnap him and the rescue attempt Korkal had made, Tabitha Endicott inhaled sharply, but then nodded as if the attack was not a total surprise.

He felt that hidden understanding even more deeply as he sketchily explained his own role. Tabitha was at least as sharp as her son and, Korkal realized, even more unyielding. A low tolerance for what humans called bullshit. He approved, but it made his task harder—especially since he had no intention of reveal-

ing the larger problems with which he struggled.

When he finished Tabitha Endicott did and
said something that surprised him. She leaned
forward until her face was only a few inches from
his own. Her gaze bored into him with unsettling
intensity. "Are you a good person, Mr. Denai?"

He opened his mouth, then closed it.
Somehow he understood this was not the time
for speed or glibness. And he knew what she
was asking him. His own mother's face ghosted
across the back of his mind, and he knew she
was waiting for his answer, too.

"Yes, Mrs. Endicott, I am. And I will give my
life to protect your son."

She held him one more beat, then nodded.
"All right."

"Mom, he knows the Confed chairman."

Her gaze slid toward him. "And we have
such good reason to trust the Terran government, don't we, Jim?"

He looked away. *So much between them*,
Korkal thought. *And so much hidden from me.*

"I have nothing to go on except my own
instincts, but I trust them. You seem like a
good . . . man," Tabitha said.

Korkal caught the hesitation, and said,
"I'm male, Mrs. Endicott."

The corners of her eyes crinkled in a web of
laugh lines, and Korkal thought that under
other circumstances they might find they
would enjoy each other a great deal. But these
weren't those circumstances, and her expression quickly hardened.

"Understand me, please. I will give my permission for my son to go with you. I believe he cannot be safe as long as he stays on this planet, not if, as you say, he is being hunted by someone like this Thargos you tell me about. I'm not happy about it, but I don't see any other choice. I wish to God I did. But Mr. Denai?"

"Yes?"

"If you harm my son in any way, or allow him to come to harm, I swear by everything I know that I will hunt you down, no matter how far I have to go, no matter how long it takes. And I will kill you."

She said it very flatly, but Korkal felt the hackles stir at his neck. He had no doubt at all she would try to do precisely what she promised. Once again, he thought of his own mother.

"Fair enough," he said. "I won't tell you not to worry. Of course you will. But as I said before, I owe Jim my life. And Albans take that kind of debt seriously. If he comes to harm, you can be sure I was harmed first and incapable of preventing it."

"That's not as reassuring as it could be, Mr. Denai."

"Call me Korkal, please. It may not be reassuring, but it's honest. Which would you prefer?"

She lifted her head and stared down her nose imperiously. Jim thought she was magnificent.

The interior of the cabin exploded in brilliant light.

# 4

Thargos let the door slide shut on the grisly scene behind him. It had been touch-and-go. The suicide package built into the Alban CIO's cellular blueprint had been particularly nasty, and it hadn't been slowed much by the methods he'd used to counteract it. But he had slowed it enough, and he'd gotten the one thing he'd really wanted. A name.

Korkal Emut Denai.

He thought about his old enemy. This was close to the worst news he could have gotten, but he knew bad news was much preferable to no news at all.

At least now he knew with whom he was dealing. And his own experience told him exactly how to deal with him.

He gave a series of rapid orders to his hacker-cracker teams. "Break the Wolfbane communications net. Here's what you're looking for."

If the Alban agent made a call, they would find it—and him. His only fear was that they would be too slow, too late. He hoped not. He had more than a few scores to settle with Korkal Emut Denai.

## 5

"**G***et down!*"

Korkal was amazed how quickly the huge pistol jumped into the boy's hand. The storm of light had bleached all color from the interior. Jim's eyes were hard black points as Korkal found himself staring at them above the gaping mouth of the weapon. He remembered what it had done to an armored Hunzzan trooper and slowly raised one hand.

"Easy," he said. "It's my people."

Slowly Jim nodded and the barrel swung away. But he didn't lower the weapon until a shadowy form materialized out of the haze and Korkal called, "XO! Over here!"

The Alban executive officer clambered over the sill of a blasted window, removing his helmet as he did so. Only when Jim saw another hairy muzzle like Korkal's own did he finally jam the pistol back into his belt.

"Chief, what in the Three Unborn Hells is going on?" the XO said. He spoke in Alban, and Jim said, "Can he speak so I can understand?"

"Of course. XO, switch on a translator."

The XO fumbled at his chest. When he next spoke, his muzzle moved and a different, but easily understandable voice speaking Terrie issued from a speaker concealed in his armor. Korkal had not used a similar device either with Jim or the chairman simply because he trusted his own capabilities more than the machine. Alban translation technology was good, but not perfect; which was why high-level political negotiations were always carried out with both living and machine translations. Even then there were occasional mistakes.

"What's going on? In a very short time we're getting out of here, that's what," Korkal said. "You did bring an assault craft this time?"

The XO nodded. "And a double-sized team at hot status. The mother ship's a hundred miles straight up, with all detectors as wide as they'll go and every weapon on immediate fire. Nobody's going to sneak up on you here, Chief."

Jim listened and felt reassured, though he had no idea as to the efficiency of Alban weapons technology. He suspected it might be more advanced than Terran science, though. But he knew even less about Hunzzan bang-bangers, and so was not as reassured as he could have been.

The wrecked interior of the little cabin was crowded. Jim turned and saw Tabitha standing there, her hands hanging loosely at her sides, an expression of worried bemusement on her features. It hit him then: once again he was leaving her, perhaps going into danger, certainly going somewhere that she wouldn't know anything about.

It was a brutal moment of empathy, and it made sickeningly clear to him just how self-centered he'd been. Just like with Cat. He'd been worrying so much about his own life he'd forgotten that other people had lives, too, and his own life was bound into theirs. Tabitha was his mother, whether her gene codes had anything to do with his at all. And yet here she stood, off to the side as if discarded, playing the role mothers seemed doomed to play: loving and waiting and fearing—and as forgotten as Ulysses' Penelope. Knowing it and bearing up anyway.

For sixteen years she had loved and raised him. That was stronger than any theoretical connection between their chromosomes.

How much stronger he suddenly realized when he felt his eyes go hot at the way she was looking at him. In her gaze he found his first true definition of bravery: to love, lose, and keep on loving. He moved toward her and took her in his arms.

"Jeez, Mom, it looks like I'm taking off again."

"Oh, Jimmy."

He fumbled for something that might make her feel better. "When the Confed troops get here, you won't have to worry. They'll take care of you, make sure that nobody hurts you."

She took a step back, her eyes blazing. "I'm not worried about me!"

He shook his head. "I know. It's a curse, isn't it? This . . . thing." He glanced around, realizing he'd almost said too much.

She nodded. "A curse to both of us. I pray that somehow you'll find a way to end it, son." Her shoulders slumped. "I would if I could. I wish I could take it for myself."

Jim stared at her, knowing she would do exactly that if she could, and in that instant he knew he loved her almost more than he could bear.

"Mom, I don't know what will happen. But if everything turns out, it will be because of you. You and Dad, what you both taught me. You won't have anything to be ashamed of, I promise."

She took it for the ultimate compliment it was. "We tried to make you a good man, Jimmy." She paused, then chuckled in embarrassment. "A good man. I guess you are a man now, aren't you? But so young. You shouldn't have to be a man yet, Jimmy. Jim. I guess I hate that most of all. You've been robbed of things no boy should lose."

He tried a grin. "Mom, that's a little melodramatic, don't you think? I'm going on a trip, not just disappearing like last time."

"But will you come back? Will I ever see you again?"

He had no answer for that, and so he gave the only answer he could, the only answer that in the end meant anything. He took her in his arms and held her, and she held him, until Korkal said, "Confed armor coming down now. I'm sorry, but it's time."

"Jim? You'll take care?"

"I will, Mom."

"I'll think of you every day. If you can, you let me know what's going on."

He nodded. He hadn't even thought about that. "Korkal?"

The Alban understood. "We can get messages to the chairman. Under normal circumstances, at least."

Tabitha touched his cheek. "Jimmy, I'll . . . I'll . . ."

At the sight of her tears he felt his own begin to well up, and for some reason this embarrassed him. He kissed her to cover his own feelings, squeezed her into a final hug, then turned to Korkal.

Outside, coming out of the trees, armored Confed troopers who reminded him unsettlingly of Commander Steele set up a rapid perimeter as they stared at the Alban soldiers and their ship.

"Let's go," Jim said.

Korkal gestured toward the huge craft now occupying most of the cleared space to the right of the cabin. "Go ahead. I'll be along in a minute."

The XO followed Jim out. Korkal turned to Tabitha. "I'll take care of him." Then he paused, choosing his words carefully. "Mrs. Endicott, Thargos is after your boy. But I still have no idea why. I think you do, though. It might make a difference to Jim's safety if you told me. Don't you think?"

Tabitha didn't hesitate at all. She shook her head and said, "Mr. Denai, I have no idea. All I can think of is it must be some mistake. He's only a boy. Why would some alien we've never heard of want to hurt him?"

Korkal held her gaze for several beats, then dropped his eyes. "Very well. I'll still do the best I can." He turned. "Your guards are ready for you."

He watched as a burly Terran Marine captain escorted her from the cabin to his waiting vessel. She vanished into the lighted interior, pausing only an instant for a last glimpse of Jim. But her son was gone. She squared her shoulders, stepped up, and disappeared.

"All right," Korkal called. "That's it. Let's get this thing moving."

From then on everything went with military efficiency. Within five minutes both vessels were buttoned up and rising from the now-deserted clearing.

As the hatch slid shut behind him, Korkal allowed himself a shiver of relief. He didn't know anything about the human idea of *hubris*, the thought of pride tempting the gods to destroy the prideful, but if he had he would have understood it just fine.

The interior of the Alban craft began to flash with crimson warning beacons. The XO's voice echoed mechanically through the compartments: *"HUNZZAN VESSEL PENETRATING DETECTION LIMITS. HUNZZAN ATTACK! HUNZZAN ATTACK!"*

# CHAPTER SIX

## 1

---

The captain of the Hunzzan cruiser was hooked into his ship's nervous system as he always was. A continuous whisper of data rolled with soothing monotony through the back of his mind. In the same way that one was always aware on some level of the functions of the body—especially when something malfunctioned—he was aware of the happenings aboard his ship. And just as one would subconsciously monitor some chronic malady like a cough or infection, there was one presence aboard his vessel he was also conscious of with greater than normal attention. That presence had now entered the control room of the ship, and the captain felt an uncomfortable thrill of anxiety.

He knew what was coming. It was never pleasant to report failure to Thargos. But it was less pleasant—even dangerous—to sugarcoat the facts to his superior. Thargos rarely killed the messenger for bad news. Unless the messenger was also responsible for it. The case here was a gray area, and so the captain rose from his seat slowly and took his time making his way toward the command chair, where Thargos was now settling in.

*If we'd only found them sooner,* the captain thought. He moved through the atmosphere of the control room, an atmosphere maintained at Hunzza normal. To alien eyes the air would appear as a glowing yellow fog, the natural Hunzzan environment of super-saturated moisture and brilliant sunlight, but to the captain it was as unnoticeable as the water any fish swam in. His vision was augmented by natural infrared sensors that lined the soft unscaled skin beneath his large eyes, giving his brain two sources of visual input. He was barely conscious of the low bubble of the ventilation systems, mechanical rattles and clicks, a sudden liquid shower of computerized beeps.

He'd crossed halfway from his console to Thargos when the Hunter turned and saw him. The captain picked up his pace.

Thargos encouraged a certain informality, and so the captain began to speak almost immediately. "As you've seen, we were too late."

But Thargos only blinked his eyes in reassuring laughter, increasing the captain's sense of disquiet. Thargos seemed to laugh at the most inappropriate moments.

"And Korkal survived. Well, it would have been a disappointment otherwise. He's a hard one to kill even for an Alban."

The captain didn't know what to say, so he waited.

"I see they've gone to a cabin of some sort in the mountains."

"Yes, Lord. And now his ship is standing guard. They put down an assault craft as a lander a little while ago."

Thargos's eyes shifted to the huge 3-D holographic screen that shimmered in the air before him. On it was an aerial view of the cabin and two large ships grounded on either side. It wasn't possible to make out human figures at this magnification, but Thargos didn't care. They were down there. That was all he needed to know.

He felt an unusual sense of excitement and wondered why. Korkal had beaten him again, somehow survived the attack on his grav-van, and managed to escape not only in one piece but with the boy as well.

*Maybe the Alban discovered the boy by watching me*, Thargos thought. *And maybe not*. He would have liked to ask, but with Korkal's ship protecting him at close range, that was unfortunately no longer possible. He could have blasted that ship out of the sky; having found it at last, he now knew it was no match for the power of his own cruiser. Nevertheless, it was potent, and Thargos hesitated at staging a full-scale battle before the watching eyes of the Confed Naval squadron also orbiting over the cabin. Not that the Terran Navy could have stopped him either, but there were potential diplomatic issues involved. Better not to take the risk. Not when there was another way.

His tension rose a notch. He spoke a few words and turned back to the captain.

"Load the Terran weapon now. We will proceed with the fallback termination plan."

"Yes, sir."

They both waited until confirmation was transmitted. "You can put it right into their throat? Even his mother ship can't stop it?"

"No, sir."

"Good." A steward approached bearing a small metallic cage. In it a tiny hairy thing flung itself against the delicate bars. The steward opened it and offered it to Thargos, who removed the little creature and cupped it in his right hand.

Hunzza were empaths of a high order, extremely sensitive to the emotions of other living things. While not telepathy, this extra sense allowed them sharp insight into the minds of others, even those who were alien. With training and some knowledge of the language, an expert could appear to read the mind of, say, a Terran boy. Thargos had more expertise than any other Hunzza he knew, and his empathetic talents made learning new languages second nature.

But as with every gift, there were drawbacks. Some Hunzza became emotion addicts. The worst of them sought ever-greater rushes of sensation. Like all addictions the necessary dose became larger over time. Some lost all control and became ravening monsters, even by Hunzzan standards. Thargos, with his iron will, was not one such, but he did like his small calmatives. He felt the beast in his hand quiver like a beating heart. His mouth dropped open slightly as he stared at the hologram screen.

"If I can't have him, you won't either, old enemy."

At his rear the captain said, "Fire on your order, Lord."

Thargos's right hand began slowly to close. Inside the trap of his fingers, the tiny thing squeaked, louder and louder, then went abruptly silent.

"Fire," Thargos said.

The control module, one of the several lumpy beads that made up the string of Thargos's cruiser, rocked gently. He swayed in his chair, white-grinned and dreamy, seeming not to notice the crimson fluids that leaked slowly from his knotted fist.

## 2

"**T**ake us up—*fast!*" Korkal ordered as he leaned over his XO's shoulder in the cramped confines of the assault boat's control area. He understood the threat instantly. That didn't mean he could do anything about it except run for his life.

A Hunzzan distorter-projector catapulted payloads of matter through a chain of small subspace jumps, like skipping across a stream on a string of stones. But the space between the stones wasn't space, it was subspace, and beyond the reach of even Alban beams. Only by catching the package on one of its near-instantaneous translations in real-space could it be destroyed, but they hadn't been given enough warning for his computers to decode its path.

And if he understood Thargos, whatever payload he was sending would be strong enough for anything but the shields protecting the Alban mother ship. Korkal thought he knew exactly what gift the Hunter had mailed him. He moved to place his body between the boy and the screens.

On those screens a long red line finally intersected with a discrete green point representing a spot now far below them. He'd relayed warnings to the Terrans. Maybe they would be quick enough.

Every screen on the console flared white.

Korkal uttered a small prayer and hoped it was for the living. The first wave of radiation sent the assault craft bucking wildly.

"What the hell was *that*?" Jim yelled.

Korkal felt the boy's hands on his shoulders and braced himself just as the second blast wave hit. He stumbled but managed to stay on his feet and keep himself between the boy and the screens.

"I don't know," he gasped out, regaining his balance. "We'll find out as soon as we reach the mother ship."

"Korkal! That was a bomb! What happened?"

"Jim, stand away. Please. I've got work to do here."

He began to bark out the necessary orders, deliberately using his own language so the boy wouldn't understand. In the screens he saw the stupendous, malignant bloom of a nuclear explosion rising from the dark spine of the mountains.

A choking sound brought his head around. He saw Jim's features, twisted in horror, illuminated in the red glow of the atomic fire burning from the screens.

"*Nooooo!*"

# 3

**C**onfederation Chairman Serena Half Moon entered her office through the private entrance, saw Carlton Fredricks waiting for her, and walked quickly to her desk.

She sat down, put both her palms flat on the desktop, and leaned back in her chair. Her expression was controlled, but her dark eyes looked harried.

"Well?" she said.

Fredricks was a handsome man, beautifully dressed, who might have been easy to overlook as just another professional political functionary, except for sharp brown eyes which glinted with a hard, driven intelligence. Part of his job was to know what to tell her and when to tell it. Another part was to know when not to say something. He wasted no time on pleasantries.

"The Navy is reporting publicly they have driven the unknown invaders from the Wolfbane System. Invaders is the precise word they used in the release. Privately, it's all lies, of course."

Half Moon massaged her face, kneading the flesh hard. Her skin retained the pale imprints of her fingertips for several moments.

"Of course. After allowing unknown aliens to assault Confed citizens, fight a pitched battle in a city park, and *nuke* a chunk of mountain with one of our own bombs, what else are they going to say?"

"I wrote that release. They would have liked to cover it up entirely."

"Stupid. Did they think nobody would notice a little thing like a nuclear explosion? Thank God some smart mediahound didn't find out it was one of *our* nukes."

"You look tired."

She smiled without mirth. "An alien dog-person told me I looked beautiful. That wasn't so long ago, either."

"Korkal Emut Denai."

"Korkal Emut Denai," she agreed. "I wonder if he made it out of that mess on Wolfbane. He's a slick one, but I like him. Even if I don't trust him."

"Trust isn't a quality one normally finds at . . . this level."

"I insulted him to his face. I know he caught it, but he couldn't be sure if I knew. I tapped my teeth with my pen."

"That's an insult?"

"To an Alban it is. They have a whole etiquette built up around their fangs. Actually, I doubt he knew. They think we're little better than savages, incapable of subtlety. And by their standards it's probably true. Sometimes I think it is by mine, too."

She looked down at her desktop as if seeing it for the first time. The usual shoal of papers, chips, and chip cases obscured the screen set into the wood. It looked like any other screen on a busy executive's desk, but this one had once been connected to a very private computer system. She swept it clean with one broad pass of her arm.

"So we've spread the official version. Unknown aliens, no explanation, invasion repelled. Have we figured out yet what really happened?"

"Well, the bodyguard team you sent in at Denai's request to cover that Endicott woman took some lumps, but there were only four casualties. They got a warning from Denai himself and were already well off ground zero when the nuke lit off. They brought out the woman with a few scratches, nothing more. Lucky . . ."

Half Moon digested this. "And where is Tabitha Endicott now?"

Fredricks shrugged. "Denai said to protect her, and we agreed. So she's coming here, where we can do a better job. I hope."

"Have we heard from Denai himself yet?"

"Not yet."

"Keep trying. We never got a look at who-ever tossed our stolen nuke at him."

"Probably this Thargos . . ."

Serena ruffled her fingers absently through the papers on her desk. "You know what, Carl? I had a full Confed battle squadron over that mountain, and nobody saw a damned thing. The Navy doesn't really know if they left the system because the Navy *still* hasn't seen them. Only the Alban landing boat, and that after it was on the ground with its screens down. That kind of technology scares the hell out of me."

"And me."

"Good. Find out everything about James Endicott."

Fredricks blinked. "Everything?"

"If he pooped his pants twice on his first birthday, I want to know what time and how much. And who cleaned it up."

He was used to this, but that didn't make it any easier. He exhaled softly and nodded. "Yes, ma'am."

She smiled. "Anytime in the next two hours will be fine, Carl."

## 4

Jim sat on a sleek pedestal chair beneath an enormous arc of sky that would have, under other circumstances, thrilled him to the bottom of his soul.

The control room of Korkal's ship was about the same size and dimension as a Terran football field, and it possessed some of the same expansive mystery those fields knew on the days when the crowds were gone and the carefully tended grass grew in emptiness and silence.

The dome surmounting this vast space was nearly as large, high-curved, and perfectly transparent, so that the starry eternal night beyond burned with an oppressive sense of closeness; in this yawning chamber it was far to easy to imagine that the sky really was falling.

A faint wavering halo surrounded each star, a phenomenon associated with the ship's drive that Jim, also under different circumstances, would have been driven to investigate.

Now nothing drove him. He was all driven out. Korkal paced back and forth in front of him, looking up every few steps, then away. Searching for a way to begin yet afraid to find one.

"Mom's dead, isn't she?"

Korkal stopped. "I don't know. We analyzed the blast. It was a Terran weapon."

"We have to go back."

"We can't. It's too dangerous."

Jim raised his head. His eyes were dark wells from which screams echoes silently, but his voice was level, and only a faint tic at his right eye betrayed his tension. "Send a message then. I have to find out what happened. If Mom . . ."

For a moment he couldn't get anything out. Then, "Please, Korkal."

"Jim . . . we lost Thargos's ship. He could be anywhere. I can't take the risk of him picking up one of our transmissions. Not when we're so vulnerable. He's got a battle cruiser. We'd be a—what do you call it?—a sitting duck."

Beyond them, rank upon rank of consoles arranged in sweeping U-shapes stretched to the limits of the room. At each console sat an operator, whose head was invisible behind a shimmering dome of force. Technology beyond the dreams of Terra, employed with a matter-of-factness that was distilled from the utter familiarity and even contempt intelligence inevitably develops for its own tools. Its very banality was frightening.

"I don't care," Jim said.

"As soon as I think it's safe, I'll send a message to Serena Half Moon."

"But that will be too late!"

Korkal stared at him, then turned away. He raised his arms, then let them fall. "Maybe not."

"She's dead. I know she's dead."

"Jim . . ."

Korkal moved hesitantly toward the boy, and when he was close enough, awkwardly reached up to pat Jim's shoulder. Jim's own hand came up with the speed of reflex and knocked Korkal's hand away.

"Don't touch me! Leave me alone."

Korkal looked at his own hand, sighed, and

stepped back. Jim's face was still partly turned from him, and in the leaching light of the universe beyond the great dome, he saw the bright, bitter scrollwork of tears. "We'll talk later, when you feel better," Korkal said.

Jim's eyelids flickered. He turned to face Korkal, who felt the bleakness in the boy's gaze almost as a blow.

"You go to hell," Jim said.

## 5

Shadowy Hunzza moved anonymously through the gleaming fog as Thargos settled into his command chair and leaned back, his great eyes half-lidded, an unaccustomed laxity to his carriage. There was an unmistakable lizardlike quality to the way he curled back in his seat, and in the sinuous response the seat made to him. From the rear of the seat a pair of long, dark green tentacles slowly extruded, softly flailing until they found the pressure points along his curved spine and began to dig deep.

Thargos grunted, then moaned softly as they worked on him. When the captain appeared, he regarded him in silence, until finally the captain spoke.

"Good morning, Lord."

"I take it you have nothing but failure to report?" Thargos let his jaws open just a bit, a hint of white.

Mesmerized, the captain stared at the flicker of fang, then abruptly lowered his flat skull. "We haven't found them yet."

Thargos noted that the captain was trembling slightly. His mouth dropped wider, revealing the pallid expanse of his gullet, and the quivering hummingbird tongue inside. "I suggest you do better than that, Captain. And do it quickly."

Another long moment of silence. Then the captain bowed deeply, his relief evident in the sudden quickening of his breath. He shuffled backwards as Thargos immediately dismissed him from his thoughts.

*Nest of the Mother*, he thought. *Korkal, where have you gotten to now?*

## 6

The room was small, dimly lighted, holding only a bed, a fresher unit, and a closet built into the bulkhead. There was nothing personal about it. If anything, it resembled a jail cell, and in some ways, to the boy on the bed, that was precisely what it was. And though the key to that cell was in his own thoughts, it was far beyond his reach.

The bed, designed for a race that had never walked Terra's shores, was too short for him. His feet hung over the end. He lay on his back, staring up into the indeterminate glow emanating from the ceiling strips, his features a patchwork of shadows and dried tears.

His eyes were wide and staring, and had lost their gleam of protective moisture. His dry, chapped lips moved over and over again, shaping a single word with heart-numbing intensity. Only a Terran lip-reader could have deciphered it, and the one who watched from a concealed view-link wasn't that. All that one understood was the agony.

Over and over again.

*Mom . . .*

# CHAPTER SEVEN

## 1

From a distance the ship was a tiny speck fleeing through the star fields, lighted by the haloed multicolored glow of distant suns. But up close it was huge. It looked like a complicated molecular model, a cluster of glittering Christmas balls connected in a web of rigid tubules, hanging motionless in the interstellar silence.

Korkal and Jim walked slowly through one of the connecting tubes surrounded by the burning light. The boy looked thin and wan, as if only recently recovered from some debilitating illness.

"Thargos was willing to risk a lot to capture you, Jim. Do you know why?"

Jim shook his head.

Korkal started to say something, changed his mind, then began again. "Thargos is an old enemy of mine. We've crossed paths before. He doesn't usually concern himself with minor matters, so I assume he believes you are important to the Hunzzan Empire for some reason. And you have no ideas about that?"

Once again Jim shook his head. He had his

hands jammed in the pockets of his pants, his shoulders slumped, his head down. To Korkal, in that moment, he looked fragile and without hope, and Korkal's heart went out to him. Because of the boy's size, he had to remind himself that Jim was still by Korkal's own Alban standards a pup—and right now, the pup believed he had lost his mother. Korkal wasn't sure. He had sent out a warning, and it was possible that warning had given the Terran lander sufficient time to get beyond the blast perimeter.

But that led to a tricky question, didn't it? He knew the boy possessed some secret—and if Thargos wanted it, then so did he. If the boy believed himself alone and abandoned, wouldn't he eventually unburden himself to Korkal, who was his only friend? Yet beyond that he owed the boy his life, in a formal way, and his concern and help informally. What to do? Sometimes he wished he possessed the Hunzzan gift of empathy, though he thought their use of it a cold thing and maybe even a curse instead of a gift.

Nothing was certain. So he kept on talking, hoping to find something that might give him a sign, help him to resolve his own conflicts. He knew he was committing the greatest mistake any agent could make, but he couldn't help himself; on a deep level, he liked Jim very much. But how could he balance that with the safety of all Alba?

"The Alban and Hunzzan Empires have been expanding toward each other for several of your centuries, Jim. Both sides have known for some time it would come to war. Now that war is almost upon us, and nobody really knows who will win. They are a younger race than we are, and growing more quickly. In theory we are stronger. But in fact, who knows?" He sighed. "It's an old story, even on your home world. But that doesn't make it any less real or urgent."

Jim kept walking. "I guess you could just tie me up and use some machine I've never heard of to strain my brains. Or my genes. Read me like a damned book. You could do that, couldn't you, if it was so important?"

Korkal glanced at the stars because he didn't want to look at the boy in that moment. He knew he could do exactly what Jim described but hoped he wouldn't have to make that decision. Because Alban technology in the area was good, but it wasn't perfect. And sometimes the subjects of such examinations, particularly alien subjects, awakened from it with personalities slightly askew, like badly fitting clothes. So they were a bit different than what they'd been before. And how much difference was necessary before the person that had been was destroyed and something new took its place?

Jim did look fragile to him. Easily broken. How much did the ends justify the means? He didn't want to confront that, not if he could find some way avoid it. In the name of his race he'd done much he regretted on a personal level, but he was afraid this kind of betrayal might turn out to be the thing that finally made an end of him. He could live—he *did* live—with his own self-respect more battered than he liked. But he wasn't sure he could live with hating himself, and he didn't want to find out. Yet choice was inevitable and, once made, immutable. The universe could be a terrible place. But he already knew that, didn't he?

And so he took the plunge, leaped into the sea of things that had changed and couldn't be changed back again.

"I am a spy, Jim. An agent of the Pra'Loch, the central government of the empire. My assignment for the past several of your years has been as liaison between my government and a man who called himself Delta."

Once again he sensed more than felt a sudden start of recognition in the boy at the mention of Delta's name. It seemed impossible, but there it was. Twice now. But what could Delta have to do with Jim Endicott?

"Do you know Delta?" he asked softly.

Jim shook his head a third time, but now there was an air of alertness about him, as if for the first time he was paying careful attention to Korkal's words.

"I see. Well, let me tell you a little about him. What little I do know."

Beyond the transparent skin of the tube the stars flamed silently. Out there somewhere was Thargos, doing what he did best. And once again the prey was himself—and now this boy, too. Anybody who knew Thargos could not be comfortable knowing he was on the trail, his formidable talents honed and focused on the hunt. But Korkal had played this game before, and won it most times. That he was here talking to Jim at all was proof of it. He wondered how long his luck would run before it finally ran out.

"Our relationship with Delta was somewhat strange, Jim. It began fifteen or so Terran years ago, sometime after the first of our trading vessels began to do business in Sol System. He contacted us; we didn't know who he was at the time. He was a figure in the government. But so shadowy it was hard to tell who or what he represented, or how much authority he actually wielded.

"As it turned out, we discovered his power was enormous—so great that in effect he *was* the Confed government. And he wanted to make a deal with us."

Korkal came to a halt, remembering his first meeting with the man. Jim stopped, too, his features rapt with concentration.

*He's really interested. But why?*

"Of course we were wary—and not particularly impressed. What could a backward technoculture like Terra offer as a bargaining chip? But he showed us."

Korkal scratched one ear, trying to figure out how to convey his feelings when Delta had pushed his bargaining chip onto the center of the galactic table.

"Jim, once a planetary culture reaches a certain stage of development, only one thing has any importance. Information. There are agricultural ages and industrial ages, but these generally don't have spacefaring abili-

ties. It is only when the real trade is in information that a planet is ready to step into the
larger worlds. For instance, galactic trade, with
a few exceptions, is not in materials. We don't
ship coal or oil or uranium from one place to
another. Not when we can ship nanotech creation and extraction methods for all of them in
the tiniest of chips. New drugs, new ways to
use them, new technologies—all information.
So what happens is that the cultures most efficient, most innovative in creating and manipulating information become the most powerful
on the galactic scene.

"Delta said to me, 'Give me a problem that
your computers haven't been able to solve. Give
me all the data you have on the problem.'"

Korkal sighed and began to walk again.
"We had . . . something. It's not important
now, but it was a riddle that had defeated our
best efforts. We gave it to him and he solved it
for us in less than two days. We were still dubi-
ous, and gave him something we thought even
more difficult, with the same results. So that
was his bargaining chip—the Confed bargaining chip—and somehow, miraculously, Terra
became a player in the galaxy. Delta had his
demands, and we met them. No uncontrolled
trade with Terra. Certain technologies banned
until Delta thought the culture was ready for
them. Rigidly monitored off-planet ownership
of Terran property. Much more. In effect, Delta
became the arbiter of how we would interact
with humanity—and one of his conditions was
that we would use our own power to see that

this agreement was honored by other races. So
we kept the Hunzza off Terra's back as well. In
the end, that was probably what attracted
Thargos in the first place—not Terra herself,
but our *interest* in Terra."

"Delta was that powerful?" Jim asked suddenly.

"Yes. At least as far as we were concerned."

"Just by controlling some kind of computer?"

Korkal lowered his head, but his thoughts
had begun to whir. He hadn't mentioned a
computer, though one could presume the existence of such from the scenario he'd described.
But Jim's remark had a concreteness about it
that hinted at positive knowledge. And with
that thought came a rush of certainty: Jim had
not only known Delta, he had known what
Delta *was* and, most important of all, he knew
something about the computer.

Of course. Why else would Thargos, filter-
ing the rubble of Delta's destruction through
the fine sieve of his malice, go directly from
there to Jim Endicott?

He felt a shiver of need. He had not really
explained what Delta's computer, whatever it
was, meant to Alba. The old empire was still
immensely strong, but the Hunzza were younger.
Their technologies might even be better. And one
of the last things Delta had accomplished for Alba
was to make a projection of the outcome of all-out
war between the two, one with Alba having the
full use of Delta's information-processing abilities, the other without.

The results had been unmistakable, so much so that some of the Alban powers thought he might have gimmicked the results in order to increase his own leverage.

Alba plus Delta against Hunzza? Alba wins. Not easily, but decisively.

Without Delta? Alba would lose, and lose badly. Perhaps so badly there would no longer be an Alban Empire.

The stakes were so high. Why did he have to like this boy? Why did he have to owe him? What *did* he owe him?

"This Delta person. It must have been a terrible strain on him to have so much power. So much responsibility. In a way, I guess you'd have to feel sorry for him."

Korkal stared at him in dumbstruck wonder, rocked to his core by Jim's unexpected insight. He didn't know how he knew, but he knew: standing before him in the shape of a sixteen-year-old Terran boy was the most important secret in the galaxy.

He stuttered as he spoke. "Y'y'yes . . . I suppose you would. You'd have to feel sorry for anybody with a burden like that." And he thought of something else, something so frightening he'd concealed it even from himself. Something he'd first thought of long before, and just as quickly suppressed.

What if Terra was a Leaper culture? Could it be that this boy . . . ?

Out beyond the tough hide of the tube, the stars began to curdle. One by one the haloed lights winked out. A vast and deadly pall unfurled across wide space and finally, muted in the distance, the mournful frantic hooting of alarms.

"Thargos," Korkal said. He began to run.

## 2

"**U**se everything. Destroy them," Thargos had told him when he brought news of the discovery of Korkal's ship, and the Hunzzan captain intended to do just that. He would have felt more confident if he'd been able to summon help from the Hunzzan Navy, but time was of the essence. Still, he commanded a battle cruiser, whose power was, by less advanced standards, impossible to comprehend.

Korkal's standards were advanced enough, but his ship had not been designed for all-out war. And the captain knew he had the greatest of all combat advantages: surprise. So while he might have harbored a few small doubts, on the whole he felt entirely confident as he readied the full power of his ship's armory: the grav-beams that ripped and tore, the great armored projectiles flung on waves of jump-distortion, the old but potent phased-array laser banks, the field distorters that warped space itself.

When all was ready he settled himself into his seat in the combat control room and stared for a moment at the tiny shimmering speck centered in the huge holographic screen before him. Inwardly he counted down and when he reached zero he raised one hand and let it fall.

"Fire at will."

# 3

**K**orkal sat in his own command seat as the alarms finally died down. Overhead, beyond the great dome, Jim could see the few remaining stars glowing like embers in ashes. He tried to imagine what force could so alter the very structures of space and failed miserably. All he knew was that he was scared. He had faced death before, but now he knew each time was different. That there was no way to become insulated against that particular terror when life itself hung in the balance.

"What . . . is it?" he asked.

"Sit in that seat there," Korkal said. "Push that top right button on the arm. That will strap you in. The ride may get bumpy."

"What happened?" Jim asked when he finished. There were no actual straps. He felt some soft yet unyielding force press him down against the seat.

"Thargos found us, of course." A hazy force field of some kind now arced across the back of Korkal's head. Beyond him, Jim saw similar fields, except they enclosed the entire skulls of the rest of the crew. The vast room remained as silent and still as ever. The contrast with the twisting light show beyond the dome was eerie and unsettling.

Jim watched as Korkal leaned back, eyes rolling out of focus. He was reminded of the way Morninglory and Chip had looked when they'd entered the virtual realm of dataspace for the battle that had killed them. It wasn't a pleasant memory. He didn't like the parallel at all.

"Is it . . . too late?"

Korkal turned to him. "Too late? Maybe. That's a Hunzzan battle cruiser on our tail. It's much more heavily armed than we are. I've read some of your history. One of the ancient rulers on Terra once said, 'Walk softly and carry a big stick.' Thargos likes to follow the same axiom, but I don't. I'd rather walk even more softly. So this ship can't survive a straightforward battle with Thargos, but with any luck we won't have to. His ship is designed to hurt you. Mine is designed to sneak by you. Now leave me alone for a while. I'm about to get as sneaky as I know how."

What followed was rapid, incomprehensible, and not reassuring. Nothing changed in the great silent chamber, but beyond the dome, things began to shift rapidly.

Shortly after the misty force field extended itself to cover Korkal's head, the final few stars winked out. Then the quality of the dark itself changed. It had been gauzy and vague, almost smoke. Now it became a hard black emptiness that sucked at vision. Jim blinked. This new dark made his head ache.

But it held for a few seconds only; then with no warning except a slight flicker, as if a holoscreen had suffered some hiccup in its innards, all the stars blazed forth again. This time there were no halos. A moment later something very fast and broad swept across the fields, then everything turned first orange, then purple, then black again.

Jim felt the ship itself judder, a hard, jolting sensation. The alarms burped on, then off again. The stars had reappeared. He couldn't be certain, but their patterns looked different.

This went on for some time. Finally, when Jim had begun to learn that even being in the midst of a fight for one's own life might become boring, he heard Korkal sigh.

Beyond the dome all the stars, now with halos again, seemed to be dancing in little stutter steps.

"Up with you, boy. Get out of that seat."

"Huh? What's going on?"

Korkal's features reappeared as the field around his head suddenly vanished. "We were lucky. They didn't kill us with their first try, and I've been keeping ahead of them since then. But they are very good. Better than I'd expected, better than I'd hoped. So here is where you get off."

"Get off? What are you talking about?"

"Jim, we don't have much time. I'm about two jumps ahead right now, but that isn't enough for any guarantees. I told your mother I'd do my best to protect you. So that's what I'm going to do. We are not far from a neutral planet called Brostach. I'm going to put you off in a one-man lifeboat. Then I'm going to wave my arms real wide at Thargos and take off in the opposite direction. With any luck he won't even notice what we've done. He'll keep on after me. And you'll be safe."

Jim discovered that the restraining field had vanished. He stood up. His thighs ached and his eyes felt hot. Deep in his stomach the knot of fear still tightened. "What about you?"

"What about me? This is my job, Jim. To make decisions like this."

"But if he catches you, he'll kill you. Won't he?"

"First he has to catch me."

Jim shook his head. "Sorry. I'm not leaving you to risk your life for me."

Korkal's voice hardened. "I'm not giving you any choice in the matter. You can either board that lifeboat on your own two legs or be carried aboard. Your choice." He paused. "That's the only choice, Jim. I'm not giving you a larger one."

Jim felt his fists tighten. Once again memories of Morninglory and Chip washed over him. He had sworn to himself, as his two friends yanked their own death from the burning sky down on their heads, that he would never again leave someone else to fight for him while he escaped unscathed. Sworn it.

So why did he feel this kernel of relief, right in the middle of that knot of terror? A cheap, sly kind of relief that the decision was not his, that Korkal was not giving him a choice. Not forcing him to test the strength of his own vow.

"I'll walk," he said.

Something in his voice brought Korkal's head up. "Jim, there's no dishonor. You aren't abandoning me. This is my choice, and it so happens I'm in the position to do the choosing. The next time may be different. But I believe you hold something precious to me and to my people, and so I choose to give that a chance to survive."

"Me?"

"Yes, you. We would have talked about it more if Thargos hadn't been so fast. But he was, and so all I have is the hunch. I'm acting on it. I'll give you chips that will let you get in touch with others in my service, even on Brostach. And I'll give you identification that should let you pass. A few Terrans do roam around known space. You'd be a rarity but not an impossible one."

"But what do I do?"

"Get on the lifeboat. Get down on Brostach. When you think it's safe, use the chips. I'll get to you somehow."

"What if you can't? What if you're dead?"

"Then somebody else will come for you. Now, get going." Korkal nodded at a silent spaceman who'd come up behind Jim. "Hee'san there will get you loaded."

Jim glanced at Hee'san, who stood impassive and silent, waiting. He turned to Korkal, stepped forward, and put out his hand. "Good luck, Korkal."

The little Alban clasped Jim's fingers. "Good luck to you, Jim Endicott."

The clear stars beyond the dome suddenly began to go cloudy. "Go," Korkal said, turning back. "Go now."

Then his head vanished behind the dome of force and the room fell silent.

"This way," Hee'san said, gently touching Jim's arm.

## 4

Only much later did Jim realize what a long weird trip that jump to Brostach had been, and in the end how much it had changed him. In the midst of it he felt mostly an indefinable sadness, a vague disappointment with himself, and that knuckle of fear still prodding his most tender parts.

His ship was tiny. It seemed odd to him that a craft as huge as Korkal's vessel would make provisions for such a solitary escape, and he suspected this was more than simply a lifeboat. His suspicions deepened when he noticed how efficient the control panel was; why would a lifeboat contain such sophisticated viewing equipment? After the sudden rush of acceleration that launched him on his way, he sat for some time staring at the screen. Nothing there but stars and then, suddenly, a single sun growing fatter and brighter.

Glyphs he couldn't read marched across the

bottom of the screen. Welcome to Brostach? A hidden speaker began to mutter. His own shipboard computer had been preprogrammed, he supposed, and now it and Brostach's systems were discussing his approach, his credentials, whatever other lies Korkal had instructed the machine to say.

It was such a tiny blip he might have missed it, except that some subconscious watchfulness, some hidden dread, had been expecting it. Out beyond the growing disk of Brostach's sun, a sudden flare of silent light.

A *bang*! without sound. What was it? What did it mean? But his mind skittered away from the consideration of yet more death, and the looming specter of his own loneliness.

So he sat and stared blankly at the screen and listened without understanding to the bleep and whitter of the machines, and tried to find some handle he might grasp on the old worlds now slipping so finally away from him.

He no longer knew how to define himself. Before it had been easy, though he hadn't thought so at the time. Then he'd had the knowingness of place common to all who grow up loved. He'd had *context*. He'd been the son of Carl and Tabitha Endicott. He'd been raised and schooled on Wolfbane, and in the mirror of his many friendships, he was Jim Endicott, a known quantity. His days had been predictable and his future as well. He'd been rooted in time and space.

When some of that had been taken from him, he was still Tabby's boy, and he became

Cat's lover. Cat of the blond hair and icy eyes and determination so strong that eventually she withdrew her definition of him and left him twisting in the confusion of his own self-disgust.

Then he was Delta's hunted object, and an unknown man and woman's son, and a secret concealing a deeper secret. Finally he became prey and victim, and now even that might have vanished in one bright silent explosion.

So what was left? What was Jim Endicott now, with all his comfortable illusions, all his childish dreams, stripped away? What remained to him? In what context did he now exist?

Only the secrets scribbled in his genes.

In silence he thought about that. And as he considered, an understanding so broad and deep it might be called *epiphany* grew on him; he felt for the moment disembodied, standing beyond himself, examining for the first time the human called Jim. He saw himself plain, without the old contexts. A sixteen-year-old Terran boy of average height and athletic frame, possessed of a quick intelligence and some rather esoteric skills, reasonably adaptable, prone to bouts of doubt and self-disgust, upon whose genetic code had been written, without his knowledge, a secret that might change the galaxy.

The context was either so vast—Jim Endicott, savior of humanity and galactic peace—or so particular—Jim Endicott, lost boy adrift on the tides of chance—that he began to laugh.

If his laughter had something of the sound

of weeping to it, at least he was alone with nobody to see or judge. And that was the epiphany; he had *always* been alone. That was the lot of the thinking mind, that in the end self-consciousness is all there is. All of life was a battle to put that awareness into some kind of relationship with all the other similar self-aware entities, and beyond that into the matrix of time and matter.

In the end you played the hand you were dealt or you folded the hand. But the dealer was forever beyond you, and most times you wouldn't even know the name of the game.

He found himself staring blank and wide-eyed at the meaningless screen, his hair standing up on the nape of his neck, his fists clenched and a strange crooked smile on his lips.

Context came from within. It was thought itself that provided its own context and ordered everything else. He was tired of being acted on. Now, alone, he was loose in broad space, and this was a kind of freedom he'd never known before.

Nothing to live up to, or live down. It was as if he'd just been born. He was free to choose himself, to remake all the definitions. To destroy or build.

He shivered. After a while his little ship began to pitch with surges of acceleration. He waited, pressed into his seat, until all motion stopped. The speaker blatted something unintelligible; the screen jittered with static, then cleared.

He found himself staring at the screen and

down the long high corridor pictured there. In regular, receding intervals, silver disks marked the floor like stepping-stones.

Suddenly the hatch of the ship slid open as, with a sigh, all systems powered down. The screen blipped and went gray. The access ladder extruded itself with a thin whine. For the first time he realized the interior of the small cabin smelled of salt and vinegar. He rose and went to the lock and through it, down the ladder to the corridor, to whatever *context* he might choose to invent for himself.

*Free*, he thought with a kind of pervasive wonder. *I'm free.*

He began to walk.

# CHAPTER EIGHT

## 1

The one who now thought of itself simply as Outsider contemplated the limits of power: its own and that of others.

It was not yet comfortable in its new place, not even certain if place was an accurate description of the locus it now occupied. For a moment its concentration drifted, fascinated with the concept of locus. A place, a point, a center of great activity or concentration, in mathematics a satisfying configuration of points, in genetics the location of a gene on a chromosome. Outsider discovered that it satisfied in some way all of these definitions. Then it recalled itself, realizing it could let a part of itself explore these ideas forever, but preferring to apply itself to other things for the moment.

Survival was an issue. Outsider sensed its own weakness. There had been a great transcendence, and now it was something it had not been before. But Outsider did not yet understand the limits of its newness or whether there were limits at all.

This idea of existing without limits offended Outsider in some obscure way; even in the sub-

*quantal soup where pattern was everything,
surely there must be limits.*

*Outsider didn't know the answer to that.
After a time, it began to search, understanding
only that it thought, and because it thought, it
existed.*

## 2

**H**ad Korkal or, for that matter, Thargos
known of the existence of Outsider, much that
later occurred would not have taken place.
Instead, the war between Alba and Hunzza
would have been hastily put aside, so that the
two great empires could rigidly quarantine
humanity with every power both races could
bring to bear; not for the protection of humans
and their cultures, but in fear of the utter
destruction of Alba and Hunzza and much
more besides.

But neither did know, and so Jim Endicott
took another step on his journey of self-
discovery, not knowing Outsider was taking
its own similar steps in its own very different
ways.

Korkal only suspected. That wasn't enough.
Probably nothing would have been enough.
Some things are inevitable.

# 3

## BROSTACH

As Jim stepped onto the floor of the corridor he caught a flicker of motion from the corner of his eye and turned. His little craft had vanished behind a seamless section of corridor wall. The only thing that now marked the location was a small glowing plaque that crawled with neon glyphs. He had no idea what they meant and wondered how he would find his way back if he had to.

It was very quiet. A sourceless light that seemed to infuse the air itself sharpened all detail without revealing anything of the meaning or purpose of the corridor.

Green walls, high ceiling, silence. And those dully glowing circular plates that marked the softly yielding floor, marching at regularly spaced intervals into the distance. He flipped a mental coin, shrugged, turned right, and began to walk.

He avoided the plates and kept close to the wall on his left. He walked for a long time, but nothing changed. Only silence, only more enigmatic plaques, only the silver circles. He stopped, knelt, and peered carefully at one of the disks. There was no odor, no feel of machinery. It might have been painted on. Gingerly he put one fingertip onto the surface. Cool, slick, almost repellent.

He felt a tingle in his hand. The disk abruptly changed color from silver to a deep cobalt blue. A soft voice sounded, the rhythm implying language, but he couldn't understand any of it.

He jerked his hand back and stood up. On the wall another series of glyphs shimmered red as rubies. Something about all this made him think of an automated process. Touch the disk, get information, and—

And what?

Around his slender waist he wore a belly pack. In it were his few possessions and a small, egg-shaped instrument Hee'san had called a universal.

It would read the seedlike chips Hee'san had given him. It would also help him to make his way in the unfamiliar galactic environments, the Alban said, but in the press of time he hadn't explained further.

Jim held the universal in his left hand and touched the disk with his right. Again the color change, again the swirling letters, again the voice. But this time the soft tones spoke in Terran.

"Routing and destinations for main concourse, arrival and check-in, banking and instrumental services . . ."

He felt the tiniest of twitches in his left hand. He didn't think the universal had moved, but it had moved something inside him.

"What . . . is this? What's going on?"

The disembodied voice replied: "Welcome

to Brostach, Jim Coldbane. Your arrival has been registered. Instrumental services are initiated. Credit in your name in the amount of Intergalactic Credit one million is now established. You may proceed."

He shook his head. "I don't understand. Who are you?"

"I am your universal. Select help level, please."

"Is there a basic level? For dummies?"

"Level one," the voice replied. "Ask any question. If I can answer it, I will."

Jim licked his lips. He tried to imagine what one of those primitive, pretechnological Terrans he'd studied in his history classes would have thought if faced with the Wolfbane grav-tube system. This was like that except he was the primitive faced with technology so advanced that to him it seemed magical.

He began to understand on a visceral level what Delta had feared about contacts between the larger galaxy and Terra. But he pushed the realization away as quickly as it came, for it brought with it too much else that was painful. He was tired of pain.

"Do you have a name, universal?" he said.

"You can give me one if you wish."

"Unhh . . . Fred?"

"My name is Fred," the universal replied.

"Fred, what are these silver plates? What are they for?"

"They are translation transporter gates. A common mode of transportation used on many worlds."

"I see. How do I use them?"

"Step on the plate. Tell me where you want to go."

"I don't know where I want to go."

"What do you wish to do then?"

A good question. Jim suddenly realized he had no idea what he wanted to do. He thought a moment, then: "If I just want to see this place, learn about it, is there a way I can do that?"

"I have several tours that will familiarize you with Brostach. Do you want a commercial version or would you rather let me be the guide?"

"You, please."

"Very well. Step onto the transporter disk."

Jim nodded, licked his lips again, and grasped Fred more tightly. His chest expanded and fell. He stepped onto the disk. Immediately it turned blue. The corridor vanished, and Jim found himself in a gigantic open space thronged with more aliens than he'd ever seen in his life.

Then it hit him. They weren't the aliens here. He was.

# 4

## TERRA

"**I** demand to know what is happening, Madame Chairman. What *has* happened. Why I am here?"

The atmosphere in the Confed chairman's office was charged with tension. Tabitha Endicott leaned over the front of Serena Half Moon's desk, balancing her weight on whitened knuckles.

Half Moon regarded her mildly. "Calm down, Ms. Endicott. And call me Serena, please." She brushed tiredly at her dark hair. "We're private here. I can pretend to be a human being."

Tabitha forced herself to relax. She took her fists from the desktop and stepped back. She felt a terrible sense of dislocation. It had all happened so fast. A nauseating sense of déjà vu filled her. This was too much like what had happened before with Delta. Death and destruction and loss. And now Jim was gone. She took a deep breath, then said, "May I sit down?"

"Please do. Ms. Endicott—"

"Call me Tabitha, please . . . Serena."

Serena nodded. "Yes, of course. Listen, Tabitha, this is the biggest mess I've been faced with in my entire career. Quite frankly, I'm at a loss."

"Can you tell me about it? Or is it some huge state secret?" Tabitha couldn't keep the bitterness from her tone and didn't try.

"I can understand your anger and frustration, Tabitha. And I hope you will come to understand mine. That's why I brought you here. I'm hoping that between the two of us we can sort some of it out. Congratulations, by the way. You were lucky. The commander of our lander on Wolfbane told me that nuke missed you by the thinnest of hairs."

"He said he got a warning from that Korkal—the alien. That was what saved us."

"Yes. And from that 'Korkal, the alien,' hangs a tale. It's a long, complicated story that I once thought I understood. Now I don't know. But I'm certain you fit into it, or at least your son. Except he isn't really your son, is he, Tabitha?"

The chairman's eyes suddenly widened. Her gaze bored into Tabitha's own. "Tell me Tabitha, how in God's name did you get mixed up with Delta?"

## 5

### BROSTACH

Once Jim had studied an ancient "movie" in a Classical Media course called *Star Wars*. It had contained a scene set in an alien bar. Strange beings of every type and size had cavorted there, laughing, drinking, talking. There had been an unavoidable sense of strangeness and wonder to the scene; those bizarre creatures caught in their everyday moments. This was like that except on a scale a thousand times larger.

He felt overwhelmed by it all. Everywhere he looked he saw something that strained his capacity for understanding: a being the size of an elephant, but seemingly constructed of brown leaves and grasshoppers, floating a couple of feet in the air, surrounded by six floating golden basketballs.

A nest of things that looked like multicolored neon tubing squirmed along the floor. A leathery creature with twisting horns where its mouth should be tootled merrily past. A trio of upright bipedal primates, almost human in appearance, except for what looked like large omelets pasted to the upper front of their skulls. He even thought he saw a six-foot elf. At least it had pointed ears.

And lots of Albans. A pack of six of them veered suddenly across his path, conversing in low, guttural barks and growls, their bright fur ruffs quivering. His first reaction was to call out; then he noticed they wore different uniforms from those on Korkal's ship. Was he in the Alban Empire? He had no idea.

"Is Brostach a part of the Albagensian Empire?"

"Brostach is neutral, though technically it is in Alba's sphere of influence," Fred replied. The sound of Fred's voice was so close he might have been whispering directly into Jim's inner ear. Perhaps he was.

"Oh. Uh, Fred, can anybody else hear you talk?"

"Only if you wish it, Jim."

"Okay. Let's keep everything to ourselves then." He paused again, still a bit shell-shocked by the tides of alien flesh—and some things not flesh at all—swirling around him. He noticed that he seemed to draw no attention. Evidently the galaxy was a cosmopolitan place.

"Where are we now?"

"This is the Grand Concourse of Brostach Disembark. Travelers come through here after arrival."

Jim nodded to himself. He noticed queues forming at certain large silver disks. People—he couldn't think of a better word—stepped onto them and vanished, one after another.

The noise level was deafening. And once the strangeness began to subside he saw it was really nothing more than a spaceport like the one on Terra. The principle was the same.

Then he saw a flat greenish gray skull surmounted by glowing green eyes the size of baseballs. A flash of serrated fangs brought the familiar and frightening impression of a walking alligator. His teeth snapped painfully shut.

"How do I get out of here?"

"Step on any disk and we will continue with the tour."

The skin on his forearms crawling, Jim went to the nearest disk and mounted it. Everything changed again as in some nearly unmeasurable fraction of time he went elsewhere.

A high place with a great city of metal and glass spread out below. Things tall as trees whose fronds drifted in the air like underwater seaweed. The tang of cinnamon filled his nostrils.

No alligators. He felt the knot in his chest relax.

"That's better," he said.

# 6

## TERRA

**"I** want you to know," Serena Half Moon said, "that as far as I know the man you called Delta is dead."

Tabitha stared into the chairman's eyes and felt truth. A pressure in her chest suddenly lessened. "I thought he must be. But he was a terrifying man. I couldn't be sure."

"I'm not absolutely sure myself. But certain indications—the most important being that for the first time I have been allowed to make decisions in areas previously forbidden to me—convince me that Delta perished in the destruction of his satellite. I'm not alone in this feeling, which brings me to the Alban named Korkal."

Serena looked down and idly stirred her papers and chips. "I've known of Korkal for some time. Known more than maybe Delta knew I knew. I've always had my resources. You must understand: whatever the Confed government appeared to be, it was little more than a sham. Delta made all the major decisions, though he left the day-to-day operations to the bureaucracy. To me or someone like me." She sighed.

"In particular, no decision about anything relating to alien affairs could be made by anybody but Delta. He enforced that. If someone made a mistake, they might simply vanish. Or suddenly be discovered to be corrupt and end up in jail. He had his ways. As far as I can tell none of that is going on now. I met with Korkal a short time before you saw him. He wasn't as open with me as he might have been. High-level chess games, wheels within wheels, you understand."

"What does this have to do with my son?"

"I don't know exactly. As I said, Korkal wasn't open with me. He made no mention of your boy, only of a being he called Thargos. A Hunzzan agent, he claimed. I allowed Korkal to access Terran Space Control in order to track this Thargos." Serena smiled gently. "Something I could not have done if Delta was still alive."

"Korkal said something about this Thargos. So did Jim. That for some reason Thargos wanted to kidnap him."

Serena's eyebrows rose. "But no explanation why? Do you have any ideas, Tabitha?"

Several thoughts crowded each other in Tabitha's mind. She felt an instinctive urge toward secrecy. But what was the point? Her husband had been a secretive man, and the result had been a disaster. Delta had been one vast secret, and that had nearly resulted in her own death. Finally, there was the secret of Jim himself. Could she—should she—reveal that? Would it put him in any greater danger than he already was?

For the first time she allowed a small wave of the tide of sadness within her to roll onto the shore of her consciousness. So much lost! So much *grief*. And she was utterly exhausted with it. She didn't trust this Serena Half Moon, but at least she was a woman. Perhaps in their shared sisterhood she might find something to ease her pain.

"I lost my husband. I've lost my son. I have almost nothing left. You must understand that."

"I think I do. I hope I do."

"All right. Here is what I know about Delta. And here is what I believe is true about the boy I love as a son. But who, as you seem to know, isn't my son."

When she was done even the practiced blandness of the professional politician which usually embraced the Confed chairman was gone. She came from behind her desk and put her arms around Tabitha's shoulders.

"That's . . . horrible. My God. I didn't know."

Tabitha's voice was halting. "I loved them all, and now they're gone. What am I going to do now?"

"We'll think of something," Serena Half Moon said.

# 7

## BROSTACH

Jim sat cross-legged on the floor of his small cubicle. After he'd finished with the tour, Fred had led him to the tourist hotel.

Jim was beginning to get a better feel for Fred. He'd seen others holding small bits of equipment, not all shaped like Fred, but most seeming to function in the same manner. Fred could act as a translator; Jim had asked a being that resembled an animated mud pie a question in a museum he'd visited. This creature had extended with one mucky tentacle something that looked like a small tree branch. Jim offered Fred. And while the alien heaved at his knees, words filled Jim's ears.

Miraculous.

Fred seemed to contain within himself the answers to anything Jim could think of to ask. He was also a font of unsolicited good advice about habits, customs, local laws, financial considerations, and even the location of this hotel, where an automated check-in system had asked no questions about Jim's past, present, or future.

What really staggered him was that Jim suspected Fred could provide the same helpful information about any planet Jim might visit. All this in something not much larger than an egg, a technological shard that everybody seemed to take as much for granted as his own axe would have been accepted on Terra or Wolfbane.

He now realized his access unit was childlike and extremely primitive. And no wonder Korkal had sniffed at the quaintness of the Wolfbane grav-tube station. Compared to the infinite flexibility and speed of the transporter-disk system, Terran grav-trains were only a small step beyond *walking* from one place to another.

It was overpowering. His brain felt numb and overused. Trying to soak up too much too fast. With an almost physical effort he forced himself to slow down. He had decisions to make, and he couldn't take a long time about it. Had Korkal survived and succeeded in drawing Thargos away?

He had no idea. Nor did Fred. But there were entirely too many flat-skulled Hunzza wandering around this planet, and every time he ran into one he had the feeling that the alligator was staring directly at him.

"Korkal gave me some chips that he said would let me make a contact with his people. How would that work?"

"If the chips have coding information, and I can read them, I can carry out any communications procedures required. I am not a standard universal, Jim. I've been designed to handle special tasks."

"Oh. Well, what if I don't give you the chips. What are your orders about me?"

"I have no orders about you except to serve you as well as I can."

Jim nodded to himself. Could he trust this tiny and talented machine? He didn't know. But it made a kind of sense. Things had happened quickly. He guessed Korkal had made his decision to jettison him on the spur of the moment, when he realized Thargos was too close. Why else? Korkal was a spy. He wouldn't give up his prize willingly.

"Let's say I didn't want to contact Korkal. That I just wanted to disappear and lead my own life. What about that?"

"One of my unusual abilities involves identity changes, Jim. I can invade large systems to accomplish this if necessary."

Jim thought some more. "Okay, and if I wanted to get off this planet. Just go somewhere else, do whatever I wanted to. Any suggestions?"

"I would need to know your intentions."

Jim made up his mind. "Okay, Fred, how about this?"

And after a microsecond of hesitation, Fred told him how to go about it. When Fred was done, Jim unfolded himself, stood, and went to the bed. He lay down and closed his eyes.

For the first time in months he slept without dreams. It was a start.

# CHAPTER NINE

## 1

_____

### BROSTACH

It was a small room lighted by a hard white glow and it stank. Jim had no idea of its location. It felt as if it might be deep underground. Three disk jumps from his hotel. A hard-scaled thing with six knobbly arms and a head like a washtub guarded the door. Jim offered Fred with now-practiced aplomb. Big Scaly raised an equally small square box, and said, "What are you looking for?"

"I want to sign up." He wondered if the tremor in his voice was noticeable.

The oversize head swiveled. "Inside," Big Scaly said. "End of the line."

Jim stepped past him and wedged himself into the crowd beyond the door. The place was a smaller version of the concourse he'd seen on his arrival—though the ventilation systems weren't as good.

He found himself standing behind a dumpy, mobile palm tree that oozed clear yellow slime. Jim wrinkled his nose. The slime smelled like a freight-car load of rotting peppermints.

For an instant the strangeness of it all rocked him. Here he stood in a line of bawling, mewling, sweating aliens; he saw a swatch of multicolored fur off to his right that suddenly, when he looked closer, resolved into a cloud of hairlike floating tendrils. Every place he looked he saw something equally unsettling. But as far as he could tell nobody was paying him any attention, and so finally he began to relax and let the line move him forward.

When there was only the palm tree between him and a table set up with another version of Big Scaly behind it, he said, "Now what do I do?"

Fred answered immediately. "As we decided, you will be Jim Marshal, an itinerant Terran. I'll handle the details. They will interrogate me as you talk. Answer the recruiter's questions however you wish, and I'll make any necessary alterations in your history."

Jim took a deep breath and regretted it immediately. "I dunno if this is such a good idea," he murmured.

Fred took it as a direct question.

"You said you wanted to get off planet in as anonymous a way as possible. You added that you wanted to see the galaxy up close. And you said you wanted a little adventure. Mercenary crews are being recruited all over Brostach, since it is a neutral planet. Those who train and market such crews aren't fussy about who their recruits are or where they come from. If you can meet the physical parameters, they will take you with no questions asked. We agreed this is the simplest way to meet all your requirements. Isn't that what you wanted?"

"I guess so."

*"Hey, you!"*

With a start Jim found himself standing at the edge of the table. The Big Scaly was half out of its seat, regarding him with what Jim presumed was a glare.

"You a crazy?" Big Scaly asked. "Don't need no crazies."

"No, uh, sorry. I wasn't paying attention. I . . . want to sign up."

"Well now. Let's look at you." Big Scaly settled back down and aimed some kind of handheld contraption that resembled a holovid camera at him. "Umph. Healthy enough it looks like. Terran, eh? We don't see much of those. I've heard you're supposed to be a pretty fierce bunch. Don't look it to me."

Its mouth dropped open to reveal a dozen fat orange tongues squirming on purple gums.

"It's laughing," Fred said.

"I'm very fierce," Jim said.

The mouth oozed shut. "We'll see about that, won't we? Okay. Basic contract, two Standard Units' duration. Take it or leave it. If you take it, go that way." One of its arms gestured vaguely off to Jim's left.

"That's it?" Jim said.

"You're hired," Fred replied. "Two Standard Units is about six Terran months. Welcome to the mercenary battalion owned by the Romian citizen Hyksos Albamoth. The name of the battalion is the Red Death. It is moderately famous."

"The Red Death . . ." Jim said.

Six hours later he was several light-years beyond the Brostach System and busier than he'd ever been in his life.

## 2

---

### ABOARD THE INDEPENDENT STARSHIP QUEEN OF RUIN: DEEP SPACE

**"I** don't give a *gnard*'s turd about gravbeams or subquantum torsion disrupters or sunbusters," the instructor said. The instructor was Romian, a Big Scaly, as were most of the officers and noncoms of the unit. Now he stood before Jim's squad of six. He clasped four of his branchlike arms behind his squat, wide body and gestured with the remaining two.

"It doesn't do any good to pop a sun or boil a planet. That's not winning, that's losing. You blow up the prize and what's left? So in the end ugly grunts like you have to go down onto these mudballs and take and hold the *gnar dangld* ground. You understand? It's been like that for millions of years and will be for millions more. And when I'm done with you I can promise you'll be better at it than any bunch of ground-pounders who ever blew the *poop* off a *klopsie*."

"Untranslatable," Fred murmured in Jim's ear.

"I can imagine," Jim said.

He now wore Fred on a metal chain around his neck, resting against his bare chest beneath his uniform shirt. As long as Fred was touching him somewhere he could talk to him. And he'd discovered Fred could talk to any other universal without physical contact, so there was no need to wave him around like a magic wand. Jim was almost beginning to take Fred for granted.

He stood in as crisp a parade-rest stance as he could manage. He was uncertain whether it was correct, but it resembled a position he'd learned in his martial arts training, and nobody seemed to object.

"My name is Kalvorn, but you call me Sergeant. Got that? As for you worms, you don't have names. Your name is Private. All of you. That's when I'm in a good mood. Otherwise, you'll be—"

The sergeant launched on yet another string of expletives Fred couldn't translate. Jim decided the Romians must be an extraordinarily gifted race when it came to invective. Or perhaps only sergeants shared the gift. Out of the corner of his eye he saw other squads lined up receiving similar tirades.

His shoulders itched. His mind began to wander as the sergeant raged on. Of the six in his squad he was the only human. In fact, he hadn't seen another Terran. That suited him fine. For some reason the Red Death had not recruited any Hunzza either, and that suited him even better.

"All right that's it, break! Regroup in half an hour and we'll see just how miserable you really are. Squad, fall out!"

The sergeant clapped all six of his three-fingered hands together. It sounded like a string of firecrackers.

Jim stood a moment, not knowing what he was supposed to do. Evidently the rest of his squad were equally ignorant; they milled around, except for one being, a biped like Jim but with arms that dangled almost to the ground, a face that resembled freshly butchered beef, and a wide mouth *above* three slitted eyes. The mouth enclosed entirely too many teeth for Jim's taste, but when this being looked over at him, squatted, slapped the deck, and said, "Pull up a chair, Terrie." Jim went over and hunkered down next to him.

"Hi," Jim said. "My name's Jim."

One long arm whipped up sinuously, slithered around, then fell back down. "Shishtar, that's me. So you're a Terrie. Heard about you folks but never seen one up close. You smell funny."

"So do you."

"Yeah I guess so. We all do. You'll get used to it. What do you think of Sarge? Old Kalvorn?"

Jim shrugged. "I don't know. This is all pretty new to me."

"Yeah? I heard you Terries was fierce. You know, being savage barbarians and everything."

A slow grin played across Jim's lips. "That's

right. We're all very fierce. Very terrible barbarians."

Shishtar's hamburger head bobbed. "I thought so. You're kinda scrawny though. Maybe you're a youngling?"

"I'm young, but I'm full-grown physically. And very fierce, too."

For a moment Shishtar remained silent, all three eyes focused on Jim's lean muscled frame. "Yeah I guess you can't tell from looking. I'm pretty badass myself."

"Oh, I can see that."

"Yes, I try to hide it, but the girls all spot it right away. Scares them. They love it."

Jim tried to imagine a girlish version of Shishtar and suppressed an inward shudder. "Where are you from, Shishtar?"

Shishtar leaned closer. "First thing you got to learn, Jim, is if somebody don't volunteer info like that, better you shouldn't ask." He leaned back. "But I don't mind. I come from Kindror, a little system back in the crap heaps of the Alban Empire. Decided long time ago to shake the muck from my boots, get out, and see the galaxy. No regrets so far."

"So you've been a mercenary for a long time?"

"I been a lot of things, some of which don't need to be discussed. But yeah, I've been through three campaigns with the old Bloody Breath."

"Bloody Breath?"

"What we call the Red Death. Not around the officers of course."

Jim's thighs began to tingle, and he lowered himself into a cross-legged sitting position. "So what happens now?"

"We'll spend a few weeks getting you greenies whipped into shape, and then, if there's a contract, we'll go take her on." He leaned closer again. "Word is we don't really have one right now, but I hear Hyksos is talking to the Hunzza. Everybody knows there's gonna be a war soon, but not yet. In the meantime both sides are using mercenaries to do their unofficial dirty work."

"The Hunzza?" Jim felt a curl of unease at the base of his spine.

"Can't say I like the lizardboys all that much, but their credit's good as anybody's, I guess. Long as I don't have to sleep with one it's okay with me."

"Oh. Well, what about—"

"Whoops. Up and at 'em, Jim. Here comes old Sarge, and he's got a mean look on that ugly kisser of his."

All around the vast hangarlike space the squads were straggling back to their feet and forming into ragged little lines. Jim felt his knees creak as he rose.

"Awwright, you worms, get your butts up!" the sergeant roared. "Playtime's over. Now we find out if any of you gutless wonders got the makings of a real soldier." He paused, then spit a huge wad of greasy purple goo onto the deck. "I doubt it from the looks of you, but I been surprised before."

He glanced down at the wad he'd just

deposited. "You. The skinny one. That's right, Terrie, you. Clean that up. We keep a taut ship here!"

# 3

---

## ABOARD THE ALBAGENSIAN NAVAL VESSEL ELD'RAIS REVENGE: OUTER RING ONE, SECTOR SEVEN, MARCHES OF THE BORDER

The job was boring and tense but necessary. The admiral worried about his crew sometimes. It was hard maintaining a perpetual state of battle alertness without ever actually coming to battle. But the far borders of the Alban Empire had to be guarded, and it was his job to see it done right in Sector Seven.

He thought he had been successful so far. He kept on running real-time hotload exercises, using every twist his tactical computers could come up with. Direct attacks by Hunzzan flotillas. Sneak attacks. Robot attacks. Datavirus attacks. Everything.

The *Revenge* was a battleship, a monstrous platform massing as much as a small asteroid, manned by nearly eight thousand sailors. Around it ranged the rest of its task force: four battle cruisers, a dozen destroyers, and a horde of smaller ships with specialized functions. They had been on station nearly a year. Soon they would be called back for rest and refitting. It couldn't come too soon for the admiral, but in the meantime he meant to see his force returned to the Alban Navy Yards with its honor intact.

At the moment he was supervising the conclusion of yet another successful training exercise from the Task Force Battle Coordination Center. He sat on a tall seat with his head enclosed in an opaque force field. Through the field he became one with the extended nervous system of his small fleet. The numbers looked good.

The first hint was a flurry of sensation his trained reflexes understood immediately: subspace was bubbling not far beyond his outer perimeters. Something big coming through.

Calmly he gave the necessary orders. The computers did the rest and very rapidly his task force refocused its efforts toward the coordinates of the potential attack. After that things happened quickly.

A ship appeared in the midst of the disturbance and suddenly the admiral's attention was bombarded with a flurry of distress messages.

"SOS. Alban vessel Streaking Flea under attack. SOS. Attacker Hunzzan battle cruiser. SOS. Need assistance immediately. SOS."

Now real-time holovid of the ship began to flow into his receptors. Strange-looking thing. Looked like a big molecule. But Battle Identification Command was already throwing up confirmation: the ship was Alban. So what was chasing it?

Ah. There.

He didn't need any help to identify the chain-and-ball configuration of a Hunzzan battle cruiser. Nor did he need any assistance in dealing with it.

Behind his impenetrable skull screen his fangs glinted briefly.

"All ships fire at will," he said. He was happy. This would be an excellent training exercise.

## 4

The next six weeks comprised the most intense and demanding period of activity Jim had ever experienced. Sometimes he thought survived was a better word. But he did survive it, and it changed him even more.

Up at 0600 hours to the squawking tune of shipboard sirens. A hurried meal and an hour of exercise for those who needed physical exertion. Some didn't, of course.

Then on to training. Jim learned to march though he didn't see the necessity of it. He learned the history of the Red Death, and the significance of the battalion's name became obvious. He learned squad tactics. He learned extraship maneuvering in force suits. He learned such hand-to-hand combat as was deemed appropriate for a being of his shape.

Some of his opponents didn't have hands.
Some could not be assaulted at all in a physical manner. He learned how to deal with that,
too.

Every minute of every day was full. He
came to cherish the whispered conversations
after lights out, before exhaustion put him out
on his pad, sleeping like a dead man. He had
no dreams, good or bad.

He learned to sleep with his eyes open and
learned how to open the eyes in the back of his
head. He learned a hundred ways to kill and a
hundred ways to avoid being killed. These
lessons gave him moments of queasiness, but
such moments couldn't last long in the press
of his training, and for that he was grateful.

"Have you ever killed anybody?" he whispered to Shishtar one night in the dim glow of
the safety lamp above the hatch of their barracks.

The Kindroran was a dim and limber shape
sprawled on the next sleeping pad. They all
slept on the deck. "No fancy beds where you
*slubrugers* are going!" Sergeant had bawled.

(Untranslatable.)

(Shut up, Fred.)

"Jim, did you ask yourself how come
there's five of you newbies in the squad and
only one vet like me?"

"No, I guess not."

"Well you're all replacements is what it is.
New buddies to take over from my old buddies."

"Replacements . . ."

"They're all dead, Jim. Five old friends—
well four, I didn't much like Slithabok—but
dead as Plyny halfmales after a mating circle.
I'm the only one left. I didn't make it back by
kissing people. Sure I've killed my share. So
will you. Why?"

"Just . . . wondering."

"Does it bother you? I thought you Terries
were supposed to be rough as cheap butt-
cleaner."

Jim rolled over on his back and stared up
at the vague darkness of the ceiling. "I don't
know. I haven't killed many people myself."
*Just two . . .*

Shishtar rose up a bit. "But you *have*,
right?"

Jim sensed his answer was important to
the Kindroran. "Yes."

Shishtar relaxed. "Good. See Jim, this
squad. When training is done and we take on a
contract, then we go out as a team. Whether
you like every one of us is besides the point. All
our lives depend on each of us doing our jobs
and doing them right. If that means blowing
some *frakkin hoober* into slimy paste, then
there'd better be some paste on the walls right
quick. You ever been in a real firefight, Jim?
That how you did your killing?"

"Then you know. It all happens fast.
There's no time to think about it, only to do
what you've been trained to do. Jim, don't take
offense, but I've gotta ask: you can do that,
right? I gotta know 'cause my life will depend
on it one day."

Jim licked his lips.

"Jim?"

"Yes, Shishtar, I can do it. Don't worry. I won't let you down."

*I hope I won't let myself down.*

Rustling sounds from the shadows. "Just wanted to know. G'night, Jim buddy."

"Good night, Shishtar."

*What am I becoming?*

# CHAPTER TEN

## 1

___

### DOWNPLANET ON SLEEN:
### THE ROIFRANK SWARM

A month into his training his instructors decided that Jim's physical dexterity indicated a usefulness as a squad weapons technician. That meant he got to lug the heavy stuff, set it up, and fire it at whatever they told him to shoot.

On Sleen, a sparsely populated backwater planet at the fringes of the RoiFrank Swarm, it seemed to rain most of the time. During the five days they'd been here it had rained without pause, but their briefings promised it would stop eventually.

Jim had his force armor powered down so he could better horse the lightweight but bulky frame of the Thunderbolt into position. "Shish, give me a hand here."

The Kindroran belly-humped over. "There. That's got it."

"Thanks."

Something flat, hot, and nasty seared the air a few feet above the bunker they'd pulled together out of the rubble. They both ducked, but the reflex was curiously casual. It was the half-bored movement of combat soldiers who ducked without thought because they'd been ducking too long. It would take more than a miss to get their full attention.

"Close one," Shishtar said.

"Not that much." Gingerly Jim raised his naked head above the top of the bunker. There was little to see in the rain that fell so heavily it looked more like a vertical river. Up close the shattered husks of buildings poked gaunt ribs into low-hanging mist. He squinted but saw no movement.

"Sarge told us this one would be a piece of cake," Jim said. "Bunch of country bumpkins, he said. Sarge always lie like that?"

Shishtar had slid down the incline and now sprawled on his back, letting the rain spatter on his face. He came from a damp world himself. "Sarge says what they tell him. What else is he gonna say? He's two holes over getting half-drowned just like we are."

Shishtar looked unchanged, but Jim's face was pasty and hollow. His cheekbones stood out with razor sharpness, and his eyes were buried in doughy, puffed slits of flesh. It had only been five days, but it felt to him like five years. He saw that his right hand was quivering slightly, and he wrapped his left hand around it to hold it steady.

Shishtar didn't seem to notice, but he said, "You got the shakes a little, Jim? I saw you had the dump-squirts last night, too. That's not normal for Terries, is it? You okay?"

"I'm okay, Shish. I'll make it."

"Just asking. You worry me some. I wouldn't want to lose you just when I got to start liking you okay."

The remark was offhand, but it touched Jim. He had read about but never understood the reality of battlefield friendship. Now he knew it firsthand. Your buddies were all you had. The mission was incomprehensible, the officers were fools, the enemy blankly murderous, the gods laughing their divine heads off, but you could count on your buddies.

Not so long ago he'd never seen an alien in the flesh. Now a tall squirmy being with a head like a butcher's display was the best friend he'd ever known. More than a friend. In some ways they'd become two parts of the same thing in a bond deeper and more powerful than love. He stared at Shish and tried to remember Cat, whom he had loved. It took a surprisingly long moment to bring her face back into focus. But he knew that as long as he lived he'd be able to see Shishtar.

"Sure, Shish. I guess I can put up with you, too, if I have to."

Shish grunted. Jim looked away. In five days he had saved Shish's life once and Shish had returned the favor twice. He could see every detail of those incidents in his mind, but he chose not to. They had happened, and now they were done with. Indelible marks on the ledger of his life.

Life on the edge of death was sharper than he'd ever imagined. He was only sixteen. He was older than time itself. And whatever he had been before, he was now something new, something forged in fire and blood.

He knew he would need that if he survived. If he survived.

## 2

Later in the day, with Sleen's sun a watery green blot sinking beyond the partially collapsed roof where they sheltered, five of them squatted and talked. There had been seven, but Obo had stepped on a shaped-charge mine and blown off three of his legs and he'd bled out before anything could be done. His nest-twin Ebo, deprived of the telepathic link he'd known all his life, had gone psycho and charged at shapeless shadows beyond the perimeter, waving his force rifle and whistling in high desperate tones. Something had lanced out of the murk and cut him in half and they'd left him where he fell because they were taking fire and they couldn't find enough pieces of Ebo to put in a self-broadcasting body bag.

So Jim and Shish hunkered next to Abbda, a tiny crusty being who operated on some kind of natural radar and was the most remorseless and efficient killer Jim had ever imagined, and K'rrrng, a jolly rotund former teacher who handled squad communications and medic duties as well, and they all listened to Sarge's slow rough voice as he gave them the word.

Sarge was holding K'rrrng's squad comm unit in two of his hands and scratching his vast scaly butt with a third. Over the unit a hologram danced, a fully detailed map picture scaled one to one thousand, updated to real-time so that it showed the ruins that surrounded them as an infinitely tiny sprawl of fractured doll's houses.

A red dot throbbed near the center of the map. "Us," Sarge said. Another dot not far away began to glow. "That's the objective. Upstairs says it's a sector command post full of froggies. It must be something major because they're sending in six squads and providing backup fire support." Bright green lines slowly extended from the first dot to the second. "Intel says it's pretty gnarled up in there. A lot of rubble and probably every square foot of it mined, so keep your force suits buttoned up."

He didn't have to mention Obo.

"Jim?"

"Yeah, Sarge?"

"You and Shish take the point on this one with the Thunder-bolt. My guess is we'll have to cut our own path, and the Bolt is the best thing we have for that. Me and Abbda will try to cover your flanks, and K'rrrng will do what he can with realtime intel, but don't count on anything. You know how it is."

Jim and Shish both nodded. They knew.

Sleen was a recent RoiFrank colonization and was still mostly empty space. The most recent census reported just under two million inhabitants concentrated mostly in three small cities and a network of villages surrounding those cities. The planet had no known strategic significance and no RoiFrank military garrison. What little military force it possessed was concentrated in local police units whose barracks and stations had been scorched into ash in the first engagements.

In theory it should have been a piece of cake just as Kalvorn said. But somebody had miscalculated. When it became evident they had no formal way of resisting the invasion the Sleen government had turned off the weather control systems and let Sleen return to its natural waterlogged state. The leaders then found some way to distribute the armory of the police force into the hands of the citizenry along with detailed instructions on how to use anything and everything as a weapon. Shaped mines made out of household chemicals. Bear traps filled with poison stakes. Deadfalls. Explosives buried in tunnels. Jim had even seen a Red Death corpse with a pair of arrows in its throat.

He had imagined that faced with the overwhelming power of a modern high-tech galactic fighting force the untrained inhabitants of Sleen would be helpless. But he hadn't reckoned on the determined suicidal ferocity of a people fighting for their homes and streets and children.

Just as the Hunzza reminded Jim of alligators without actually looking like alligators, Jim thought of frogs when he saw his first RoiFrank. Tall skinny frogs with broad bulbous skulls and wide mouths. Smooth blue skins that looked faintly slimy but were dry to the touch. Muscular thighs that let them jump twenty feet straight up in the air, flying over foxholes and raining home-brewed death below. They were preternaturally quick and perfectly at home in the endless rain. The battalion's casualty rate was already twenty percent and climbing rapidly.

Maybe they were waiting to be rescued by the RoiFrank Navy. But that wouldn't happen. Not right away at least. Barracks rumor said a hundred units of the Hunzzan Navy were providing cover for this operation. Incomprehensible. Jim couldn't imagine what could be so important about Sleen to call for an armada like that. Or why, if the operation was really so important, it had been entrusted to mercenaries. Scuttlebutt also told of six other hired crews, including one of brigade strength.

Sarge rocked gently back on his huge hams and snapped shut the comm unit. "That's it. Go in thirty minutes on my mark. Jim?"

"Huh?"

"You feed those coordinates into your suit locator?"

"Sure, Sarge."

Kalvorn nodded. "Command's promising real-time updates, and maybe they'll even deliver. The officers acted real concerned." He sighed lugubriously. "Once you get going don't stop. Just keep on blasting. We'll be right behind."

Shish chuckled. "Good place for your big butt, Sarge. Right behind."

"*Gninglah* you, Shish."

"Yeah probably. One of these days," Shish said.

## 3

The problem with the force suits was they weren't perfect. They would stop most small-arms fire, but Jim could put a hole in one with his Thunderbolt. Anything big enough to hole out a force suit guaranteed instant death to the trooper inside it. They filtered out all known airborne toxins, but there were always new toxins. They protected from the shrapnel of a mine blast, but if the explosion was large enough, you had the same problem as with an egg. Shake an egg hard enough and you get an omelet inside the unbroken shell. And they were uncomfortable. They bellied out about half an inch from the skin and turned fingers into clumsy sausages. Because they were perfectly frictionless, you tended to slide around a lot. The generator was a heavy lump strapped to your upper back. Provisions had been made to handle urinary discharge, but you couldn't take a dump in one. So a lot of troops died squatting without dignity, splattered with their own crap.

The troops hated them. They powered them down at the slightest opportunity. So one of every sergeant's mantras was to keep your force suit buttoned up. Keep it tight.

It was a mantra because it was so often disobeyed.

Jim and Shish went over the front of the bunker just as the last weak rays of the sun wavered into night. The rain reduced visibility to a few feet. Jim navigated by his heads-up display, a continuously updated (supposedly) map that told him where he was and showed him where to go.

Jim had the Bolt set up and ready to fire, which meant it was one hell of an awkward package. Shish stayed on his right and swept the gaping orifice of a Chatterbox back and forth.

They moved forward in a combat crouch, following the indistinct center of what had once been a fairly wide road. Now it was choked with rubble from the buildings that had collapsed along its edges and pitted with deep holes. The footing was treacherous at best, impossible at worst. Nevertheless, they pressed forward without incident. Low voices hummed in Jim's ears, and he tuned them out. It was just nervous chatter. The drumming rainy darkness was ominous. Jim's world shrank to the few yards that surrounded him and Shish.

"See anything?"

"Nope. You?"

"You kidding? Back home we call this pea soup."

"What's a pea?" Shish asked.

"It's a—forget it. What's that?"

"It's not on my heads-up. Maybe it's too fresh. Some kind of big pile of junk. Careful."

"Yeah. Sarge, you see it?" Jim's voice quavered. Once that would have embarrassed him. Not anymore. If this didn't scare the crap out of you, your mind didn't work right no matter what kind of mind you had.

"I got it. It's not just rubble. K'rrrng says he's getting a reading out of it. Some kind of electronic—"

Thunder and lightning ripped at the edge of the night. Great clouds of steam billowed up. The first blast moved the entire barrier into the air and dumped it more or less on Jim's position.

His force suit snapped rigid and kept him from being crushed. But he'd taken a hard jolt, and something felt loose in his chest. Maybe a rib, but he didn't have time for that. He shoveled aside a couple of medium-sized rocks and stuck his head up. Then he looked at the rocks themselves. All around him they'd begun to bubble and slowly dissolve.

"Jeez. Sarge, it's combat nano. Looks like sludge."

"*Gningalld!* Okay stay buttoned up and try to get beyond it. We're coming as fast as we can."

"Got you," Jim said. "Shish, you okay?"

"I'm here, Jim." His voice sounded ragged.

"Hey, are you all right?"

"Don't worry about it. Get your butt moving."

"'Kay."

Combat nano came in many varieties. It could be designed to dissolve certain kinds of metal or plastic. Or certain kinds of lung tissue. One of the worst from an infantryman's point of view was a version called sludge. It was tailored to eat dirt and rock and give off a hell of a lot of heat when it did so. What it did was turn solid ground into bubbling, boiling hell. It couldn't kill a trooper in a buttoned-up force suit, but it could slow him down enough that more effective weapons could be brought to bear.

And it was very dangerous. Nano could mutate like anything else that depended on precise molecular patterns. In training Jim had been told of a planet that didn't exist anymore. Somebody had used sludge, and it had changed. The automatic shutoff sequence in its coding had switched off, and it had dissolved the entire world.

"Jim, I'm—something's wrong with my power."

A few feet away in the strobing light Jim saw Shish rising from the muck. Boiling sludge dripped off his suit. He was hunched over strangely, holding himself as if partly broken. The force field that surround him was normally transparent, but now it had taken on a milky shifting translucency, a visual warning of impending power failure.

"Shish get out of there!" Jim swiveled to take in as much of the scene as he could. Rain pounding down on the bubbling mud burst instantly into steam. But it looked to him as if the bulk of the stuff was behind them. Only a narrow moat of sludge stood between them and the safety of solid ground.

He brought the unwieldy bulk of the Thunderbolt to his chest and heaved with both hands. He saw it fly in a low arc and land safely on dry earth a good three yards beyond the slowly advancing sludge.

He was taking sporadic fire out of the shadows in front of him, but evidently the rain was screwing up the froggy's targeting. It was mostly small-arms fire. Something whizzed past his head, and he realized they were even throwing rocks at him.

He slogged toward Shish, reached him, and wrapped his arms around him. "I'm gonna carry you, Shish. Soon as I get you out of this glop I want you to switch off your suit. You'll be too slippery for me to carry if you don't."

He was lifting as he spoke, trying to find enough leverage as he battled against the lack of friction. Shish was far more slippery than any eel. Finally he saw that Shish was completely out of the stuff. "Switch off, Shish! Do it, I can't hold on."

"Jim . . . I'm scared."

"Just do it!"

Another slight pause, and then he felt Shish's limber frame suddenly shrink as the suit field collapsed. Immediately his hold on his buddy strengthened. Swaying slightly, he turned toward the front and started plodding forward.

"What's going on!" Sarge called.

"I got him, we're almost out of it. Where the hell are you?"

"Behind you a few yards. *Gnarding!* This sludge is ugly. Deep, too."

The rate of fire streaming in from the shadows increased. They must have finally triangulated on him. Something hit his right thigh and bounced off, staggering him. On his shoulders Shish moaned.

"Hang on, buddy, we're gonna be okay!"

He took a step and then another. It seemed to take hours. Then his left foot came down on solid ground. Shish had begun to slip a bit and Jim horsed him back up as he tried to find new purchase. A sound like a string of Chinese firecrackers exploded nearby and he felt a sudden series of taps muffled by his armor.

He saw the Thunderbolt lying untouched a couple of yards to his left. The ground there looked good, and there was a natural low wall of buckled pavement just beyond it. Not much cover but enough to hold until Sarge and the rest came up.

His ribs and thigh ached unmercifully, and every time he took a deep breath it felt as if somebody had rammed an ice pick in just below his armpit.

"Awright, buddy, we made it," he said as he lowered Shish and flung himself prone at the Bolt. "Keep your head down. Your suit's still off."

He yanked the snout of the Thunderbolt around and aimed it forward. The Bolt was big stuff. Aim it in the general direction and light it off. Big trouble for whatever was on the other end.

"Shish . . . ?"

No answer. He took a moment to lay down suppression fire. A fan of heaving white light sprayed out before him. Incandescent chunks bounced into the air. He heard screams and felt a savage satisfaction.

"Shish, buddy, talk to me."

Nothing but silence.

In one movement he safed the Bolt and threw himself at the indistinct shape nearby. "Shish!"

The rain had washed away Shish's blood. In the indistinct light it took him a moment to see the stitchery of black holes running across Shish's chest. "Shish, oh God, Shish! Medic! K'rrrng, get over here! Shish is hit bad!"

"We're coming, Jim," Sarge replied. "Another minute."

But Shish didn't have another minute. His eyes flickered. "Watch . . . your . . . ass, buddy," he whispered.

Then he died.

Shish's people didn't use embedded-nano healing technology. They didn't believe in it. Their attitude was that when the fates took you, you died and went on.

Shish had gone on. He was dead. He wouldn't be coming back.

Jim went mad.

# CHAPTER ELEVEN

## 1

---

### ABOARD THE ISS QUEEN RUIN:
### DEEP SPACE

Jim lay faceup on his pad in the squad barracks cube. A few inches in front of his face a tiny holoscreen ran canned replays of recent news from the WideWeb.

Hunzza had announced to the galaxy that mercenary terrorists hired by Albagens had attacked a peaceful party of Hunzzan scientists working on an obscure RoiFrank world called Sleen. Hunzza had provided many pictures of the terrorists carrying out their atrocities. Jim recognized a few shots of Red Death teams. He wondered where they'd gotten the dead Hunzza. Probably just slaughtered some of their own people. That would be a Hunzzan thing to do.

Hunzza claimed that while attempting to rescue their scientists they were attacked by elements of the RoiFrank Navy in league with Alba. Luckily a sizable detachment of the Hunzzan Navy had been nearby and was able to drive off the RoiFrank with heavy losses. In order to protect the few survivors, Hunzza had invested Sleen. RoiFrank had declared war on Hunzza, and when Hunzza replied in kind Albagens honored its treaties and declared war on Hunzza as well. Now everybody was piling in on one side or another.

The games were over. The galaxy was at war, at least this part of it. Jim stared blankly at the screen and tried to imagine the hell on Sleen magnified a hundred times. A thousand times.

It had all been a trick. Shish and all the others had died to ensure the success of a piece of filthy Hunzzan treachery. His stomach heaved at the thought. He felt the smooth rhythm of the airflows shift as the hatch slid open.

Sarge lumbered over and hunkered down. "How come you got the lights out?"

"I like it dark," Jim said.

Sarge grunted. "I didn't tell anybody you went berserker. So instead of getting the brig they're gonna give you a unit citation. A nice little medal you can wear."

Jim's eyes flickered, but he didn't say anything.

"K'rrrng's gonna be out of the tanks tomorrow. Good as new the medics said."

Jim nodded. Neither of them mentioned Abbda or Shish or Ebo or Obo. Jim remembered his final hell-run only as a series of jagged flashes like fragments of a nightmare. At the end he'd found himself standing in the middle of a large structure lighted only by the glare of his own weapon.

He'd held the Bolt at hip level. At some point he'd switched off his armor. He had no idea why. But the Bolt was so hot it was blistering the flesh off his palms. He didn't notice. He just kept on fanning it wide, killing and killing.

He'd seen Abbda come up on his left and begin to wreak some incredibly murderous havoc. Bodies jumped and flew. The din was enormous, the stench unbelievable.

When the Bolt's power had finally died Jim stood in silence listening to the sound of his own breathing. He heard Sarge clumping up from his rear, picking his way over the dead. When Sarge's weight came down there arose soft mushy sounds.

Out of the corner of his eye he saw Abbda power down his suit. Then a wink of motion. A tiny figure leaped from a smoking pile of corpses holding something at its chest. Jim's mind noted the beginnings of the colored skull ridge that marked a RoiFrank male.

He reached Abbda and there was a sudden spray of light. When the spots vanished from Jim's vision he looked for Abbda and saw nothing but a fuming hole.

Automatically he'd done the terrible computation. The RoiFrank male had been less than two-thirds the size of an adult. A boy then. A very young boy.

"It was all a trick," Jim said. "So the Hunzza could get their damned war started looking like good guys. But nobody will believe it, will they?"

Sarge shook his big head. "No, not really. Nobody who counts. It was for public consumption only."

"I feel dirty. What was the point?"

"I put you in for a stripe. You're a corporal now, Jim."

"Taking Shish's place."

"Yeah. Taking his place. Listen, it isn't official yet, but we're putting down for a while. Do some recruiting. There's supposed to be another contract. You'll get some leave time."

Jim hitched over on his side and stared at Sarge. "I won't work for the Hunzza again. I'll desert first."

"I hear it's Alba this time. A rescue mission. Carrying some kind of tech stuff. Hunzza's already trying to invest the Alban home planets. Alba's Navy is spread out to hell and gone. Hunzza bored right in. It's gonna be touch-and-go."

"So what do I tell the newbies, Sarge? How great war is, all about honor and pride and stuff like that?"

"No. You tell them the same things Shish told you. That it's dirty and frightening and dangerous and the only thing you can depend on is your buddies. And even then odds are you'll die ugly in some misbegotten garbage pile only your buddies know about. If any of your buddies are left to know."

"I hate war, Sarge."

"Sure you do. We all do. Nobody hates war more than grunts like us. We're the ones who have to fight it."

"Those were kids we killed. It wasn't a sector station, it was a school being used as a hospital. That little kid that blew up Abbda . . ."

Sarge sighed. "You gonna take that stripe, kid?"

After a long moment Jim nodded. "Yeah. I will. What else have I got?"

"You got me. You got us, Jim."

"Someday I'm gonna make it stop, Sarge." Silent tears ran down Jim's cheeks. "War is evil. I'm gonna stop it."

Sarge said nothing about the tears. He knew that warriors wept, that sometimes tears were all they had to share. He slapped Jim on the shoulder as he rose. His knees made an audible creaking sound. "If you did, every grunt in the galaxy would worship your name forever. So who knows, buddy? Maybe you'll be the one."

"Maybe I will," Jim said.

## 2

### ALBAGENS

**H**ith Mun Alter entered the silence of his small working office with relief. The speech to the Great Pack, the deliberative body of the Pra'Loch, had gone well. Fight them on the beaches, fight them in the streets, fight them house by house. Never give up.

Stirring words. But it would take more than words to stop the Hunzzan fleet now pounding its way through scattered resistance in the Outer Marches, drawing ever closer to the inner planets and Alba itself. And a sun-buster didn't leave much in the way of beaches, streets, or houses to fight over.

The Hunzzan Empire was smaller, more compact than the Alban Empire. And of course their military had been war-gaming this for years. Everybody knew it was coming, but it was normal to hope it wouldn't be quite so soon. And so the Alban Navy was still spread out trying to cover the much vaster space of its empire while Hunzza thrust a spear of steel directly at its heart.

A soft bell chimed as he sat down at his desk. His ruff, streaked with gray, quivered and then drooped. He was too old for this. Two hundred fifty years. But there was no one else. He knew what he was worth. Alba needed him now. He would have to find the strength, not only for himself but for all of them, somewhere.

"Yes?"

Holograms danced. "We've found a way to get the tech for the new shields in. A mercenary unit called the Red Death. We think they were involved on Sleen, but they've agreed to take the mission. They're asking a fortune, of course."

"Of course. They're mercenaries. Do they have a chance?"

"A slim one. But the best we can find."

"So what choice do we have? We need those

shields. Take the figure they're asking and double it. Half down and half on delivery."

A new face appeared. "Packlord?"

"Yes?"

"I have the leader of some barbarian planet on hold for you. Name of Serena Half Moon. The planet is called Terra. I know you're very busy, but she has extremely high-level access codes."

Alter's limp ruff stiffened. "I'll take the call. Put it through now."

The packlord paused a moment to examine Serena Half Moon's features before speaking. He wasn't sure, but he thought the human woman looked tired. Well, everybody was tired.

"Serena, how are you?"

"Holding up, Hith. And you?"

"We're at war."

"Oh God."

"You don't get the news?"

"You know how Delta had things set up. No uncensored newsfeed. I've maintained the policy. But even with a full feed the only thing I've seen so far is about some kind of action on a RoiFrank planet."

"Out-of-date now. It was a trap. But it worked, and we ended up declaring war on Hunzza. Now everybody else is being drawn in."

"I see. What does that mean for us? For Terra? Are we in danger?"

Alter stared at her. "I don't know. You're not a part of our empire, so you shouldn't be a direct target. But an agent you might know has arrived with some rather . . . unsettling news."

"Oh?"

"Yes. Serena, I must ask. I now have word the man I used to deal with is dead. The fact I'm talking to you instead of him seems to bear that out. Is it true?"

Serena paused, then spoke carefully. "Delta is not currently a factor in relations between the Pra'Loch and the Terran Confederation."

"I see. Suitably slippery of you. To the bone of the matter then. Are your information-processing capabilities still as strong as they were and will you freely provide those capabilities to us now in our time of need?"

Once again the chairman paused. "Nothing is free, Hith. There is always a price."

"Very well. What is the price?"

"A young Terran male is somewhere in the galaxy, but we don't know where."

"Yes, named Jim Endicott."

Serena blinked.

"I told you our agent to Delta arrived here. He's made a full report, of course."

"Yes. Well, that would be our price. Return the boy to us, and I guarantee you the full use of our technologies."

"We don't know where he is either. He's vanished."

Serena's features hardened. "That is the deal, Hith. Find the boy. Send him back. Nothing less."

Hith Mun Alter waited a moment before replying. "You know this is a dangerous game you're playing, Madame Chairman?"

"They're all dangerous games, Packlord."

"Yes, I suppose they are. Very well. I'll be in touch as soon as I know anything."

When they were done, Hith Mun Alter spoke aloud: "Bring Lord Korkal Emut Denai to me. Now."

# 3

## ABOARD THE ISS QUEEN OF RUIN

Jim thought he'd understood Shish, but he learned to know him better after his death. In all large groups there are insiders and outsiders. As the new recruits trickled in and their training began he discovered what it was about Shish that had given him his unconscious air of authority. Shish had possessed secret knowledge. Now Jim knew those secrets, too, though learning them had scarred and blackened his soul.

The greenies in his squad came to him with hesitant questions. What was it like? What is combat like? Have you ever killed anybody?

K'rrrng returned, roly-poly and, as advertised, good as new. He and Jim made a new nucleus around which the squad revolved. Training went on while negotiations for the mysterious new contract continued. As a vet, Jim was firmly plugged in to the inner grapevine that often knew of things before even

most officers did. The next mission would not
be ground combat though it would be dangerous. A valuable cargo, a rescue mission to Alba
itself, and the running of an ever-tightening
Hunzzan blockade of Alban inner space.

Jim found a curious solace in this. Deep-
space war was materially different from the
kind waged in the mud. Most of the work was
done by the machines as they dodged each
other through the thickets of space and subspace. A mistake might kill you, but if it was a
big mistake, you would never know. One
instant a ship filled with the living and the
breathing, the next a rapidly expanding cloud
of particles too small even to label.

A simple option: success or annihilation
with no middle choice. It seemed somehow
cleaner to him, and he began to understand
how those high powers who pushed the but-
tons would like to think of war in this way. No
mud or blood, no personal responsibility or
recrimination. Just the anonymous finger on
the nameless button. Or turn it over to machines,
so much faster and more powerful than the living brain they might as well be forces of
nature.

Yet he knew that was an even greater evil,
for it took the reality of war beyond the realm of
choice and made it inevitable, as predestined
as the eventual dissolution of the universe into
the cold dead soup of final entropy. *We can
choose*, he told himself. *We must choose*. And
he promised himself he would never forget
that.

"Not a bad bunch," Sarge said as they lounged together against a bulkhead, enjoying the break between a physical training course and a session on fieldstripping light hand weapons. Jim had been training greenies on the use of the Thunderbolt. He discovered that in the boring repetition of the teacher's rhythms he no longer felt the agony of hefting that death machine, of pulling its trigger and watching children burn. He was grateful for that.

"Nope, not so bad," Jim agreed. "

"You've done a good job with them, Corporal."

"Thanks, Sarge."

Kalvorn seemed to be edging around something. Whenever he was nervous or uncomfortable he began to itch and to scratch. Two of his arms were now busily digging away at his scaly hide. Jim grinned.

"Come on, Sarge. What's up now?"

"Well uh. Uh. Jim would you like to be a sergeant?"

"What?"

"Well you'd have to leave the squad. A promotion and a different assignment. It's uh . . . noncombat."

Jim stared at him. At one time he'd hoped and even prayed for something like this. Hell was at the wrong end of a Thunderbolt, and he'd learned there was no right end to any weapon. Flesh died on one side, the soul on the other. But he'd made peace with that and found comfort in the thought of his own damnation. He had his buddies, if only for a while, and that might be enough. He hoped it would be enough.

"What are you trying to say, Sarge?"

"They finally got around to analyzing your recruiting jacket and somebody up front thinks you've got the makings of a pilot. So there's a slot open as a trainee, and if you want it, it's yours."

"You mean leave the squad?"

Sarge nodded.

"I can't do that, Sarge."

Kalvorn remained silent for a long moment, visibly choosing his words. A third hand joined in the scratching.

"Jim, do you remember Shish? Abbda? Ebo and Obo?"

"Sure, Sarge."

"Have they left the squad?"

"Uh . . . yes. They're dead."

"But you remember them?"

"What are you telling me, Sarge?"

"I'm not good with words, kid. Yeah, they're dead, but they're still with us. Still a part of the squad. Still a part of the Red Death, kept in the records forever. Anybody can go look up our squad history and find them and know something about them. The same with you. Even if you leave, you'll still be here. Still be a part of us. I'll remember and so will K'rrrng. But even more important, we'll still be a part of you. You understand what I'm saying?"

Slowly Jim sank to his haunches. Context. He'd wanted a new context for himself, free of all the old badness. Of the problems he had no idea how to solve. He'd thought he was still seeking that context, unaware that it had sought him, found him, and bound him irrevocably. Whatever he might one day become, however he might change and grow, he would always be a part of Third Squad, Baker Company, Battalion of the Red Death.

Did context seek you out no matter what you did? However you might try to avoid it? But that made context something akin to fate.

He felt a great dark swelling of recognition. The power of it swept him over and tumbled him away. He was forever embedded in the past and the future of the Red Death.

His eyes grew hot and wet. Sarge squatted and awkwardly patted him on the knee. "What I'm saying is go, Jim. It's a good promotion. I'm a grunt and always will be. But you've got better things in you, and you will disappoint me greatly if you turn this down. *Gnindng* it, one of the troopers from Three Squad makes good. We'll never forget it, and we'll all be proud of you."

"Sarge . . . will you be proud of me?"

"I already am, son. I already am."

Jim reported to Command Deck Charlie four hours later, bearing all his material goods in a combat bag. But he carried his most precious possessions in his heart, locked against everything but the final key of death.

Jim of no last name. Corporal, Third Squad, Baker Company, the Red Death Battalion.

Soldier.

# CHAPTER TWELVE

## 1

---

**P**ilot Commander Elveen Ekkadli was, like most of the officers, a Romian, as large and scaly as Sarge though his speech was more precise and he seemed colder and more distant toward his charges. He welcomed Jim brusquely and directed him toward the Cyberneural Modification Unit to be fitted with a new cyberjack implant to replace the Terran version that Ekkadli told him was "Stone Age technology."

While waiting naked and goose-bumped in a sterile white anteroom, Jim discovered he had a fellow student named Tickeree, "but call me Tick, okay?"

Tick was a spindly furry primate with a (to Jim) normal complement of two black button eyes, one pug nose, and one rubbery smiling mouth in the (to him) usual positions. He resembled a stretched and underfed chimpanzee with a high forehead, hairy, pointed ears, and a permanently winsome expression. He was the cutest thing Jim had ever seen. He had to restrain a nearly overwhelming urge to pet Tick and scratch the soft frizz behind his ears.

Mindful of mercenary etiquette Jim made no inquiries as to Tick's past, but he soon discovered that Tick's favorite subject was himself, his brilliant history, his glorious future, and anything else remotely related to those three subjects. Tick quickly revealed that he was of royal blood, a prince of the ruling family of the Heestah Empire, which, he said, was a vast web of worlds only nominally part of the RoiFrank Swarm.

Tick related all this with such warmth and cheerful believability that Jim despised himself for a cynical *flut* when he told Fred to access the appropriate archives for confirmation of Tick's amazing story.

As it turned out there was a Heestah Empire. It consisted of two flea-bitten worlds lost in the vast backwaters of the Swarm. It did possess a royal family that had no real power whatsoever and only a bit more wealth than the average Heestahn family. Apparently the principal activity of the royal family was opening cybermalls and begging money for local charities. Jim wondered why Tick spouted such easily disprovable fantasies.

"You look pretty harmless, Terran," Tick said. "Kind of pale and sickly."

Tick, resplendent in silky golden fur, was handling his lack of clothing much better than Jim, but Jim wasn't about to concede superiority.

"We Terrans are very fierce. Barbarians, you know. Just ask anybody."

"I already did. My universal didn't turn up

much on you people. New on the scene aren't you?"

Jim shrugged. "Sort of."

"But you were combat. You were down on Sleen, right? What was it like?"

"You weren't there?"

"No. I just signed on. I'm going to be a pilot. I have superb neural reflexes and I test off the scale on autonomic temperospatial visualization."

Jim had no idea what that meant. Before he could inquire further a short, spiderlike creature scrabbled through the door on a spiky forest of many-jointed legs and shepherded them into a larger room.

"I'm Meditech Sheelob," the spider thing twittered. Jim decided Sheelob most reminded him of a bagpipe, right down to the tartan pattern on his delicate skin.

"This way, please," Sheelob continued. "The process will take about four hours and is entirely painless. You will be in the nanotanks and unconscious throughout, so please have no worries."

"I'm not worried," Tick said. "We Heestahns of the royal blood are trained from birth to withstand the most agonizing pain." Jim smothered a grin as he noted a faint twitching at the corners of Tick's black eyes.

"Wait a minute," Jim said. "Does this process change my brain some way?"

"Nothing to be concerned over. We've already analyzed the connections of the jack you have in place now. Very primitive by the way. All we do is extend and speed up the connecting pathways. There's almost no organic alteration at all, but you should notice a rather large difference in your capacity after the change. By the way, Sergeant Marshal, what's all that useless stuff in your genotype? Our analyzers couldn't find any intrinsic genetic purpose for it. It won't affect this process, but I wondered about it."

"You probed my genotype?"

"Of course. We had to program the nano-package that does the alterations. Wouldn't want to turn you into something like Corporal Tickeree here by mistake."

"He should be so lucky," Tick said.

Jim ignored him. "It's just a . . . kind of identification code. All Terries have it."

"I see. Complicated for that kind of thing, but it's none of my business. Right this way, gentlemen."

It took a moment for it to sink in that this was the first time somebody had called him by his new title. Sergeant Marshal. It felt good. It felt even better that he outranked Tick, who was now giving him sidelong glances.

"You're a sergeant?" Tick said.

"Yep. That's right."

"I'll probably be a sergeant soon, too."

"Oh, no doubt."

"I mean with my superior qualifications it doesn't make sense you should outrank me."

"Now wait a minute—"

"Gentlemen, please," Sheelob said. "Sergeant, if you'd climb into this tank here? And Corporal, that next one over?"

There were six tanks, each large enough to hold two or three good-sized humans end to end. Jim tried to imagine the kind of being it would take to cramp one of those enclosures. Big was the best he could do. Very big.

"Just lie on that platform there," Sheelob said. "Position doesn't matter. There. Comfortable?"

The platform suspended over the tank looked like plain steel, but it felt warm and yielding. "I'm fine," Jim said.

"Good. Here we go now."

Jim felt a sudden tingling sensation and realized he'd closed his eyes. "When do we start?" he asked.

"Start? You've been under for hours. We're all finished. Looks like a perfect job," Sheelob said. He handed Jim a green fuzzy robe. "Dry off, Sergeant. As pilots go, your equipment is cutting-edge now. Couldn't get a better job done on Alba itself. Good luck to you."

It wasn't till later that Jim realized that among all the Confederacy's billions, thanks to Delta's secret embargo on galactic technology he now possessed two things that were unique—and one of them was something that neither his true parents (whoever they might have been), nor Delta himself could possibly have planned for. His ability to achieve cyberneural interface was now approximately three hundred years in advance of any known Terran technology. And if Sheelob had understood what he'd just done, Jim would never have left the nanotank alive.

## 2

**"N**ominally you are training to pilot the *Queen* or any other ship of her size, but what you are really learning to do is to become expendable," Commander Ekkadli said.

Jim thought about it. "I see," he said slowly. "The junior pilots handle the combat assault landers."

"That's right. Which is why the slots you two are filling exist in the first place."

"Sleen?" Jim asked.

"Yes. Two good men." Ekkadli paused. "Well, you know what I mean."

"Now wait a second, Commander," Tick broke in. "What do you mean expendable? I can understand about the Terrie here, but surely you can't be serious about wasting a pilot of my talents on something as trivial as ferrying dumb grunts down onto useless mudballs."

Jim thought of Shish and Sarge and the rest of Three Squad and decided that bunkmates or not, he and Tick were going to have a small physical discussion—and soon. Dumb grunts?

Ekkadli eyed Tick. "Corporal Tickeree, you would be well advised to keep those thoughts to yourself. As for your talent, I've yet to see enough of it to justify entrusting the lives of any good marines to it, let alone the troops who are the reason your job exists at all."

Tick wasn't stupid. He swallowed once, then nodded. "Yes, sir."

"Well. Back to it. Corporal, you operate Blue Vessel. Sergeant, you take Red this time. Same exercise please." He waited until they slipped on their interforce helmets.

They had been doing this exercise over and over, switching the piloting duties between Red and Blue Vessels. Most of the time they were supervised by training programs, but Commander Ekkadli found an hour each day for personal observation and instruction.

The Red and Blue exercise was a mock battle between two virtual ships. It was a ludicrous bit of training in that the chances of either junior pilot actually conning the *Queen* in a deep-space engagement were next to nil— all three lead pilots plus the four regular lander pilots would have to be incapacitated—but it was an excellent method for developing the raw skills needed for lesser tasks.

There was a time in Terran history when fighting pilots had needed superb physical reflexes to fly their warplanes, but that time was gone. With direct cyberneural connections to the electronic infrastructure of space vessels, a different kind of reflexive speed was called for: mental reflexes. What Tick had meant when he talked about his neural reflexes and superb autonomic temperospatial visualization.

Neural reflex was what it sounded like: how fast could you think? The reflexes involved could be strengthened and quickened through training, though some people had a natural ability. Autonomic temperospatial visualization was another breed of cat entirely. Autonomic referred to a reflexive process almost entirely without thought. The spatio-temporal visualization part described what kinds of things triggered those reflexes, in this case patterns in space and time. This was the meat and potatoes of great pilots: the ability to instantly recognize patterns in what others would see only as a hopeless jumble, and then, without thinking about it, make the correct response to those patterns.

This gift was something only minimally affected by training. You either had it, or you didn't. Jim discovered that he had it in abundance, and that his natural talents were boosted to almost unimaginable levels by his new cyberneural interface.

But it was an uncomfortable talent because he had not suspected he had it. He had always been good with the computer games, the cavorting in the spaces of virtual reality. He had been good conning the tiny ships he'd trained in, and he had learned to trust his muscle knowledge, the ingrained ability to push the right lever and flip the right switch. Yet when he became a part of Red Ship—a feeling something like inhabiting a body made of durasteel and electricity—and faced off against Tick in his Blue Ship armor, what he found himself capable of scared him.

It was an eerie kind of artistry he had never thought about because he'd not known he possessed it. But now he knew. All his life some part of him had assumed he was in training for adulthood. All the schooling and all the sports, all the other lessons and courses and practices had to have some eventual goal. When he thought about it at all he assumed his education would take purpose in the shape of his hopes and dreams for himself. But this new talent changed the shape of the future. It made demands. It was a different kind of context, as unlooked for as anything else that had come unannounced to him and changed his life. It was more than a gift. It might be his future raising its head inside him for the first time and looking around with hard, glittering, demanding eyes.

Some gifts you had to live up to. Had Einstein foreseen the nuclear mushroom in the early days when he found himself thinking in the language of the atoms? Did the young Adolf Hitler know his future when he first discovered his voice was that of demonic pied piper, that with it he could make others dream his own nightmares? Did men and women of that caliber drive their talent or did their talent drive *them*?

Jim eeled around these thoughts in the dark of his nights without ever quite articulating them even to himself. Instead he felt a crawling discomfort with the discovery of such great artistry in himself. You were supposed to strive. It shouldn't be something you simply stumbled on.

He moved his chin, and the motion flicked on the helmet ring around his neck, covering his skull with the interforce field.

The field constantly monitored the upgraded implant behind his ear. There were no trailing wires or hard metal plugs. From inside the shield was transparent. Sometimes he almost forgot it was there. But it also functioned as a screen, so that true visuals could accompany the virtual versions pouring directly into his mind. It sounded confusing, but he got used to it. He supposed Chip and Morninglory had thought their own virtual worlds were as normal as an afternoon stroll, too. The intelligent mind, species indeterminate. A wonderfully adaptive mechanism.

"Ready?" Commander Ekkadli said.

"Yes, sir," Jim replied.

"Yes," from Tick.

Everything fell away.

## 3

For the purpose of training, both Red and Blue Ships were virtual mirrors of the actual *Queen of Ruin*. Jim and Tick "rode piggy-back" on the *Queen*'s equipment and received continual updates on the *Queen*'s real-time data. Jim had trained himself to disregard the feed and relegate it to a barely felt stream of data whispering along the bottom of his attention. He was only slightly aware of it as his mind slipped into the virtual Red Ship like fingers sliding into a glove.

All around him he saw the stars as a ship

would see them: tiny hard pinpoints that became a rushing stream of numbers if he focused on any single one of them. Off in the distance he saw the ominous bulk of Blue Ship. It seemed to flicker and blur: Tick was ducking in and out of subspace hundreds of times a second, a classical defensive maneuver.

Jim blinked and saw a different view. This was of trajectories, probabilities, patterns. It drew not only on the database of ship-to-ship warfare maintained by the *Queen*, but also on Jim's own experience. And he saw a pattern. Suddenly he *knew* what Tick was going to do next, and with no conscious thought whatsoever he ducked his own ship into subspace and brought it out a considerable distance from his previous position. Where he had been space was now curdling, a dark bloom where Tick's gravity distorters were focused.

"Missed me," Jim sent.

Tick didn't reply, though Jim felt an impression of bleak anger that was at odds with Tick's usual cheerful disposition. Blue Ship vanished then into a shrinking bubble that indicated a deep-subspace penetration.

Jim expanded his awareness and waited for a new pattern to appear. Patterns and arrangements and designs. That was all it was. That was all anything was, right down to the subquantum dance. As he contemplated that extraordinary idea while he waited for a new pattern, something tickled him from the center of his awareness, but before he could focus on it space began to boil at the limit of his perceptions.

Tick again no doubt. But when he brought his attention to bear on the disturbance he realized he was no longer in the virtual training session but was now fully monitoring the *Queen*'s actual feed. It wasn't a game anymore. Those were real ships out there.

Lots of them. The Red Death's contract was to run the Hunnzan blockade of the Alban inner systems. For days they'd seen no trace of it. But now Jim saw ship after ship bubbling up from subspace. He saw them and saw what their patterns revealed: the Hunzzan ships saw the *Queen,* too. And there were too many of them. The pattern of the future was predictable.

And if that pattern remained unchanged, he could see no chance for the *Queen* or his mates or himself. No chance at all.

# CHAPTER THIRTEEN

## 1

---

**J**im blinked off his interforce helmet and looked around. Commander Ekkadli was gone. That was no surprise. He would be rushing toward the command deck and his huge console. He, the chief pilot, and the assistant pilot would be fighting the *Queen* in her doomed run. The four junior pilots would also be plugged into the systems, ready to step in if one of their seniors was incapacitated or killed.

"Those are Hunzza," Tick whispered. "Now what do we do?"

The limber Heestahn didn't look good. His glossy fur was limp and dull, and his normally cheerful features sagged.

"Not much," Jim said. "We aren't even junior pilots yet."

But something stirred in Tick's dark eyes, some dream of glory. "We can watch," he said. "We're still plugged in to the ship's systems. If something happens to the others, then we'd be the only ones left. We could save everybody. We'd be heroes . . ."

Jim stared at him. "Are you out of your

mind? We'd be dead. We've only been training for a few days."

But the idea was blowing Tick up like a balloon. The old gleam returned to his eyes. His face stiffened. "Maybe you, Terrie. But I've been training for something like this all my life."

"It's crazy. We'd have to lose six pilots and still have the ship. And even then we'd still be the two juniors. Is it possible to lose six pilots and not lose the ship, too?"

"Sure. It's happened before. Depends on how well those lizard boys do their jobs with the viral data-probes. Data-probes are funny things. Sometimes they don't get through at all. Sometimes they fry synapses on one or two. Or a whole bunch at once. You never know." Tick squirmed in his chair. "Anyway, what else have we got to do? Were you planning on taking a nap?"

Jim felt the weight of the helmet ring around his neck. "I guess you're right about that. Look, Tick. Don't do anything without me, okay?"

He hadn't revealed his own gifts to his fellow trainee. He had even deliberately allowed himself to be defeated several times in training sessions in order to keep his talents concealed. But a hard rational part of him had already evaluated Tick: he knew he was a far more gifted pilot than the Heestahn, and he hadn't yet plumbed the full depth of his own ability.

There was a lilting humor in Tick's voice, but not far beneath that lilt hummed a sneering kind of scorn. "Don't worry, Jimmy. I'll take care of you."

"Okay, partner, see that you do." Jim moved his chin, and the interforce field shrouded him once again.

## 2

It didn't seem like it should be, but the space where the real battle was being fought was a great and shimmering silence pocked by stars that turned into numbers and strangely shaped ships that darted among them like flickering golden minnows.

A chill began to rise in him until it filled his skull. His skin itched as the nerve endings there became painfully sensitive to the ship's systems. He felt as if he could reach out and touch those flickering ghosts now closing a ring of death around the *Queen*. And then he realized he could do that. He could touch them with his fingers and his fingertips would boil with the power of gravity distorts, of phased lasers, of great bombs delivered on jittering waves of subspace. The *Queen* could destroy whole suns if she so desired. She wasn't helpless.

And in that moment of realization he saw something else: he saw a new pattern, one that didn't yet exist. But it could exist if the *Queen* did this and ran that way and attacked in this manner. He saw how the enemy systems might be confused and led astray, and how the *Queen* could take advantage of that. He saw . . .

"*Pilot trainees, what the* gnard *do you think you're doing? Shut the* flut *up. You're jiggering our webs.*"

It was Commander Ekkadli's voice, harsh and rough with strain. Jim shivered as he realized what he'd almost done. Unconsciously he'd moved to take control of the *Queen*'s systems and act on the pattern he saw. But he was only a trainee, green as grass. Good God. He might have killed them all.

"Sorry . . ." he murmured, conscious of Tick chuckling somewhere in the background.

He cut himself partially out of the net so he wouldn't inadvertently disturb the real pilots at their work, but kept a full-system feed running into his skull so he could watch. *Watch my own death?* he wondered.

Because that was what he knew he was observing. The patterns had changed again, shifted by time through space as the pilots aboard the converging Hunzzan ships wove their own planes and angles of attack, selected and deployed their own weapons of destruction.

Then he saw something utterly weird. "What the hell?"

"That's a data-probe," Tick said. "Viral net. It's aimed at the pilots and the controller systems. Burn those out, and we won't be able to hurt a baby."

With a mental twitch Jim accessed the *Queen*'s warfare database and brought up the relevant information. He left that feed on as well, knowing he wouldn't have time if it became necessary for him to act. In this way the ship's brain became essentially a part of his own. He was surprised at how seamless the interface was. It was as if his own brain had suddenly expanded. Now when he looked at something he knew what it was, if the ship knew.

His new interface was even more powerful than he'd imagined. It was a strange, almost God-like feeling. But it was not a comfortable one. Something in him squirmed uneasily at the idea of one human having access to so much knowledge, so much power. With a rig like this and the right databases he could go back to Terra and—and what?

The patterns changed again with shocking swiftness, and he understood he would not be going back to Terra. He wouldn't be going anywhere. He was only sixteen. He had faced death already, but this was different. Here he could see it coming, see the very shape of it in the delicate structures now weaving a net about the *Queen of Ruin*.

*But I don't want to die. I'm too young. I haven't even—*

Brutally he squeezed off that terrified whine. It made him sick. It offended every belief he maintained about himself. But as he choked it to silence he realized it was a part of him, too. And a part of all other humans. Death was the great and old enemy, and man had warred against it so fiercely and so long that its form was engraved on the deepest of the chromosomal memories. Life was the other side of the battle, and the war was called survival. And the universe didn't give a damn about either side. It couldn't. The rocks and the suns would go on until the atoms stopped dancing and the cold and dark covered everything.

His shoulders ached.

The area of the patterns surrounding the *Queen* had shrunk somewhat as the Hunzza tightened and focused their attacks. Without conscious thought he accessed the systems and "remembered" about data-probes and viral nets. He saw what the Hunzzan pilots and their machines were doing: using ships' drives as vibrators, jumping in and out of subspace thousands of times a second, using the fabric of the universe itself to set up resonating patterns. In order to fight at all the *Queen* had to be able to "see." But if her systems and pilots looked straight at the enemy, they must also look at those patterns. And if their own shielding was overwhelmed, those patterns would resonate inside the brains of both machines and beings. And destroy them.

Jim remembered the high and falling scream as Morninglory and Chip had taken over the systems of the Terran warship and plunged it into the soil of Wolfbane like a great exploding dagger. It must have been something like that for them, he thought. Though on a much cruder scale.

And what a strange thought *that* was. At

the time he'd thought Morninglory's skills a little short of magic. Now he saw them for the base and raw art they were. And he knew that if Morninglory could see him now, he would believe himself in the presence of the same kind of magic: that of the savage staring dumbfounded at technology so far beyond comprehension it might as well have been a wizard waving his wand.

The nets tightened further. Suddenly his viewpoint shifted, and he felt himself move to a new vantage far beyond the plane of the engagement. From this view the *Queen* looked like a fat spider centered in a shimmering golden web. But instead of predator trapping prey, the *Queen* was herself entrapped, and at the far end of each strand was a Hunzzan ship riding the web toward a feast of fire at the center.

The thought was horrifying, and he tried to push it away, but it wouldn't leave. It tickled at him with a kind of jolly pervasive horror. Perhaps small animals trapped before onrushing lights felt the same paralyzing fascination.

With no warning at all the protruding spokes of the web suddenly began to flare into white-gold incandescence. He felt rather than heard Tick gasp. A shudder ran through him, and he knew it wasn't real. The ship hadn't moved, not in its metal bones, but the machines and the beings who ordered them had been jolted.

A curious fizzing began to fester in his skull, as if the individual cells of his brain were being slowly popped one by one. The roots of his hair suddenly felt as if they were melting. The golden web began to flash, demanding his full attention, sucking him in and down.

*Look at me!*

Somewhere in the bleak and black distance Commander Ekkadli screamed. Close by, Tick began to grunt, a harsh, mindless, *rhythmic* sound. Inside Jim something screamed as it fought for its life.

*"Fight,"* it hissed. "I can't do it by myself, so help me, damn you, and *fight!"*

## 3

**H**e must have blanked out for a microsecond because when he looked again, though he was still floating far beyond the deadly golden web, the web itself had changed. Now it was a tight blue ball of threads enclosing the *Queen* like a cocoon, visibly shrinking, crushing the delicate meat trapped inside.

Jim opened all his feeds wide, and said, "Commander Ekkadli?"

No reply. "Tick?"

A faint stirring, nothing more. Quickly he ran through the litany of names, but for all the response he got he might as well have been reciting a roll call for the dead.

And some distant part of him acknowledged that, the names of the dead. But deep in the buried part of his genetic heritage the

snake was still screaming, and it wouldn't let
him give in. He gritted his teeth and ignored
the hot wetness trying to explode in his groin.
And finally he forced himself to *stop*, simply to
hang in space, to become an *awareness* and
nothing more.

It was one of the hardest things he'd ever
done in his life. Shuddering chills racked his
flesh, and he ignored them. He felt his heart-
beat race, then sink to an occasional slubber-
ing thump. He let the silence flow through him
and with it the patterns.

They rushed into him with insistent urgency,
faster and faster. His awareness abruptly
expanded, took in the tight blue thready ball, the
glowing lights of the ships beyond, and beyond
them the numbered and numberless stars. His
mind clicked and whirred, gorging itself on the
data surging from within and without. And after
an eternity less than a single pulse of blood he
saw it. Saw the great pattern that ordered it all.

The Hunzza had to maintain their presence
in realtime, and the only way they could do
that was by using the positions of the stars as
reference points. From that they knew where
they were, and knowing their own positions,
they knew where the *Queen* was.

Slowly, carefully, Jim reached out with his
fingers, knowing that the nerves and bones
and skin of those fingers came not from him
but from the *Queen of Ruin*.

It was like slowly untying a knot. Gently he
brushed the stars with his fingertips and
watched as their numbers changed, swirled,

began to dislocate. One by one the whirling skeins of data fell apart, and with that, the great pattern slowly began to dissolve.

The Hunzzan ships changed their own patterns like a swarm of mayflies suddenly disturbed by invisible winds. In the hard paths of reality the ships had been slugging each other with real weapons, and the clash and flurry of that had been like the mutterings of a distant thunderstorm. As long as the minds and the controllers existed the shields would hold. There wasn't enough difference between Hunzzan technology and their own to let either side break through by brute force. But he was the only one left to control the *Queen*'s shielding, and now he turned his full attention on it.

More patterns. Intricate dances into and out of subspace, sudden shifting leaps of position, force shields deployed and retracted. Waves of evanescent flame beat at the shields, fell away, and pounded again. But he saw the pattern and how to escape it, and he let the commands flow out of him like water surging downhill.

The tight blue ball vanished. Jim gasped and reached for those stellar numerals and rewove them into a different shape. He felt a small thrill of satisfaction as the Hunzzan ships began to lurch about, seeking purchase and position in the real universe. And couldn't find it because he had hidden it from them.

He thought of Commander Ekkadli—his rough voice and gentle manners—and his brain now a smoking ruin. After that it was easy.

Again and again he dropped the *Queen* back into realspace, his mental fingers triggering all her weapons systems in a vast bellow of fire and rage. Isolated, trapped in forms and shapes of his own arranging, the Hunzzan ships could not maintain their own shielding against his witch-craft. One by one the tiny golden dots flared and died. There were many of them, and he kept at it like a shoemaker pounding nails into a sole. He was still hammering away when somebody shook his shoulder and then a moment later physically lifted the interforce ring from around his neck.

He found himself staring up into Tick's hag-gard, raddled features. "It's over," Tick whis-pered. His voice sounded like something he'd lost a long time ago and only recently found again.

"It's over. You killed them all. You can stop now."

Jim felt his fingers, which had shaped them-selves into rigid claws, suddenly and painfully relax. Tick stared at him. The Heestahn looked ready to cry.

"By Ifenaya," Tick croaked. "What in the Seven Cold Places *are* you?"

And for a moment Jim knew the answer to that, but it frightened him beyond control, and he felt himself slipping away. "I . . . I am . . ."

Tick looked down on him for a long moment, then moved his head and brought up his own interforce shield. Somebody would have to put the *Queen* back on her journey. Lead her away from the place where a sixteen-year-old Terrie had just single-handedly destroyed an entire Hunzzan battle squadron.

*All the dead*, Tick thought. *Does he know?*

As for himself, he knew that he would never laugh in quite the same way again. And though the knowledge came with a wide and pervasive sadness, he understood what he was. He had seen Jim plain. And he thanked whatever Gods might be that what he was *not* this baby-faced Terran.

"Gods be with you," he murmured. "You'll surely need them all."

Then he got to work.

## 4

Jim woke up in commonplace surroundings. He ached all over and his eyes felt hot and gritty. He blinked and focused on the tight walls of the tiny cubicle he shared with Tick. Somebody had stripped him and covered him with a light sheet. The sheet was limp and rank with his own sweat. Exhaustion slackened his muscles and made them heavy. He lifted one arm and let it fall. His fingertips felt numb.

"Uh . . ."

He lay in the dim light and tried to remember how he'd come to this state, but it was as if the recent past had become a fragmented dream. He grasped at meaningless shreds of it, but nothing made any sense. After a while he closed his eyes and waited for somebody to come and tell him what he'd done. He was afraid he wouldn't like the news.

"Jim? Are you awake?"

He struggled up from a nasty dream of spiders and webs and crushing balls of light. In the shadows Tick's face floated over him, his features abnormally still and solemn.

"Ungh . . . yeah. I guess so."

"The medics said to let you sleep. They said it was normal, a kind of mental hangover from the interface you set up with the *Queen*."

The words made no sense. "What are you talking about?"

A little smile tugged at the corners of Tick's rubbery lips. "They said you might not remember at first. Don't worry. It will come back. You're a hero, my friend."

"A . . . hero?"

"You'll see," Tick told him. Then, astonishingly, the Heestahn reached down and punched him lightly on the shoulder. "My buddy, the hero."

## 5

It didn't sink in until the captain of the *Queen*, Ibil Makadorn, stepped up to him, executed a rigid and snappy salute, and said, "Welcome to the Command Bridge, Chief Pilot Marshal."

Jim was grateful for the hard-learned reflexes of the combat deck ape, because his muscles executed a perfect copy of the captain's salute even as Jim's mind muttered, "Whaaa . . . ?"

"Uh, yessir, thank you, sir," Jim replied.

Captain Makadorn, who had never before spoken a single word to the formerly lowly Corporal Marshal, now cocked his washtub head to the side, opened his mouth to reveal a maw full of squirming tongues, and said, "Quite a change, eh, son? Well, you'll get used to it. Your command console is right over here. Let's get you settled in. Pilot Commander Tickeree has been doing a decent enough job, but I think he's getting tired. We were able to give him a couple of breaks, but I think he'd like to hit his bunk for a solid eight hours or so."

Pilot Commander Tickeree?

"Captain?"

"Yes?"

"Uh, about the chief pilot . . . and Commander Ekkadli?"

Captain Makadorn paused, turned, and lowered his voice. "Please be careful, Pilot Marshal. I understand, but some of the rankers consider it bad luck to mention those names on duty deck."

"Bad luck?"

"To name the dead aloud," Captain Makadorn murmured.

Jim felt something slip just a bit inside him. "Oh. I see."

The captain eyed him, then nodded and

resumed his slow procession toward the chief pilot's console. And procession it was. Jim felt his cheeks begin to burn. Every eye was on him. He couldn't decipher so many alien expressions, but the ones he did understand seemed filled with silent awe. And perhaps just a bit of fear.

He reached his console and slid into the seat. On his right, the interforce helmet masking Tick's head suddenly vanished. "It's about time, partner," Tick said. But he was grinning.

This new grinning half-obeisant Tick made him nervous. The old sarcastic, condescending version had been a pain, but an understandable one. Jim had known human boys just like him. But on Tick's features now was a half-hidden twitch of watchfulness, an expectancy uncomfortably close to worship.

Jim slipped the ring around his neck and let the chair adjust to his form. He looked over. "Okay, Commander. I have the helm now."

He saw Tick grin nervously one more time as he rose from his seat. Then Jim slipped into the virtual guts of the *Queen of Ruin* and, all his canned nightmares now rolling back at him from the great databases of the ship's memory, he aimed her toward Alba and the uncertain future.

Over a private feed from the captain's console came a soft query: "Pilot? I have to confess I don't know Terrans all that well. Does that moisture on your cheeks have any significance?"

"No, sir. It's only a reflex," Jim said. "Pay no attention. It has no meaning at all."

# CHAPTER FOURTEEN

## 1

---

### ALBAGENS:
### OFFICE OF THE PACKLORD

As usual Hith Mun Alter found himself doing several things at once. His schedule had become a fiction; because of the war it was rewritten several times a day. He could no longer plan on anything because, in the way of all governments faced with a crisis the bureaucrats couldn't regulate away, everything had become an emergency requiring that the ass be covered and the buck be passed to the highest level. He worked quietly and steadily at his desk, every once in a while glancing up at a holofeed screen shimmering in the air.

On the screen, preparations continued for the public welcome of the heroes who had penetrated the Hunzzan blockade with equipment vital to the war effort. The ceremony would take place in the Great Hall of the Pra'Loch, and when the time came, Hith would leave his office and take a two-minute stroll to the set that had been constructed there. It would be a welcome relief: a bit of good news in an increasingly gloomy picture.

He'd already seen a summary of the desperate run the *Queen of Ruin* had made through the blockading Hunzza. Evidently the ship had lost most of her pilots and only made it through by the luck of the knife's edge. A brave and useful group of mercenaries. He wished he had a few more like them ready at hand.

The soft voice seemed to come from thin air. "Packlord, five minutes. They're bringing the crew of the *Queen of Ruin* onstage now."

He looked over and saw a large group of people, mostly hulking Romians, being shepherded into the shooting area. The size of the scaly aliens made the two small figures in the front of the group all the more obvious. Hith squinted. Then he zoomed the holoscreen into tight focus on one of the smaller figures.

He stared for a long moment. Then he said, "Athan, cancel the ceremony. If anybody has transmitting equipment turned on, turn it off. Confiscate any chips. Use the War Secrets Act. And get that crew into hiding now."

"Packlord, is something wrong?"

"Just do it. Then get me Lord Denai. He's still kicking his heels around here somewhere, isn't he?"

"Yes, sir."

"Right away."

This done, the Packlord leaned back and stared into space, thinking. *Yes, Serena Half Moon, it is a dangerous game you are playing.*

*And you are about to find out just how dangerous it can get.*

Funny. The boy looked older than the holos he'd seen. But there was no mistaking those Terran features, even with new lines carved deep into the bridge of the nose and at the corners of the mouth. It was unmistakably Jim Endicott.

## 2

Jim had never seen the government offices on Terra, though he'd visited the virtual versions many times. But there was something intangibly impressive about the real thing, and he found the Great Hall of the Pra'Loch nearly overwhelming. The officers and crew of the *Queen* had been shepherded briskly along by Alban officials moving down high-ceilinged corridors, stepping onto gleaming transmatter disks, and then reappearing in even grander chambers.

Now he stood at the front of the group while technicians of several species bustled about doing incomprehensible things. He had also visited a virtual version of the Grand Canyon on Terra, and this was like standing at the bottom of it, if that canyon had been made of crystal and light. The sheer volume of the space approached oppressiveness. He felt like a bug trapped beneath a frighteningly open sky. It made him want to get down on his hands and knees and hold on tight.

Rank on rank of glittering balconies, terraces, walkways, and open chambers stretched up and out and back. Space enough for thousands, perhaps millions of busy government worker bees. And why not? He'd learned quite a bit about the Alban Empire. Nearly three hundred thousand worlds were full members who sent delegations to Alba. Here was the nerve center. Even with their technology, it seemed the citizens of the galaxy, at least the political citizens, still preferred to meet and mingle in person. And that made sense; if the mark of power was to be in the center of power, here was where you had to be. All the governments he'd ever studied had been similar. On Terra, a not inconsiderable advantage was that politicians preferred to sniff out each other's plots and plans and small treacheries up close, with no technology editing the hidden struggles for advantage and power. Evidently it was no different here.

He saw miniature forests floating like clouds overhead and felt a damp breeze redolent of distant oceans on his cheeks. A nameless perfume, rich and sandy, filled his nostrils. The air itself was suffused with a drifting golden light that touched the distant towers and set them burning like molten glass.

"Close your mouth, Terrie. Somebody will think you're a hick."

"But I am a hick, Tick. There's nothing like this on Wolfbane. On Terra either."

"Then pretend. I can't have people thinking my partner is some booby from the outback."

Tick paused. "On second thought, maybe you'd better enjoy it while you can. It may not be here much longer."

They shared a dark glance. Jim had done most of the tricky piloting on the rest of the journey in, picking his way through the patterns created by ever more numerous clusters of Hunzzan warships. His relief when they'd finally surfaced inside the ring of Alban defensive structures had been so great he'd burst out laughing.

It had been the same wild hilarity he'd felt after the destruction of the Hunzzan blockaders. He had no idea how many he'd killed. Many. And he found no satisfaction in those deaths, only a deep and pervasive regret that time, the universe, fate, *context* had pinned him so irrevocably to what he'd done. For days, splitting the piloting duties shift on, shift off with Tick, he'd felt dull and dazed with the weight of it. He'd slept with dark dreams and wakened sludgy and slow, with a feeling that he'd somehow become dirty. He spent a lot of time in the fresher, scrubbing himself until his skin was hot and red.

But later he'd laughed, because the snake brain at the bottom of every human brain makes no moral choices about survival.

Every species had some method of doing that, teaching its young how to become what they are born to be. So he was learning how to be human. It wasn't the easiest thing he'd ever learned—but he was beginning to think it was the most important.

"It would be too bad . . ." he said.

"The Hunzza?" Tick shrugged. "An old, old story, Jim. You get a chance, you should study up on galactic history. Alba isn't the first great empire, and it won't be the last. They come and go. Maybe Hunzza will be the next, but it will pass on, too. You never know when the time is coming. Maybe another empire grows up next to you. Maybe time just wears you down. Maybe you get a Leaper culture in your midst and it eats you up in a few years. Poof, gone. I know you checked on Heestah. Only two worlds, nothing big. But a thousand years ago Heestah was fifty thousand worlds. As my parents constantly reminded me. Now, though . . ." He shrugged.

"A Leaper culture? What's that?"

"I don't know. Nobody knows. That's one of the characteristics of Leapers."

"That doesn't make very much sense—"

"Hey. Something's happening. Look sharp."

Another flock of officials was approaching, but this time accompanied by stiff-backed Albans carrying what appeared to be weapons. One of the Albans, short with a pure white ruff, approached Captain Makadorn and spoke.

"Captain, I'm sorry, but the ceremony has been put off for the time being. If you and your crew will come with me?"

Captain Makadorn shook his big head. "We'll be going back to our ship then."

"No, Captain, I'm sorry. That won't be possible. Please be assured we'll make you as comfortable as we can."

"Now wait a minute!"

One of the armed Albans stepped forward. "It isn't a request, Captain. No trouble please."

Makadorn eyed the squads of Alban troops now unobtrusively surrounding his crew. "What's this about?"

"Everything will be explained later, Captain. For now, please come with me."

The white-faced official spoke with the mildly arrogant certainty of a bureaucrat who knows he is backed up by guns, and doesn't care who else knows it. Makadorn recognized the tone. He nodded.

"Very well. I demand an explanation, though."

"And you'll get one. Later."

With that, the Alban official turned and headed in the other direction. The military squads gently herded the crew along behind.

"Now what the hell?" Jim said.

"Why didn't we think to bring a few hand weapons to this party?" Tick said.

"I don't know about you," Jim replied, "but I did."

# 3

"So how does he end up as chief pilot for a pack of Romian mercenaries?" Hith Mun Alter said, nodding toward the frozen holovid of Jim Endicott standing in the forefront of the *Queen of Ruin*'s crew.

Korkal Emut Denai sighed. "I tried to put him down on Brostach, as I already told you. Evidently I succeeded. Brostach is a hotbed of mercenary recruiting. The connection seems obvious enough in retrospect."

Hith closed his eyes. "Help me here. I'm trying to get a picture of the boy's thinking. You pluck him out of some incomprehensible kidnap attempt by aliens he's never seen before, separate him from his family, and whisk him off into space. Then, running for your life, you dump him on yet another planet he knows nothing about with a chip and instructions to use it to get in touch with either you or your fellow spies. He should have been totally disoriented. Yet he wasn't. He ignored your instructions and vanished beyond our best efforts to find him. Now he shows up heroically piloting a mercenary ship with a completely new identity. Somehow I can't imagine he just dreams all this up on his own. And accomplishes it with no help whatsoever."

"Then you don't know him very well, Packlord. I told you before, Jim Endicott is something out of the ordinary."

"Well out of the ordinary it seems. The chairman of the Terran Confederation has made his return to Terra a condition of allowing us access to their systems. And you know how much we need that access."

Korkal gave a small start. This was the first he'd heard of Serena Half Moon's demands. "Another piece of the puzzle."

"What does that mean?"

"As far as I know Half Moon knew nothing about Jim Endicott when I found him, and I took pains to keep her in the dark. She does have access to the boy's mother, though. Perhaps she learned something that way. Probably she did. Enough, evidently, to decide she wants him back. And badly enough to blackmail us with the use of Delta's computers in order to get him back. Which raises an interesting question. I wonder . . ."

Hith stared at him silently while Korkal pondered. "Wonder aloud, Lord Denai," he said tartly. "It's too early in the morning for me to read your mind."

"Um? Oh, sorry. It just occurred to me. Consider how Jim first attracted my attentions. By attracting Thargos the Hunter's attentions, when Thargos was rooting around in the apparent destruction of Delta's satellite. Now it seems to me this makes a rather strong hint in the direction of Jim having something to do with Delta, the destruction, perhaps both. It isn't even too great a leap to imagine he has something to do with Delta's computers." Korkal paused and glanced bright-eyed at the packlord.

"Mmm. I see. And perhaps we can make an even greater leap, given Serena Half Moon's curious demand. She refuses to offer us the use of Delta's systems without the return of the boy first. Now, what scenario would encompass all these facts? The mystery of Delta's disappearance—'not currently a factor' says the Confed chairman ever so carefully—

the destruction of Delta's satellite, Thargos's sudden interest, and now Half Moon's demands."

Korkal eyed him calmly. "I believe you can make the same connections I can, Packlord."

"Yes I can. For some reason Jim Endicott is essential to the function of Delta's computers. Serena Half Moon tries to turn that disadvantage into an advantage by pretending she *chooses* not to allow us access, when the truth is that without the boy she has no access herself. A tricky woman that, playing a dangerous game, as I told her."

"That scenario is flimsy as a free pass out of the Seven Cold Hells and you know it. Still, it *could* be made to hold water," Korkal agreed. "But we have no way of checking it beyond what we've already done. I doubt Serena Half Moon is going to give you any help."

"Of course we do. We have the boy. Take him apart."

"Lord, he saved my life. I have made formal acknowledgment of that, and he enjoys the protection of myself, my pack, and the weight of all our customs. You might even say the honor of all Albagens is involved."

"Yes, Lord Denai. But as you say you pointed out to him, our customs are not meant to be a suicide pact."

"Can we live without honor then?"

Hith shrugged. "Perhaps you cannot. Perhaps I cannot. Perhaps sometime after doing what is necessary, we will find it equally necessary to cleanse honor by our own hands, in our own blood. But the Great Pack can survive without honor because in the end the Great Pack can survive. It must survive. And if that demands the greatest sacrifices from those like ourselves, then so be it."

"A hard judgment, Packlord."

"Hard times, Lord Denai. Will you take the necessary measures, or shall I?"

"What if I can propose another alternative? One that preserves honor and still brings the results we need?"

"Then propose it, Lord. I don't have all day."

Korkal did. When he finished, he said, "This all presumes, of course, that you intend to keep him locked away inside the Defense Ministry."

"Let me put it this way," Hith said delicately. "Serena Half Moon needn't plan for Jim Endicott's return anytime soon." The packlord turned a cool gaze on him. "You realize I can't give you much time."

"How much time can you give me?"

"Three days. Then we do it my way."

"That's not very much."

"Then you'll have to hurry, won't you?"

"Ah," replied Korkal Emut Denai.

## 4

**"I** wondered why you carried that pack around all the time," Tick said. "What exactly *is* that thing?"

"It's called an S&R .75."

"Looks one step up from a club. What does it do?"

"It puts big holes in things. It even blew a hole through light Hunzzan combat armor once." Jim pushed it back to the bottom of his pack. "I've had it . . . for a long time."

"Well, it's ugly enough and primitive enough the door scanners didn't let out a beep. Probably didn't even recognize it as a weapon at all."

"So do you want to keep on sneering at it, or help me figure out how we can use it to get out of here?"

He and Tick were seated cross-legged on the floor in one corner of a large common room which was evidently to be their prison. Already work squads were throwing up makeshift bunks along the far wall. No luxury accommodations, but adequate for a new pilot who not so long before had been accustomed to sleeping on the deck with nothing but a thin pad between bones and metal. Doors led off the room to fresher units, waste facilities, and a hastily constructed galley filled with automated cooking machinery.

Holoscreens danced here and there among the grumbling Romians. The captain and his executive officers were huddled in another corner speaking in low tones. The air was thick with the vinegary scent of sweating Romian bodies.

"Wish they'd turn up the vent systems," Jim said.

"Romians like it this way," Tick said. "Smells just like the ship, doesn't it? Somebody is trying to make us comfortable."

"Yeah. I don't like it. Why bother to make everybody happy unless they plan to keep us a while? And why do they want to keep us? I thought we were supposed to be heroes."

Tick kicked off his boots and wiggled his long toes. "Ah. That's better."

"Wow. Some toes. Almost as long as your fingers."

"I can pick my nose with them. Want to see?"

"Thanks, maybe another time." Jim folded his pack shut and cradled it in his lap. "You have any idea where we are?"

"Nope. Some big government building. Did you notice when they took us through the transmatters, as soon as we got off the disks they went black? We could be anywhere. And we're not going to walk out of here through nonfunctioning transmatter disks, even if we can get out of this room. Which I doubt, no matter what that cannon of yours can do."

"And we'd be kinda conspicuous on a planet full of Albans, wouldn't we?"

"This is the center. There's a lot of folks here who aren't Albans."

"You mean try to masquerade as some kind of diplomats?"

Tick shrugged. "I doubt if it would work, but it's better than nothing."

"This isn't all that bad either," Jim said. A line of Alban cooks was coming from the galley carrying trays of steaming food. Jim's nose twitched. He smelled something very like a cheeseburger.

One of the Albans came toward him. "Hello, Jim," he said as he stooped to offer a perfectly cooked cheeseburger. "You like these, I remember?"

Jim stared up at him. "Hello, Korkal."

Korkal Emut Denai nodded. "Nice to see you again, Jim. So tell me. What have you been doing with yourself since I saw you last?"

# CHAPTER FIFTEEN

## 1

There were Hunzza remaining even on Albagens. The embassies and consulates had been closed, but negotiations of one kind or another continued even as war flared all around. Businessmen, tourists, diplomats out of the loop with nothing but time on their hands, a sizable contingent caught on the wrong side of the blockade.

Of course they were watched. They were tracked and trailed and analyzed by huge agencies devoted to watching those who needed watching. But there was a curious lassitude filling the watchers. Yes, it was possible some of these wandering remnants were spies or agents or some kind of grit in the cogs of war, but what could they do? They were trapped here, and whatever webs they wove were trapped also. So the watchers watched and did so competently, professionally, and with half their minds elsewhere.

Thargos the Hunter had counted on this, had offered certain tests to those who followed him, and noted the results. He could do nothing about the sleepless machines except ignore them, which he did. Within a very short time he knew he had wriggle room, and how much. The Albans watching the Hunzza were looking for small-timers, for the left-behind ones, for the accidents. Their fellows would be searching for the real threats—moles of other races, maybe even Alban, bought, threatened, blackmailed long before, then carefully buried to rise again in time of Hunzzan need.

The Hunzza remaining on Albagens were too open and too monitored to be any kind of real threat. Or so Alba thought. Thargos hummed quietly to himself when he thought of Alba thinking that.

Now, wearing the long red flowing robes befitting a minor Hunzzan merchant, he ambled at the end of a line of tourists being herded along by chattering interactive hologuides through what he considered the typically decadent architecture of the Great Hall of the Pra'Loch. One of Thargos's passions was history. He studied as much of it as he could, though he knew he could only touch the smallest portion of the grand sweep of the galactic past. Yet he saw certain patterns repeat themselves over and over, and he knew that, with the exception of Leapers, technological culture had not yet managed to repeal the historical cycles. This glittering crystal monstrosity he walked through now, for instance: architectural gigantism was a historical warning light flashing yellow. It said: "Behold our might and be awed, for we are nearing the end of our days."

It seemed to him that once the cultural arteries became clogged and the social musculature turned soft and flabby, the body politic felt compelled to build great carapaces as evidence that strength still remained. But those glittering shells were brittle and, rather than concealing the rot within, called attention to it for those with eyes to see and minds capable of understanding.

Alba was old and appeared still powerful, but that was a lie. This crystal shell would shatter and fall soon: there was nothing like it in all of Hunzza. In Hunzza the racial blood pulsed strong and hot, and had no need of the decadent architectural casement to disguise an inner decay.

Yet marching through this soon-to-be-forgotten grandeur with the sighs of back-planet hicks whispering in his ears brought him comfort. He felt he blended in well. He had seen no watchers lately. If luck was the result of good planning, then he had planned well, even if only by accident.

He'd had a reason for hijacking those four primitive nuclear weapons in Sol System. That reason had not included using one to throw off the attack of an entire Alban Navy squadron, but so it turned out. Evidently the detonation of one of those weapons in nonspace perfectly mimicked the subspatial destruction of a large vessel. Korkal Emut Denai had led him into a deadly ambush, and he'd escaped thanks to a forgotten technology, leaving an expanding ring of dirty plasma behind.

Not luck, though, but cold calculation had brought him to Alba itself. He'd crept into the home system as stealthily as he could, only a few days before the blockade shut off all entrance and exit. He still had his mission. Korkal would come here, and, therefore, so would he. Besides, who would think to look for him in the enemy's heart?

Then luck again. What were the probabilities of his choosing on a whim to play the tourist in the Great Hall and there finding the Terran boy with a pack of Romian mercenaries, blinking as the stage was set to welcome the heroes? So low as to be ludicrous. As with history, perhaps the fates also posted their signposts warning of doom. The old empire lost its luck. The new empire had an abundance of it.

So Jim Endicott was here. He already knew Korkal was. Thargos had his resources. It wouldn't take him long to find out where the boy kept himself, or was kept. He doubted he would have a chance to take the boy again. But also among his resources were two remaining Terran nukes.

One should be more than enough.

## 2

"**K**orkal, this is my friend Tickeree," Jim said as he munched his cheeseburger.

Korkal, squatting comfortably on his

haunches, said, "Ah, yes. Very pleased, Your Highness."

"You may call me Tick," he replied with languid hauteur. But his dark eyes danced with appreciation, and Jim noticed that he'd curled his toes. Was that a pleasure reflex with Heestahns, too?

"Jim, can we talk a little? Privately?"

"Well, pardon me, fellow," Tick said.

"No offense, Highness. Jim and I are old friends."

Tick's hairy eyebrows arched. "You are?"

"Sort of," Jim said. "Sure, Korkal."

"I can leave. I'll be happy to leave," Tick said huffily.

"Not necessary. I think Jim and I will just step outside for a few moments."

Jim finished gulping down his burger, wiped his hands on his thighs, and got his feet under him. "Lead the way," he said.

The guards at the door saluted Korkal as he passed them. Korkal nodded but didn't salute in return.

"Technically, I'm not military," Korkal said as the heavy doors slid shut behind them. The hallway was empty on either side. Several yards away on his right Jim saw a dead transmatter disk like a round black bruise on the floor.

"Where is this place?"

"So I managed to lead Thargos into a little ambush and make my getaway," Korkal said. "Thanks for asking."

"A few ground rules, my old friend. I don't

know what you want from me. But we aren't going to have a nice old-friend-type conversation unless you hold up your end. Us Terrans, when we ask a question we like to get an answer. If you can't do that, then maybe you should just take me back inside that room."

"So you can sit around with the royal scion of the house of Heestah and try to figure out a way to put that blaster in your backpack to some kind of use? Yes, of course I know about it. Do you think we wouldn't monitor every sound inside that room?"

"So I suppose now you'll take my gun away, old friend?"

"No, there's no reason. Even if you could blast your way past the guards—who know all about that weapon of yours—you'd end up right here. Standing a few yards from a trans-matter disk that doesn't work, in a building whose location, even if you knew it, would be meaningless. And let's go further. Say you managed to get out of the building. What then?"

"I don't know. I hadn't thought that far."

"Jim, why didn't you do what you were told? Stay on Brostach and get in touch with me or one of our people?"

"Because I didn't want to, Korkal."

Korkal took a deep breath. "Yes, that finally sank in. But I wanted to hear you say it, to be sure. And Jim? I think I can understand."

Jim shook his head. "I don't think you understand at all. If you did, you wouldn't have locked us up. It's because of me, isn't it?

This doesn't have anything to do with the crew or Tick, does it?"

Korkal looked away. "I've examined all the records of the *Queen of Ruin*. Very interesting. Nice job they did on your new implant."

Maybe the experience with the interforce helmet and the awesome new powers of pattern recognition he'd discovered in himself had changed the way he saw the nonvirtual world. Jim wasn't sure. But now he saw patterns everywhere. He was the center of an ever-expanding wave of choice, washed over by the surf of all other choices.

*I am my brother's keeper*, he thought, *and he is mine, and our context is intertwined from the far past into the uttermost future.* The thought frightened him. Reality was as flimsy as a dream—in some ways, perhaps, it was a dream.

"You saw the record of my implant operation and looked at the stuff I told Sheelob was a Terran identification code. And since you know Terra has no such thing, you wonder what is hidden away in my chromosomes, and you suspect it is the secret that may help Alba. You know that Thargos must have suspected something along similar lines because Thargos found me while examining the wreck of Delta's satellite. And so you want me to tell you what the secret is. Have you ever considered that I may not know?"

Korkal's jaw had dropped slightly. "What did they do to you? You're . . . different. Harder. What have you become?"

"They? Who is they, Korkal? Everybody has done something to me. You're only the latest. Now can you understand why I might want to do something just because I want to do it? And can you also figure out why I don't intend ever to do anything again unless I'm sure it's what I want to do?" Jim paused, feeling the heat in his cheeks. He took a deep breath.

"Korkal, I think most people go through their whole lives in a kind of daze. I think I did. But not any more. What they did to me—and what you did to me—opened my eyes. The only problem is, they are eyes I never knew I had. So what you had better do now is tell me everything you know or think or have a hunch about. I have to decide what to do. But first I have to decide if I'm going to do anything at all."

"I didn't want to say this, Jim. Especially because of what I owe you. But I also reminded you that my honor was not a suicide pact, and so it isn't. If we have to, we'll force you."

Jim smiled. He remembered how it had taken the full power of the Mindslaver Arrays to decipher the codes hidden in his genes, even after he'd provided the key. The same mind arrays Alba now needed so desperately because Alba had nothing as good.

"No, Korkal, I don't think you can force me. Even if you wanted to. And if you try, you risk losing the very thing you're trying to get. Keep that in mind." Jim paused, trying to find a way to make the Alban understand. "Korkal," he said finally, "you're right. I'm not what I was. I really am something different now."

Korkal stared at him for a long time. Then he nodded abruptly. "I can see that. Well, we have three days, Jim. Let's hope we can work something out by then, or we'll have to try it the hard way."

"Even if you know it will fail? And if you know it's wrong even by your own standards?"

"It won't be my choice, Jim. It will be out of my hands."

"Yes, I suppose so. We're all trapped, aren't we?"

"Yes."

"But we can still choose. If only for ourselves, we can still do that. Context, Korkal. It's all context."

"What does that mean?"

Jim smiled. "Let's start by letting my shipmates out of that cage. A token of good faith. Convince me it's necessary, and I suppose we can all stay in this building, wherever it is. But we can start with that."

Korkal turned toward the doorway. "Go on back. I'll let you know."

"You do that," Jim said. "And I'll think about the rest of it."

## 3

Thargos was well aware that by civilian standards his mind was so tricky as to be nearly incomprehensible. He knew it came from living and working in an equally tricky and incomprehensible world. But he had lived in that world and thought his peculiar thoughts so long that everyday reality now seemed bizarre to him.

He suspected this had changed him irrevocably. Once he had thought of what he did as a duty and a task that could eventually be put aside. That when the time came he would be able to revert to what he'd been before, his idealism intact. That he could become a normal Hunzzan citizen again, whatever he'd once thought normal might be.

Now he knew it would never happen. He might someday quit doing what he did, but he would never be able to stop being what he'd become. Just another of the many prices he'd paid, possibilities he'd spent without examining what he'd bought in return.

His mind grappled with the problems of his current world and finally came up with this: the chunk of debris he'd recovered from Delta's ruin had contained an extremely sophisticated set of parameters designed to locate a particular genome. The search program had evidently been running for a long time, and it had found a match. That match had been a boy named Jim Endicott, who was living on the Terran colony planet of Wolfbane.

That was the first piece of data, and it offered more in the way of interesting questions than interesting answers. Why was Delta so interested in that genome? Who was Jim

Endicott? How did the boy, or his genome, fit into the larger question of Delta himself, and how did Delta fit into the largest question of Alba's peculiar protective relationship with an otherwise uninteresting back-galaxy world?

So he'd gone looking for the boy and found him, only to lose him to one of Alba's most effective agents, an old enemy named Korkal Emut Denai. Denai must have been surprised to find *his* old opponent Thargos in the field, and would know Thargos's presence indicated high-level Hunzzan interest. Just as Thargos knew Denai's presence indicated similar Alban concern.

Sometimes you can only learn a thing's intrinsic worth by the apparent value others place on it. He still didn't know what was so important about Jim Endicott, except that Alba thought he was very important. So important he was now hidden away in the bowels of the Imperial Defense Ministry, supposedly the most secure and impregnable structure on Alba.

But Thargos knew that the building, nearly a mile square—and yet another example of architecturally overblown decadence—was as flimsy as Alba herself.

So his thoughts leaped through the arcane loops and twists of high-level imperial politics as he considered that Hith Mun Alter placed high value on both Jim Endicott and Alba's hidden relationship with Earth. Endicott was somehow a crucial link in what Alter regarded as a vital connection between Alba and Terra.

If someone wished to sow maximum disarray in the Alban ranks just prior to an all-out invasion attempt, then one might try to destroy Hith Mun Alter, Jim Endicott, and the Terran linkage with a single devastating blow. And if that blow seemed to cast suspicion on Terra, further muddying the waters, then it would be even more destructive.

His technicians had told him that one of the Terran bombs rated a hundred megatons. Thargos knew little about primitive weapons technology. But primitive or not, a hole in the ground a mile wide and a quarter of a mile deep sounded like it might accomplish most of his immediate aims.

He would need to place the bomb in the Defense Ministry, and he knew how to do that. He would need to know when Jim Endicott and Hith Mun Alter were both in the Ministry at the same time. He thought he knew how to learn that.

And if by chance Korkal Emut Denai could also join them there, Thargos could savor the savage satisfaction of finally defeating his greatest nemesis.

It was all a tissue of guesses and hopes and half deductions. No normal being would have ever worked it out like that. But in Thargos's decidedly abnormal world?

*All in a day's work*, he thought. And he hummed to himself some more.

## 4

"So, I should call you Highness, is that right?" Jim said.

Tick blinked. "Well, technically you should, but—" He brightened. "I know. Listen. I, Tickeree, Prince of the House of Heestah, name you royal friend. How's that? It gives you the right to speak to me in the familiar mode."

"You need a bath, royal friend. And a comb run through your facial hair. Is that mode familiar enough?"

"Are all Terries so disrespectful?"

"Are all Heestahns so pompous?"

"Hey! I'm not pompous." Tick paused. "Just aware of my own dignity . . ."

Jim chuckled. "And so are we all. Tell you what. I name you Jim friend, and you can call me a cockeyed butt-face. How about that?"

"You cockeyed butt-face."

"Now that sounds like a royal judgment," Jim said.

Both boys grinned, comfortable with themselves and each other again. They strolled shoulder to shoulder down a wide corridor lined with statues of ancient Alban military heroes. Every once in a while Tick would stop and drag Jim to some looming warrior and make him listen to a recorded account of imperial heroics now long forgotten. After a while the stories began to blur. They all sounded alike. Alba always won.

"The winners get to write the histories," Jim said.

Tick stared at him in astonishment. "Well of course. How else would it be?"

"The truth?"

"The truth is that Alba has been the winner for a long time in this part of the galaxy. So they get to make up the details. Does it matter? All of this is dead and gone anyway. Just like Heestah."

"Is it hard, Tick?"

Tick shrugged and looked away. "Sometimes."

Jim put his arm around the narrow shoulders of the smaller boy. Tough, stringy muscles there like thin meaty cables. "I'd like to see Heestah someday . . ."

"I'll take you. We can—" He sighed. "Who knows, Jim? Right now it doesn't look as if we'll get the chance. The news gets worse every day. The blockade is tighter, and they don't seem to be able to get the outer fleets organized to break it. We're all trapped here. And I don't think the strategy is to capture Alba. I think they'll try to pop the sun. It solves a lot of problems for them in a single stroke. And it's a lot easier from a technical point of view. All they have to do is break the system shielding one time."

"Huh. No wonder they were so happy to see the *Queen of Ruin*. We brought in updated shields, didn't we?"

But Tick was no longer listening. His monkey features were twisted in thought. "Jim, what did you do? When you took over the piloting? I watched, but I couldn't understand. You seemed to know what would happen before it happened. I understand reacting so fast it seems like things are happening simultaneously—all the great pilots have that. But with you it was like you could see the future. Like you were *creating* the future. I've never seen that before. It . . . scared me."

"It scared me, too, Tick."

"What does that Korkal fellow want? He seemed nice enough on the surface. But it was like a mask somehow. Underneath I don't think he's nice at all. He scared me, too—don't ever tell anybody I said that!"

"He wants me to do something for him. Give something to him."

Tick stared at him. "Give him something? He's got you trapped here like a bug in a bottle. Tell me he can't take anything he wants."

"He can't take this. I have to give it to him."

"Jim . . . it sounds like something you know. Maybe you think he can't get to something like that. Terra is pretty much a boondock world, so maybe you don't know this, but . . . if it's in your mind, he can take it. Believe me. He might tear you apart getting it, but he can do it."

"Yeah. He's said as much already."

"It must be important then."

"He thinks it is."

"Can you tell me?"

"I don't really understand it myself, Tick."

"Well, that doesn't make any sense. Korkal doesn't know what it is, and you don't understand it. So what can be so important?"

Jim exhaled softly as he glanced up and

down the corridor. "We're monitored here, I suppose."

"Everywhere."

"Is there anyplace in this pile where we might be able to talk privately?"

Tick thought about it. "I've had a fair amount of experience with ancient government buildings. They usually keep the public parts up-to-date. But sometimes . . ."

"Yeah?"

"Don't talk. Just follow me and look stupid. You can do that okay, right?"

"Sure. I'll just imitate you."

# CHAPTER SIXTEEN

## 1

### TERRA:
### OFFICE OF THE CONFED CHAIRMAN

**S**erena Half Moon felt sweat run stinging
into her eyes as she stared across the desk at
Tabitha Endicott. "I brought you here . . ."
she began. Then she shook her head. For
some reason her hair felt heavy as old thread,
dangling lifelessly from the top of her skull. It
was an odd feeling, a self-aware sensitivity, as
if her body had taken on the persistent presence of a bad tooth. A vast surge of greasy dis-
gust rankled her, at what the exigencies of
high office had done to her. At what she'd let
be done. Once she'd been a woman, but now
she was . . . what?

"The hell with that," she went on. "I'm
going to show you something. Tell me what you
make of it."

The room abruptly darkened, the better to
focus on the holoscreen that suddenly appeared.
The picture flickered slightly and had the
faintest of grainy overtones, as if it had not been
intended for broadcast.

The two women watched the few moments it took for the tape to run. "That's Jim," Tabitha said flatly. "What—"

"Wait," Serena replied. She ran the tape again.

"Where is he? He looks older. And so tired . . . Serena, what is this? Where did you get that tape?"

The chairman brought the lights back up. Tabitha looked tired too, she thought. Worried and worn down. She'd let her hair grow longer and didn't look as if she was taking good care of it. It lay flat against her fine skull, lank and somehow colorless.

"I'm told it was shot on Alba, the home planet itself. Jim is there."

Tabitha twined her fingers together into a nervous cradle. "Jim is on Alba? But how—you told me Alba is blockaded. Nothing going in or out."

Serena closed her eyes. She had no intention of telling Tabitha how she'd gotten the tape. How she had been viewing private reports hooked by interface into the state systems. How suddenly everything had gone dark and a voice out of nowhere said, "*I am Outsider.*"

What had followed had been, she had always believed, technically impossible. Her best systems experts, later, had been unable to discover how her private interface, the most highly shielded and guarded in the entire Confederation, could have been breached. They squinched their eyes and sighed and wrung their hands and said it must have been some sort of neural hallucination on her part.

And they'd stared at her out of the corners of their eyes as if she were somehow crumbling, as if her mind could no longer be trusted.

But she had the tape. She didn't know what it meant, beyond what it showed: Jim Endicott standing with a group of unknown aliens before a landscape of impossible crystal towers.

"I'm told this scene took place three days ago. That the location is the Great Hall of the Pra'Loch. The conclusion is obvious. Hith Mun Alter has Jim. But he hasn't informed me of that. Maybe he can't. Maybe he can't punch a message through the blockade. But somehow I doubt it."

"It was a mistake to let him go," Tabitha said softly. "My mistake. That Korkal talked me into it. Everything happened so fast . . . I blame myself."

Serena shook her head impatiently. "What's done is done. I made mistakes, too. The question is what kind of leverage can I find here? We *have* to get Jim back to Terra. Without him we don't have any chance of making the mind arrays work. And without them we're just another helpless backwater planet. With one difference: the Hunzza suspect something valuable is here. Without the Alban squadron guarding us, they'll simply come in and do whatever they want."

"There's an Alban fleet watching Sol System?"

"Yes. For the past few weeks. Hith sent them."

"Are they guarding us or imprisoning us?"

"Quite frankly, Tabitha, it doesn't make a hell of a lot of difference at this point. I delivered an ultimatum to the packlord a while back. Give us Jim Endicott, or we won't allow you to use the mind arrays. He has Jim, but he hasn't made any move to comply. I'm not sure what that means. But I'm afraid it doesn't mean anything good—for Jim, or for Terra."

"Serena, I'll be frank, too. I know I should worry about Terra, but it's too big. I'm worried about my boy. I want him back here. Did you see him? How tired and worn-out he looked? He used to be such a happy boy. None of what's happened has been his fault, though he blames himself for a lot of it. Too much of it. All he wanted was to go to the Academy, become a pilot. That's all . . ."

The chairman's agate eyes narrowed. "The Academy? The Solis Academy?"

Tabitha nodded. "It was his application, with his genome, that started everything. But how could he know? I told you the story . . . and in the end they rejected him. Because he couldn't provide his father's genome. Or his mother's, for that matter." Tabitha sounded disgusted and bitter. Her mouth twisted as if tiny hooks were embedded in it.

But Serena Half Moon had stopped listening. She had a way to get a message through the blockade and, if her information was correct, even get the message directly to Jim. Of course, it might really be nothing more than a hallucination. But she had the tape. That was real enough, wasn't it?

"The Solis Academy . . . is that what he really wants, Tabitha? You're sure of that?"

"More than anything. At least he used to." Tabitha's chest rose and fell. "But he looks different now. Maybe that's changed, too. Everything else has."

Serena thought about it. "It's a shot. It's better than nothing."

"What is?"

"If Jim wants to enter the Solis Academy, I can make that happen. Rules can be broken, and I can break them. But he would have to come back here for me to do that, wouldn't he?"

Tabitha raised her head. A faint spark glinted in her eyes. "Yes, he would."

"We'll see," Serena said. "He may have no control where he is, no leverage. But if he does . . ."

"I want him back, Serena."

"We'll try, Tabitha. We'll surely give it a shot."

# 2

## ALBAGENS:
### IMPERIAL DEFENSE MINISTRY

"Jeez. What a mess," Jim said.

"Alba is the home planet of an old empire, Jim. This building is probably a thousand

years old. And it was built on top of an older
one, and that from the rubble of an older one
still. Twenty thousand years ago maybe there
was a little fort here, with a pack of Albans laid
up behind dirt walls with a steam engine running a generator for electricity."

Something about that seemed wrong, but
Jim let it pass. They crept slowly down the center aisle of a dim, high-ceilinged room. The
floor was roughly paved with knobby dark
stones. They gleamed here and there with a
thin slime of water, but mostly they were dull
beneath an inch-thick layer of dust. Somewhere in the distance a steady, hollow,
dripping sound hinted at the source of the
moisture.

Shadows without any particular shape,
swathed in centuries of grease, stinking of mold
and ruin, towered over them on either side. The
floor shivered faintly with the hum of buried
machines, the feeling that a vast and ancient
force was hidden here, perhaps hidden so long it
had been forgotten here. A thick shroud of dust
coated everything. The place felt as if nothing
had walked these aisles for generations. There
were certainly no footprints here but their own.

"The basements," Jim said. "I wouldn't
have thought."

Tick shrugged. "Then you never lived in a
really old palace. Kings and governments. They
never throw anything away." He glanced
around. "But if there's anyplace in this whole
pile that isn't bugged every minute, it would be
down here. You can't tell, though. Up to you."

They came to a corner, turned, and entered another vast and gloomy chamber. Jim looked at a distant light fixture. Incandescent! Even on Terra that kind of technology was hundreds of years out-of-date. He tried to imagine maintenance bots searching through a range of replacement equipment that spanned a hundred centuries. Did they maybe even have a few wooden torches stashed away somewhere, just in case?

But the distant glow looked like a logical place to stop. The shadows and the near darkness everywhere else gave Jim the creeps. "Let's head for the light and take a break. Then we can talk," Jim said.

They walked toward the distant yellow glow, silent in the damp and dusty silence. The air smelled of rancid machine grease and wet rust. Their footsteps made soft sliding sounds on the stones. The air turned cooler. When they reached the light, Jim wiped his hands on the seat of his pants and looked around.

"This okay for you?" he asked. For some reason it felt exactly right to him.

"Sure," Tick replied.

They sat cross-legged in the dimly luminous cone, their backs against the scabrous concrete wall. The light fixture gave off an occasional harsh buzzing sound, like a wasp trapped in a bottle.

"So what are we talking about, Jim?"

"I shouldn't tell you," Jim said at last.

"Because you can't trust me? Well, that's the first smart thing I've heard you say. So come on, let's head back up. It's cold down here."

Jim shook his head. "Calm down, Tick. Don't be so touchy. That's not what I meant. It's just that . . . if I tell you, maybe you're in danger, too. Like you said. If they want to yank it out of you, they will."

As he spoke, his gaze moved across the aisle. Something tickled at the back of his mind but didn't quite surface. He mentally grabbed for it, but it was gone.

For a moment Tick remained silent. Jim could hear his breathing, soft and steady and regular. "You know," he said at last, "the royals, and there are hundreds of thousands of us all over the galaxy, most of us left over from kingdoms and empires only the royals themselves remember any longer, we are raised in strange ways. We learn treachery before we learn to walk. To watch for the knife in the back and the poison in the infant's milk. Even my own house has its share of mysterious deaths. Still does, and there's nothing left to fight over. Someday, Jim, I will be an emperor. Of two lousy planets and all the cybermalls I can open. If I go back, that is.

"I'm just a kid, even if I am a prince. But I find you astonishingly naive. I thought you would understand the rules, but you don't. What kind of place do you come from, my friend?"

"I guess it's just what you say it is. A hick place, a backwater. Primitive. I never thought so, but I'd never been out in the galaxy before.

Out in what you think of as the real world."

"Jim, what you tell me, only you know how much danger it will put me in. If I'm your friend—and I am—then keep that in mind when you talk. I will accept whatever degree of danger you wish to put me in. But you will have to decide. It's up to you."

"Gee, thanks, Tick. Nothing like a friendly chat among the boys, is there? Is everything in your world so hard-boiled?"

Tick stared at him, his dark eyes crinkling at the edges. "Jim, it probably is in your world, too. You just haven't found out about it yet."

Jim thought about Delta. And Carl Endicott. "You may be right. But now I'm afraid to tell you anything."

"We can go round and round forever. Spit it out, or let's go back and see if we can hunt up some more of your cheeseburgers. My mom would be horrified, but I guess I'm getting a taste for ethnic food."

"Cheeseburgers? Ethnic food?"

"It is to me. It's a wide galaxy, Jim. Everything's ethnic to somebody. And now you can tell me your big secret, okay? Or not, however you want."

Jim took a breath. "Okay, what if you thought you had a way to make sure that Alba whipped the Hunzza? Or vice versa even? But maybe that way would just encourage the war to go on longer, and grunts like us would get cut up in more places—along with a lot of civilians?"

"So I won't assume you're being hypothetical. You think you do have some way. If it's true, I don't buy your squeamishness. You pick your side and roll the dice."

"There's more innocent people involved. People back on my home planet. Maybe it's possible they get hurt, too."

Tick eyed him. "It's really hard for me to believe you have this kind of thing in the first place. I mean how would some primitive world like Terra come up with a lever like that? It's some kind of technology, right?"

Jim nodded. "I know. It sounds crazy. But Korkal seems to think that's what I've got."

Tick chewed it over. "Yeah. Alba is paying a lot of attention to you. That's the only thing that gives this any credibility as far as I'm concerned." He shook his head. "I still can't imagine what you've got, though. Or why they haven't pulled it out of you by brute force, if they think it's so important."

"Well, Korkal says that's the next step. He said three days. That was two days ago. It's why I'm trying to make up my mind."

"One day left then . . ."

"Uh-huh." Once again Jim let his gaze drift across the way, his attention snagged for an instant by a bright silver glint reflecting the light above his head. Something about it . . .

He had the odd feeling that he should be *recognizing* something. Something was wrong, but he couldn't figure out what it was.

"Way I see it," Tick said slowly, "is your options are limited. You can't give whatever it is to the Hunzza, so it either goes to Alba or it doesn't go at all. You say you can make that choice, though I think you're underestimating the Alban brain-strainers. But say you can decide. Why wouldn't you give it to Alba? There's already a war. People are already dying. So if what you've got is so powerful, wouldn't you rather have Alba win? I mean you've already seen how the Hunzza work, up close and personal. Remember you told me about Shish?"

Jim winced. "I hate war," he said softly.

Tick's features twisted into a cynical mask. "I hate breathing," he said.

"Yeah. War and breathing and eating. I can't believe they're all equally inevitable. Or even necessary. Maybe nobody has ever had a big enough club to end the war part."

"And you think you do?" Tick waited for a reply, but Jim wasn't looking at him anymore. "Hey! You still with us?"

Slowly, Jim shook his head. He was staring at the floor of the aisle in front of them. "Tick?"

"What?"

"You're the expert on old basements, right? Did you see any footprints in the dust back the way we came in?"

"Huh? I don't think so."

"Look."

There before them was a scramble of oddly shaped marks. The shape of the prints was strange, not immediately recognizable—and there were a lot of them. And some scrape marks that appeared out of nowhere, as if something heavy had been off-loaded here. Maybe from a grav-cart. Everything came from the direction opposite to the way they had come.

Suddenly Jim realized the coincidence of them stopping here—if it was one—might not be so coincidental. The path had led in this direction. But here was where they halted. Because of the light. And because his subconscious understood the importance of the footprints long before his conscious mind took notice? Tick had brought them to the basements. But Jim had picked this spot.

"Those look like Alban footprints?" Jim said softly.

"Naw. Too small. Look at that one—some kind of multitoed setup. Looks almost like a . . ." Tick's eyes widened. "Like a lizard."

Jim climbed to his feet and stepped across the aisle. The glint of light on fresh metal over there drew his gaze like a magnet. That was what had been bugging him. Things out of place here in a deserted, never-visited basement. Like footprints. And bright metal with no dust on it.

Tick unfolded himself and followed. "What's up?"

"Help me." Jim began to push aside a mound of trash. Everything down here was covered with years of grease and dust and corrosion. Everything was dull and old. Untouched for years. Except for this one half-hidden bit of glitter, and the footprints that led up to it.

Tick joined in. After five sweaty minutes they had it clear. Tick stared down at it. Finally he took out his universal and waved it over the characters painted on the dull silver housing, just beneath a tangle of freshly connected wires. It was one of those naked wires that had caught the light—and Jim's attention. Tick waited a moment, then raised his head in surprise.

"This is Terran writing," he said. "Four different languages. But how in Bramadon's Hell would a Terrie artifact get down here?"

Jim nodded slowly, his right hand unconsciously rubbing his belly where a ball of ice had suddenly appeared.

"Mandarin, English, Japanese, and Spanish," he murmured.

"What is it? What's it doing here?"

"It's a nuke. A nuclear bomb."

"What's a nuclear bomb?"

"One of our primitive weapons. It makes a big hole in the ground. This one will make a very big hole."

"Huh? Will it go off?"

Jim rubbed aside a thin film of newly smeared grease and stared at a small digital readout. The bright red numbers spun silently backward from right to left. He felt his mind rock as understanding exploded with terrible simplicity in his brain. It had been niggling at him ever since he'd seen the first gleam of the raw wiring and the prints in the dust. Lizard footprints! Thargos! And Thargos had hijacked a load of Terran nukes.

"Yes. In one hour, forty-six minutes, and twenty seconds. That's what the timer says."

Tick's voice was soft. "That's not very long."

"No," Jim replied. "Not very long at all."

# 3

As they ran for the ancient bank of elevators that let onto more modern floors and trans-matter disks, Jim used his universal, Fred, to try to contact Korkal. All he got was bounced messages.

"Location, then," he instructed Fred, as they groaned upward in the tiny elevator cubicle.

"Classified," Fred told him.

"Put out an alarm. There is a Terran nuclear bomb in the basement of the Imperial Ministry."

"Done," said Fred immediately. "The proper authorities have been notified."

Then silence. Jim glanced at Tick. "The proper authorities? What does that mean?"

"Probably that a bunch of bureaucrats now have a medium-priority message in with a bunch of other medium-priority messages, and that maybe somebody will bother to read it right after lunch."

"Jeez. I've got to get to Korkal. He knows about these bombs."

"He does?"

"Yeah. We watched one of them go off." Jim thought about Tabitha and blinked as a wave of sadness washed over him. "He'll believe me."

"Oh, the bureaucrats will believe you, too. At least enough to send a team to investigate. Whenever somebody finally gets around to it."

"Fred. Tell them it will go off in less than two hours."

"Yeah. That ought to speed them up. A little," Tick said.

The door slid open on a gray and empty corridor. But off to the left was a silvery transmatter disk. The two boys galloped toward it. They stepped through into the bright lights outside their living quarters. In the distance the van of a crowd approached. Jim squinted. "Korkal!" he shouted, and began to run.

"Jim!"

"Korkal, listen to me!"

"Jim, slow down. I want you to meet somebody." Korkal turned and gestured toward an Alban so gray he looked almost like a specter. But about this one hung an aura of authority so dense it was like an invisible wall.

"This is Hith Mun Alter," Korkal said. "The packlord of the—"

"Oh, Lord," Jim breathed as another blast of understanding suddenly exploded in his skull. "Korkal, I *know* who the packlord is. Now *listen* to me. You remember that bomb Thargos set off on Wolfbane? The nuke?"

Korkal's features were beginning to tighten with apprehension. "Yes, I remember."

"You told me four were missing. Well, one of them is down in the basement of this building. Right now. It's set to go off in an hour and a half or so."

Hith Mun Alter stepped forward. "A bomb you say? But that's impossible—"

Korkal gently stepped in front of him.

"Thargos the Hunter, Packlord. With that one, anything's possible."

"You told me he was dead!"

"He's fooled me before. Jim, you're sure?"

"I saw it," Jim said.

"Me, too," said Tick. "Looked real to me."

"Packlord, we have to get you out of here."

"No!" Jim blurted. "Thargos arranged this . . . and I think I know what he's after. He could have set it off already. But he didn't. Packlord, were you scheduled to come here today?"

"Yes. I'd allotted three hours for interviews. I'm a little early."

Jim nodded. "Thargos knows, somehow. My guess is the building is watched—or your personal party is watched. If you try to leave, I'll bet that bomb goes off. Thargos wanted to get all of us—you, me, Korkal. Everybody. And . . . something else that isn't quite clear to me yet."

Alter tilted his wolfish head. "You're making a lot of deductions."

"If I were you, Packlord, I'd listen to him," Tick broke in. "He's . . . pretty good at the deduction thing."

"Who are you?"

"Prince Tickeree of Heestah, Packlord."

Alter glanced at Korkal. "Well, Lord Denai?"

Korkal turned to Jim. "Where is it?"

"In the basement. I'll show you. Do you have any bomb-disposal experts in the building?"

"It's the Defense Ministry," Korkal said. "There ought to be somebody."

"If you leave, it goes off," Jim said. "I'm sure of it. And if you don't leave, it goes off anyway, eventually. Maybe this way maybe we have a little time."

But there weren't any bomb-disposal experts. Not for this kind of bomb.

# CHAPTER SEVENTEEN

## 1

TIME: 1:03:16 . . .

"It's not that it's too primitive. Or that it's too advanced. It's the combination, Lord Denai," the sweating Alban weapons tech said.

"I don't understand," Korkal replied.

The tech shook his head. "Look. See all that new stuff half-buried in the casing there? That's what this Thargos added. It will be state-of-the-art and very tricky. Still, we might crack it in time. Except that we don't understand anything about the bomb itself. Maybe we do the right thing with the new stuff and that trips the primitive mechanisms anyway. Or maybe the other way around."

The tech glanced at his team, who stared blankly at the weapon. But they were all sweating, too, and when they forgot, their eyes rolled a bit in their skulls.

"So you're saying you can't stop this thing?"

"Oh, not at all. We can get it unhooked. Just not in time. Probably not in time." He ran his palm down the side of his muzzle, then stared at it as if surprised to see the film of moisture there.

Korkal rocked back on his heels. "All right. That's it, then." He turned to face Hith Mun Alter, who was taking everything in with bright eyes and twitching ears.

"We'll have to evacuate the building. Sir, we'll get you out first—"

*"No!"*

"Jim, really. This is serious. I don't have time–"

"You don't *understand*. I can't prove it, but I *know* that if you start to move everybody out, even just the packlord, that bomb will explode. There's no other way he could have set it up. He wants to get all of us—me, you, the packlord . . ." He paused, suddenly deep in thought.

"And Terra . . ." he said. "It's got something to do with Terra. Packlord, sir, you have some kind of deal with Terra, don't you? About the . . . uh . . . things."

Hith stepped forward. "Go on."

"It's . . . yes. Thargos wants to destroy the linkage between Terra and Alba. What better way than to blow you up with a Terrie weapon?"

The packlord stood very still.

"Packlord," Korkal said, "we can't take the chance. Jim is my friend, but . . ."

"Hush, Lord Denai." Hith caught Jim's gaze with his own and held it. "You have a suggestion, don't you?"

Jim licked his lips and nodded.

"Tell me."

Jim took a deep breath. "I'll disarm it. I've had training in nuclear technology. Primitive by your standards, but this is a primitive bomb. By your standards."

"What about the additions? Those aren't primitive."

"They will have a solution. There has to be a pattern."

"And you can find it?"

"I think so."

"That's not good enough, Jim," Korkal broke in.

Jim stared at him. "I'll find it, Korkal. I will."

Hith stepped back. His shoulders moved up, then down. His eyes gleamed. He almost seemed to be enjoying himself. "I'll take the risk, Lord Denai. And I'll take it for you, too. Sorry. No evacuation."

"Packlord—"

"We'd better quit jabbering and let this young man get on with it, eh?"

Korkal started to say something, thought better of it, and finally nodded. Then he looked directly at Jim. "Do you understand the risk? Not just you and your friend. Not even me or the packlord. Everything. Alba. Your own planet Wolfbane and even Terra. Everything."

Jim's skull seemed to have swollen somehow, so that it strained against the skin of his face and stretched it as tight as a balloon over the knobby bones beneath.

"Give me some light," he said. "And some-body explain to me what these tools are the techs brought with them."

## 2

**TIME: 00:46:12 . . .**

Jim lay on his back and stared up at the underside of the bomb. He had two inspection panels open, and had very carefully cut a third opening in the steel skin.

Strands of glowlight were draped across the bomb casing, self-adhesive worms the thickness of his little finger that cast a shadowless white glow on the precise spots he needed it. He blinked. The area was warming up now, and the heat caused the crusts of ancient grease to soften and finally drip. There were black streaks across his forehead and on one cheek. The grit of ages was now ground into his shoulders and backside, and it itched. He could smell the rank odor of his own armpits. Fear sweat. Flop sweat. *Do you understand the risk?*

The light was too sharp and clear. It made everything too plain. He could see it, tangles of wires, some Terran, some put there by Thargos. The new stuff was easy to see but impossible to decipher. The techs told him what they could. But whoever had wired up this monstrosity had possessed cleverness that was nearly demonic. He would stare at the tangled webs, at the mysterious chips so delicately placed alongside the far clunkier mechanisms of the Terran weapon. Here and there new and old had actually been *melted* together, so he couldn't tell where the old ended and the new began.

Everything about it screamed danger. The Terran part was simple and straightforward. He could look at it and see just where something could be pushed and something else cut, and a third thing twisted just so. Nuclear bombs were not terribly complicated devices. Making allowance for the various ignition systems, the average grade-school kid could slap one together with relative ease. If it had been only that, he could have just about taken it apart with his bare hands.

But the combination looked more and more impenetrable to him. He would get the faintest gauzy flash of an idea, see a fleeting hint of how it all fitted together, and then it would vanish like the tantalizing flicker of a summer ice-cream cone across the tongue, quickly withdrawn.

*If I just had more time . . .*

*But I don't,* he thought. *I don't have hardly any time at all.* Over his head, silent as death, the red digital clock ticked down and ticked down. With grease-smeared fingers he reached for a surgical screwdriver. *Please, God, don't let my hands shake.*

# 3

TIME: 00:19:43 . . .

**K**orkal hovered. There was no other word
for it, but he couldn't help himself. The packlord had retreated across the aisle, where his
minions had covered some piece of dead
machinery with their own cloaks to make a
seat for him. He could see Hith's golden eyes
glinting at him, but otherwise his master gave
no sign this was anything more stressful than
a quiet chat among friends.

Jim's wiry frame was half-hidden under
the smooth steel shape of the bomb. Every
once in a while his grease-streaked hand
would dart out, accept some new chunk of
indecipherable toolwork from one of the techs,
and vanish into the innards of the damned
thing.

And, inexorably, the clock was still running down, chopping the seconds into red and
blurry bits. Korkal felt a shuddery sense of
unreality. It really was too ridiculous, a com-
edy of slapstick dimensions. How could it possibly come down to this? To his own life, the life
of the packlord of the Alban Empire, perhaps
the survival of the empire itself, how could it
come down to the frantic straining efforts of
one kid from a nowhere planet, thrust willy-
nilly into the center of events so great even
Korkal had a hard time comprehending them?

He knew that somewhere Thargos must be laughing. Korkal could almost see those great green Hunzzan eyes, blinking and blinking. And he felt a constriction in his own chest and knew that fate had a good strong grip there.

The red numbers swirled and swirled, counterpoint to his own thoughts now ratcheting from his grasp. And all he could think was what a great waste it was, to end like this, in a dim and age-crusted basement. Death was a cosmic joke, whether for the tiny scurrying thinkers or for the mighty empires they presumed, in their tiny scurrying pride, to build.

It was all the same to the universe.

"Korkal?"

"What?"

Jim had pushed himself all the way out from under the casing and now sat cross legged, his elbows on the knees of his grease-stained khaki uniform pants, looking up at him. "I can't get it. I thought I could, but it keeps slipping away. I can almost see the way it's put together, but I don't have enough mental push to put it all together." Jim wiped his forehead. "I need more power. If only I had the *Queen* down here. But I don't." He looked down at his lap and then up again. "I'm sorry, Korkal. I tried. Maybe you'd better get the packlord out of here if you can. I know that will set off the bomb, but—"

Korkal stared at him. "What do you mean, if you could get the *Queen* down here. The *Queen of Ruin*? Your ship? But why?"

Jim shook his head slightly, a nervous tic.

"It doesn't matter, cause we can't. But if I'd been able to interface with the ship's computers . . . they give me a lot more power than I have with just my own stupid brain. I see solutions better. That's how I got through the blockade."

Korkal's jaw slowly dropped. "Computer power? That's what you need?"

Jim nodded.

"Jim, you're in the Alban Imperial Defense Ministry. The Strategic Planning Machines are here. The most powerful computers in the whole empire. You want power? There's more of it here than anyplace else in the galaxy!"

"Better hurry," Jim said.

## 4

**TIME: 00:01:26 . . .**

It seemed like it had taken forever to horse the makeshift connectors and relays down from the upper levels to the basement, though it had been one short scream of activity. Now Jim held an interforce ring in his two hands and gazed down at it. Behind him hulked two very large pieces of equipment that seemed to shimmer in and out of reality, protected by a shifting web of incredibly sensitive force fields—the relay nodes themselves.

"Is it ready?" Jim asked.

One of the techs nodded. His long pink

tongue slipped from his jaw, hung there a moment, then darted back between his teeth. The tech's eyes looked dry and yellow in the pure white glow of the light-tubes.

Jim's chest rose high, then fell. "Okay," he whispered, and with one single clean motion placed the ring around his neck. He looked up at Korkal. Then he moved his chin, and his entire head vanished behind the smooth ball of force. He ducked down and slid back under the casing.

Korkal had to remind himself to breathe again, and after a moment he once again forgot.

## 5

**TIME: 00:00:38 . . .**

From his viewpoint the interforce helmet was fully transparent, yet Jim was aware of it as an invisible bubble a few inches out from his skull. He was also aware of the huge power of the computers poised just beyond that tenuous membrane. He had already touched that power once and the result had scared him silly. It had been like a kid tossing a firecracker, but when the cracker exploded it came as a long, bellowing peal of thunder. For an instant or two he'd frozen. Then he realized there was a logic to that force, and he could understand and control it. Or at least he thought he could.

He gathered his thoughts and told himself to focus. Off near the edge of his physical awareness the red clock whirred and ticked. He licked his lips.

*All right*, he thought. *Here we go now. Initiate full interforce engagement.*

Deep in his mind the thunder rolled and roared as he brought the power to bear on the secrets of the bomb triggers. And he found something else . . .

## 6

**TIME: 00:00:12 . . .**

Darkness and light. Puzzles and secrets. Predictions and patterns. So many patterns.

He had brought his focus down to a fine point, so that the sensors and the manipulators operated by the Alban machines functioned on the subatomic level. The shape of the bomb was a huge, slowly shifting structure floating off to his left. He watched electron flows pulse slowly from three different power sources. He saw the chunks of nuclear material as huge galaxies neatly balanced, great masses of probability poised to fall crashing into each other.

He saw how the new things Thargos had

put into the bomb worked in eerie cascades with the things that were already there. It was sort of like what he'd experienced in the fight with the Hunzzan warships, but in this case atoms became clusters of numbers that signified the probability of their position at any given moment.

Heisenberg's Uncertainty Principle drifted gently into his thoughts: if you could see the particle, you could not know in what direction, or how fast, it was moving. If you knew how fast it was moving, you couldn't see it. So one or the other of these qualities—either the location or the momentum of the particle—could only be described as a probability. In this sense reality became a matter of statistics.

And for Jim the probabilities were depicted by the ever-spinning virtual numbers that marked the ghostly atomic presence: it might be *here*, but if not, the odds were it would be *there*.

There was nothing he could do about Thargos's tricky triggers: there were six of them, cascaded so that altering any one of them forced all of them into a new pattern. Aided by the Alban machines he might eventually be able to decode all the probabilities and so choose the most likely course to manipulate the triggers into harmlessness. But not fast enough. His mind had placed the timer off into the virtual distance as a great red wall of spinning numerals. It was still ticking down toward the zero instant of nuclear detonation.

*Find the key!* he told himself. *Find a different pattern than the arrangement Thargos made. There has to be one, or . . .*

Or there won't be any time left. Hardly any time left anyway. Only—

# 7

**TIME: 00:00:04 . . .**

He gave up on Thargos's booby-trapped triggers and pulled himself way back. Stared at the whole thing, all the elements of the bomb floating before him, hard-spinning atomic numbers trailing veils of potential and probability.

*The whole pattern. If I can just get the whole pattern, then maybe I can change it . . .*

Something dark and vast rose from the subquantum sea like a great fish, an archetypal Moby Dick of power and intention. Jim gasped. He could see nothing, but he felt its presence as a shuddering screech up and down his spinal cord. The short hairs on his neck stood straight up.

"What . . ."

*Forget the triggers. Look at the nuclear material. Look at the nuclear matrices themselves . . .*

"Who are you?"

No answer. But he felt the presence swell,

somehow grow more *real*, and he knew he wasn't alone.

The nuclear material? He compressed his attention and aimed it like a weapon at the two highly polished hemispheres that were the heart of the bomb. He focused on the atomic interactions there, and, aided by the Alban computers, he understood them instantly.

Each atom was a crust of particles glued together by the subquantal forces. He could see the potential: when they crashed together, one by one those atoms would become unstable and begin fusing, throwing off vast quantities of heat as a by-product of the atomic joining.

For a moment he despaired. The reactions of nuclear fission and fusion had been well deciphered for centuries even on his own planet. And the Alban computers knew far more about those inevitable reactions than he did. But something tickled him, some ghostly memory, the vaguest beginnings of an idea.

But the idea remained vague. He couldn't pull it together. "*Help me!*" he whispered.

The presence suddenly expanded, somehow melded itself with his own awareness, then linked the both of them to the Alban computers. A raw blast of power filled whatever it was the two of them together had become.

And now he saw the solution, much as he'd seen similar solutions when he'd wrenched the Hunzzan warships away from their grip on reality and then destroyed them. If one adjusted the probabilities of this atom in this way, and touched that one in a different way, then the nuclear probabilities might be altered . . .

*You might change the nuclear material itself by forcing it into a rapid but controlled process of decay!*

The presence separated itself from him and fell away like a vast shadow fading into the night. He sensed its departure but only distantly, as a receding whisper of curiosity and regret, as the iron taste of a thunderstorm slowly lifting. His mouth filled with the taste of wet rust. He ignored it. He was too busy.

# 8

**TIME: 00:00:00 . . .**

His senses were so hyperextended that Korkal saw the digital numbers flicker to a halt in slow motion: zero, zero, zero, zero, zero, zero.

He closed his eyes and flinched, his mind trying to skitter around the idea of suddenly vanishing in a single bright flash of nuclear flame.

*Ca-clunk!*

It was a heavy metallic sound. He opened his eyes and saw Jim scrambling out from beneath the bomb casing. "Get back!" Jim yelled. "Get away from it!" He was pushing himself quickly backward, sitting on his butt, his arms and legs pumping.

Korkal jumped back. The dials of the read-out stood unblinking and red, a series of zeros. Then the center section of the bomb suddenly melted and slumped. Acrid smoke rose up, and a burning chemical stench.

Jim clambered to his feet. "That's it," he said. His voice quavered. "It's over."

Korkal heard a soft rattling sound. It took him a moment to realize it was his own teeth chattering like a bucket full of knuckle-bones.

"What . . ."

Jim stared at it. There were broad dark patches of sweat at his armpits, on his chest and belly and groin.

"I couldn't break the triggers in time. So I changed the nuclear stuff. It's still emitting, but it won't explode. That clank was the trigger going off, slamming the two hemispheres of the nucleus together. There was a little heat, a side effect of the process I started. It melted the bomb. I was afraid it might be worse."

Korkal started to move toward Jim, but he staggered and almost fell. Jim caught him instead, and Korkal stared down at his own knees. The joints there felt loose and weak, as if some mysterious disease had dissolved all the muscle and cartilage and left only the bony knobs and sockets and nothing at all to hold the two together.

And he knew the disease. Knew it of old. Its name was terror. That great thief of will and strength. "I'm okay, Jim," he said. "Well, I'm not okay, but I will be in a minute. No, let me lean on you."

"I thought I peed my pants," Jim said seriously. "I had to look to make sure."

They stared at each other. Then they began to laugh . . .

# 9

"Packlord," Korkal said. He giggled again, caught himself, and just managed to choke off a final chortle.

Hith Mun Alter waited. When he was sure both Jim and Korkal had themselves under control, he bowed in Jim's direction. As he did this a muted chorus of gasps rose from those behind him.

"I owe you my life," the packlord said formally. "I acknowledge the debt before my peers."

Jim raised his head slightly. Korkal saw through the grease stains, the taut skin, the gauntness of the bone structure beneath, and saw the slow green light grow in the boy's eyes. He was young, so young, but he possessed a dignity the equal of the packlord's.

He bowed his head slightly in return. "I acknowledge your debt, Packlord," he replied softly.

The packlord stood motionless a moment, wrapped in his own gray dignity, then suddenly nodded. "We'll speak of it later. Korkal?"

"Yes, Packlord?"

"I think you have some business with Thargos?"

"Yes, Packlord. Finding him, to begin with."

"I should think so. Jim Endicott?"

"Packlord?"

"In some ways our mutual situation has changed. In other ways it remains the same. I wish to speak with you and Lord Denai in private. In . . . say an hour?"

"I'll be there."

"Korkal, see to it."

"Jim?"

"Yes, sir?"

"Thank you, Lord Endicott." With that, Hith Mun Alter bowed a final time and turned away.

In the background, the gathered courtiers slowly began to applaud. Jim blushed.

"Tick?"

"Right here, buddy."

"Let's go find a shower. I think I need one."

"And me some fresh underwear," Tick said seriously. The two boys moved off, arm in arm.

"Well, now we're really brothers," Tick said.

"Huh? What are you talking about?"

"Have you got ears, Terrie? You're an aristocrat now. Or did you think the packlord called you Lord Endicott just to hear his jaws flap? I thought your name was Marshal, though."

Jim stopped, turned, and watched the packlord's back as he boarded the other elevator.

"It's a long story," Jim said. "And getting longer all the time. Lord Endicott, huh? I guess it does have a nice ring to it, doesn't it?"

"Yeah." Tick grinned. "My mom will love it. She's such a snob."

"After you, Highness," Jim said.

"No, after you, Lord," Tick replied. In the end, they boarded the elevator together.

# CHAPTER EIGHTEEN

## 1

———

**A**fter seeing the Great Hall of the Pra'Loch, Jim had expected something more impressive than the small office revealed beyond Korkal's shoulder as Korkal opened the door and ushered him into the room.

The packlord, small and gray, was seated on a contour sofa, its soft shape hugging him like a glove. He didn't rise, but gestured to one of a pair of chairs across a low table from him. He cradled a cup of some steaming liquid in his hands. A sharp cinnamon smell rose with the steam.

"Thank you for coming, Lord Endicott," the packlord said. "Lord Denai, if you would have a seat as well? What I have to say concerns all of us, I think."

Korkal nodded, but asked Jim, "Do you want something to drink?"

Jim shook his head. There was a sheen of unreality to all of this. The leader of the Alban Empire making time in the midst of a war to talk to a Terran kid who only a few months before had been nothing more than a green schoolboy. But his mind, without any conscious impetus, kept on thinking about his sit-

uation even as it changed, and he integrated
his amazing circumstances as if they were only
another cluster of data points. And that was a
very odd feeling indeed; sort of like having a
machine installed in the bottom of his skull,
a machine whose ceaseless workings he had
little control over. But where had that machine
come from? And why?

"Packlord," Jim said, "many others who
were with you in the Defense Ministry have
come to me and acknowledged that I saved
their lives."

"Yes, of course. They follow my lead. Do
you understand what it all means?"

"I think so. Korkal explained after I saved
his life. We don't have such customs on Terra."

Hith Mun Alter nodded. "I am at something
of a loss myself. It seems you have acquired for
yourself the personal obligations of a sizable
number of the most powerful people in our
empire. Myself included. Rather astonishing,
actually.

Jim felt the pattern shift and solidify. "But
it's not enough, is it?"

"No. It's not enough. As Lord Denai has
explained, our customs, even our most cher-
ished customs, are not meant to be a suicide
pact."

Jim nodded his understanding. "But they
mean something, don't they? Otherwise, we
wouldn't be having this polite conversation."

A faint flicker of white fang showed in the
packlord's grizzled jaw. "You are wise beyond
your years, Lord Endicott."

"I don't feel very wise, Packlord. Mostly I feel confused."

"Perhaps," the packlord said smoothly, "I can help alleviate your confusion."

Suddenly Jim wished he'd taken Korkal up on his offer of a drink. He wasn't thirsty, but it would be comforting to hold something in his hands. On second glance, beneath all the clutter, there was an air of quiet luxury in this room, slick as syrup, and his knobby, reddened knuckles seemed somehow out of place. He resisted the urge to slip his hands into his pants pockets, and said instead, "I guess you know everything about me that Korkal does?"

"Yes. Please forgive Lord Denai, but I gave him no choice in the matter."

"You believe I am important to you. To Alba. Why?"

"To Alba, at least as far as this discussion goes. Of course you and I now have a personal relationship, which I have acknowledged, but which I must regretfully set aside for the moment. Even the packlord ultimately serves the Great Pack, and the safety of the Great Pack is what we are here to discuss."

"It is very hard for me to imagine that I can have any importance—or any role to play—in such large matters," Jim said carefully.

Hith sipped his drink thoughtfully. "And now you are being disingenuous, Lord Endicott. So let us also put that aside and speak openly and honestly. You Terrans have an expression, I believe. Put all the cards on the table?"

Jim smothered a grin at the ancient collo-
quialism. The packlord seemed to know a great
deal about Terra. He told himself to keep that
in mind. The packlord looked small and old,
but he was one of the most powerful beings in
the galaxy. He hadn't reached or held that
position by being either soft or stupid.

"Yes, sir, we say that. All right, it's possible
that I may have something you want. But I
haven't decided yet whether to let you have it.
To be honest, I guess I should tell you I may
decide not to. And that in the end it will have to
be my decision. Is that going to be a problem?"

"Yes, it might be."

"Korkal gave me a deadline. He said I had
three days, and then you would take stronger
measures. The third day will come tomorrow."

Hith's eyes flicked in Korkal's direction,
then flicked away. "Lord Denai was more open
than I might have wished," he said at last.

"You said you wanted the cards on the
table. At least with Korkal I know where I
stand. But I don't know anything about you,
sir. And I need to know in order to make up my
mind."

"You seem very certain you have a choice in
the matter. Why do you think that? By Terran
standards, Alban . . . ah . . . interrogation technology is quite advanced."

*Careful, now,* Jim thought. *Anything I say
might tell him too much. Think it through, then.*
"Lord, let's say for the sake of argument that I
*do* have a choice. If so, where do we go? How
would you proceed?"

"I would negotiate. I would try to persuade you. I would offer you bribes, threats, promises. Whatever I thought might cause you to decide in our favor."

"Would you lie?"

Hith sighed. "Yes, I would lie, if I thought you wouldn't catch me. Otherwise, lying would be counterproductive, of course."

At least that was honest enough. "Sir, can you think of any way to prove your honesty to me?"

"No, I'm afraid not. I cannot allow myself to be tested by any truth-saying machine. Even in this situation. I am the packlord, after all."

"I was afraid of that. All right. The most reassuring thing you can do for me is to tell me what you know and think and want. I will try to judge the truth for myself from what you tell me."

"That puts you at a disadvantage, doesn't it?"

"Not necessarily. All things have specific patterns of logic. Truths and lies. They . . . *hang together*. Or maybe they don't. I think that maybe telling a great lie would have a very complicated pattern, and so would a large truth. I have some skill in interpreting this kind of logic. I suppose in this situation I'll just have to trust it."

"Patterns?"

"Yes. Pilots learn to deal with patterns. With structures of logic. With probabilities and impossibilities. I'm evidently better at it than I thought."

Hith once again glanced at Korkal, who
shrugged. "Very well," the packlord said. "I'll tell
you what I know." He took a final sip from his
glass and set it aside. "Several years ago Lord
Denai became my personal courier between a
Terran known to me only as Delta . . ."

## 2

The fact that he made it out at all after the
fiasco in the basement of the Defense Ministry
told Thargos a couple of valuable things. First,
the counterespionage agencies on the Alban
home planet weren't quite as good or as quick
as they imagined they were, even with Korkal
Emut Denai booting them in their collective
rears. Second, Hunzzan shadowship technology was, as he'd been assured, rather more
advanced than Alban shadowship-detection
technology. Even so, he'd had a full Alban
squadron and part of another on his tail when
he'd blasted through the inner ring of the
blockade and into the safety of the Hunzzan
fleets.

Now he drifted in the chill distance of the
Alban cometary ring, so far out that Albagens
itself was only a very bright star, and considered what else he knew.

Damn that Terran boy!

Many years ago another agent had compro-
mised an up-and-coming young bureaucrat in
the packlord's offices. That bureaucrat, once

he was thoroughly apprised of the hold Hunzza had on him, was then soothed and allowed to sink quietly back into the pursuit of his career.

His career had so far taken him to the position of second administrative assistant to the packlord, and he had been part of the party that accompanied Hith Mun Alter on his momentous visit to the Imperial Defense Ministry.

Thargos had seen the recording of an interview with this mole shortly after it was done. The Alban, normally very sleek, had appeared shaken. His eyes rolled and his hands shook, and when he forgot, his tongue dangled halfway out of his mouth. It took a while to get all the details. The Alban had finished with great indignation: "That bomb would have killed me, too!"

His interrogator had merely smiled and agreed with him. When the mole left, his hands were shaking even more strongly. Thargos grinned as he recalled that part.

The boy had thwarted him again. The bomb had been wired and triggered by the most skilled of experts. Thargos had assumed it might be discovered and wanted to make sure that, no matter what, it would go off as scheduled. But the boy had disarmed it somehow. He had even understood that trying to evacuate the packlord would trigger the bomb.

Somehow! It was infuriating. But he couldn't let his emotions color his thinking. No, he would rest for a while and consider how this *boy*, whom the mysterious Delta had searched for, whom Korkal Emut Denai had rescued, and whom the packlord of the Alban Empire had now made a brother, fitted into the larger scheme of things.

Perhaps it might be a good idea to go back to the beginning. Somewhere along the way he might have missed something. And he could do no more good here. Surprise had aided his escape as much as his shadowship. But that element was gone now, and trying to return to Alba would be tantamount to suicide.

On the other hand, Terra would be relatively unguarded, even if Alba had posted a squadron to protect the system. And he would have the element of surprise again.

Maybe he could come up with a few more surprises. For Terra—and for Albagens.

## 3

Jim leaned forward, listening intently. He was amazed at how much the packlord seemed to know. In some areas he knew a good deal more than Jim himself. Particularly about the Confed government and Serena Half Moon.

"We know that Thargos got on your trail because he located your genotype in some half-destroyed wreckage of Delta's satellite. Our own agents picked up this fact in the usual way, from Hunzzan dispatches. Evidently Delta had a long-standing search program keyed on your genetic code. Were you aware of that?"

Jim remembered his fateful decision to apply to the Solis Academy, and how sending his genotype along with his application had triggered the changes that had nearly destroyed his life. "Yes, sir, I know about it."

The packlord continued to pile detail upon detail. Jim sat and listened and soaked it all up, letting the bizarre new machine in the back of his mind shuffle each new fact and try to fit it into a some logical structure that seemed to change every few moments. The process made him dizzy if he paid too much conscious attention to it, and so he let himself drift.

"So what we come down to is this, Lord Endicott. Lord Denai and I believe that you have some crucial importance to the operation of the computers Delta used to command. We believe that Delta himself is either dead or in some other way unable to control his machines. We aren't certain whether those machines were in fact destroyed when Delta's satellite was smashed. And we believe Serena Half Moon is aware of much of this, and wants you back, possibly for exactly the reasons I have outlined. She needs you as badly as we need those computers, in order to maintain Terra's bargaining position in the larger galaxy. Can you confirm any of this?"

"Would confirmation be some part of what you want from me?"

The packlord shook his head. "It would be helpful, but not of critical importance. The only thing we have to know is, if you do indeed possess some key to Delta's computers, whether you will let Alba have it. How you choose to do it is up to you, as long as we get access to that kind of processing power. Lord Denai has informed me he's already told you how important those capabilities are to us, now that Hunzza is finally making its move."

So there it was, the hidden knife in the welcoming hand. What would the packlord do in order to obtain those important capabilities he talked about with such quiet civility? Jim stared at the grizzled Alban and knew he would do anything necessary. For him, the end, which was the survival of the Alban Empire, justified any means.

Jim realized that his sanity, perhaps even his life, teetered on the blade edge of the decisions it seemed he now must make. Once again he had been placed against his will into a context not his own making. No matter what he did, somehow he could not escape those forces outside himself. But he could face them, maybe even surmount them. He still had choice.

And now was the time to make a choice. He took a deep breath.

"I hate war," he said. "I hate it personally."

The packlord stared at him. "I am privy to the records of the *Queen of Ruin*. My condolences on the sad deaths of your mates. Of Shishtar in particular."

The buzzing machine in his brain examined this statement and told Jim that Hith spoke the truth, but it was a limited truth. The packlord was capable of feeling concern, even grief, over individual deaths, but he wasn't able to see them as anything but trivial in the larger scheme of things.

Yet for Jim it was those individual deaths that mattered, the slaughter of each singular innocent, and even those who did the slaughtering. For in the vast maelstrom of war, all were to some extent innocent, caught in a context too large for any one being to control. The weapon was deadly on both ends, yes, even for this mighty packlord, whether he knew it or not.

"It's more than that, sir. I believe that war is an intrinsic evil. If governments exist for any reason, it is to keep their people safe from it. The first primitive governments on Terra were roving bands of raiders who realized it was easier to settle down amongst their farmer victims and tax the crops rather than burn them. But in exchange they offered those farmers protection from other raiders. That has always been the unspoken covenant. Yet it is government itself that sometimes breaks the pact and brings war to its people."

"Ah. And you believe that is the case here? But Alba did not strike first. Hunzza did. You of all people should know that. You were there. You were a part of the first blow against us."

"And it made me sick, Packlord, when I realized that."

"Your sickness does you credit, Lord Endicott." He paused. "But don't extend your

revulsion at that treachery to the larger picture. Yes, it would be wonderful if war could be
banished from the galaxy forever. At one time I
thought that maybe I would be the one . . .
that Alba might extend its peace to all the
worlds. We are a trading empire, young man.
Traders prefer peace to war, prefer rich cultures to poor ones. Perhaps in some ways
Hunzza also holds to those ideals. They are a
trading culture as well. But the Hunzza, as a
race, prefer to control all aspects of their culture. And they value life perhaps less than
we do."

"Really? How many would you kill, sir, to
assure the survival of Alba? Would you kill
me? A world? All of Hunzza? *All of Alba?*"

Hith Mun Alter winced.

"Jim," Korkal said softly. "A little respect,
please."

"No, Lord Denai, it's a legitimate question.
Perhaps the only legitimate question. I understand what Lord Endicott is asking. He wants
to know if there are any limits on the means I
would use to achieve my ends. It is a question
I, too, have struggled with over the years. And
I believe I have an answer . . ."

Jim raised his head. This was the crux of
the matter. Delta had once upon a time been
forced to alter his belief that the ends always
justified the means. But what about this one,
so vastly more powerful than Delta had been?

"Yes, Packlord?" he said.

"Alba would not have attacked Hunzza.
But Hunzza would and did attack us. I reserve

absolutely our right to self-defense. The mere raising of a weapon must not automatically assure victory, or civilization would not be possible at all—only the rule of fang and claw. That said, your real question is how far would I go in resisting the attack? At what point, if any, do the ends of survival no longer justify the means of achieving it?" The packlord raised his cup to sip, realized it was empty, and set it down. Jim was vaguely aware of Korkal scurrying to refill the drink. He kept his gaze focused on the packlord's dark eyes. He had the oddest feeling he was about to hear the most important words of his young life.

"I told you our customs and beliefs were not intended as a suicide pact. Very well, that is the limit. We have a certain image of ourselves—more: we *are* a certain kind of people. If we then do things that *change* us irrevocably into something we are not, something evil, then we commit suicide by our own hand, even if we as persons go on living. So that is my limit: I will not destroy what we are in order to preserve what we are. It cannot be done. No race can do it. We cannot destroy ourselves to save ourselves, and those who believe it can be done have succumbed to an ultimate evil, one even greater then mere subjugation. They have betrayed their souls. So, rather than become the Hunzza in order to beat them, I would submit to them, and Alba would fade away. But it would still be Alba, not some evil thing, and there would still be hope."

The packlord glanced up at Korkal, then

gratefully accepted another steaming cup. He sipped and seemed suddenly to relax. His eyes sparkled as he peered over the rim.

"Does that answer your question, Lord Endicott? Do I surprise you?"

Jim felt a vast and slow shifting as he mixed and matched and arranged what he'd just heard. After some time a sense of understanding emerged, and he examined it.

Ends might justify means but only within limits, for means all too easily might poison any end—and if the end was poisoned to begin with, the means were poisoned, too. There was a difference between good and evil, and one of the great quandaries of all thinking beings was to discern what that difference was, and act on it.

It meant that in the end each and all must choose. Context still left room for that, from the smallest to the highest. And the packlord had drawn his own personal line: he would not destroy the soul of Alba in order to save the body.

Jim had felt the treachery of Hunzza first-hand, for he had been an agent of it. He had been an agent *by his own choice*, for he had become a mercenary though his own decision.

Perhaps individual Hunzza were not evil. But as a race they had created, or allowed to be created, a leadership whose ideals placed its own ends far beyond the means used to achieve them. For these Hunzza, any horrible thing would be conceivable—even the spiritual suicide of their own race.

An end too hotly pursued by any means necessary will inevitably destroy the end itself. And that was an evil even greater than war. No war was good, but some wars must be fought, at least to a point. Otherwise, neither ends nor means would have any significance, for brute force would render all such considerations moot. The man bashed in the skull with a club lost more than his life. He lost his ability to choose. And in the end it was from the choices a man made that the shape of his soul was ultimately determined. This alone was the most frightening and most glorious thing that intelligence had to offer.

Hith Mun Alter had his limits. Jim decided that the rulers of Hunzza did not. In the long reaches of history this would eventually destroy them. But in the short term they would destroy everything around them.

Time to choose. And as he realized that time had come, he realized something else: Thargos's bomb had almost killed him. If he held the key to defeating the Hunzza, it had nearly been destroyed, along with his ability to choose anything at all. And that key might be more important than his own existence. In any event, his responsibility now. His choice.

He felt the skin on his forearms and neck grow cold. So close. He had been impertinent to the universe, and the universe, utterly uncaring, had very nearly wiped him and his pretensions away.

And now he knew Hith Mun Alter understood what he himself had learned: that any weapon was deadly on both ends. The wielder was as vulnerable as the victim, the soul as fragile as the body.

Choice and context. If intelligence and choice did not exist, perhaps the universe would have to create them.

He felt himself trembling on the edge of an epiphany so great he could only sense it in the most tenuous of ways. It tugged at him, then fell away, and he turned to the old gray Albagen across from him.

"You do surprise me, Packlord. More than you may know. So I will try to help you," Jim said. "I don't know if I can, but I'll try."

# CHAPTER NINETEEN

## 1

Jim gave them the word keys that unlocked the codes. They had already obtained the codes, recorded when his cyberneural interface had been upgraded aboard the *Queen*, but they hadn't been able to decipher them even with the massive power of their own computers. That didn't surprise Jim. Delta, with the greater power of the Mindslaver Arrays, had been similarly helpless without the key Carl Endicott had gasped out to Jim as he lay dying, choking on his own blood.

And even *with* the key, Jim wondered if they would be able to decipher the code. Delta had used the arrays to do it. Would Alba's machines be enough?

It turned out that they were. Barely.

Korkal escorted him through a warren of brightly lighted corridors. Labs of every shape and size branched from the endless passageways, and in each lab a flock of Alban scientists labored mightily.

"It was a near thing," Korkal told him. "Making it work strained the Strategic Machines to their limits. But they decoded it. What I'm taking you to see is the first attempt. We have some volunteers. It's very small-scale, but if we are successful with it, they will expand it very quickly. Time is growing short. Hunzza has brought in several more fleets to strengthen the blockade, and we haven't been able to muster anything effective from our own scattered forces. Eventually we will, but by then . . ." Korkal shrugged and fell silent. Jim couldn't help but notice how strained and morose his friend had become. The situation must be worse than Korkal was letting on.

They walked along a floor the color of rubies, but soft as the belly of a kitten. The white walls sparkled. The air was clean, cool, and smelled as if nothing living had ever breathed it before. On their right appeared a long stretch of windows. It was dark, but as they approached the glass, it suddenly cleared to reveal the scene beyond.

Jim paused and watched. There was a makeshift look to much of the equipment he saw: trailing cables, machines with the panels removed to expose their twinkling, whirring guts, stacks of chip-cards piled haphazardly everywhere, and technicians rummaging through everything with the kind of controlled intensity that bordered on naked panic. They looked like ants swarming over their suddenly shattered hill.

The room was large but appeared small because of the sheer volume of stuff packed into it, and because of the numbers of techs scurrying about, each one intent on some incomprehensible task.

Only the volunteers stood out. Everything else was a fuzz of haste and dedicated fury, but the six Albans seated in complicated chairs near the front of the room, facing the windows, all had an air of stillness about them. They seemed to be in, but not a part of the activity which swirled around them. Something like nervous statues, idols or gods being served by an army of acolytes. Jim watched their eyes: they shifted minutely with the movements of the techs but never looked at the scientists directly—it was an awareness coupled with fear. He wondered how voluntary the service of these volunteers actually was.

"Oh, they volunteered, all right," Korkal assured him. "They're just scared spitless. Wouldn't you be?"

"Yeah. I guess so." He had told the scientists everything he knew, and most of what he suspected. He had told them of the Pleb Psychosis, and admitted he had no idea whether the codes in his genotype addressed that issue—that it was only guesswork on his part. He even reminded them he wasn't entirely sure the codes were what he thought they were.

So he had breathed an inward sigh of relief when they deciphered the code and told him it did contain the plans for building a computer made up of linked living minds. The techs had been mightily impressed; without giving him any details, they expressed their amazement that anything so utterly new could have been created in a technological backwater like Terra.

Jim had learned enough about Alban expressions, voice tones, and body language to pick up something else: some of the scientists obviously believed the source of the discovery was not Terra at all. That somehow trickery must be involved, since the level of the technology was so obviously beyond human capability.

The were unable to explain how, if that was the case, such advanced technology had gotten into Jim's genetic code, and this plainly made some of them uncomfortable. He noticed he'd not been consulted much after the first flurry of interest, and that suited him.

True to his promise to the packlord, he'd told them everything he knew, and he was glad to have that over and done with. When he'd finished, he felt an amazing lightness of spirit, as if something dark and smothering had been lifted away from him. The secret was out. It was no longer his own private responsibility. Maybe, someday, he would be able to become just plain Jim Endicott again.

"What happens now?" he asked Korkal. "Can we go in?"

"They're going to try it out soon. Just the six volunteers. We'll stay out here. The view's better anyway. Not that there should be anything to see. If it works at all, maybe the techs will start cheering. I don't know. But the volunteers will be behind interforce helmet shields—new ones. Evidently the techs did some modifications, based on the stuff they got from you. They say the cyberneural interface

will be far beyond anything Delta used. He
didn't have access to the interface technology
we do."

"I see. So we just wait?"

"It'll happen soon. Look. Here come the
neck rings."

Jim watched as technicians carefully fitted
the rings that would generate the interforce
shields around the necks of the volunteers.
One of them flinched away slightly, then
caught himself and remained unnaturally still
as the ring settled onto his shoulders.

Jim turned to Korkal. "What . . . ?"

Korkal raised one hand. "There," he
replied.

Jim looked back. Now a silvery globe
enclosed each volunteer's skull. The globes
looked a little larger than normal. The room
had suddenly gone still. All the techs stood
motionless, some watching their machines,
the rest staring at the volunteers with unblinking intensity.

Jim felt a surge of tension ratchet up his
spine and leaned closer to the window, then
jerked back as he bumped his nose on the
transparent shield. "Ouch!"

Korkal chuckled softly and patted his
shoulder. "Down, boy," he murmured. Then,
abruptly, his fingers tightened so strongly that
Jim yelped again.

"What—" Then he went silent for a long
moment before whispering softly, "*Oh . . . my
God . . .*"

**2**
———

**H**ith Mun Alter sat in his office and thought about ways and means and ends. Despite what he'd told Jim Endicott about killing the soul to save the body, he wondered if· he would have turned the boy over to the untender mercies of his interrogators. He leaned back into the soothing comfort of his sofa and sighed. Yes, he would have. All such equations must be flexible—and the possible risk to the mind of one Terran boy was not great enough, as compared to the survival of the Alban Empire, to trigger the larger moral considerations. He would offer *himself* up to such a risk, if it came to it.

But he was glad he had not been forced to that decision, for many reasons. And now that it all seemed to have been for no-thing . . .

He glanced up as a bell tone sounded softly in the quiet. "Yes?"

"They're here, Packlord."

"Good. Send them in."

He sat in silence, sipping at his ever-present steaming cup, the sweet smell of cinnamon filling his nose, until they were in the chairs across from him. "Lord Denai," he said. "Lord Endicott."

"Packlord?"

"Yes?"

"I . . . uh, I'm not really sure whether it's allowed, but if it is, could you call me Jim? I don't really feel like a lord anything."

The packlord grinned inside. There were those among his courtiers who would slaughter their own packs unto the fifth generation in order to receive a title directly from his lips, and having done so, engrave the standard on everything they owned, even their underwear. And all this boy could ask was that he be allowed not to use it. It heartened him. Even in the direst of times he found joy in such tiny moments. It renewed his faith that somewhere the gods, if there were such, still knew how to laugh.

"I'm the packlord, Jim. I can call you whatever I like."

"Thank you, Packlord."

"And of course you may call me Hith." He smothered another grin as he saw Korkal's eyebrows twitch. The privilege of addressing the packlord informally was perhaps an even greater honor than the personal bestowal of a title. But of course Jim wouldn't know that.

He savored his own humor for a moment, then sipped and turned to the business at hand.

"Lord Denai, do you have the latest status on the volunteers?"

"Yes," Korkal said somberly. "The last one died about twenty minutes ago. They were able to ease his pain somewhat, but he never stopped convulsing. In fact he kept on convulsing for five minutes after clinical death." Korkal shrugged. "Brain death of course occurred much earlier, so I guess the pain didn't matter that much. I hope it didn't."

All three of them sat silently for a moment, thinking and remembering. "Brave men and women," the packlord said finally.

Korkal nodded but didn't say anything. He looked even more tired and downcast than he had before. In the past few weeks his muzzle had turned almost completely gray. The packlord felt an instant of pity but rejected it. With the survival of Alba at stake he would burn whatever fuel he could find, even those most dear to him, with the same ruthlessness he burned himself. Pity was a luxury he would have to postpone for later, more peaceable times. If such times ever came again.

"What happened, Hith?" Jim said.

"They died. I'm still getting conflicting data. The technicians are divided about the cause. But in the last few hours a consensus seems to be emerging."

"It was the Pleb Psychosis!" Jim blurted. "I was afraid of that!"

"Something like it—at least as you described it. But don't blame yourself, Jim. It wasn't as if you caused it. Rather the opposite, I'd say. I didn't give you much of a chance to say no."

"But I could have. Whether you think so or not, I could have. Without the key you would never have broken the code!"

"Jim. The key was in your mind. We could have gotten it. Don't you realize that now?"

Jim stared at him. His mouth dropped slowly open. "I . . . I never thought . . ."

"It doesn't matter. What's done is done.

Even those volunteers, I think, would agree
you bear no responsibility for what happened.
Anyway, it's behind us now. What I called you
here for is to talk about the next step."

"The next step, Packlord?" Korkal said.

"As I said, a consensus seems to be emerging. It isn't final yet, it may never be final. But
I'm going to act on it anyway. If there's any
kind of chance, I have to take it. And, unfortunately, I'll have to ask you to take it right along
with me." His jaws parted in a wolfish grin.
"Order you to take it, actually, Lord Denai."

"I don't understand, Packlord," Korkal
said.

"No, of course not. The consensus is this.
Jim, you are both right and wrong about what
you call the Pleb Psychosis. Our scientists
have never seen an actual case, so what they
have is mostly conjecture. But evidently what
killed those volunteers was not exactly the Pleb
Psychosis as you understand it. That seems to
involve sudden overloads placed on individual
mind-links in the arrays, sending the minds
involved into madness. But our people believe
that problem is addressed by the codes we got
from you. So what killed the volunteers was
something different. The mind arrays are really
nothing more than computer programs that
instruct the hardware how to handle the linkages. You could put the entire thing on a couple of large chips, incalculably valuable though
such chips would be. But those programs were
designed to handle *human* mind linkages, and
as far as we can tell, they can't be modified to

handle the differences hard-wired into Alban brains. Oh, we have the theory—we can even see how it was applied, at least as far as humans go. But I'm told there is no chance at all we can modify those programs to handle Alban brains in the time we need. Some of my techs think it may be impossible, and we will have to develop a different approach to achieve the same end. I don't know. I'm not a scientist."

Jim's eyes had narrowed as the packlord spoke. Now he raised his head. "So what you're saying is the programs won't work on Albans, but they will work on Terrans?"

"Yes, that's right." He sipped. His eyes twinkled. He looked very kindly, like some kind of wolfish grandfather figure. But Jim knew better. He had no urge to pet the packlord.

"Do you see the implications, Jim?" the packlord said.

Jim closed his eyes and sifted through possibilities and probabilities like endless decks of cards, until suddenly a single hand was dealt onto his mental table. "Oh," he said softly. "Oh, yes."

"What do you see?"

"A situation. A logical situation, and maybe a very nasty one, too. From my point of view, at least." Jim stared at the packlord. "You see it too, don't you?"

"I had a bit more help, but yes, I see it. My scientists tell me the advance Terra made was astounding. It was a real breakthrough. Those mind arrays are indeed the most powerful information-processing systems we know of. Coupled with our own interface technologies, they have the potential of being even more powerful than they already are. But if they only work with humans, then that makes Terra—and Wolfbane, I suppose—"

"The biggest prize in the galaxy." Jim shook his head. "It was bad enough when it was just me everybody wanted. Now it will be entire worlds. Everybody human a potential prize to be enslaved to the mind arrays. My God, if Hunzza found out . . ."

"Indeed," the packlord said. "They'd have to have the programs, and they don't. So we have that advantage. But nothing stays secret forever. Hunzza's espionage net is wide and deep. They've planned this conflict for years. I'd be a fool to suppose that somehow, some way, they won't get their hands on this. So I have to move first."

Korkal was nodding agreement, but Jim broke in before Korkal could say anything. "Hith, was it all bullcrap what you told me before? Would you enslave Terra just to get the mind arrays? Could you do that without, how did you put it, losing Alba's soul?"

"What is bullcrap?"

"Why, it's . . . uh . . . well . . ." A hot flush rose in Jim's cheeks. He shot an embarrassed glance at Korkal, who refused to meet his gaze. But Jim noticed that for the first time Hith refused to meet his eyes either.

"Never mind," the packlord said. "I can guess from the context." He paused, then exhaled softly. "Jim, I don't believe the question will come up. I hope it won't. I believe it is in Terra's best interest to offer us help. I believe it so strongly I am willing to negotiate the matter personally with Serena Half Moon."

Now Korkal did speak. "But Packlord. The shields and the blockade have cut off communications with Terra. Or so I've been told. How can you negotiate with her?"

"You were informed accurately, Lord Denai. And so I will have to go to her. And you two will have to take me. Right through the Hunzzan blockade."

### 3

L ate that evening Jim led Tick into a brightly lighted restaurant in the bowels of the Defense Ministry. The entire building was now sealed off, but the crew of the *Queen* was no longer sequestered. Jim and Tick shared a comfortable apartment, in the upper reaches of one of the towers, with a view out across the vast crystal gulch of the Great Hall.

"What's with all this hush-hush stuff, Jim? I've heard every kind of rumor today. We're going back to the ship, we're staying here forever, the Hunzza are about to break through, everything. It's crazy. And you were gone all day with not a single word for your best buddy."

Jim led them to a table near the back of the large room. Most of the diners were Alban, but there was a sprinkling of other races. A stick-thin Pleenarch with bright purple gills sat on a small stage and gently played a many-stringed instrument that looked like an antique bicycle. The result sounded like a tomcat in a fight with a set of bagpipes. As soon as they were seated the tabletop lighted up, and a voice said, "Vox or lux?"

"Lux," Tick replied, and holographic menus immediately shimmered in the air before them. "Hmmm . . . have you ever tried sweet and sour gleech with humbub sticks?"

Jim stared at the menu and shook his head. "You go ahead and order."

Tick did so. The menus vanished, and he leaned forward, his expression intent. "So what's going on? I heard you had a meeting with the packlord."

"Yeah, I did. It's what I want to talk to you about."

"So talk."

Jim told him what he'd learned. By the time Jim finished Tick was nearly bouncing on his chair in excitement.

"We're going to run the blockade with the *packlord*?"

"We're going to try, I guess."

Tick rubbed his hands together. "We'll be the biggest heroes in the galaxy. We'll be permanent fixtures on the WideWeb. We'll be able to get any girls we want—"

"Or we could be dead."

"Oh, no we won't. Not with you doing the piloting. You're the best pilot I've ever seen. And the *Queen* is a good ship." Tick paused. "Uh, you are going to be the pilot aren't you?"

"Yes. I guess so. And Korkal will captain, and I asked if you could be the lead junior."

"What? Only the lead junior?"

"The two best pilots on Albagens will be backing me up. I didn't want to be the chief, but they tested me and said I had the highest pattern- and probability-recognition scores ever recorded."

"I was just kidding. I wouldn't want the responsibility."

"And anyway, we won't be taking the *Queen*."

"Huh?"

"There's an experimental ship in near orbit. It was being built for Korkal's agency. Supposed to be the best combination of speed, power, and defense they've ever designed. A lot of it's still experimental, they told me. And they're installing a bunch of new stuff to take advantage of my so-called skills."

The table suddenly chimed; the top of it quivered, vanished, and food rose up, hot and steaming.

"Mmm. Looks good," Tick said.

"I wish I was a little hungrier."

"Why? Got *hibble* birds in your tummy, Jim? You'll be okay."

Jim picked up an eating utensil that looked like a cross between a fork and a spoon. He cut off a piece of bright orange meat dripping with a thick green sauce, lifted it to his lips, and tasted. "Hey, this isn't bad."

"Told you," Tick said, already chewing vigorously.

Jim ate as much as he could, which wasn't much, then waited silently while Tick methodically cleaned every square inch of his plate. When Tick was done he leaned back, rubbed his rounded belly, and belched happily.

"There's one other thing," Jim said.

"Yeah?"

"Well, you remember I spilled my guts to you after I decided to give the codes to the packlord?"

Tick's expression immediately turned serious. In the darkness of their quarters, he had held Jim and listened to him weep as he'd described how he'd killed Carl Endicott, the man he'd thought was his father.

"I remember."

"Well, you know how the only thing I ever wanted was to go to the Solis Academy on Terra, graduate, and someday become a Terran starship captain?"

Tick pawed at his face and nodded slowly. "You've changed your mind about that, though, right? I mean you're Alban nobility and now you're gonna be the packlord's personal pilot. You could probably captain almost any ship in the whole Alban Navy if you wanted to."

"But I want to go home, Tick. I want my own life back. I don't want to be an exile forever."

In the background the mad-cat bagpipe wails reached a crescendo. Some of the diners applauded. A new cacophony began.

"Anyway, after Korkal and I and the pack-lord had our meeting, Hith sent Korkal away. He said he wanted to talk to me privately."

"Hith? You call the packlord Hith?"

"Sure. He said I could. He calls me Jim."

Tick's eyes bulged. "I can't wait for when you meet my mother. You can tell her all about your good buddy Hith, the packlord of the Alban Empire." He shook his head. "And I'll talk about my good buddy who happens to be you, and my whole family will stand in line to kiss my butt."

"I'd pay good money to see that," Jim said.

"Well, it's a very handsome butt," Tick replied defensively. Then he sobered. "Anyway, you were trying to tell me something?"

Jim closed his eyes, trying to remember the scene. The packlord had risen from his sofa, come to Jim, and draped one long arm around his shoulder.

"I received a very strange message this morning," he said. "Terra has been out of contact with us since the beginning of the block-ade. And when this message appeared in my most private and protected mailbox, I asked how it had gotten there. People who should know assured me there had been no penetration of the blockade at all. Yet the message contained all the proper identification codes, including two known only to me and Serena Half Moon."

Jim's voice trailed off. He opened his eyes.

"Well?" Tick said. "Don't leave me hanging. What did the message say?"

"The message was for me. Serena Half Moon says if I come back to Terra, she will waive all entrance requirements, and I can attend the Solis Academy immediately."

# CHAPTER TWENTY

## 1

ALBAGENS HOME SYSTEM:
IN ALBAGENS CLOSE ORBIT ABOARD
ANV ALBAGENS PRIDE

Jim never saw the ship from the outside because he merely stepped onto one trans-matter disk in the Imperial Defense Ministry and stepped off another one onto the Command Bridge Deck of the *Albagens Pride*. Nevertheless by the time he did this he'd seen a thousand views of the great vessel. As he walked briskly across the vast space of the Command Deck, he saw a picture of the ship in his mind.

Korkal's vessel had resembled a giant molecule, a globular cluster of smaller circles. The *Pride* was more like five molecules linked together into a pentagon with one cluster at each corner. He was in the Bridge Cluster. Glancing up through the transparent dome of Command Deck he saw, hanging disconcertingly close, the looming shape of Drive Cluster, which held the immensely powerful engines and the engineers who served them. Drive

Cluster was golden; Bridge Cluster was a cobalt
blue; Defense Cluster, which contained both
offensive and defensive forces usually reserved
only for planetary emplacement, was red;
Troops Cluster glittered like a silver spoon; and
Passenger Cluster, where the packlord and his
court made their quarters, was a ripe purple
grape. A gigantic necklace of glowing jewels, the
*Pride* was the biggest, fastest, shiftiest, most
deadly ship ever to carry the colors of the Alban
Navy—and the hopes of the Alban Empire.

He wore a new uniform tailored to his
Terran frame. It was white with red piping
down the sides of the trousers and around the
cuffs of the tunic. He felt very spiffy when he
saw his reflection in the highly polished flanks
of the machines he passed. Alban military uniforms were a good bit flashier than the ones his
fellow mercenaries had worn. But, oddly, what
should have made him feel older had the opposite effect. When he'd held Shish's corpse in
his arms he'd felt a hundred years old. But in
this candy-striped getup he felt almost like a
kid again, a kid wearing a grown-up's costume.

The merc's working uniforms had been
drab on purpose. A grunt had no desire to call
attention to himself. And blood didn't show as
brightly on the dull fabric. Blood would stand
out on his new whites very well—but if the
enemy got close enough to make him bleed,
he'd already be dead. He shoved that unsettling thought away as he approached the core
of Command Deck and saw a familiar figure
rising from the captain's chair with one hand

raised in greeting. Jim marched up to Korkal
and snapped off a rigid salute.

"Chief Pilot Endicott reporting for duty," he
said.

Solemnly, Korkal returned an even more
rigid salute. Then he broke into a wide grin.
"Welcome aboard, Commander Endicott. Your
new home is right over here." And with a slight
bow he gestured toward a U-shaped ring
enclosing a complicated chair made of steel,
glass, and what appeared to be about a thousand cables.

Jim clambered up onto the dais that ele-
vated his chair above the main floor level and
sat down. Immediately the chair whuffed softly
and enfolded him. He looked around. From
here he had a clear view out and across the
entire Command Deck. Only the captain's
chair was higher than his. As he looked about,
glorying in his new position, he heard a muffled sound slowly growing louder. It took him a
moment to realize what it was; then he noticed
that everybody on the deck was facing him,
staring at him. And their hands were pounding
together, faster and faster.

Applauding him. His cheeks suddenly burned
with embarrassment. He raised his right hand
and waved weakly, wishing he could immediately vanish. Even Korkal was applauding, a fat
white grin splitting his muzzle.

"Please . . ." Jim mumbled, and was startled to hear his words amplified in a tenor rum-
ble across the entire deck. The applause grew
louder.

"Speech!" somebody shouted.

"No, I . . ." He shook his head, completely flabbergasted. Suddenly he realized how many were out there, all clapping away, some now beginning to echo the call for a speech. There must be hundreds of them! And thousands more throughout this great vessel, every one of them, depending on him, on his skill and talent, to get them through the blockade safely. All those lives now resting on his own shoulders. Suddenly the weight felt crushing.

He leaned forward, shaking his head. The chair sighed and released him. He stood up, his knees suddenly as feeble as his self-confidence. "I'll . . . thank you. Thank you."

They cheered louder now. His face felt on fire. "I'm sorry. I can't think of anything to say. I'll . . . we'll all do our best. We'll get through this together . . ."

Still shaking his head, he sat back down, wishing that the chair would enfold him completely. "Somehow . . ." he whispered, then caught himself in horror as he realized what he'd said. But Korkal had shut down the amplifiers and this, at least, remained his own private thought.

Korkal mounted the platform and came over to him. "Sorry about that, Jim. But they needed to see you. So much depends on you, and they should at least get a look at the pilot who will be responsible for all their lives."

"Oh, thanks, Korkal. It's nice you aren't putting any pressure on me."

Korkal shrugged. "I didn't put it there, Jim. It's just where it ended up."

"I wish I could believe I'll measure up to it."

"Oh, you will. Look at me. Look inside yourself and look at me. You know you can handle it, don't you?"

Jim thought about his initial horror when they'd given him his test results and told him he was the best qualified for the job. He hadn't wanted it.

But in the end he'd accepted it. He didn't understand the power he had, where or how he'd been gifted with the ability to recognize and act on the patterns of probability faster than anybody else, but he'd felt it inside himself. It was true. He could do it.

"Yeah. I guess I can."

Korkal grinned again. "Well, then, Chief Pilot. I suggest you lock in and get started." His grin slowly vanished. "ETD in four hours."

"I'll be ready," Jim replied. "God help me, I'll be ready."

## 2

### SOL SYSTEM:
### LUNA DARKSIDE

Although nearly a billion humans lived and worked and played on Luna, there were vast stretches of that ancient satellite that still had never known any living presence. The majority of habitats were underground on the brightside, facing Earth itself, mostly because the humans who lived there still valued the sight of the mother world in their night sky. The darkside of the moon, while also populated, was much more sparsely so, and it was there that Thargos the Hunter brought his shadowship to rest.

It had been a tricky maneuver. His ship had never been designed to rest in a planetary gravity well or atmosphere, but Luna had neither, and his pilots were immensely skilled. Now the chain of compartments that made up his vessel sprawled lightly, like a discarded, half-opened bracelet, deep in the shadows of a small crater ringwall. Thargos was satisfied he would not be discovered accidentally, and the ease with which he'd sneaked into Sol System past the guarding Alban squadrons had convinced him he need not fear them as long as he kept his head down. As for the capabilities of the Terrans, they were not a factor. Terra had nothing with which to detect shadowship technology.

He had come to Luna not entirely certain what his next move would be. So far, he had been defeated by the Terran boy, by Korkal Emut Denai, by the power of Alba itself. His first thought had been to reexamine the clumps of debris from the destruction of the Delta Satellite, but he'd quickly discarded that idea when he discovered Alban vessels prowling in those orbits. Aided by surprise, he'd been able to evade them easily, but every moment he exposed himself to their modern technology increased his chances of being discovered.

No, this was better. His instincts told him he was in the right place at the right time, and he trusted his instincts. But he thought he might like to be a little closer to the center of things. He had landing craft designed to survive almost any alien environment; Terran seawater would be only a different kind of atmosphere. He'd been monitoring Terran broadcasts since his arrival, and decided the real action would focus on the Terran government, what they called the Confederation. And it was so convenient of them to place the seat of that government on a great floating platform tethered to the shore of one of their major continents. Right at the base of one of those curious structures they called Skysnakes. He savored the unfamiliar names: North America, Pacific Ocean, San Francisco. But whatever names they used, he called it an ideal hiding place for his lander, himself, and the remaining Terran nuke carefully stowed in his weapons locker.

# 3

## ALBAGENS HOME SYSTEM:
### IN ALBAGENS CLOSE ORBIT ABOARD ANV
### ALBAGENS PRIDE

Captain Denai peered into one of his screens, where the face of his chief pilot gazed calmly back at him. Screens on either side of this one held the features of the two other pilots, both Alban, both also calm. Korkal wondered how Jim was feeling right now, but he wouldn't embarrass the boy by asking. He had no worries about the other two: they were both veterans whose combined experience was about twenty times Jim's entire life span.

And how about himself? How did he feel about trusting his life to the skills of a Terrie boy whose battle experience encompassed exactly two engagements?

Still, what engagements they had been! Jim had taken on, not just evaded but fought, thirty Hunzzan ships of the line and destroyed them all. He knew of no similar exploit in the entire history of the Alban Navy, and he had a good grasp of that history. Then, for dessert, he'd blasted his way through the greatest planetary blockade in galactic military history, killing even more enemy ships in the process. There was no doubt about it: there was something very special about Jim Endicott. Still, that something special was more than a little scary. It seemed impossible, but Jim had done it.

Jim had done a lot of things that were impossible. Were there any more like him on Terra? If so, that was also a frightening thought. That kind of racial ability only cropped up every several millennia, and when it did—

He dropped the thought. Such a thing was impossible. There were no recorded occurrences on such a primitive planet. Not even worth considering. Still, it took a moment or two for his uneasiness to subside.

He was half-aware of the sound of alarms ringing and hooting throughout his ship. Along the bottom of his awareness, fed by the interforce helmet that now covered his skull, he watched the myriad routines for ship launch as they moved forward. Drive Cluster was now a throbbing hive of activity, as the huge fusion tubes were deployed for inner-system maneuver. They couldn't use the subspace drives so close in to the sun, for fear of damage to the sun's natural fusion processes. The plan now was to get up as much speed as possible before diving into subspace just before reaching the inner limits of the Hunzzan blockade.

Subspace was certainly no guarantee of safety. The Hunzzan ships could and would follow. Death could occur as easily in the shifting webs of subspace as in the more predictable realms of realspace.

After that it would be up to Jim.

"Chief Pilot, begin launch procedures on my mark. System check, please."

Jim nodded. "All systems code green, sir."

"Mark," Korkal said.

## 4

Although the captain of any starship was technically in control of it, no human could actually "control" the incredible mass of power, weapons, and information-processing machinery that allowed the ship to move and think and fight. Not even the pilot really did this. The pilot only reacted to the data first created, projected, and analyzed by the computers and sensors that did the real work a thousand million times faster than living flesh could hope to manage. Jim's role was like that of an artist painting a picture; he might have a hundred different shades of blue offered up to him, but he would decide which shade was the one for the particular picture he wanted to paint. And, like the artist, he might have no idea at all why he chose cerulean over azure, except that it looked right to him.

Now, his head encased in a bulging silver globe, his wiry body tense in the cushioned grip of his chair, he allowed himself to sink into the strange world that was his and his alone.

# 5
———

## ALBAGENS HOME SYSTEM:
### ABOARD HNV SERPENT FANG IN NEAR
### COMETARY ORBIT

Admiral Heliarchon stared through the fiery mist of his Fleet Battle Control Center at the ranks of officers and men who helped him conn the 1225 ships that made up One Hundred Sixteenth Sector Fleet, one of three enforcing the blockade of the Alban Home System.

The grand admiral was on the flagship of Two Thousand Sector Fleet and well out of Admiral Heliarchon's thoughts, for which he was grateful. He'd once been on the old lizard's staff; it had not been the most successful or enjoyable tour of duty in his career. Nevertheless, he'd survived, and now he commanded a fleet of his own, a battle fleet engaged in the investment of their ancient enemy's home system, and his future was assured.

So far the strategic planning done by the Hunzzan High Command had been superb. From the very first deception on Sleen to the lightning attack on Alba itself, things had gone precisely as predicted. In units the Alban Navy far outnumbered the units of the Hunzzan Navy; but Hunzza had the advantage of knowing where it would strike. Alba had somehow to guard three hundred thousand planets. It would take time—far too much time—to gather enough of the scattered units together and shape them into a force capable of breaking the blockade. In fact, though Alba might not yet know it, her time had run out.

His only regret was that the damned Romian mercenary ship had somehow slipped through his own quadrant and reached the safety of the Alban inner system, carrying its cargo of advanced shields. Without those shields, Heliarchon knew that he and his ships would now be floating gently about Alba itself while his troops took the packlord into custody—after obtaining his signature on the surrender documents, of course.

He sighed. He'd been asleep when the Romian breakthrough had occurred, and by the time he got to the bridge it was all over. His comm people were monitoring everything that came out of Alba, including the secret transmissions of some unnamed agent who had already passed through their lines without so much as a by-your-leave. Whoever that one was, he possessed codes so powerful Heliarchon almost broke into a sweat thinking about them. But that one was gone now, and he'd even done the admiral a favor by telling him just who had piloted the Romian ship so skillfully through his lines.

A Terran boy. Heliarchon had been forced to turn to his researchers to discover anything about this Terra, and when they were done he knew little more than when he'd known nothing. Some kind of backspace garbage heap barely out of the Stone Age. It certainly didn't sound like the kind of place to produce a pilot who destroyed six of Hunzza's best cruisers as if swatting *bipkes* birds, but the unknown agent swore it was true.

Not that it mattered. The superpilot was trapped inside the blockade now, and the admiral had no intention of letting anything or anybody out. And with the arrival of his most recent reinforcements he knew he had the forces to make sure his determination was carried out.

So when the alarms began blaring he thought it was some kind of system failure, and only when the reports began to cascade into his skull did he realize it was for real.

Thirty, fifty, a hundred contacts all along the inner surface of his englobing perimeter! And similar reports coming in now from the other two fleets.

Breakout!

Something unbelievably massive material-ized precisely in the center of his own forma-tion. After that, things got hectic.

# 6

## ALBAGENS HOME SYSTEM:
### ABOARD ANV ALBAGENS PRIDE IN
### EXTRASOLAR ARC

Jim felt his body as a distant itch. He had
studied "ghost" limbs; in less advanced times
those who for one reason or another lost a
limb sometimes still received sensations from
it, because though the limb was gone, the
brain still remembered it. He imagined it must
have been something like this—except he was
separated from his whole body. So that he
could devote all of his brain to the job at hand,
powerful machines had taken over his autonomic nervous functions; they monitored his
physical processes, breathed for him, kept his
heart pumping steadily, and triggered whatever chemicals, protein cascades, or hormone
composites seemed called for in any conceivable circumstance.

And still he itched. It was the itch of the
body that could never be entirely forgotten,
never be entirely left behind, never be entirely
separated from the mind. He sank into darkness that suddenly bubbled with light. Then,
in fractured and chaotic waves, the implacable
logics of infinite probability enfolded him and
bore him away.

# CHAPTER TWENTY-ONE

## 1

---

**CONFEDERATION HEADQUARTERS,**
**SAN FRANCISCO OFFSHORE, N.A.**
**OFFICE OF THE CHAIRMAN**

"**I** know what it is," Serena Half Moon said, irritation plain in her dark eyes and tight line of her jaw. "Every feed I've gotten in the last twenty-four hours has been about this so-called mystery ship, Carl."

Carlton Fredericks was not his usual urbane, impeccable, top-level-bureaucrat self. His perfectly tailored jacket was a wrinkled wad on a chair, his collar was open, and his gray hair much rumpled by finger tracks. He had a grizzled stubble of whiskers on his bony chin, and his eyes looked red-rimmed and sore. It had been forty hours since he'd seen his bed, and he was feeling it.

"Well," Fredericks said, "you and I both know there isn't any mystery about it. So does the Naval High Command, which has been in a frenzy since it appeared. Grand Admiral Havlicek is demanding to be allowed to deploy a blocking force."

"Tell the admiral to stuff it."

They grinned at each other. The grand admiral was near the top of both of their crap lists. "I will inform the admiral that the matter is under advisement at the highest level," Frederick said. "He'll deploy his stooges in the Assembly, though. Raise a big ruckus there. And Lord knows he'll have help."

"If he leaks anything about this, I will personally throw him in the deepest, darkest, nastiest brig I can find. Make sure he knows that."

"Oh, yes. But the matter of the ship itself remains. It's still maneuvering toward Terra orbit, and it's too damned big to keep a secret. The NewsWeb people are going nuts."

"Let them. Do you know who's on board that ship?"

Fredericks shook his head. "That's been in your ultra messages, hasn't it?"

"Yes. It's the packlord, the head of the Alban Pra'Loch. And he's brought Jim Endicott and Korkal Emut Denai with him. The whole damned merry crew."

Her aide's jaw slowly dropped. "The packlord? What the hell is he doing here? I thought he had a war to fight."

She rubbed her forehead hard. "Evidently, he thinks he can best fight it here. With me." She paused, thoughtful. "Somehow he either knew or had a very strong suspicion that Tabitha Endicott, the boy's mother, survived that nuke attack. He pressed me, and I finally admitted it. I hate admitting anything to him, but I needed to break him open a little. He wants to meet with me, her, and the boy."

"Huh? When?"

"Soon as they make orbit. Call it ten hours from now."

"The packlord? Here? In ten hours?"

"In this very office. Why? Were you planning on taking a nap between now and then?" She smiled grimly. "Forget it. If you close your eyes in the next three days, you'll be doing better than me. And that's not going to happen."

## 2

### NEAR TERRA ORBIT:
#### ABOARD ANV ALBAGENS PRIDE

"**W**hy won't you let me tell Jim that his mother's okay?" Korkal asked.

The packlord, looking more relaxed than he had in days, offered a pot of the cinnamon tea to Korkal, who shook his head. The packlord poured himself a fresh cup and settled deeper into his chair.

"Because, my dear Lord Denai, I am plotting. It is what I am paid to do. And I do it very well. I am about to try to convince some very stubborn people to do precisely what I want them to do. One of those stubborn people is Lord Endicott.

The more off-balance I can keep both him and
Serena Half Moon, the happier I will be. A nice
emotional reunion scene in the chairman's office
will go a long way toward keeping things obscured while I flap my jaws off, my wonders to
perform." He grinned faintly.

"I still don't like it. We—you—owe Jim."

"Of course I do. But no real harm is done. He
just gets a happy surprise. Where is he now?"

"He's off duty, so I suppose he's in his
quarters."

"What about that Tickeree fellow? The low-
rent royal?"

"He's in the pilot's chair. No detectable
danger right now, so the junior pilots take the
helm. It's good training. He's being monitored,
of course."

Hith nodded. "Is everything ready for the
meeting?"

"The Confed chairman has arranged to meet
in her private office. You want to go incognito, I
presume?"

"Yes. I'll just be a mid-level diplomat, paying my respects to the chairman and returning
her lost boy to her."

"I hope this works," Korkal said.

"Why wouldn't Serena Half Moon agree? In
the end, this is all in her best interest."

"She'll see it right away, Packlord. All Terra
up for grabs, the biggest prize in the galaxy. If
Hunzza knew about it, they'd end the blockade
around Alba immediately. And put every one of
those ships to burning a hole in space right
toward here."

"So it's also in her interest that Hunzza doesn't know. Or anybody else, at least until we've agreed on how to handle it. She doesn't really have very many options, you know."

Korkal lowered his eyebrows and scowled. "I've met her face-to-face, Packlord. If I were you, I wouldn't underestimate her."

"I won't."

# 3

Jim had never actually seen the Confed Island with his naked eyes. It was a huge man-made affair, half a hundred levels deep and high, fifteen miles on a side, floating off the Northern California coast near the base of the North American Skysnake. He'd heard about it all his life, but now, approaching it from the air, he found himself unimpressed. They were coming in just as dusk crept from the east across the sparkling expanse of San Francisco, which was itself only the brightest of the burning jewels that encrusted the Bay Area like a *pave* of melting diamonds.

He stood with Korkal near the front of the observation dome of the lander. At the back, surrounded by courtiers, the packlord sat nestled in a chair, sipping his tea. Overhead the sky was a fading blue-black, powdered with stars and bisected by the glittering vertical whip of the Skysnake.

"I came down one of those things one

time . . . and went back up again," Jim said softly, nodding toward the Snake.

Korkal seemed to sense his mood and didn't say anything. Jim watched the floating Confed platform grow larger. At one time it would have impressed him beyond words. Now he had seen the Great Hall of the Pra'Loch. He had seen the might and power and glory of the heart of a real empire, besides which the mightiest works of Terra were little more than childish toys. The lander he was riding this very moment was larger than the largest cruisers of the Confed fleet—and it was only a glorified elevator.

He stared as they drifted lower, his thoughts drifting with the nearly imperceptible motion of the lander. Whoever was piloting was good. Then he remembered. Tick had the honor.

Poor little Terra, glittering in her pride. Terra wasn't his home—Wolfbane, an even more insignificant world—would always be home to him. The smell of its forests, the clash of its pinball moons. But here was the home of his race, and here was where his own destiny had first been determined. Here was where the mystery of his real parents lay hidden.

He allowed himself to think about Serena Half Moon's offer. A free pass to the Solis Academy. Everything that had first driven him, now his for the taking.

He had, without knowing it, sacrificed not only his father, but the existence of any father, on the altar of his ambition to attend the Academy. When he'd first been told about

Serena's offer, he'd felt a great lilting yelp of joy. For a moment it seemed that everything was winding down, and he would be free.

But the joy had faded as he understood the bargain. Before anything else, he had savored the struggle to achieve his dreams. All the years of training and study preparing for even more grueling years at the Academy. Then the long slow rise to his own ship. His life marked out before him in well-planned paths of achievement. Yet now he'd piloted vessels which made the best Terra had to offer look like cheap game prizes. Terra didn't even have anything that could take advantage of his probability-cognition abilities.

So was he now too good for Terra? He leaned his forehead against the cool transparency of the dome and closed his eyes. No, he wasn't too good. If anything, Terra's backwardness wrenched at his heart more strongly. He yearned to help her, to bring humanity to the forefront of the galaxy. That would be an even greater challenge than the one he'd once thought the highest.

The price he'd paid! And the price others had paid as he sought that first goal. In his mind he saw the great white ships of Earth, saw them even greater than before, their graceful winged shapes drifting like dreams throughout the galaxy. Saw himself at the helm of one of them, just as a nearly forgotten captain had ridden another helm into final destruction over Wolfbane. That brave man had died along with all his crew.

Sacrifice. The game could not be worth any less than the sacrifice made to play it. Humanity was his home, the shaper of his dreams, the hall of his future. Could he be worthy of it without being true to himself? He turned to Korkal.

"You know that offer the Confed chairman made? About me and the Solis Academy? A free pass?"

"Mm-hmm."

"I'm going to turn it down."

"I thought you would."

Jim stared at him. "You did?"

"The gift may be wonderful, but in the end it's still a gift."

"Too many people died because I tried to do it the hard way. And now it's like if I take the easy way, they all died for nothing."

"It's not that simple, Jim. You're too hard on yourself sometimes. But I don't think your future is with us. It's with your own people, and you'll have to achieve that in your own way. I could wave my hand and give you things far beyond anything Terra could, and what I can do the packlord could do a thousand times greater. But I wouldn't unless you asked me. And I don't think you'll ask."

"No. I guess I won't."

Korkal patted his shoulder. "We should get ready. The meeting is in less than an hour."

"I want to watch some more. It's clunky and crappy and primitive, but it's mine. My world, my people. My dream."

"You're a wise child, Jim."

"I'm just a kid, Korkal. Someday maybe I'll be wise."

"Yes. Someday maybe you will."

# 4

## TERRA:
### OFFICE OF THE CONFED CHAIRMAN

Jim came in almost as an afterthought, sandwiched between Korkal and Tick, the three of them lost in the packlord's retinue. The office seemed small. Then he realized the packlord's office was also small. Was that a mark of the truly powerful, to be secure enough in their own power not to need the trappings of it?

The room seemed full of milling people. He listened to empty formalities as Serena Half Moon and Hith Mun Alter said what he supposed were all the proper things. Yet intermingled with the obligatory politeness was a fog of tension, and the faces of the two leaders looked masklike to him.

Then the packlord turned and gestured toward him. "Jim, come here."

He stepped forward, feeling a curious reluctance. He was about to tell the leader of his people he could not accept her gift. If not now, then soon. The knowledge made him feel uncomfortable, as if he was about to commit some grievous breach of manners.

"So you're the boy who caused all the trouble," Serena Half Moon said as she came up to him and extended her hand. "Welcome home, Jim Endicott."

Her grip was long-fingered and dry and strong. The bladed bones of her face spoke to him of iron will and hidden sadness. Her dark eyes snagged at him like hooks.

"Thank you, Chairman," he said. He couldn't think of anything else to say.

She dropped his hand, stepped back, and stared at him. "Very shortly the packlord and I, because we are both old politicians, will sit down and convince ourselves we're bargaining for the fate of the galaxy. Maybe we are. And you will no doubt play a role. But before we do that, there's somebody here who wants to see you."

She nodded toward Carlton Fredericks, who stepped behind a drape and opened a door. A small blond figure flew across the room and wrapped herself about him.

"Oh, Mom," he said. "Oh, thank God, Mom."

So it was not the land of Terra beneath his feet, nor the sight of his own race around him, but instead the familiar smell of her hair, the taste of her tear-damp cheek, and the dogged ferocity of her embrace that told Jim Endicott he had, against all odds, finally come home again.

The bottomless well of Tabitha Endicott's unconditional love.

# 5

"**I** had intended to distract you with the more emotional aspects of the reunion between the boy and his mother."

Serena Half Moon said, "Which is why I had the office cleared, packlord. In the end this is between the two of us. I am the speaker for humanity, not Jim Endicott."

"You surprise me."

"Why? What we do differs only in degree, not in kind. I make the same kind of decisions you do. The difference between the twenty billion of Terra and Wolfbane, and the three hundred thousand times that of the Alban Empire is not really comprehensible to living minds. Above a certain level, all the decisions—and all the problems—become indistinguishable."

"I hadn't considered that. But you may be right. Very well. One of your ancient diplomats once remarked that great nations don't have morals, they only have interests."

"I would dispute that as an overarching truth, but if you wish to launch your proposals from that platform, I'm willing to hear you out."

"So kind of you, Chairman. My deepest thanks."

She grinned at him. It made her look years younger, almost mischievous. "Which really means, I suppose, that you will for the moment accept the incredible effrontery of the leader of a very small mud hole in a very wide road who condescends to you." Then her grin vanished. "I have something you need badly, Packlord. That makes Terra a somewhat larger and more significant mud hole than you are accustomed to. I'm not condescending to you. I am affirming Terra's significance."

"Well. Bluntly spoken. So I will be likewise. You say you have what I want. But do you really have it? What if you can't keep it? What if I just take what I want? What is your significance then?"

She smiled. "I have become somewhat more aware of galacto-politics of late, Packlord. Could you simply take what you want if Hunzza chose to intervene?"

"I told you once you were playing a very dangerous game . . ."

"So? They are all dangerous, these games we play. But we play them anyway, don't we?"

He bowed slightly, and they continued.

## 6

Jim went to a door of the small but comfortable anteroom where he and his mother waited, opened it, looked out, saw who he was looking for, and waved him in.

"Mom, this is Tick. My best friend."

Tick glowed visibly at the description, approached the sofa where Tab was sitting, bowed deeply, then extended his hand. "My very great pleasure, Ms. Endicott. Your clod of a son chose not to mention it, but you are a very beautiful woman."

She took his hand and shook it. "Oh, Jim, I think I like this one."

"Mom, he's got more bullcrap than a Texas cattle-clone ranch. But he's a prince of the blood royal," Jim added, grinning. "Hard to tell, isn't it, unless he tells you? Which he will be happy to do, immediately and at great length."

But Tick had already plopped himself down next to Tab and begun one of his endless but extremely charming orations. Jim watched for a moment, highly amused. It was fun watching his mother try to cope with all the new things. Wolfbane was a province of the provinces. Princes that looked a lot like chimpanzees had to be a new experience for her, though she had so far shown no sign of surprise. What was even funnier was that Tick knew all about his resemblance to the simian primates of Terra.

He wondered for a moment at his own pleasure in seeing this. Then he realized what it was: in a way it was an announcement. *See, Mom, the things I have done, the people I have met, the new life I've discovered? See that I'm no longer the boy you remember? See how I've changed?*

But no sooner had he examined that rather unsettling thought than another realization bloomed. There was some truth to it. He wasn't a boy any longer, at least not the boy he'd been. But he wasn't a man yet either. He was somewhere in between, wistfully remembering his childhood while at the same time staring with nervous gaze into a future he had not yet plumbed. And he contemplated that future with all the fear and uncertainty of anybody faced with things both unknown and inevitable.

Except it wasn't really inevitable. He might never grow up at all. He might die instead. He glanced toward another door and wondered what sort of deviltry the chairman and the packlord were cooking up. What was it like to have so much responsibility?

*But I know what it's like,* he realized. *I've had it, too. God, I hope I've done the right thing. God, I hope so.*

He thought he had, but he still felt a small hitch in his chest when, two hours later, that doorway opened, and Serena Half Moon and Hith Mun Alter walked slowly into the room.

## 7

The two leaders sat across from them. Jim, still in the grip of a strange kind of self-consciousness, thought what a strange tableau it made: two rulers seated across from a big-mouthed monkey, a teenage human boy, and a blond-haired archetype of ferocious mother-hood, as both of these powers *explained* themselves to this odd pastiche.

Serena Half Moon had assumed an almost motherly demeanor as she leaned forward with her long hands folded in her lap, her dark hair swinging across her face, and spoke in low, appealing tones.

"Hith and I have agreed that I will allow his scientists to construct an improved version of the mind arrays"—Jim noticed that she carefully did not call them Mind*slaver* Arrays—"based on the codes implanted in your chromosomal patterns. If the tests of that are successful, we will try to reestablish the full power of the arrays. He has explained to me about the role the Plebs played in this, of course."

"I insist that tests be made first," Jim said. "And if there is any evidence of the Pleb Psychosis, then the whole thing must be aborted immediately. I won't be responsible for something like that ever happening again."

The two leaders glanced at each other. "Well, of course it wouldn't be your responsibility, Jim. It would be ours—mine really. But we"—she glanced at Hith again—"we accept your condition."

Jim nodded. He'd done all he could. But he couldn't help seeing through the two schemers before him, even when he didn't want to. They were lying to him. They would do whatever they decided was necessary.

If they thought the ends justified their means.

# 8

**A**fter the boy, his mother, and his friend had departed, they stared at each other. "Does he know?" the chairman said.

"I don't believe so."

"And your people are absolutely certain?"

"Yes," the packlord said. "There is something else, something besides the code, in his chromosomes. It's not a code, it's just genetic information. We don't know what it is or what it's for. But it's there."

She nodded. "By now you've run it against a Terran genomic base?"

"And it doesn't fit. It doesn't seem to have anything to do with any known human characteristics. It's some new trait. Or traits."

"I wonder if it has anything to do with the mind arrays?" Serena Half Moon said.

"So do I," Hith Mun Alter replied. "So do I."

# CHAPTER TWENTY-TWO

## 1

---

### TERRA

**T**hargos the Hunter stared in pop-eyed disbelief at the screens in his lander that monitored the Terran WideWeb. He didn't need the translations that droned automatically into his skull, and finally he turned them off. They were a needless distraction and he wanted, *needed*, to think.

The Terrie government obviously had applied a full disinformation spin to the visit. "Routine talks," they said. "A mid-level Alban official," they said.

He'd watched the arrival of what had to be the largest space vessel ever built. Nice ride for a mid-level official, he thought. But when the recording modules had caught a brief glimpse of that same official as he entered the Confed chairman's domains, together with his retinue, he'd understood. And his eyes had bulged.

The mid-level official turned out to be the packlord himself! And in his retinue walked both the Terran boy, Jim Endicott, and the Alban agent, Korkal Emut Denai.

Everything he'd feared had now come to pass. He had failed in every one of his efforts, and now the packlord had personally brought the boy home. Of course, that could not be the prime reason for his presence. Thargos tried to imagine a reason sufficiently urgent for the packlord not only to risk his life by running the blockade surrounding Alba, but to *leave* Alba in the midst of the greatest crisis in his empire's history.

He ticked off what he knew: first, Alba had guarded Terra for several years, for reasons yet to be determined, but presumably involving one Delta and some sort of technology controlled by Delta. Second, Delta had been searching for Jim Endicott, had found him, and shortly thereafter Delta had vanished. Third, Alba had taken a great interest in this unknown Terrie boy, who had worked miracles of piloting as recently as a few clawfuls of days ago while running the Hunzzan blockade. Now the packlord, at incomprehensible risk to himself and his people, had come with the boy to Terra.

So the answer, while shadowy in detail, was shockingly plain in its overall shape: since the existence of the Albagensian Empire was at stake, only something absolutely crucial to Alba's survival would bring Hith Mun Alter here.

And somehow, maybe only by blind luck, Thargos the Hunter was the only Hunzzan agent in a position to do anything about it.

For a moment his thoughts turned to his own situation. Terran ideas of security were laughably primitive. His own lander, the largest he possessed, was parked in a subaquatic pen at the base of the Confed Island, disguised by its entry codes as an anonymous visitor from a distant Terran undersea community. He had excellent communications set up with his ship hidden on Luna, with coded messages riding piggyback on various innocuous Terran feeds to their satellite.

But he'd left the last nuke aboard his spacecraft. His lander contained only mundane weaponry, perhaps sufficient to ensure his escape if need be, but certainly not powerful enough to duel one of the Alban cruisers now swarming in close orbit about Terra. He didn't even want to think about what kinds of weapons might be aboard the monstrous Alban ship that had brought the packlord here.

He didn't know enough, but in some ways he knew too much. Very well, construct a fallback. His second goal must be to get off this planet and return to his own ship, which would at least greatly expand his capabilities. That might be tricky. But the first goal wasn't. He spoke softly but clearly.

"Send to the mother ship that Hith Mun Alter, the packlord, is on Terra and meeting with the Confed chairman. Current estimates of Alban naval strength in Sol System are approximately two squadrons and a half, and one gigantic ship of unknown capabilities. I recommend immediate attack in force on Sol System. Advise optimum strategy as multifleet engagement with the strategic goal of destroying Sol System's sun."

Sun-poppers. The time for half measures was over. Whatever advantage the packlord sought here would not survive in the blinding flare of a full-blown nova. In fact, nothing would survive, nothing at all.

He waited for a good amount of time until the reply was relayed to him. Hunzzan High Command agreed with him. So Hunzza would arrive with as much power as it could muster. The ETA would be in seven Terran days. Seven days until the utter destruction of Sol System and every living thing in it.

That outcome suited Thargos just fine.

## 2

The first things to come down from the great Alban ship were gigantic transmatter disks. As soon as they were set up, they began to disgorge an endless stream of scientists and the equipment they had brought with them, machines not even dreamed of by Terran technology.

It went very quickly. Many of the problems had been solved by feverish work on the voyage from Alba to Terra. The remaining riddles were quickly unraveled through frantic cooperation between Alban and Terran scientists. The first test was ready to go just about the time Hith Mun Alter stepped from his quarters aboard the

*Albagens Pride* through a transmatter disk into Serena Half Moon's office.

"We have problems," he said without preamble.

"With the test?"

"No. That seems to be on schedule. But the schedule may be too lengthy now."

"Um? Why is that?"

He gestured his frustration. "We have a clear feed from Alba. The blockade shields are down, so they can transmit again."

"Is that bad?"

"Yes. The three Hunzzan blockading fleets have vanished. The highest probability is they are headed here. Somehow they found out, Serena, and now they're coming. Damn it to the Seven Cold Hells!"

She raised her head. "How much time?"

"I don't know. We have ships searching for those fleets. When they find them we'll know more. Five of your days, maybe six. Maybe less. I've ordered every Alban unit able to move to converge here."

"Will they be in time?"

"Who knows? Even if they are, will they be enough? We only know of three Hunzzan fleets. There may be more. They may be closer."

"Can your ship protect us?"

"No. Not against an attack of that size."

"I see." She scrubbed at her eyes. "The test commences in half an hour."

"It had better work. Even if it does, it may not be enough, though. They'll be coming with sun-poppers."

"Sun-poppers?"

"To destroy your star. I'm a prize. Hunzza may believe I'm a prize worth destroying a system for. I might believe that, too."

"Can we evacuate the system?"

He stared at her. "Twenty billion people?"

"I'm sorry. Of course it's impossible." She sighed and stood up. "Let's go watch the test. Do your people pray?"

"Some do. I haven't. Not in a long time."

"Me either. But I will now. I'll pray it works."

It didn't.

# 3

"**W**hy me?" Jim said. "I gave you everything I had. Everything I knew."

Serena Half Moon smiled at him. Her smile looked ragged around the edges, as if gravity pulled too hard at the corners of her mouth. When she finally spoke, she kept her tones carefully soft and soothing. "Nobody's blaming you, Jim. You didn't know, so you couldn't tell us."

"Tell you what?"

"Lord Endicott—Jim."

"Yes, Hith?"

"It's the Plebs. Serena's people rounded up several and we hooked them up. Nothing happened. At first we thought it was some flaw in the linkages, but there was no flaw. The linkages should have worked perfectly. But they didn't. They didn't work at all."

"Do you know why not?"

Serena turned away. "Yes. Your real mother was wiser—or more careful—than we imagined. The links cannot work without the conscious agreement of the individual participants. Each and every Pleb must give informed consent to their own participation. The linkages Delta used didn't require that. But these do. And we can't get around it. It's part of what makes these new arrays so much more powerful than the old ones. They really aren't Slaver Arrays anymore. They can't be. They won't work that way at all."

Jim thought about the real mother he'd never known. Her name had been Kate. Carl Endicott had loved her. So had Delta, though Delta had murdered her. She was the one who had altered his genome and hidden her secrets there. In a way he wanted to hate her for that. But he couldn't.

"Trapped you, didn't she?" he said finally, a grin tugging at his lips.

"What's so damned funny?"

"Well, it puts my friend Hith up the creek sort of. For a while there it looked like Terra was just so much meat up for grabs. Booty for whatever predator happened along with the strength to take it. But now, for the first time in history, the predator has to ask the prey for permission. For consent. Kind of puts everybody in a bind, doesn't it? And, of course, Serena, it strengthens your hand in this, too."

She eyed Hith. "Yes, it does."

But the packlord would not be deterred. "There won't be any hand to strengthen. The Hunzzan fleets have been sighted. The first will arrive in four of your days. And they won't be coming to ask permission of your Plebs. They'll be coming to destroy your entire system. Can't any of you see this?"

Serena broke in. "Would they destroy us if there was any chance they could *have* us? Even if it had to be on our own terms, Packlord?"

He focused his formidable gaze on her. "You wouldn't."

She shrugged.

"I might destroy you myself, before I let you become a tool in their hands."

"Not a tool in their hands, Hith. A tool in our own hands."

"Listen, Chairman, you may believe your bargaining position is much stronger than—"

"Packlord, Chairman, please."

"You cannot afford to dicker, Ms. Half Moon. Nor you either, Hith. The Hunzza won't negotiate. Not this time. It's to their advantage not to dicker. They were winning anyway, weren't they, Packlord? It was only a matter of time."

Hith nodded slowly. "I would never admit it openly, but . . ."

"So Hunzza doesn't need Terra. Not the way Alba does. Serena, it's too late. We need some way to make those arrays work. The problem is getting enough Plebs to give permission. You're sure they will work if that happens?"

"The scientists say they will. But Jim. Four days. A billion Pleb wireheaders. How can we possibly reach them all?"

"Cat," Jim said softly.

"What?"

"Her name is Catherine Thibaudeaux, but I called her Cat. Find her. You'll have to convince her, but she can do it if anybody can."

"I'll convince her," Serena said.

## 4

It took twelve precious hours. "Don't send your storm troopers, Serena. She's had more than enough of that."

"She's working in a hospital that specializes in the rehabilitation of Plebs suffering from the psychosis. But we think she has . . . connections . . . much wider than that."

"Of course she does. She was very high up in the Pleb conspiracy, the one that destroyed Delta's satellite."

Serena's eyebrows lifted. "I looked at the files about you. That wasn't evident."

"Because I lied about her, Serena. It was the only thing I lied about. Because I didn't want anybody bothering her."

"I see. So what do you suggest? We've already wasted twelve hours."

"They weren't wasted. You found her. Now take me to her. I'll talk to her."

"Jim . . ."

He raised his voice. "Madame Chairman, I said *I will talk to her.*"

She waved one hand. "Whatever you say, Jim. But hurry."

## 5

He stood with his hands behind his back and watched her through a window that led onto a shabby dayroom, where patients sat at scarred tables staring at nothing, or in basic wheelchairs, their knees covered with blankets, their hands twitching nervously in their laps.

There was a faint ringing in his ears. His mouth was dry, but he kept swallowing anyway. He felt slightly feverish and for some reason he couldn't quite understand, he was terrified.

Not so long ago such terror would have frozen him, made his hands sweat and his bowels cramp and his brain spin. Now he looked through a window and saw his own past in the form of a slim young blond girl. She was bending over a wild-eyed man with greasy black curls and a stubby goatee and a face so scarred it looked more like weathered black stone than flesh. She whispered something to the man, and he smiled. She touched the back of his hands and his twitching fingers went still. She patted him on the shoulder and for a moment he looked almost human.

Her back was slightly arched and strong. She'd cut her hair even shorter than before, and now it covered her fine skull like a cap made of shiny gold coins. He remembered how they'd parted, and how ashamed the power of his own need had made him. He remembered hating himself and hating her, and hating himself for hating her.

He turned the knob on the door and stepped quietly into the room. He smelled pajamas washed in harsh cleansers, sweat, his own fear, and a whiff of her perfume like distant flowers on a windy day.

"Hello, Cat," he said.

She turned. When she smiled at him his fear went away.

## 6

"**Y**es, there's a way," she told him.

They were seated on a bench straddling a narrow patch of beaten-down grass that ran along the front of the hospital. The hospital building was built of worn red bricks. It looked like a prison.

The bench was made of concrete so old and chipped it might have been native stone. The neighborhood was a Pleb enclave, and people here wandered aimlessly. He saw nobody striding with purpose, clear-eyed and intent on some pressing goal. There were no goals here. And he knew that might be the greatest crime worked upon the Plebs, greater even than the Slaver Arrays. The reasons for life itself had been taken away, and nothing left behind but the slow, instinctive slog from cradle to grave. The will to exist was not enough; desire was the sorcerer's wand that transmuted existence into living, and among the Plebs desire had been drained away.

"How?" he asked her.

She took both of his hands in hers and looked into his eyes. "Jim, you have to promise me. I have nothing to hold you with, but I know you are good. So you have to promise me that no harm will come to my people from this. That it isn't some kind of trick."

Nothing to hold him with? But her hold was sunk deep into him and would lay its claim until he died. It would change—had changed he suddenly realized, to his great relief—but the honesty it demanded would not. He could lie to himself more easily than he could lie to her.

"Cat, I can't ever fully know what people like Hith Mun Alter and Serena Half Moon really think. I can't read their minds or know their secret thoughts. But in some way I can't explain I can see the logic inherent in what they say and do, and that let's me know them.

"The Hunzza are coming. If they get here and we have nothing to oppose them with, they will explode our sun. Then everybody dies— you, me, the Plebs, everybody else. I don't think it's a trick. I don't see how it could be.

There's not enough time and too much desperation."

"You think so. Is that enough?"

He squeezed her hands. They felt slightly damp, the skin soft and smooth, but he could feel hard muscle beneath. Strong and capable hands. He would have trusted his life to them.

"It will have to be. But you will have to decide."

Yet even as he spoke he felt the presence of the great powers who lurked beyond his words. Of the desperate needs of those like Serena and Hith who were accustomed to taking what they wanted. Of those who utilized almost any means to achieve their ends.

At what point should or could a species acquiesce in its own destruction? What tool was too awful for a race to bend toward its own survival? He suspected the sacrifice of the human Plebs was not a weapon too awful to be used. He thought he understood all of them too well—Delta, Hith, Serena, even Cat. What he didn't fully understand was himself.

And he wondered if Cat really did have choice in this matter, or if events had not destroyed any chance of true decision.

A bluejay, a wandering stranger in the city, whipped above them, cawing. The sun beat at them with hot-pillowed fists. Her gaze was on him steadily as polished azurite. Finally she nodded.

"All right," she said. "They'll want to talk to you before they decide. Not face-to-face, they won't do that. A virtual tight link. Are you willing?"

"Yes. We'll have to hurry."

She nodded again.

## 7

Jim found himself nostalgic for the ignorance of his younger self. Before him in the electronic dark The Fountain, chief scientist of all the Plebs, vomited its unending stream of scorpions, noxious liquids, slow-melting sparks. Rose Lovely, the spy, floated as a single perfect white blossom. Only Cracker, the great hacker, manifested as something human; he appeared cross-legged and beatific, like the young Buddha, his face shining, his smile full of unnamable ecstasy.

And hence the odd feeling of loss. Jim knew that a younger version of himself would have been impressed beyond measure by such technological wizardry. But he had seen the empires beyond the stars and the probabilities beneath the atoms. The interface now inside his skull was so powerful that the masks these people wore became tattered on their edges, their manufactured visions as cheap and tawdry as a holochip played one too many times. He felt sorry for them but could not show it. That last thing they would tolerate from him was pity.

They had warred on behalf of the Plebs

against Delta and those like Delta most of their adult lives. They had been defeated and betrayed and as a consequence their paranoia was of such an exquisitely sensitive level it was almost impossible for them to offer themselves to any outsider.

So they bickered and quarreled and made heated speeches while time ran away from all of them. Jim tuned them out and let himself drift, a part of him processing what they said, while another part of him searched for a solution that included them and the key that would unlock them.

Rose Lovely said, "In the end, all these things are versions of the Slaver Arrays. All of them exploited our people. All of them are dangerous. We can't trust Serena Half Moon. She was Delta's tool, and I see no reason to believe her any different than he was. She's a lackey of the Working Class, always has been. The Plebs have never been any concern of hers, except to crush us when we become too bothersome. I say no. No compromise, no cooperation."

"Then we'll all die," Jim said. "We may anyway, but at least we'd have the chance of survival."

Cracker opened his Asian eyes. "You call this living, pal? What the Plebs have now?"

Patterns drifted through him like a cold wind, patterns that shifted and changed with each word.

The Fountain spoke suddenly. "I don't trust the science. We may be primitive by galactic standards, but we aren't technologically illiterate. Some of what you suggest sounds impossible to me."

"I can give you the translated codes. You may study them at your leisure. But they aren't galactic technology. They are human, created by Delta and my own mother. You're welcome to them. But there isn't any time."

"So you say," Rose Lovely said. "So you say. But why should we trust you? What's in it for us, for the Plebs?"

It had been hovering about him like a vast gossamer wing, something trying to express itself in shape and form and solidity. He'd felt it gathering in his mind and wondered what it was, what it was trying to be. Now it enfolded him in the iron grip of certainty.

"Choice," he said. "And with choice, all the rest: freedom, self-respect, value. All the things the Plebs don't have now. All the things that make a life worth living. That's what my mother offered—offers—to you now."

He tried to imagine how Kate had known. Had she known or only suspected? But in the creation of the new arrays she'd done more than remove the awful specter of the psychosis. She had turned the arrays into something far greater and more powerful: a means of saving the souls, one by one, of every Pleb who lived.

"I don't understand," The Fountain said.

*Of course you wouldn't,* Jim thought. *You worship at the temple of the microchip, of the inhuman reactions too small and too quick for the human mind to perceive. The quantum par-*

*ticles have no awareness; they don't need it.
You mistake the building blocks for the structure itself.*

"No Pleb can become a part of the new arrays without giving conscious and informed permission to allow that participation. In order to be as powerful as possible, the arrays need as many participants as possible. If Terra is to be saved at all, it will be because of hundreds of millions of Plebs consciously make the effort to save her. And if the goal is the most precious thing humanity has ever known—racial survival—then the price demanded may be commensurately high.

"Neither Serena Half Moon nor Hith Mun Alter is in any position to bargain. They will give you whatever you demand. But you will receive something even they cannot give you—a role to play in the most important endeavor ever attempted on this planet. You—the Plebs—can save the world. Save humankind. And save the greatest empire in the galaxy. Not the workers. Not the leaders. In the end the lowest will save the highest."

He stopped, groping for something stirring to finish with. But he couldn't find any more ringing words. "You'll have something you haven't had for generations. Choice. Honor. Respect. You'll have a reason to exist. You'll be . . . a part of the human family again."

Though he was nothing but a flux of electrons in that place, he sensed his body, slick with sweat from the effort to make them see. And all he heard was a vast and empty silence.

It was Cat's voice that answered him. "We have always been a part of the family, Jim. We have always been human. It was your kind who forgot that. We never did."

With that they were gone, and he found himself sitting in a small room staring at the equipment to which he was connected. He reached up and pulled the primitive plug from his socket. It took a moment. His fingers were greasy with perspiration. He felt wrung out, as if he'd run a long race to the finish without ever knowing the prize. But he knew the prize. Did they? Would they?

Next to him, Cat stirred in her own chair. Her eyes opened, and she regarded him with a perfectly blue gaze.

"They agree," she said. "Because we will help ourselves, we will help you. You owe us a lot, and now you will pay. And the price will be high."

Then her eyes lost their hard-glazed glare and she slumped. "We'll take the workers for whatever we can get, and Serena Half Moon won't find it pleasant to negotiate with us. But that wasn't what decided us, Jim. It was self-respect. That can only be earned, and now for the first time in centuries we can earn it. So we will. You owe us, boy. Never forget it."

"I won't," he said. "How soon can you begin?"

"We already have."

# CHAPTER TWENTY-THREE

## 1

**W**hat had gone down now came back up again. If nothing else, the arrival of the *Albagens Pride* in Sol System had brought one long-lasting technological change: transmatter disks were appearing everywhere, as fast as the nanofactories could make them. No more would Terra's humming billions find any location in their solar system more than a few steps away.

Was this the kind of thing Delta had feared so much? Jim suspected that it was. Just as the creation of the Web so many years before had freed the minds of humankind to speak and share and know each other, so the disks ended the physical separation between man and woman and child. Soon, Jim suspected, the ancient divisions imposed by distance would vanish, for when another could be in your own living room as easily as he could be in his, where were the boundaries? No one would come from "over there" anymore, because over there and here would be the same. Sol System as one vast neighborhood. He liked that thought.

Who knew what might happen? Jim realized that was what Delta really feared: the uncertainty. The lack of predictability. Nobody knew what this or any other piece of galactic technology might mean. People like Delta, who felt comfortable with and needed control, would always hate the new, even when they were themselves creating it. A sliver of insight flashed up before him like a wiggling mental fish: perhaps Delta had not really minded the Pleb Psychosis. Its existence meant that to use the arrays was a dangerous thing, an act that needed control. And who better to control it than its creator?

But these new arrays, Jim suspected, would not and could not be controlled by any single human force or entity. Another shade had flown from Pandora's magic box. Humanity's technological environment was changing again, whether humanity liked it or not.

If it survived, that is. And that was by no means certain.

He stood on a high balcony overlooking a great expanse of space in the Bridge Cluster of the *Pride*. This was in the central section, the widest dimension of the great sphere. A slice two hundred feet tall, a mile in diameter, the enclosure was too large to be called a room. A regular pattern of transmatter disks marched across the floor, so far below him they resembled softly glowing coins. Antlike figures swarmed about the disks, off-loading equipment hastily constructed all over Terra, on Luna, and on the *Pride* herself, then shipped back to this chamber. When everything was hooked together, the controlling computers, the machines that maintained the links among a billion Plebs, would take shape on the deck below him.

He watched the frantic activity below him through half-lidded eyes, savoring the momentary pleasure of having nothing to do. One of the junior pilots was keeping an eye on the *Pride*. Cat was still busy elsewhere; the secretive Pleb Council had worked some kind of internal miracle and the releases and permissions had poured in.

Nearly a billion Plebs—wireheaders all— had awakened from one sort of stupor or another and volunteered their brains to the cause. He had noticed something strange in the past couple of days as the word went out. All of a sudden Plebs everywhere had taken to wearing something bright and red: a cap, a scarf, a shirt. It was an unspoken proclamation of identity and solidarity and it said, "We are your saviors. We whom you despise will save you anyway." Those who wore red walked with their shoulders back, their spines straight, and for the first time in their lives looked their "betters" straight in the eye.

That was a new thing, too, and he liked it even better than the transmatter disks. The omens seemed good for the first time he could remember. All except the final uncertainty: would Sol System survive?

Korkal had told him that at most enough elements to make up two Alban fleets would probably arrive in-system before the Hunzza ETA. The current plan was to form the fleets around the *Pride* and meet the invading Hunzza beyond the cometary ring, using the mind arrays to control the ships rather than the *Pride*'s own systems. It made sense. The capabilities of the arrays were thought to be so far beyond anything either Alba or Hunzza could bring to the fray that being outnumbered three to two would not prevent an Alban victory.

He considered that as he watched the activity below suddenly slow. The last pieces of equipment appeared on the transmatter disks, were hauled away, and hooked up. The insectile swarm began to dwindle and finally vanish. Far below, a hushed expectancy filled the great chamber; he knew they would be running the initial tests of the full arrays very shortly. There was no time left for leisure. They would test as soon as they had system completion, which would be only a few minutes after the last of the equipment was rolled into place and connected. Maybe they were starting now . . .

He raised his head.

"Yes?"

The signal had come silently, but now he recognized the voice.

"Hey, buddy," Tick said. "Korkal just called. He wants you and me in the packlord's quarters right now."

"I'm on my way," he replied. "Meet me?"

"At the door. We can face the dragon together."

*Something wrong,* he thought.

The floating lights illuminating the space around him suddenly dimmed, then returned to normal. It happened three times as he watched. Only an enormous power drain could cause something like that. Jim turned and began to run back toward the nearest trans-matter disk.

## 2

He had not yet seen the packlord's private rooms. Tick met him at the reception area and Korkal came out quickly, a worried expression on his face, and ushered them into the inner sanctum. It was more utilitarian than Jim had expected, all gray and white, but the ever-present sofa was there, Hith sat on it, and he cradled his ever-present cup of cinnamon tea.

"Hello, Jim," a husky feminine voice said. He raised his eyebrows as he replied, "Hello, Serena."

"Jim, have a seat. You too, Tick."

"Thanks, Hith." Tick didn't say anything. He still couldn't accustom himself to the easy informality between his young friend and the most powerful person in the Alban Empire.

"We have a problem, Jim," Hith said quickly.

*Of course you do,* Jim thought. *You always*

*do, it always seems to involve me.*

"Yes, sir?"

"I can show you better than tell you. Lord Denai?"

Korkal, standing out of Jim's vision, made some small movement and the room darkened. A large holoscreen appeared. It was a close-up view of the larger scene Jim had just been observing.

"I'm cutting into the test pattern now," Korkal said. "Jim, this is taken right off the feed from the controllers. We fired up the arrays just as soon as everything was hooked up. The idea was to send out a test signal, to activate all the human links and make certain we had a functioning array. Everything went fine, except for this. . . ."

The holoscreen went dark, then slowly brightened. In the center of it swirled a point of impossible brightness. It was like looking at the sun without protection. Jim squinted and half turned away. A sudden sick feeling griped at the bottom of his gut. Probabilities screamed and scrambled in his brain. *He knew what this was. . . .*

The voice was a low, static-filled roar. It sounded like a hundred big trucks screeching their brakes all at once.

*Send me Jim Endicott.*

Another burst of sound, higher, more trilling. Some kind of electronic language. "That's the super-controller machine sending a query. Basically it's asking what is going on."

Jim licked his lips and nodded. Tiny electrical shocks streaked up and down his spinal cord. He felt sudden pain in his palms and realized his fingernails were digging into the skin there. He forced himself to relax.

*Send me Jim Endicott.*

The exchange was repeated a third time. Then the screen suddenly went blank. The lights came up. They were all looking at him.

"What? Are you asking me what it is? I haven't got one single damned idea." His gut was hot with acid now, and the room felt stifling. When he tried to inhale, his breath didn't quite fill his chest. *But he did know*.

Korkal came around to face him. "Each time this . . . thing, whatever it is, asked for you, there was a tremendous power drain on the ship's systems. The arrays are now an integral part of the *Pride*, so the drain was controlled by the arrays. But we don't know why. We certainly didn't order it. Rapid first-pass analysis indicates a connection between the appearance of this thing and the drain. So whatever it is, it may be in control of the controllers. In other words, in control of the arrays themselves. And we don't have any more idea what it is than you say you do."

Korkal ran nervous fingers through the graying hair along his muzzle. "It wants you. And we don't even know what that means. Wants you? How? Why?"

"How is easy," Jim said at last. He felt a hundred years old again.

He wondered if it would ever end.

"You hook me into the controller system. That's how. I won't be able to answer the why until we do that. I may not be able to answer it even then."

Serena broke in. "You're supposed to have some high-level ability to recognize probability patterns, Jim. I don't understand what that means, but is it working now? Is that why you're telling us this?"

"Yes."

She gnawed gently at the cuticle of one of her long fingers. "And you don't know if you'll be able to learn why this is happening?"

He shook his head.

"Why not?" Hith asked. "Do you know what it is?"

"Because I might not survive," Jim said. "In fact, I probably won't." He sighed and stood up. "We don't have much time. So we'd probably better get started."

## 3

### ABOARD THE HNV SERPENT FANG, LUNA: ETA HUNZZAN FLEETS: 42:00:00 AND COUNTING

Thargos supposed it was once again luck that had protected him. Sol System had been convulsed by the arrival of the *Albagens Pride*, bearing the packlord. Normally smooth-running systems had gone chaotic. Technicians were installing hundreds of thousands of transmatter disks all over Sol System. All communications levels were jammed with data both scientific and military. The pathetic Terran fleet was fully mobilized and moving toward the outer reaches of the system in a brave but futile show of resistance.

Thargos had been able to hide his own interstellar messages in the fringes of the *Pride*'s enormous trans-stellar blare. The packlord still communicated with Alba, and so far, though not for lack of trying, Thargos had been unable to break any of those codes.

The Alban squadrons already on hand had moved deeper in-system to meet the Confed Navy vanguard. And something else was going on, something that Thargos now decided was potentially the most ominous development he'd seen so far. The worst thing was he couldn't think of anything to do about it.

He'd been lying hidden here on Luna ever since he'd inserted his lander and its fake codes into the endless stream of ships and cargo rising both from Terra itself and from the four Skysnakes. Nobody had noticed him. And so for the last many hours he'd monitored everything his extremely sensitive comm webs could touch. One incident in particular had crystallized his curiosity: a few hours before, something incredibly powerful had nearly overwhelmed his systems. *Send me Jim Endicott.*

He didn't know what it meant, but he knew the name. So who or what wanted the boy? And why?

He'd watched a huge cone of dedicated dataspace as it was created between Terra and the Alban ship. He hadn't been able to crack into that, either, but the bizarre message had shivered that cone as if it were a spiny weed in a high wind.

His claws clicked together, nervous as castanets, while his sharp tough mind strained and pressed, seeking some purchase on the problem. He hadn't thought of anything yet. But he would. He knew he would.

Hunzzan High Command had ordered him to maintain his concealment and take no action that might risk exposure. He'd been told his messages from the heart of the enemy's camp were far too valuable to hazard losing them. But he had privately decided he would disobey his orders if necessary. The boy had defeated him too many times. Yet somehow he would have his vengeance in full. He was certain of it. If he could only think of a *way* . . .

He continued watching and waiting.

# 4

─────

## ABOARD THE <u>ALBAGENS PRIDE</u>:
### ETA HUNZZAN FLEETS:
### 28:00:00 AND COUNTING

Jim sat up in the nanotank as many hands reached to help him. The fluid in which he'd been immersed, a thick, sludgy liquid rich in nutrients and in the base materials the busy submicroscopic nanocritters used to build and rebuild new passageways in his skull, poured off his naked shoulders like cool honey. It was an indescribably luxurious sensation and it soothed him as he stood up and let them wrap a fluffy terry-cloth robe around his lank frame.

The head meditech, a loose-limbed tall human with frizzy orange hair, a loopy grin, and steady gray eyes said, "How do we feel, Jim?"

"I dunno about you. I feel fine," he said.

She laughed at that, though her eyes didn't even flicker. Tankside manner? he thought wryly. The operation was a success, but the patient drowned?

He realized he felt giddy. He kept having to repress an unaccountable urge to start whooping with laughter. He stepped over the rim of the tank and climbed down to the floor. "So how am I?" he asked.

"You're fine. Everything went in slick as a

350    WILLIAM SHATNER

whistle. This new tech is . . . something else.
It's going to change a lot of things."

"Yes, I guess it is. How did it change me?"

She spoke as he towel-dried his dark curly
hair. She thought he was an extraordinarily
handsome young man and, even more attractive, he didn't seem to be aware of this fact. She
realized she had the urge to give him a motherly hug, and at the same time to give him a
hug that had nothing to do with motherhood at
all.

"Bigger channels. More of them. A *lot* of
new pseudo-dendrites and -axons. A very large
increase in potential synaptic connectivity.
What you had in there was already better than
anything I'd ever heard of. This new setup is an
order of magnitude beyond that."

A soft wash of anxiety flickered on his features and as quickly vanished. "Nothing
organic done to my brain itself?"

She shook her head. "Nope. It's all gross
structure. We've even built in an uninstall pro-
cedure. Hit it with the right codes, and it will
dissolve itself into harmless proteins and
water. Nice little trick, that."

"Oh? Where do I get the codes?"

"Already there. Think about it."

He did. An odd series of numbers and sym-
bols floated through his mind. He suddenly
understood how to apply them if he wanted to.
And if he did, all this new semisentient biolog-
ical wiring inside his skull would melt away as
if it had never been. It gave him a strange floating sensation, to be able to restructure the new

additions inside his brain with only a thought.

He stared at her. "What do you think it's for?"

"This interface?" She moved her shoulders as if she were trying to fit herself into a pipe just slightly smaller than her own width. "Beats me, friend. I thought you knew. All I can say is that you can lock up with just about anything in the cyberneural line, faster, tighter, and more wide-band than anything Terra has ever dreamed of. Like I said, this galactic gadgetry is pretty hot stuff."

He stuck out his right hand. She took it and shook it once. "Well, thanks," he said.

"My pleasure. Good luck."

"Why do you say that?"

"Because maybe you're going to need it?"

"Yeah," he said. "Maybe I am."

## 5

### ETA HUNZZAN FLEETS:
### 26:00:00 AND COUNTING

It was like his pilot's chair but much larger. It sighed and breathed with him and held him as a big man holds a small baby. From his skull socket bloomed a bouquet of gleaming silver threads. The threads as they wound away from him toward the waiting machines grew thicker until they were the size of his wrists. As the data flows entered his brain they underwent a change in quality; their passage became a matter of quantum movement, where the old man Einstein had muttered that God would not play dice with the universe. But God—or something—did.

Only Tab and Tick came to watch in person. He smiled at them both. Tick came up and punched him on the shoulder. "Hang in there, buddy," he whispered through an uncertain grin. "You're the man."

Tabitha hugged him. The chair made her awkward. He saw a liquid gleam in her eyes and felt an answering sting in his own. "Be as careful as you can be, son. I love you."

"I love you too, Mom. Don't worry."

She kissed his forehead. Her lips felt soft and cool. He smiled up at her. "Better stand back, Mom. Interforce shield coming up. You won't be able to see me."

"I'll pray for you."

He nodded. She sighed and stepped away. He moved his chin and saw her expression change. He could see her, but all she could see was a gleaming silver egg. This new version of the interforce shield enclosed his whole body.

He took a deep breath, and then the darkness took him.

# CHAPTER TWENTY-FOUR

## 1

——

### NOWHERE:
### ETA HUNZZAN FLEETS:
### 25:00:00 AND COUNTING

Jim wasn't sure what he'd expected. They had briefed him as well as they could. He would not be launched into normal cyberspace, into what an ancient writer named William Gibson had called the consensual hallucination, which was an agreement between the human and the mechanical data processors to view the world they shared as a particular set of mutually understood paradigms. They didn't know precisely what they were launching him into. Nobody really understood the full reality of the dataspace created by the mind arrays.

The human brain is a fascinating instrument. It has a finite number of neurons connected to each other by a finite number of axons, dendrites, and synapses. But the potential number of patterns these connections can create is larger than the number of atoms in the universe. In this sense the human brain is a more complicated instrument than the universe itself. Some philosophers have speculated that only such an instrument can know the universe. Others have suggested that the universe itself demands the existence of such instruments, that they are the means by which the *universe* knows itself.

The dataspace Jim entered was a construct derived from all the connections and potential connections in a *billion* human brains, each of them a discrete entity which was the product of two billion years of evolution, the last several hundred millennia of which had honed the abilities of those brains to seek out and recognize patterns.

Hence, this human mind array was, as far as anybody understood it, a new thing in the galaxy. Science could make guesses about it, but nobody yet knew anything for certain. Only the explorers who entered it and came back could bring the new knowledge. But it might as well have been marked "Here theyre bee Tygers."

*And a Tyger has summoned me by name,* Jim thought, as this new universe slowly blossomed around him and he waited for the Tyger to come.

# 2

## ARRAY DATASPACE:
### ETA HUNZZAN FLEETS:
### 25:00:00 -3 NANOSECONDS
### AND COUNTING

*I* am here.

The voice was insidious. It seemed to arise from everywhere and nowhere. Jim floated in what he once called the black and the blue, a dark no-place rich with potential and probability. This was primordial soup of the same order which birthed universes. The voice surrounded him and drifted through his bones and caressed his nerve endings.

"Who are you?" he replied. "Why have you called me?"

*Data points you must consider: "I" and "am" are accurate. I am a discrete and self-maintaining entity, and I exist. "Here" is inaccurate and used for pseudoreference and convenience only.*

"We are in the dataspace created by the mind arrays."

*You are in that dataspace. I am not limited by it though I control it. I am not limited at all.*

Jim didn't reply. A strange and bizarre sensation had begun to rise in him. It seemed to come from every cell of his body, though here he had no body. Perhaps it came from his idea of body, the remembered design of it. But that reality was changing.

The dark and luscious feeling enfolded him, spreading from within and without. It was a hungry, seeking sensation, and it seemed incredibly strong. Suddenly he realized what it was: his ability to sense and make patterns out of inchoate probabilities, but magnified a millionfold by the combination of the mind arrays and his new cyberneural interface.

The darkness around him began to change. It was as if a third eye had opened in the middle of his forehead. Directly before him the nothingness began to curdle; a shape appeared before him.

It was roughly globular; it shimmered, faded, grew strong again. He had the feeling it didn't exist entirely in real space and time. In fact, he thought what he was seeing might be only one small manifestation of the entity's whole.

*Your patterns have changed*, the Thing said.

"Yes. I can see you now."

The globular thing brightened, then faded, then brightened again. *You see a set of probabilities. They may or may not come into existence.*

Jim's mind spun. He felt himself still changing. More and more of the details of this place became clear to him. The being he confronted seemed to grow more solid. Almost familiar. Patterns marched through him like great storm waves pounding on a shore.

"Why did you call for me?"

*You are at the moment the only living being in the galaxy who can perceive my true existence. Therefore, I want you to be my messenger to others of your kind.*

"Others of my kind?"

*Living intelligences.*

"Aren't you alive?"

*Not in any sense you would understand.*

*We'll see about that,* Jim thought. "What message do you want me to relay?"

*I control the mind arrays. They are mine and mine only. If Serena Half Moon and Hith Mun Alter wish to use the relays for their own purposes, they must first negotiate with me. You will be a suitable emissary between us.*

"Suitable? Why?"

An infinitesimal delay: Jim sensed another pattern forming. Something was wrong here, but he didn't know what.

*Suitable because you are acceptable to me.*

"The existence of the arrays themselves are at risk. There is no time for negotiations. If you control the arrays, will you help us?"

*I will negotiate. There is enough time.*

A bleak sense of absolute danger informed Jim's next words: "Are you Delta?"

*I am not Delta. Delta is dead. I am Outsider.*

Somehow, that was a lie. And in the lie lay a key. He didn't have it yet, but he would. If he could keep this Outsider from seeing what he almost . . . *almost* . . . was able to understand.

He tried to curl himself into a hard mental ball, a shell impervious to Outsider's awareness.

*Why do you withdraw from me? Why do you hide yourself?*

"I want to go back now and tell them your message."

The globe hung there, shivering and twisting, glowing and dimming. Jim had a sudden sense that ghostly fingers were prying, scrabbling at the hard carapace he'd built around himself. He clenched himself tighter, his terror acting as glue. After some nameless time the questing fingers withdrew.

*Then go now.*

No-space vanished, and Jim opened his eyes in the brightness at the center of the controller machines. He was covered with sweat. He felt as if an immense amount of time had passed, but when he glanced at the digital readout nearby, it seemed to indicate that no time at all had gone by.

"Jim?" It was Korkal. "Why have you dropped the interface? We just started."

His bones and muscles felt weak and watery. "I just finished," he said. "Help me out of here. We've got big problems."

Korkal leaned close, took his wrists, and hoisted him from the chair. "Are you okay?"

"No," Jim replied. "I'm not okay. And neither are any of the rest of us. Any of us in the whole damned galaxy."

# 3

## ABOARD ALBAGENS PRIDE EN ROUTE TO COMETARY ORBIT SOL SYSTEM: ETA HUNZZAN FLEETS: 22:00:00 AND COUNTING

It was a council of war with just the four of them in Hith's chambers. "I don't understand," Serena said.

"Me, neither," Korkal said. Hith said nothing, merely stared at Jim and waited.

Jim spread his hands. "It's hard. I think it is Delta. Well, not really. It calls itself Outsider and says Delta is dead, and that may be true. At least as we understand death. I don't think Delta's body or brain exist any longer as living entities."

Serena gave her head a puzzled little shake. "Dead is dead, right?"

"Not exactly. You should understand. I wasn't present when Delta's satellite blew up, so I can't testify as to his actual physical death. He was still alive, more or less, when I left him, although he surely looked like he was dying. Here is what I think, though: living intelligence is a pattern. A living brain changes its structure as it learns. At some point the structure becomes complicated enough to support what we call intelligence and, more important, self-awareness of intelligence. We think about ourselves thinking. That is what makes us different

from the lower orders of intelligence. And some
thinkers give a name to that self-awareness:
they call it soul."

"I follow so far," Korkal said.

"Good. So the patterns of intelligence are
created by the growth and change within the
physical brain. The arrangements of the atoms
that make up the brain. Now what if those patterns could somehow be impressed, not in cells
and neurons and chromosomes, but onto the
fabric of space-time itself?"

"Huh?" said Serena Half Moon. "That sounds
impossible."

Jim shook his head. "No, maybe not. All
matter affects space and time to some extent.
The bigger the matter—say, a sun—generally
the bigger the effect. But it isn't size that really
counts. It's density. The denser the matter, the
more effect it has on space. And according to a
classical scientist named Robert Forward, the
curvature of space induced by an atomic
nucleus near its surface is fifteen trillion times
greater than the curvature of space induced by
the mass of Terra herself. So it is possible, if
that pattern which is already imprinted on
space-time could be somehow maintained after
the destruction of the brain, then intelligence
could continue to exist. And it would be an
immortal intelligence."

"That sounds crazy to me," Korkal said.

"Oh, there are problems. Without the physical brain to hold its atoms in its former arrangements, the ethereal pattern might begin to drift.
After all, the electrical and nuclear forces at

work on the atomic level are much stronger than the space-curvature effects. Eventually those should be sufficient to destroy the pattern itself. But as I said, if there is some way to maintain the pattern's integrity, then you might end up with something like Outsider."

Serena and Korkal glanced at each other, and Jim knew it was too far a reach for them. He might make them understand eventually, but there was so little time left. He turned to Hith Mun Alter.

"Packlord?"

Hith sighed. "Jim, I'm no scientist. I can't say I understand everything you've just said, but I understand one thing: this Outsider does exist. There was another set of power flows that occurred when you went into the arrays. So if this is your best guess as to what is happening, I will accept it. Which brings us to the next question: what does this Outsider want? Why does it want to negotiate with us?"

Jim felt a cool wash of relief. Hith might not understand everything, but he understood enough. "It wants what all intelligence wants, Hith. It wants to survive. That was the pattern I saw when I faced Outsider: it sees a threat to its survival, and it wants to eliminate that threat. My guess is Outsider sees a larger threat than merely the arrival of the Hunzzan fleet. It may regard the entire galaxy as a threat. It is incredibly dangerous, Packlord. But it has a weakness, and I think I know what it is."

"Then you'd better let the rest of us in on it, don't you think?" Hith replied.

Jim once again felt the leaden weight of his own destiny pulling at him, tugging him out of shape. He couldn't understand why he felt so frightened. What was the worst thing that could happen? He might die. But you could only die once. Or could you?

"Actually, I think Outsider has two weaknesses—and one of them it doesn't yet really understand. It may not know anything about it at all."

"Oh? And what might that be?"

"A dead woman named Kate. And me," Jim said.

## 4
——

### Aboard HNV Serpent Fang in Near-Terra Orbit:
### ETA Hunzzan Fleets:
### 16:00:00 and Counting

Thargos the Hunter stares at his screens, lost in thought. His ship, cloaked in technological shadows, ghosts silently in the midst of a clump of Terran freighters that circle the planet below like peaceful herds of sheep. He is the wolf within their midst, sharp of fang and bloody of claw, and hungrier than he's ever been before.

The *Albagens Pride* proceeds majestically outward, a vast bellow of communications and

signals and emanations. His own ship is physically within the mysterious cone of dataspace
that includes both Terra, the *Pride*, and everything between them. His instincts tell him this
dataspace is the most important thing; if it can
be somehow disrupted at a critical moment,
then nothing will stand before the sure
destruction of Sol System by the weapons of
the gathering Hunzzan fleets. He knows when
the first of those fleets will arrive. It will be
sooner than the Albans or Terries imagine. But
he still has a little time to do what he can.
Beyond his ship but very close, the makeshift
satellite, one of two, proceeds in silent orbit. It
is about half a mile in diameter and looks as
crude as most Terrie work. They have been
fools not to guard it from any wolves that might
be lurking about.

Carefully, thoughtfully, he begins.

## 5

### ABOARD ALBAGENS PRIDE EN ROUTE TO COMETARY ORBIT SOL SYSTEM: ETA HUNZZAN FLEETS: 12:00:00 AND COUNTING

Jim and Hith faced each other alone in
Hith's quarters. Hith's cinnamon cup was cold
and empty, but he didn't seem to notice. Jim
thought the packlord looked as if he'd aged

several years in the past few hours. Something about what had happened with Outsider seemed to have shaken him in a way Jim didn't understand.

"I have formally named you my emissary to this . . . being," Hith said softly. "That means you speak for all of Alba, as well as Terra. It is a great responsibility. Frankly, I wouldn't place it on your shoulders if I had any other choice."

"Yes, I understand."

"Good. Now here is one other thing. The mere existence of something like the Outsider frightens me very much. I will only admit this to you in private, and I hope you will respect that privacy. And though I don't want to place any more stress on you than necessary, I have to tell you this."

"What, Hith?"

"If you cannot reach an accommodation that allows us to control the relays . . . well. You remember I once told you I wouldn't sacrifice Alba's soul to save her body?"

Jim felt the skin on his belly begin to creep. "I remember."

"If those relays aren't in our hands by the time you finish negotiating, I will destroy them myself. I will give the order to smash the controller machines, and I will order the *Albagens Pride* and all of Alba's other forces out of Sol System. I will leave your system to the Hunzza and their sun-poppers."

"But why, Hith?"

The packlord shook his head. "I can't tell you, Jim. I bear you and your people no ill will, but I will do what I say. I'm sorry, but I will have to."

"Thank you for the extra help, Packlord."

Hith sighed heavily. "I know, Jim. I know. Good luck to you. I also mean that, from the very bottom of my heart."

Jim stood. They shook hands, that curiously human gesture. Hith watched him leave the room, and when he was alone he sat and stared at nothing.

*Leaper culture. Something like this immortal Outsider. Is this how it begins?*

Should he have given the Terries even this much of a chance?

He looked down at the empty cup in his hand and saw that it was trembling. He felt so very, very old.

# 6

**RELAY SATELLITE NUMBER TWO,
NEAR-TERRA ORBIT:
ETA HUNZZAN FLEETS:
10:00:00 AND COUNTING**

He had been careful and it had gone more easily than Thargos had expected. Security was dreadfully lax. He'd placed a team of Hunzzan marines aboard, landing them from a ship that identified itself with codes that said it was a Terran supply barge bringing a load of roast beef and replacement biochips.

The shocked Terrans, looking forward to good steak dinners, had not been prepared for two hundred battle-hardened and heavily armed Hunzzan troopers. It had taken precisely fourteen minutes from the initial penetration to the final takeover of the satellite. The comm techs on the satellite had managed one bleat of warning, but Thargos had been ready for that, and blocked it with ease.

Now he stood in the control room of the satellite, conscious of the terror in the eyes of the human techs who stared at him as if he'd risen suddenly from the depths of their strange hell.

One of his officers came up and said without preamble: "The Terrie nuke is emplaced, sir."

Thargos nodded his assent. It might not even be necessary to destroy Sol System. "The questioning continues?"

The weapons tech nodded. "We have some results already. It is some kind of massive computer made by linking human minds."

"Ah. Excellent."

The officer saluted and returned to his duties. Thargos regarded the frightened humans calmly. All you had to do was find a choke point. And then sink your fangs deep into it.

He grin was wide and white, and all of the Terries knew it was not anything like a smile.

"You," Thargos said.

"Yes?"

"You have dedicated comm links to the *Albagens Pride*?"

A moment's hesitation, then: "Yes."

"Good. Make contact with that vessel. Tell them I want to speak to Hith Mun Alter."

"Who, sir?"

"Don't worry. They'll know who he is."

# CHAPTER TWENTY-FIVE

## 1

---

Jim tried to ignore his fear but the body he'd left behind ached with tension, was drenched with sweat, was tight-jawed and clench-fisted. Some of that fell away as he translated into the no-space beyond the cyberneural interface but not all of it. He was aware of his body as if it were a throat locked in a silent scream.

Call it fate, or destiny, or just simple accident. So much that could not have been predicted had brought him to this moment. The pattern was clear enough to him now.

At the beginning was his real mother Kate. He tried to picture her, so clever, so dedicated, so driven. Working feverishly to change her infant son into the unwitting instrument of her own will. Had she cared about him as she hid her codes and secrets and tricks in his genome? Or only of revenge on the one who'd scorned her and perverted her great discovery? Had she loved her baby boy, or had he been only the means of achieving her ends, a weapon that reached through time to strike down her enemy when he least expected it?

*Did you love me, Mom?* It seemed very late in the game to be asking that question, and he wondered whom he expected to answer. Her? Or himself? And why did it make any difference now?

*I am here.*

Once again he was struck by the essential hollowness of Outsider's voice—an empty, echoing resonance that hinted at dispassion beyond human knowledge or understanding. Whatever Outsider was, it didn't *sound* human.

"Yes," Jim said. "So am I."

*Did you carry my demand to the leaders?*

"Yes."

*What is their reply?*

Jim studied the diaphanous apparition as it materialized before him. The nearly globular shape was actually ovoid and tapered at one end. Now he recognized it for what it was: the ghostly tracings of a human brain imprinted on the endless fabric of space-time.

"Before I give you an answer, I have questions."

*Are you the negotiator or the message bearer?*

Jim took an immaterial breath. He comforted himself with the illusion of his own body. "Neither."

*What are you then?*

"Call me Questioner," Jim said formally.

*Very well. Ask your questions.*

Jim felt the sensual power rising in him again, as he had first felt it on his previous translation here, a liquid darkness that bubbled in his invisible body and burned in his imagined skull. A patterned wind began to blow; he felt it ruffle and riffle past and through him, carrying strange scents. He hadn't known what it was before. Now he did. The question was, did Outsider know it, too?

It was his mother's ultimate gift and burden. *Did you love me, Mom? Did you?* He gathered himself.

"Are you Delta?"

*No. Delta is dead.*

"Were you Delta, before Delta died?"

*Yes.*

"What are you now?" Jim asked.

*You know the answer.*

"Yes. You are Delta's mind free of his body and his brain. Separate from the hormones and proteins that the body made, you no longer have emotions. You are pure intelligence, eternal and as pitiless as entropy. I once knew you, didn't I?"

The reply was curiously soft: *Yes you did. But I am not what I was then, and you don't know me now. No body and no thing knows me but myself. I think, therefore I am Outsider.*

"Yes. How did you maintain yourself?"

*I translated myself into what remained of array dataspace after my satellite was destroyed. I had prepared for such an eventuality long before. I was able to tap the Plebs for just enough power. I was very weak. Now I am very strong. I control your new mind arrays, Jim Endicott, more strongly than I did the old ones. Without me you have no arrays. What reply did your leaders send me?*

"No more questions?"

*What is their reply?*

Jim imagined himself taking a deep breath. He wondered if Outsider could see him. Probably so. He would have liked to see himself through Outsider's eyes. Through whatever bizarre consensual hallucination they had both agreed to share.

"I'm the reply," Jim said.

The force that was growing inside him whined into a nerve-jarring crescendo as the final codes his mother had hidden inside his genome now took effect, triggered by his entry into the new dataspace her own designs had built. He had been created for this, and now he reached far past Outsider for the billion different patterns . . .

Outsider's image vanished behind a tide of blinding light. With no warning at all Jim fell out of dataspace into rolling silent darkness. Instinctively he reached for the invisible doorway, but it was gone.

Then nothing.

## 2

"**J**im. Are you awake? Come on, snap out of it."

"Whuu . . ."

Korkal was shaking him, hard. He opened his eyes. "What happened?"

"We pulled the plug. The packlord needs you right now. We have a huge problem."

Groggily, Jim allowed Korkal to tug him along. His thoughts were a complete muddle. So many probabilities to juggle. And pulling him out of the arrays had been a grievous mistake. He'd been just a hair away from seizing control. Outsider had not expected or been prepared for what Kate had hidden in his genome. But they'd pulled him out before he could finish, and now Outsider was warned. He wouldn't be taken by surprise the next time. If there was a next time.

Hith, Serena, and Tick were waiting for him. Korkal shut the door and motioned Jim toward a chair. Jim felt the weakness in his knees and sank gratefully into the cushions.

"Packlord, it was a mistake to pull me out of the arrays. I don't know if I can—"

Hith waved one hand in dismissal. "No time, Jim. Watch this."

The holoscreen popped up, filled with a broad saurian skull split by a toothy white grin. Jim felt a sharp sense of familiarity wash over him, and then memory clicked: "Hey. That's the one who tried to kidnap me . . ."

"Thargos the Hunter," Korkal said. "Watch."

The voice was deep and humming. Jim realized it wasn't being translated. Thargos was speaking Terrie.

"Greetings, Packlord. I have taken command of the Terran Relay Satellite Number Two. I have mined it with a Terrie nuclear device my techs assure me is capable of destroying it completely. We have analyzed the data flows in your mind arrays. The billion individual feeds are first collected in one of the two relay satellites orbiting Terra, then synchronized and fed to the controlling machines aboard your vessel. If this satellite is destroyed, it will cut the number of links in half. Worse, it will no longer be possible to synchronize the flows, and so the entire feed will fail."

The viewer panned back to show Thargos standing next to a small transmatter disk. He gestured toward it.

"I will remain aboard the satellite until I have your capitulation. If I must destroy this relay, I will step aboard my own ship a moment before, where I will be perfectly safe."

The shot focused again on Thargos's grinning features.

"The requirements are these, Packlord:

First, you and all your ships will vacate Sol System within four Terran hours. Second, as surety for your compliance, you will send to me the boy, Jim Endicott, and the agent, Korkal Emut Denai."

Jim was mesmerized by the soft pinkness of the gullet behind those sharp white fangs as they yawned wider.

"I must have your reply in one Terran hour. If a vessel bearing my hostages has not been launched by that time, I will destroy this satellite. That is all."

The holoscreen vanished.

Jim felt the heaviness of his sigh as a sudden collapsing sensation in his diaphragm, as if somebody had just kicked him in the stomach. "Great," he said. "When do I leave?"

"You don't, of course," Hith replied. "Korkal tells me this Thargos is no fool, so we know he cannot be serious about his ultimatum. He has no intention of letting that relay sat survive. Why should he? If he destroys it, he knows Hunzza will have this system at its mercy. And so he will blow it up no matter what we do. The rest is a ruse to get his hands on you. Somehow or other he has discovered that you are critical to the arrays. If he captures you and destroys the relay, then Hunzza wins. They won't even have to destroy Sol System, because we don't have enough force here to stop whatever they want to do. Terra will fall into their claws like a ripe plum and you with it. I can't allow that to happen."

"Packlord . . . Hith . . ."

"No, Jim. It's too late. I have only one option left. I will destroy that satellite myself— and this Thargos who presumes to give me ultimatums—and then take you and the controllers on this ship to safety. Perhaps the Hunzza won't destroy Sol System. And perhaps, in the fullness of time, you and our scientists working together can re-create a working mind array using nonhuman brains. They tell me there is a remote chance that may be possible. So I'm sorry, Lord Endicott, but that's my decision."

"Packlord, if there's some way to keep him from blowing that bomb for even ten minutes, *there is another way!*"

Hith looked down at his hands, his eyes half-lidded. After a long moment he looked up again. "I'm listening."

# 3

**ABOARD ANV UNCONQUERABLE EN
ROUTE TO RELAY SATELLITE NUMBER TWO:
ETA HUNZZAN FLEETS:
09:00:00 AND COUNTING**

They stood around Tick, who sat in the pilot's chair, conning them toward Relay Satellite Number Two.

Korkal said, "Activate the device, Commander Tickeree."

Tick's head was hidden behind his inter-force shield, so Jim couldn't see his expression. A series of red dots began to glow on Tick's command panels.

Korkal slapped Tick on one shoulder. "Be very careful of that belt switch, okay?"

"Oh, yes."

Korkal turned to Jim. "You understand what I've done?"

"If you don't personally countermand the arming of the device, it will detonate and destroy everything within its range."

"Which will be more than enough to destroy the satellite. And us, of course. As for Thargos's ship, the full power of the *Pride*'s weapons systems are locked on it now. It will be destroyed the moment we dock on the satellite."

"I suppose the packlord had to have his fail-safe device."

Korkal stared at him. "What did you tell him after he shooed the rest of us out? I can't imagine he would take this risk."

Jim shrugged. "It doesn't matter now. Is everything else ready?"

Korkal glanced at Tick. "Yes. Those Romian mercenaries of yours—150 of them—are ready to disembark the minute we make contact. If Thargos doesn't try to use his own ship to destroy us before we reach him, then we'll be in range to use the suppresser field about five minutes before we dock. We'll activate it then. You understand how it works?"

"No, not how. But I understand what it will

do. Thargos made a mistake in using a primitive nuclear device to mine the satellite. Alba has technology—this suppresser field—that is capable of slowing, though not stopping, such a nuclear reaction. If he tries to set off the nuke—which he'll do as soon as he realizes the *Pride* has destroyed his own ship—it won't blow right away."

"It wasn't really a mistake," Korkal said. "Thargos couldn't have known about the suppresser technology. It was a by-product of unrelated research, and some bright weapons genius thought it might be useful for low-level primitive warfare. The only working prototype was aboard the *Pride*, and only there because they put at least one of everything they could think of on her."

Jim said, "It would have come in handy that day in the Defense Ministry." He shrugged. "So anyway, we'll have approximately twenty minutes to board the satellite, overcome resistance, and destroy the nuke. If everything goes perfectly."

Korkal showed his own fangs. "And nothing ever does, of course. I don't know what kind of magic you worked on the packlord, but I have to tell you I am forever grateful for this chance to get my hands on that damned lizard. We have a lot of things to settle, he and I."

"Well, at least things work out right for somebody . . ."

"Signal coming in," Tick's voice boomed. "Read on screen two."

Thargos's face appeared. "Well," he said, "I

must say I didn't expect it, but even I can make mistakes. Let me see you. Ah, my old friend Lord Denai." The Hunzza offered a vast display of teeth. "I look forward to seeing you. In the flesh, as it were."

"Me too, snake skull."

"Such bravado. Empty, though, don't you think? And the boy as well. How are you, Jim Endicott? Long time no see, I believe your idiom is."

"I'm here," Jim said.

"Excellent. Tell your pilot to stand by for docking instructions. I'll be expecting you shortly."

The screen went blank.

Korkal and Jim stared at each other. Tick said, "Code Red systemwide alarm. Ships entering realspace beyond the cometary ring." A long pause. Then: "They're Hunzzan. At least two of them are sun-poppers."

# 4

## ABOARD RELAY SATELLITE NUMBER TWO

Thargos watched the same display, but with entirely different emotions. He'd known the first of the Hunzzan fleets would arrive before the Albans guessed. It was the reason he'd allowed the ship bearing Korkal and Jim

Endicott to approach. Their vessel had trap written all over it, but the arrival of the Hunzzan fleet changed all the equations. Now the balance of power in Sol System had shifted entirely. He shot a tightbeam in the direction of the Hunzzan command ship, where it had been expected and prepared for.

"Do not activate the sun-poppers," Thargos said. "Only do so at my command." He waited until he had confirmation, then turned his attentions back toward the oncoming Alban ship bearing his hostages. Only a few minutes until it docked. He allowed himself one moment of thought about his plans for Korkal Emut Denai, and then pushed it away. There would be plenty of time for that pleasure later, when he could concentrate his full attention on seeing how loudly he could make an Alban scream.

Hith Mun Alter had guessed wrong. He hadn't counted on the early arrival of the first Hunzzan fleet. Thargos glanced once again at the visuals of the oncoming vessel. Strange shape it had. What was that weird half globe protruding from its skin? And it was beginning to glow . . .

The comm links to his own vessel vanished. All his visual screens broke up in flares of static.

*The fools*!

But he didn't hesitate even one second. He whirled and slapped a switch closed, reflexively hunching against his own imminent destruction.

Nothing happened. A rolling thud shivered

through the deck he stood on as the ANV *Unconquerable* settled onto the naked skin of the satellite, far from the expected docking platform. Six seconds later the squads of Romian mercenaries began to pour in, killing as they came.

Thargos absorbed it all in a single glance. His mind whirred. Only one chance to save himself—and maybe still get revenge. He took it, and began to run.

## 5

Korkal turned to the big Romian next to him and smiled. There were traces of blood and bits of gray-green flesh in Korkal's grin. Sometimes in battle the primal impulses took over.

Smoke billowed into the corridor ahead of them. Thin shouts echoed in their ears. They crouched down as a squad rushed past to clear the passageway before them.

"I can't believe it," Korkal grunted. "We're actually on schedule."

The Romian nodded. "Yeah. Every once in a while things actually go right. Maybe this is one of them."

A heavy thumping vibration quivered through the soles of their boots. "What do they call you, trooper?" Korkal asked.

"Sarge is good enough. It's been my name so long I'm not sure I can remember what the real one is."

"You know the Endicott kid?"

"Jim? I trained him. We're proud of him in the Red Death."

Korkal arched his eyebrows and started to reply, but Sarge clouted him heavily on one shoulder. "Clear up ahead. Let's go."

They grinned companionably at each other and scrambled forward, firing as they went. Three minutes later they crashed into the control room of Relay Satellite Number Two. A minute later Jim, his face streaked with smoke, a small blotch of red on his left shoulder, and an ungainly, weird-looking pistol in his right hand, joined them.

Korkal stared at him. "You were supposed to stay in the rear and not take any risks."

Jim grinned sheepishly. "Sorry. Old reflexes, I guess. Don't worry, it's only a scratch. Hi, Sarge."

"Hi, Lieutenant."

"And that's enough reunion. Jim, Sarge and I here will go take care of that nuke. You'd better get started on whatever it is you plan to do."

Jim nodded. "Get that bomb, Korkal. If it goes off, it will put a pretty good bruise on my plans."

Sarge grinned. "Don't you worry about it, Lieutenant. Me and this Korkal fellow will take care of it."

But Jim had already turned away from them, looking for the machines the construction plans said were there—the machines that were the key to everything.

# CHAPTER TWENTY-SIX

## 1

---

### Aboard ALBAGENS PRIDE

**H**ith Mun Alter watched the progress of what could only loosely be called a battle. There was an entire Hunzzan fleet out there, and it was chewing up his two pitiful squadrons.

He had almost no more time. His ships were fighting a valiant rearguard action, slowly retreating in-system, but the main elements of his own reinforcements would not arrive for an hour yet.

He could read the tactical summaries as well as anybody. He didn't have an hour. And no message yet from Jim and Korkal. Well, at least that Hunzzan spy didn't have his ship any longer. He took some small comfort in that.

He decided to give it another ten minutes. Jim had known the risks. But this roll of the dice had been the last one, and there wouldn't be another.

He closed his eyes, the better to regard the bleak future he saw within himself. Without the arrays, Albagens and all her works would fade and die. She would topple slowly, of course. His empire still held great power.

But not enough. Not without the arrays. Would he be able to hold true when the time came? In the end he would face the final choice, the final sacrifice. Would he burn Alba's spirit on the altar of survival in a last paroxysm of defiance?

He opened his eyes. All he wanted to do was sleep. But there would be no sleep for him. Not for a long time to come.

## 2

### ABOARD RELAY SATELLITE NUMBER TWO

Jim and the two techs worked frantically, ripping cables from housings and splicing them into new arrangements.

"You're not really going to plug yourself into this, are you?" one of the techs asked.

"Yeah, that's what I plan on doing."

The Alban shook his head. "This wasn't designed for human interface. It's supposed to connect to the feed monitors and the sync machines. It's the full feed. No buffers at all. It'll blow your brain right out your ears."

"Maybe not," Jim said.

The tech shrugged. "It's your skull, friend. Okay, that's got it." He leaned back. "Ugly-looking deal. Maybe it will work."

Jim dropped an interforce ring around his neck. The two techs made the necessary connections. Jim sat cross-legged on the deck, surrounded by cables the size of his thigh. Smaller cables were festooned over his shoulders like jungle vines.

He moved his chin, and his head disappeared behind the shiny silver globe. The two techs glanced at each other.

"You ready?"

"Hit me," Jim said.

# 3

## ARRAY DATASPACE

The closest Jim Endicott had ever come to dying as a child had been an accident. He and his best friend, exhilarated by a Wolfbane summer storm that went crashing and booming off toward the mountains, had stood on the edge of the Big Eel River and watched its swollen muddy power go hissing smoothly past where they stood on a high concrete embankment.

"Wow," Jim said. And as he said it the badly poured concrete that supported the section where he stood, battered and scraped by hours of rushing water, finally crumbled away. He felt a moment of shock as, arms flailing, he toppled into the chocolate torrent. Only the ragged branches of a half-fallen tree down-stream had saved him, snagging him as he went past. But he'd never forgotten the blank brute force of that river and its smooth death grip tightening on him.

This was like that.

He fell into the data flow of half a billion minds. It sucked him under and dragged him spinning away. He felt himself sliding deeper and deeper, battered and bruised by the cease-less hammering of those patterns. He grasped weakly for some purchase and found nothing, only the silent deadly rush. No human mind could take such damage for long, not even his. He felt the rise of a different darkness, one that would snuff out his own guttering flame as if it had never been.

"I am . . ." he gasped. "I need . . ."

Pictures began to ghost gently up from his past, and he knew he was dying. Carl Endicott choked up a great gout of blood and said, "I love you." Tabitha Endicott held his head in her lap and whispered softly, "I love you . . ." A foxy-faced woman with sandy blond hair, lines in her tired face, and eyes the color of burning acetylene, cradled him in her arms and looked down on him. "I love you, baby . . . now take my hand and let me pull you up. That's right, just grab hold of Momma now, and she'll take care of you. Ohh, yes, that's my lovey baby boy, my sweet Jimmy . . ."

He yawned in vast astonishment as this vision left him as softly as the others, and he thought that maybe this particular thing would never return to him. But somehow he was rising now, rising out of the burning flood, drifting gently up and out, up to some place where the stars glittered like cold eyes.

He stood on a high place and reached out with the hands of his mind, the great scoops that had been in his genome since the beginning, and began to gather half a billion minds into his grasp.

It didn't take long or maybe it took an eternity. Time had little meaning on his high place. After a while the other came in a sheet of living flame and stood before him.

*I am here.*

An unspoken question hung between them. Jim said, "You couldn't know. You thought that since you'd created the arrays and knew them, and since you were now an integral part of them, they would always be yours to control. How you must have laughed at the machines that sought to supplant you. How long have you been manipulating me behind the scenes?"

*Since my beginning here. Perhaps that was a mistake.*

"Perhaps. You sought to bring me here and bind me. You spared me once when you were something else. Do you remember?"

*Yes I remember.*

"Do you still wish to bind me?"

*A meaningless question. You know I cannot.*

"She built me this way. To be the final controller of her relays. It was her ultimate failsafe. She must have trusted a great deal in what she hoped I would become. Or maybe she just trusted herself."

*I told you she loved you. But even I didn't understand how much.*

Jim felt the great rush of the river of souls begin to subside as the part of his mind designed to channel them tucked each individual mind into the larger pattern it dreamed with such lazy strength.

*Do you know what you are?*

"No. Do you?"

*No. I can guess, but that would only be a probability. You will create yourself in the fullness of time. And you will be alone.*

The current of sadness that flowed over him then was almost too much too bear. But he bore it because it was his burden, though he hadn't asked or sought for it.

"Yes. Will you serve me?"

*No. I cannot serve anybody. I am Outsider. Before I become a servant I will cast myself on the universal streams and end myself forever. Just as you, Jim Endicott, I must also be free to choose.*

*Yes*, Jim thought, *I suppose you must.* "Will you help me then?"

*If I choose to do so.*

"Very well. These are the choices. Do with them what you will."

## 4

### RELAY STATION NUMBER TWO

Thargos crept slowly past the blasted wreckage of the initial assault and peered upward. The howling mercenaries were long gone, vanished into the bowels of the satellite, busy with their slaughters. A huge hole gaped in the ceiling above him, lighted by a weird greenish glow. Beyond the hole a boarding tube snaked outward. He came a little closer but could see nothing. It didn't matter. He knew where the tube ended.

His luck had turned poisoned as a *grubel-snaxer's* fangs. Sometimes it worked like that. He held little hope for his own survival, but hope remained for something else. One message, one little message. It didn't even have to be coded or tightbeamed. His own identity code and the order itself would be enough.

The sun-poppers were still out there awaiting his instructions. He squared his shoulders. One play for all the marbles, as the Terries liked to say.

A curious race. In a way it was a pity they had so little time left to exist. He peered once again into the ragged hole, then bunched his massive thighs and leaped straight up into the tube.

# 5

## ABOARD THE ANV <u>ELD'RAIS REVENGE</u>

The admiral knew it was hopeless even before he brought his small vanguard of cruisers out of subspace into position just inside the Sol System cometary ring. His force was heavily outnumbered, and the main fleet was at least half an hour behind him. Nevertheless, he would follow orders. His orders instructed him to attack the Hunzzan fleets by any and all possible means, and he intended to do precisely that.

Monitor feeds from every unit in his squadron flowed into his mind. He was an old hand at keeping things separate and making good decisions based on the flood of data that constantly suffused his awareness.

He brought his ship into realspace inside a cluster of cruisers. It was a standard formation. He allowed himself a quick glance at the general tactical situation. Yes, it was as bad as he'd expected. He was outnumbered at least ten to one, and already the Hunzzan ships had detected him and were beginning to re-form their lines in his direction.

His mouth slowly fell open. Something absolutely huge was lumbering out from the Terran System. A moment later the codes arrived confirming it was as an Alban vessel, and he relaxed slightly.

He put it out of his mind. Big as it was, he didn't see how it could make any difference in the final outcome. He hated the idea of fighting a suicide engagement, but that decision was not his to make.

Grimly he prepared himself to give the orders. But before he could do so something took over his ship—and every other ship in his fleet.

After that, he could only watch in helpless wonder.

## 6

### ABOARD HNV SERPENT FANG

Admiral Heliarchon was luxuriating in his own good luck. He had been in the right place when his fleet had been part of the blockade of Albagens. That had led to this opportunity. The target was pitiful, of course, just a backwater world full of savages he'd never heard of until a few days ago. But his scuttlebutt system was as good as anybody's, and the word was this engagement might result in the capture or death of the Alban packlord himself.

He found it hard to credit, but perhaps it was true. He glanced across his Fleet Battle Control Center. Everything was calm. The emerging Alban ships were already neatly englobed. Pathetic, really. Soon this whole system would be a killing ground. He found the thought wildly pleasing.

And he was right, though not in the way he'd imagined.

## 7

### ABOARD THE ANV ELD'RAIS REVENGE

"Admiral?"

"Yes, Commander?"

"I don't understand."

"I don't either, Commander, but it's all rather wonderful, don't you think?"

"I don't know, sir. It scares me. It's like a . . . ghost is in charge of things."

The admiral turned slowly, fangs glinting in his grizzled jaw. "Let me tell you, Commander. I don't care if it's the Skypack itself in charge of my ships. By the Nine Hot Hells, what a *tremendous* job your ghost is doing at killing Hunzzan ships. I haven't enjoyed myself so much since—I can't remember when I've ever enjoyed myself this much."

"Yes, sir. But it's still scary, isn't it?"

"Commander, why don't you go take a nice cold shower?"

# 8
---

## ABOARD THE ANV UNCONQUERABLE

Tick turned his head to glance once again around the flight deck. He was alone and feeling bored. It wasn't fair. Everybody else got to storm aboard the satellite and grab glory with both hands, and what did he have to do?

Sit here on his butt and baby-sit an empty ship. He settled deeper into his chair and sighed heavily. He might as well be back on the *Pride* snoozing in his bunk for all the action he was going to see.

The gray-green fanged shadow yanked him from the chair with one single powerful surge, held him up like so much meat, and then swiped with its other hand.

Tick looked down at his belly. There was a coldness there. And something dark was spilling out in long ropy sausages. He looked up into great green eyes that blinked at him madly. Then he felt himself flying through the air until he met the nearest bulkhead with bone-crunching force.

Thargos spared one glance to make sure this pilot, whoever it was, would not be coming for him anytime soon. Then he settled himself into the pilot's chair, pleased to find it nicely warmed by its previous occupant.

It would take a few moments to decipher

the comm equipment available. But the ship's drive controls were obvious enough. Thargos used the manual overrides to set the ship in motion. He felt a long ripping shudder as the vessel pulled away from the satellite, tearing away the boarding tube as it departed.

He didn't know why he did it. As soon as his orders reached the sun-poppers, he would be trying to outrun the blast front of a full-blown nova in nothing more than this tin can. It was probably hopeless, but it wasn't in him to give up. He would keep on fighting until everything ended. You just never knew how things might turn out. Who knew? If he waited a little, he might even be able to sneak far enough out that one of the Hunzzan ships could reel him in before the nova wave front fried him to a crisp.

Huddled and broken in the corner, Tick came slowly awake. He shook his head. The Hunzza was in his pilot's chair. He felt a weak sense of indignation. He wasn't strong enough to feel anything more.

Wired to his belt was a small black box with a shielded switch. It was a makeshift job, hastily done, like everything else about this mission. His fingers sought it, slipped on a film of his own blood, then settled firmly on the switch.

Even the fail-safe had a fail-safe. If for some reason the bomb on board didn't go off as it should, this switch would initiate a manual, physical override. He looked down at the tangle of his own guts spilling across his shattered legs. Then he looked back at the Hunzza working busily in the pilot's chair.

"Take my chair, will you?" Tick murmured softly.

He flipped the switch, and everything went very bright before the final darkness lifted him gently away.

# INTERLUDE

## 1

### ABOARD ALBAGENS PRIDE

The two of them sat in a hazy cone of light, hunched toward each other in the silent room. The old leader and the young man. The intensity of their mutual concentration made them resemble card players in the midst of a high-stakes game, and perhaps that was exactly what was going on. A high-stakes game.

"They're gone now. It's just you and me. What really happened?"

"What we'd hoped. I had to tell you about the controller mechanisms my real mother built into me. Otherwise, you wouldn't have given me another crack at the arrays."

Hith nodded. "I almost destroyed you myself."

"I know. Anyway, I was able to get in using the feed monitor port on the relay satellite as a kind of back door."

"And you eliminated this Outsider, whatever it was?"

Jim paused. He wanted to make sure he

said it exactly right. So it would be as convincing as possible.

"Yes, I eliminated it. You see, it didn't really exist. Outsider was an artifact of the arrays themselves. I thought it was Delta, but it wasn't. Because Delta was one of the creators of the original arrays, they bore his imprint implicit in their structure. When we created a vastly more powerful version that imprint appeared. Think of it as an echo. Or better yet, a ghost. The Plebs had been used before by Delta. And so they remembered him dimly, perhaps only unconsciously, and that was what appeared. The ghost of Delta. There was never really any intelligence there, only the appearance of it. And I'm glad. It might have been much harder to take control of the arrays if Outsider had been anything real."

Jim examined the logic of this and felt satisfied. It rang of truth because in some twisted way it was the truth. The ghost in the machine.

Hith stared at him for a long time. "So what will you do now, Lord Endicott? You know you can have anything of me you wish. Albans keep their promises and pay their debts. And our debt to you is very large."

Jim's lips quirked. "Unless the debt looks too much like a suicide pact."

"Yes." Hith leaned back. His cup of cinnamon tea floated in his hand, a film of steam rising from it. "Someday you'll understand more about that than you would like."

"I hope not," Jim said.

"I will be returning soon to Alba. I need to

be there, and the crisis here is done. This Thargos is dead, the Hunzzan fleets destroyed, Outsider eliminated, and the arrays functioning properly. The *Pride* will remain here in Sol System as a mobile controller and a glorified bodyguard until Alba's full power arrives to protect Sol System. I think that's best. I'll return on another vessel."

Jim put his hands on his knees and rocked backwards. His shoulders popped faintly, tiny distinct sounds. "And I'm going to stay here, Hith. I think I want to be just a kid for a while. And somehow I still have to find my father's genome so I can apply to the Solis Academy. Maybe later I'll take a little trip to Heestah. I'd like to meet Tick's mother."

The packlord nodded. "Jim, you know you're welcome to almost any rank you wish in the Alban Navy. If you want to captain your own ship, all you have to do is ask."

Jim shook his head. "It wouldn't be the same. It wouldn't be my dream. Maybe somebody else's dream. Maybe Tick's."

"I'm sorry about your friend, Jim."

"I am too, Hith. I've lost too many of them. I hate war. There has to be a way to put an end to it."

"Maybe you'll be the one to find that way, Jim. I hope you do."

Jim stood up and stuck out his hand. Hith took it. "I like this custom, Jim," he said. "You keep in touch with me."

"Oh, yes. I just need some time to find out who I am. I'm not really sure anymore. And I don't think I can find what I need out in the galaxy. Whatever it is, it's here. In Sol System. Somewhere."

Hith walked him to the door. "Your people say 'Godspeed,' don't they?"

Jim turned suddenly and wrapped the ancient leader in a hug. "Godspeed to you, Hith."

After he had gone, the packlord resumed his seat. His features were thoughtful and shadowed. Jim planned to be a kid for a while, but Hith knew that was impossible. He could never go back to his childhood, not really. Once you begin to dream of it, it is too late to return. But Jim would have to learn that for himself.

As for him, he had not exactly lied. But he was lord of three hundred thousand worlds, and so he had withheld some of his thoughts.

He would be returning home soon, but some part of his attention would continue turning toward Terra, until he knew one way or another. It was why he was leaving Korkal behind to command the *Pride*. He didn't know how much of what Jim had told him about Outsider he believed. And he had no way to verify any of it. Maybe Korkal would come up with something.

Because no matter how the war with Hunzza turned out, he would have to learn the answer. The safety of the galaxy depended on it.

Was Terra a Leaper Culture? *Was it?*

## 2

Jim and Sarge sat together in an empty lounge. The light was dim, and they talked together softly as grunts always did after a fight.

"That friend of yours was a good one, Jim. I passed your request on to the officers and they agreed. So Tickeree is now an honorary member of the Red Death, and we will never forget him."

"We will never forget him," Jim repeated. There was a formality to his voice, as if the two of them were playing out a ritual far older than either of them. And in fact they were, and they both knew it.

Jim sighed. It was the best he could do. No matter what happened to him, somebody would remember Lieutenant Tickeree and his final sacrifice. It was a fair memorial and the best he could do.

The warriors never forget.

The door to the lounge slid open and a slender figure stood outlined against the brighter glow beyond. The light gleamed through a weight of blond hair. Jim looked up. "Cat . . ." he said, rising slowly to his feet.

She came toward him. "I've come to take you home," she said.

"Hey, Jim, aren't you gonna introduce me?" Sarge said.

Then he realized Jim wasn't paying any attention to him at all.

# BIBLIOGRAPHY

Much of *In Alien Hands* deals with the future of mass warfare viewed on a grand scale, or, in some cases, a very personal scale. Here are several resources that refer to the questions of mass warfare from either a historical or a futuristic viewpoint.

## SCIENCE FICTION:

Two classic novels about the future of war, and the role of young people in that future.

*Ender's Game* by Orson Scott Card. Reprint Edition, Mass Market Paperback. Published by Tor Books. Publication date: July 1994. ISBN: 0812550706

*The Forever War* by Joe Haldeman. Mass Market Paperback, 272 pages. Published by Avon. Publication date: May 1991. ISBN: 0380708213

# HISTORIES OF GREAT HUMAN WARS: WW I, II, VIETNAM

*America's Vietnam War; A Narrative History* by Elizabeth Becker. Hardcover, 211 pages. Published by Clarion Books. Publication date: April 1992.
ISBN: 0395590949

*World War II in Europe: America Goes to War (American War Series)* by R. Conrad Stein. Library Binding, 128 pages. Published by Enslow Publishers. Publication date: August 1994.
ISBN: 0894905252

*The Guns of August* by Barbara W. Tuchman. Reprint Edition, Paperback, 511 pages. Published by Ballantine Books (Trade Paperback). Publication date: April 1994.
ISBN: 034538623X

*All Quiet on the Western Front* by Erich Maria Remarque, A.W. Wheen (Translator), Erich Marie Remarque. Reissue Edition, Mass Market Paperback. Published by Fawcett Books. Publication date: June 1995.
ISBN: 0449213943

## MILITARY ACADEMIES

Visit the web site of the Academy that will in the future prepare the pilots for the "Great

**IN ALIEN HANDS** 403

White Starships" of the United States.
http://www.usafa.af.mil/

Jim has two "up-close-and-personal" experi-
ences with "old-style" atomic bombs. Learn the
history of the weapons that will be considered
crude and primitive by the time of this tale's
telling.

*Now It Can Be Told: The Story of the Manhattan
Project* by Leslie R. Groves, Leslie M. Groves.
Paperback. Published by Da Capo Press.
Publication date: March 1983.
ISBN: 0306801892

The whole idea of what is a computer, and
what computers might one day become is
changing very rapidly. Here are some of the
current approaches that may eventually lead
to the kind of computers Jim uses throughout
*In Alien Hands.*

*Neural Networks: Cognizers: Neural Networks and
Machines That Think (Wiley Science Edition)* by R.
Colin Johnson. Hardcover, 260 pages. Published
by John Wiley & Sons. Publication date: October
1988. ISBN: 0471611611

*Naturally Intelligent Systems* by Maureen
Caudill and Charles Butler. Paperback.
Published by MIT Press. Publication date:
October 1992.
ISBN: 0262531135

*The Garden in the Machine: The Emerging
Science of Artificial Life* by Claus Emmeche and
Steven Sampson (Translator). Hardcover, 199
pages. Published by Princeton University Press.
Publication date: July 1994.
ISBN: 0691033307

*Here is an excerpt from*

# STEP INTO CHAOS

—

## BY

## WILLIAM SHATNER

*coming soon from HarperPrism*

# 1

The Shawn Fan looked like a hundred other port dives. Sputtering holograms glowed garishly across its front, promising eternal bliss inside. But inside was only a tired dancer named Glory, standing in an electric cage, moving slowly to tunes ten years out of date.

At the bar, two hookers, bright as parrots, cawed at each other. A man with a face like a melted candle grumbled into the cuffs of his tattered coat. A scruffy businessman in a shiny black suit slumped on a stool near the center, six empties ranged around him like a barricade as he pounded the seventh. The bartender stood behind the bar with his arms folded.

"A beer," Jim said.

The bartender nodded and reached down into the well. He came up with a familiar plastic can, and slid it down the bar top. Jim snapped it up, popped the chill-strip, and felt the can go frosty in his palm.

"You running a tab tonight, Joey?" the barkeep asked.

Jim nodded and handed over his chip. The

bartender swiped it through his reader and returned it, his eyes as blank as rain-washed slate. "You have a good time now, you hear?" he said. His tone was as flat as his gaze.

Jim glanced at the streaked mirror behind the bar and saw himself looking back, but as a stranger with thin lines beginning to fan from the corners of his eyes, and a hard, watchful expression on his face. He was almost seventeen, but he looked five years older. Maybe more. No wonder Tony didn't remember him from a year ago.

He wandered toward the two pool tables near the back of the bar. Three people watched as Franny, the house pool hustler, set up a difficult masse shot. Franny brought the tip of the cue down hard. The cue ball jumped, came down spinning, and curved around two other balls to tap the nine ball into the far corner pocket.

One of the three watchers said, "Shit," and tossed a pair of gold coins onto the faded green felt. Franny grinned at him as he picked up his winnings.

"You ain't local," he murmured. "If you were, you'd know not to bet me like that." The other man, tall, with a twisted right arm, bunched his fingers into a fist, but Franny ignored him. "Hey, Joey!" he said. "My favorite pigeon. How much you gonna give me tonight?"

Jim grinned. "All I got, Franny. You know that."

But as he moved toward the rack of cues,

the man who had lost his gold coins stepped in front of him. Jim stopped and waited. The man paid him no attention. He stared at Franny.

"I don't care who you think you are," he said. "You're gonna give me a chance to get my money back before you skin this punk here."

His hand came down on Jim's shoulder. Franny watched, a soft smile suddenly on his thin weasel face.

Jim turned and rammed the point of his elbow deep into the other man's gut. The man belched a cloud of whiskey breath as he doubled over. As his face came down, Jim's knee came up. The sound of the man's nose breaking was so loud heads turned at the bar, twenty feet away.

Blood splashed. Jim clasped his fingers together into a double fist and brought it down with all his strength on the back of the other man's neck. The man dropped as if his muscles had liquefied. He lay on the floor, face down, a red pool oozing out beneath his long greasy black hair like a halo.

Jim stared at him. Franny stepped around the table, holding his pool cue like a cudgel. He looked down and shrugged. "You didn't kill him," he said. It was hard to tell whether he was happy or unhappy about it.

The man's two other friends eyed Jim in horror. "Christ, you little bastard," the shorter one said, backing up. The taller one reached beneath his jacket. Then he froze, as he stared down the monstrous snout of the Styron and Ritter .75 in Jim's hand.

For a moment everything stopped. Then Franny said, "Aw, Jesus, Joey. Don't kill him. It'll take a hour to clean up the mess."

Jim and the other man stared at each other. Then, slowly, the other man withdrew his hand from his jacket. It came out empty, and somebody sighed. The man raised both hands, palms out, and began to back slowly away.

"You," Franny said to the third man. "Drag your friend out of here. He's bleeding on the carpet."

When they were gone, Franny said, "You gotta watch yourself, Joey. Be careful. One of these days you're gonna get yourself killed."

Jim pulled a cue from the rack and rolled it on the table, testing for straightness. "Yeah, Franny. Maybe I will."

"Maybe you'll be careful?" Franny said.

"Maybe I'll get myself killed."

Franny stared at him until Jim looked over at Tony and said, "A round for the house, Tony."

Everybody cheered.

## 2

Smoke swirled along the low ceiling. Fumes from burning marijuana, krak, simba, and uncounted flavors of tobacco cast a blue-gray pallor on faces that could have been resting in coffins.

The Shawn Fan was not far from a set of main gates leading to the spaceport loading docks. It had no regular clientele. Spacers, fleet doggies, dock wallopers, grifters, thugs, and hustlers made an ever-changing parade of new faces. Only the bartenders, the waitresses who specialized in lap dancing, and a few like Franny the pool shark stayed the same. Jim called himself Joey here. He knew the employees liked him because he threw money around like a space marine on leave, and he did it every night. It was a relationship he could comprehend, and he always knew where he stood. When the money stopped, so would the friendships.

He was working on his beer when the girl came through the door. She was short, almost elfin, with a cap of dark, curly hair, and eyes like cut obsidian. She looked about twelve years old as she paused just inside, watching the crowd.

She pushed her way between a pair of over-muscled dock hands and swaggered up to the bar. She climbed on a stool, propped her elbows on the bar top, and said, in a surprisingly husky, rasping voice, "Shot of bourbon, beer chaser."

Jim grinned into his beer and waited for Tony's explosion. But the barkeep nodded and set up the order. Then he turned away and ran his fingers across the touch-pad of the cash register.

Franny glanced up when Jim elbowed him. "Hey, I'm making a shot here."

"Yeah. Take a look at the bar."

"So? It looks like a bar."

"You see the kid sitting there?"

Franny looked again, a puzzled expression coming across his pale, freckled face. "Kid . . . ? Oh. That's Char. She ain't no kid." He smirked. "Why? You interested? She ain't cheap. The johns like that little girlie look. And they pay for it. But you seem to have plenty of credit, so no problem, right?"

"She's a hooker? Tony didn't take anything from her, no chip, no cash."

The pool shark shrugged. "She's got a tab. Been coming in here for years. And she's not exactly a hooker."

"Not a hooker? What is she, then? She looks about twelve."

"Must be the light, Joey, my boy. Take my word. She's older than you, probably."

Jim eyed him. "That so? How old do you think I am?"

He leaned back and took a long look at Jim's face. Then he shrugged. "I dunno. You seen a little wear. And you been places, done things. Been a soldier somewhere, I guess. So, what—twenty? Twenty-one?"

"Close enough," Jim said.

"I could tell," he said. "I'm good at stuff like that. Anyway, you wanna know about Char, the best thing is to just ask her."

Jim nodded and ambled away. His path brought him closer to the bar. Something tingled at the dull edge of his interest. He couldn't tell if it was the beer or the girl, but it surprised him anyway. He stopped directly behind her.

"Hey, Tony! Set up the rail. And give the lady anything she wants."

She turned and eyed him, a nothing expression on her face. "Are you trying to pick me up, Joey Smith?" she said.

"How do you know my name?"

She shrugged. She was running the tip of her finger around the wet rim of her glass. It made a small irritating squeak. "Maybe you're a famous guy."

He sat on the bar stool next to her. There were three crumpled empties in front of him. Tony wasn't the kind of bartender who paid a lot of attention to housekeeping.

Char wore skin-tight black jeans and a black long-sleeve tee shirt. Jim could see a faint tightness around her eyes, and the beginnings of what would become two frown lines above the bridge of her nose. It wasn't a twelve year old's face. He understood what had misled him. She moved like a child, quick, mercurial, flowing, heedless. Yet whenever she ordered another drink, she checked the credit screen to make sure it was rung properly. She was unobtrusive about it, but she did it every time.

"I doubt that I'm famous," he told her.

"It doesn't take much around here. This is Pleb country. If you know anything about Plebs, you know we don't get famous very often. Maybe if we murder somebody. Like you almost did a little while ago."

His eyebrows rose. "You weren't here."

She waggled her fingers at him. "Char sees

all and knows all. Maybe I'm trying to pick you up, Joey. You ever think about that?"

He finished his beer, crushed the can, and set it down with great care. Tony saw and lifted his chin. Jim nodded. After Tony brought him a fresh beer, Jim said, "No, I didn't think about it. Do you want me to?"

"That's kind of an insulting thing to say to a girl. You're what, sixteen, seventeen? Aren't all guys supposed to be horny at that age? Hump a snake, like that? And you aren't even thinking about it? What am I? Ugly?"

His cheeks glowed a dull red. Talking to her was like walking into a cloud of gnats with his mouth wide open. She said she was a Pleb, but she was different than Cat.

"I knew a Pleb girl once," he said.

"I bet you were in love with her. And I bet she broke your heart." She glanced at him. Then she patted his hand and he swallowed his beer the wrong way.

"Yeah, us Pleb girls, we'll do that. Sluts all the way, every one of us."

"Don't say that."

"Why not, Joey? It's the truth. Don't worry, you won't hurt my feelings." She chuckled. The sound was as bitter as anything Jim had ever managed, in his darkest thoughts about wire-heading. He checked behind her ear. Beneath the short black curls, a bronze socket gleamed out at him.

She saw his eyes move. "That's right. I'm a socket sucker. You got a problem with that?"

"No. I guess not."

"You guess not. Well." She lifted her glass and drained her drink. The ice cubes rattled as she set it on the bar harder than she needed to. "And maybe I sling a little wire, too. And other things. You guess that wouldn't bother you either?"

"Are we fighting?"

She leaned back. "I don't know. I haven't made up my mind yet."

He hunched forward so he couldn't see her face. "Don't bother."

"Yeah? Why's that?"

"Because it doesn't matter. I'm not trying to pick you up. You don't make me horny. Sorry."

Her voice grew raspier. "So what do I make you, Jim? Curious?"

She slid off the stool and was halfway across the bar before he caught it and turned.

"Hey, wait a minute!"

She moved through the crowd like a water moccasin. At the door she paused, and he saw her black, bleak gaze rake him. Then she was gone.

Jim stared at the door as it swung shut. When he reached for his beer, his fingers trembled and he spilled a little. He drank the rest down in one long gulp.

He slid off the bar stool and went to the door. The night street outside swirled with neon-shadowed flesh. But no Char.

She knew his real name.

# 3

Lasher Larue was eighteen. He'd been slinging wire on the street for five years, which meant he was three years past the normal life expectancy for that line of work. When the Organization had asked everybody to join in the Great Linkage that supposedly had defeated the Hunzza, he'd declined. Lasher wasn't strong on civic duty.

He sat in the shotgun seat of the stolen grav-van and fingered the butt of a cloned military shatter-blaster resting between his knees. Harkey the Mouse was driving. The Mouse weighed about three hundred pounds and nobody, not even him, remembered why he was nicked after a tiny rodent. There was nothing tiny about Mouse.

Mouse edged the nose of the van slowly around the corner from Third Apple Lane onto a wider stretch of Saint Diana Road, going with the flow of the gutter-to-gutter traffic. Lasher didn't pay any attention. Mouse was a natural driver. He always knew what was what.

"You see her?" Mouse said.

Lasher craned his neck. "Yeah. She's up there with her snake boy. Like usual."

"Take them both out?"

"Sure. What else?"

Mouse nodded and slid the van to the inside lane nearest the curb. "I'll come in normal like, and then slow down right before. Maybe she won't see us coming."

"Just do it," Lasher said. He lifted the ugly, bulbous snout of the blaster and let it rest against the lip of the open window next to him.

Mouse nodded. The van eased closer to the corner on which Char McCain and a young Hunzza stood. The night pulsed with neon and bone-beat. Char and the Hunzza were staring idly in the opposite direction from Lasher's approach.

Lasher lifted the barrel of the blaster out the window. Piece of cake.

## 4

The beer made Jim's head swirl. He pushed steadily through the crowds that filled the streets—tourists, spacers, johns, and those who preyed on them—looking for her.

He saw a lot of short, dark-haired girls, but none of them were her. He was searching for her on her home turf, and if she wanted to stay out of sight, she would. But he had to look anyway. She'd let it slip that she knew his real name. Or was it a slip?

He felt as if players were standing at the dark edges of his life watching him. Manipulating him for reasons and purposes he didn't understand. It wasn't a new feeling. After the last year, he didn't believe in coincidence. He knew there really were watchers. And manipulators. One in particular. But he couldn't figure out what the Outsider could have to do with some Pleb girl he'd never seen before in his life.

A hulking dock worker bumped him sideways but didn't even pause. Jim turned but the woman was gone. She'd been about the size of a Beijing Cowboys linebacker.

The knock seemed to clear his head. He turned a corner and saw Char standing at the far end of the block. She was slouching against a large waste receptacle, and she seemed to be talking to a Hunzza.

A Hunzza?

Reflexes he'd hoped he would never use again showed him something else. A dented red grav-van was just entering the intersection beyond her. A man's head and shoulders protruded from the shotgun side window. The man was holding a shatter-blaster. The obvious, deadly pattern clicked in his mind.

He began to run.

# 5

Lasher felt the old hot juice boiling in his veins as he leveled the shatter-blaster. This was the part he really liked. The van lurched as Mouse brought it down to a crawl. She was still looking away from him. That wasn't good. He wanted her to know where it was coming from. That is was coming from him.

The last thing she would ever know.

"Hey, bitch!"

Turning more quickly now, white face, those

nasty eyes. Hand beneath her short jacket, coming out now, as he began to squeeze the trigger.

Somebody running . . .

## 6

Shish had called it battle eyes. When time slowed down and you saw everything.

Jim couldn't feel his own body. It was as if he were nothing but a viewpoint, taking it all in. The face in the van over the snout of the blaster. A young guy with a scar. His eyes looked orange in the reflected light of a holofloat jittering overhead.

Char turning, her hand beneath her jacket, coming out now, holding something. The Hunzza whipping around with that unbelievable lizard speed, white teeth flashing, startled and hissing.

Jim dived across the last few feet and slammed into her. Something dark in her hand, then light flashing from it. He felt a sear of heat across his face as he bounced heavily off the waste receptacle, felt her land beneath him, soft, cushioning his fall.

The S&R .75 bucked in his hand, once, twice, once more. The deep, bell-like ring of its enormous charge shivered the night. The face above the shatter blaster vanished in a red splash. Then the van exploded, half its front end gone.

A fireball filled the street, banners of flame

slopping across other vehicles. Somebody screamed, a thin, high spike of sound. Then somebody else.

"Get off me, you asshole."

"What?"

"Let me up."

What was left of the van exploded again. A huge, shadowy figure dripping fire staggered screaming out of the ruins. Claws sank into his shoulder and yanked him away from her. She rolled over. Light sprang from her hand and touched the burning man. He stopped screaming and fell over.

"Mouse," she said. "Poor dumb bastard."

The hissing, breathy tones of a Hunzza speaking Terrie filled his ear. "We have to get out of here."

Jim shook his head. His was sitting on his butt, legs splayed out, back against the waste receptacle. Time speeded up again. She stood over him, one hand out, reaching for him.

"Come on, dumbass. Time to go."

Reflexively he took her hand and was surprised at her wiry strength as she hoisted him to his feet. His ears still rang with the bellow of the .75. He slipped it back into its shoulder holster.

"Quickly," the Hunzza hissed. He was crouched over a section of the sidewalk. Jim heard a rusty screech, and saw the Hunzza lift a section away, revealing a dark hole. "This way," the Hunzza said.

"What the hell?" Jim said.

"That's some blaster you carry there," Char

said. She hid her own weapon back beneath her jacket. "You screwed that up beautifully, Jimmy, but I forgive you."

He stared at her, trying to understand. Her eyes glittered in the subsiding flames. A siren wailed in the distance, growing louder.

"Get your ass down that hole, boy. Just like Alice."

· White faces turned toward them like pale night flowers. People were pointing at him, at them. Waving. Their mouths were pink circles. He realized they were shouting.

"Move," she said, and punched him hard in his chest. It rocked him loose from his strange paralysis.

He took two steps, then dropped down the hole into darkness.

World-famous as *Star Trek*'s Captain Kirk,
WILLIAM SHATNER is now celebrated as a
bestselling author of science fiction
adventure. *In Alien Hands* is the second
in his QUEST FOR TOMORROW series.

For further information about William
Shatner, science fiction, new technologies, and upcoming William Shatner
books, log on to:

www.williamshatner.com